One Minut

Surviving the Evacuation
Book 23

Frank Tayell

Surviving the Evacuation, Book 23: One Minute More

If you don't stand up for the weak, you have to bow down to the strong.

Published by Frank Tayell

ISBN: 978285133056

Science Fiction

Brawl of the Worlds 1: First Contact, 2: Wish You Were Here
Work. Rest. Repeat.

Strike a Match - A Post-Apocalyptic Detective Series

1. Serious Crimes, 2. Counterfeit Conspiracy
3. Endangered Nation, 4. Over By Christmas, 5: Thin Ice

Surviving The Evacuation / Here We Stand / Life Goes On

Book 1: London, Book 2: Wasteland, Zombies vs the Living Dead
Book 3: Family, Book 4: Unsafe Haven, Book 5: Reunion
Book 6: Harvest, Book 7: Home

Here We Stand 1: Infected, Here We Stand 2: Divided

Book 8: Anglesey, Book 9: Ireland, Book 10: The Last Candidate
Book 11: Search and Rescue, Book 12: Britain's End, Book 13: Future's Beginning
Book 14: Mort Vivant, Book 15: Where There's Hope
Book 16: Unwanted Visitors, Unwelcome Guests

Life Goes On 1: Outback Outbreak, 2: No More News
3: While the Lights Are On, 4: If Not Us, 5: No Turning Back

Book 17: There We Stood, Book 18: Rebuilt in a Day
Book 19: Welcome to the End of the Earth
Book 20: Small Cogs in the Survival Machine
Book 21: Our, Home, Too, Book 22: Letters From Yesterday
Book 23: One Minute More

For more information, visit:
www.FrankTayell.com
www.facebook.com/FrankTayell

Authors Note

This book is set in the Pacific Northwest, around the time the first Canadian exiles returned to the north, while the European refugees are still camped in Nova Scotia.

This story began as a prologue to a novel that continued directly from Book 22, with Sholto setting out to explore the Pacific Northwest. Maggs's journey was supposed to be a brief introduction to a few important locations and critical characters. When the prologue hit ten thousand words, I decided to make it the first part of the book. When it hit sixty thousand, I realised it had to be a novel in its own right.

Though Maggs did appear in the prologue of Book 22, and through the letters she left for her husband, Etienne, we glimpsed her life, everyone that she's travelling with are new characters. As such, there's no story so far in this book. In the prologue, we finally meet Grandpa Jack, the patriarch of the family Kim lodged with during her semester abroad in Oregon. From the moment Kim told Bill about this part of her life, I'd wanted to include Jack and his family in the series. It just took a few more books than expected for them to appear.

At its heart, this story is still a prologue to Sholto's upcoming journey, featuring the places he'll visit, the people he'll meet, and those he must overcome. But it is also a story of friendship, a tale of boundless love and petty tyranny, the importance of hope, and the danger of despair.

Happy reading, Frank.

Prologue - Grandpa Jack
March 12th - Year Zero

Jack Harper briefly raised his eyes from the telescopic sight to take in the floral calendar that was still stuck on February. He hated the mud months. Gone was the stark beauty of winter, replaced with an untidy mess of budding trees and rampant lawn. During his long years of farming, he'd been too busy to notice the quagmire beneath his feet. Now that he was retired, he had nothing to do but look out on the swamp and dream of a harvest that, this year, wouldn't come.

He leaned forward, training his rifle on Harvey Johnson, president of the homeowners' association. The mouth-breathing carbuncle stood in the open doorway of his two-bedroom cottage on the far side of the floral clock. And there was his mosquito of a wife, Dr Jane Pleasance-Johnson. Woe betide anyone who didn't use her title and hyphen. The couple had been the bane of his existence ever since his unwanted retirement began. There she was, by her prized trellis, staring vacantly at the empty greenhouse. At least that was an improvement on her weekly séances.

Séances! It was enough to make him spit. The concept was nothing but quackery inflicted by con artists on the hard of thinking. What soul, on being released from their earthly bonds, would want to hang around this planet? None, he was certain of that. Not his wife, his daughter, or his precious granddaughter. He released the safety. Adjusted for wind. Waited until she turned to face him. Fire? No. He took his finger off the trigger. Not today.

He got up from his chair, wincing at the drumroll crack from his joints, and walked into the small kitchen where his wedding-gift coffee pot perched atop an equally ancient camping stove. Two cups a week, the doctor had said, and never at home. It was just one of the many diktats that would drag out his increasingly miserable life. He'd compromised with himself and stuck to one cup a day, first thing in the morning, but today he'd accidentally-on-purpose made too much. Since it'd be a shame to waste it, he poured himself another cup. After all, what was the worst that could happen? He added a spoonful of sugar and wished he had cream. He certainly wasn't going to spoil his morning prescription with that blasted oat milk his other granddaughter, Dessie, had sent him.

For fifty years, he'd greeted each new day with one cup of coffee and one pipe of tobacco while fact-checking the previous day's newspaper. Cup in hand, he stretched out in his chair, staring into the swirling vortex at the top of his coffee, looking deep into the past at the world he'd known and seen disappear. Who would have thought it would be newspapers that would vanish first? And then the farm, when he'd become too darn old to be of any use there. He should have stayed. He *could* have stayed. Conrad had asked him to stay, and he'd kept on asking even after Jack had moved. But the boy didn't need his father around telling him the whys and wherefores of all his mistakes. Besides, he'd built that retirement cottage by the stream for his wife. With Leanna gone, he couldn't sleep there. He'd not even been able to set foot in it after she'd died in that crash, or in the orchard, or by the lake, or in the barn they'd built together on their honeymoon. No, it was right that he'd left and let his son stamp his vision, however misguided, onto the land bought with the blood of his friends. But moving into this wretched hovel had been a mistake.

He wasn't sure which was worse, that his retirement home was in Washington State, or that it was all so damned new and yet already filled with so many ghosts. He should have spent more time looking. He should have stayed in Oregon, or maybe he should have travelled. Maybe visited England, except that had been Leanna's dream.

He picked up his pipe, hand-carved by an old man who'd seemed ancient at the time, but must have been younger than he was now. He'd bought the pipe fifty years ago, give or take a month or three, and he'd stopped counting those when he'd turned seventy. They'd each got a pipe, everyone in the unit, all because of a stupid joke he'd not understood then and couldn't properly remember now. He was the only one who'd come home. Julio had made it back to America with a medical discharge, but he'd shot himself six months later. No, Jack was the only one who'd truly come home. The good died young, while the old clung on.

He'd run out of tobacco last week, but he still had coffee, so he sipped his cup, sucked on the stem, and looked out the window, across the street, and towards his neighbours. The first time he'd met them, while he was still unpacking, they'd handed him a list of infractions committed by the previous owner and which needed rectifying. That said it all really, all that was wrong with this place, and wrong with the country.

Back on the farm, every time he'd got a new neighbour, he'd taken them a basket of produce or eggs, and some freshly made bread. He'd make sure they knew they were welcome, and that they could rely on him, because in this crazy world, you had to rely on your neighbours. Now, most of his neighbours had left.

Domingo, the on-site caretaker, had escaped at five in the morning, three days after the crazies completed their takeover of Manhattan. Jack couldn't blame him. He might have had free rent, but no wage could ever be sufficient compensation for the round-the-clock headache the elderly residents caused. The Sorensons had gone by noon on the same day. The others had left soon after.

The government had told them to stay put. Not that he put much faith in the current bunch of delinquents squatting in the state house, not since they'd taken his licence. If Conrad hadn't taken his car, maybe he'd have left, too. Maybe not. Out on the road, away from safety, away from food and the familiar, that's where you got in trouble. It was how the Meisners had been infected when they'd gone out to look for food. They'd come back, of course. Rushed home. Shut the doors. Pulled the curtains. Hoped. Prayed. He'd had to shoot them both after they'd turned. They hadn't been the first, though. No, the first was poor old Clint Hoffenbaker.

As far as he was concerned, Clint was one of the few normal people in the retirement commune. The palaeontologist was a little slow in his speech. As a consequence, some of the residents here, mostly those who thought palaeontology was a new-fangled diet, thought that made him slow in the head. He wasn't. Clint had learned to be cautious in what he'd said, and to whom, conscious of what ingrained bigotry might lay beneath a stranger's smile.

Jack finished his coffee; it was time to begin his patrol. He went from room to room, peering through the single narrow slit he'd left in each of the wooden boards otherwise covering the windows. Outside, he'd strung wires high and low around the house. The living might be able to duck under or step over, but the undead would drift right into them. None of the wires had been disturbed. It wasn't much of a precaution, but what else could he do? Attach bells? Sound brought zombies. Bells would bring more. Install motion-sensitive cameras like he had on the farm? He had none here. To find some would require a trip to a store. That would mean leaving. Clint's car was still under its tarp in the lot. The 1965 Ford Mustang was fun to drive. He'd had a go, twice, before they'd taken his licence. But it would be like blaring a come-hither siren all the way there and back, defeating the purpose and probably hastening his end. Nope. If you left, you couldn't come back, so he'd stay put, shepherding his supplies, hoping everyone else was doing the same, and that, somewhere, someone was pulling order out of this chaos.

After his visual patrol came the radio check. Conrad had given him the ham radio as a post-moving gift after one of their regular stilted phone calls. He'd not used it before the outbreak. He *had* owned a set before, buying it when Conrad had been just a boy. To the best of his recollection, and his was better than most, they'd powered up the set on nine occasions over three years. For Jack, it had been one of his many failed attempts to spend time with the boy, while coping with what, these days, would be called PTS. They'd tried astronomy, bat-tracking, bee-counting, and a host of other semi-scientific activities, but it was the handful of times spent trying to speak to strangers that had stuck in his boy's mind. Over the years, the memory had grown into some elaborate father-son tradition, at least to Conrad. Jack's only memory was of clutching his hands together so his son didn't see them shake.

"This is Jack Harper, broadcasting in the clear. Anyone talk back?"

He waited, thinking about that half cup of coffee he had left. Conrad would always have cocoa with extra marshmallows when they'd sat at the set. When was the last time he'd had a marshmallow? Or any candy? Years.

"This is Jack Harper, Washington State. Still alive, still reaching out. Is anyone out there?"

What was the name of that fancy candy the English girl brought over? Marks and someone. No, he forgot. Nice taste to it. Really clear flavours. That was five years ago now, wasn't it? Or was it longer? Six years? She'd come over on a university exchange programme. Dessie had volunteered to be her local guide. Kim had come to live on the farm because her campus accommodation was a scandal. Or was it seven years? It didn't matter. One of the lessons of getting old was that time was a lot more elastic than it had seemed when young.

"Hello? Is anyone there?"

He sat bolt upright. The voice was unfamiliar but came through clearly.

"This is Jack Harper. Who's this?"

"Micky Stanislov. You're not the firefighter I was talking to last night?"

"No, son, I'm Sergeant Jack Harper, retired. What's your situation?"

"Bad," Micky said. "Real bad. There are seventy-five of us, and we're nearly out of water. Seattle was hit by a nuke. Did you know that?"

"No. No, I didn't."

"We're surrounded. There are thousands outside. Zombies."

"Are you armed?"

"The soldiers left us a few guns, but there aren't many bullets left."

"Are the zombies likely to get in?" Jack asked.

"No. The walls are sound. For now. But some people are talking about leaving. Some of us might survive, and that's better than everyone dying."

"You've got to stay put," Jack said. "Stay put for as long as you can, and that's a lot longer than you think. People can go weeks without food."

"We're almost out of water."

"Knock holes in the roof and gather rainwater. We're due a deluge."

"And then what? How long do we have to wait? When's help going to come?"

Jack could hear the desperation in his young voice. Twenty winters old, if that. Just a kid terrified out of his wits. Jack's gaze fell on his rifle.

"Micky. Tell me where you are. Give me your position, over."

He waited.

"Micky?"

He leaned back, listening, waiting, wondering what he would do if Micky replied. What *could* he do? Get in that old Ford Mustang, drive like hell, and hope he made it in time for… for what? What could one person do against thousands? Nothing, if he didn't have the address.

In frustration, he stood. Of their own accord, his feet returned him to the coffee pot. No, he was already feeling a little jittery. He'd reheat it later. Or maybe tomorrow. He needed to preserve water, too. His supply came from the rain barrels behind his property and the communal greenhouses. It had rained last night, heavily enough that he'd spared some for a wash, and it was certain to rain again within the week, if not within the hour. He went through to the pantry, giving it a once-over check for mice. It was fine. He had enough food for another ten weeks, but he didn't have much of an appetite anyway. What would he do after ten weeks? His gaze fell on the radio set, sitting on the small kitchen table. He didn't think Micky would reply. One person going to help seventy? It should have been the other way around.

It was nearing ten, and he'd been up since five, but he still called it breakfast, and today he was finishing the last packet of cereal. He almost cheered. No more cereal meant that tomorrow he could start on the pancakes. There was enough mix for two weeks. After that, he might as well push breakfast to eleven and start calling it lunch, because no one ate rice for breakfast. The milk was the long-life oat-based swill Dessie had bought for him. Milk by mail? Surely that was a sign that the world was due to collapse. Three cartons a week for six months. It was a good thing it had a long shelf life; he'd kept it in the pantry, only bringing it out when she visited. It wasn't so bad, not with cereal, but he did so miss adding a splash of cream. One for the cup, one for the bowl; it was another of his morning rituals, now but a dream. He took the bowl back to the kitchen table and slowly ate, trying to lose himself in his book, but unable to take one eye from the radio.

By noon, his book had been abandoned. He'd tried to reach Micky, but to no avail. It was just like the handful of other people he'd managed to connect with. One minute they were there, but the next, there was only silence. He stood, half-heartedly stretched, and headed over to the part of the open-plan space mockingly called a living room. He opened the flap in his blinds and looked across to the Johnson-hyphens. Their front curtains were open. That was unusual, and anything unusual was dangerous.

After ten minutes, they came outside. Technically, both were armed. In trained hands, a hammer or a lawn-edging tool could wreak havoc. In hands driven by fear and rage, they could still cause a lot of damage. Those two would be lucky if they didn't drop them on their own feet. They had some bags, too, but those looked empty. Where were they going? Here? No. Ah, number nine. Of course. Ruben's house.

Ruben wasn't a solid citizen like Clint, but he had some interesting travel stories. He'd lost all of his money and most of his family in one of the dot-com booms. But he'd stayed in touch with one grandson and had made enough in the years since to send him to film school. Ruben was gone now. Not dead. Well, *maybe* not dead. He'd left three days after Manhattan, driving to Northern California and his grandson. He'd left nearly everything he owned behind, and now the Johnsons were going to steal it.

Jack sat behind his rifle, and lowered his eye to the scope, tracking the husband, and then the wife, as they walked, jogged, and then walked up to the front door. The keys were in the lock. Jack had put them there himself. Each time someone had left, Jack had taken the emergency key from the live-in caretaker's house and gone to clean up. Any open food went into the trash, but there was never much. And then he'd left the key in the door, in case someone needed to reach safety quickly.

Stay inside, that's all they had to do. Just stay put, stay inside, and you'd be safe. If everyone had done that, the world would be putting itself to rights about now. Go outside, and you became a target. Zombies followed sound. The houses were well insulated. As long as you were sensible, you wouldn't be caught. But no. The hyphen worshipers had to go out. Again. Because they thought they were special. Only children had the luxury of thinking they're special, and only because grown-ups who knew better kept an eye out for them. Adults who thought they were special, who thought rules were only for others, tended to have reality smack them square between the eyes. He'd learned that in the jungle.

And here was reality, right on cue. The creature was young, with that shaved-sides, long-on-top haircut that made every kid look like a pineapple. The clothing was barely more than pyjamas. Then again, maybe he'd been asleep when he'd been infected. Blood covered his long-sleeved top and most of his face. Jack was glad of that. He hated when he recognised the people he was about to kill. The zombie was on the drive, approaching the floral calendar. It had heard something, but it hadn't identified where. Not yet. Maybe it'd turn around and go back the way it had come.

The zombie spun towards Ruben's house. It had definitely heard something. Be quiet, Jack thought. Why couldn't they just be quiet? It wasn't so hard, was it? He picked up his rifle, carried it to the front door, and checked that the homemade suppressor was firmly attached. He opened the door and stepped forward, checking his nine and his three, but there was no danger nearer than that young zombie. In one fluid movement, he raised the rifle and fired. Even with the suppressor, the shot sounded louder than a slamming car door, and far louder than the sound of the corpse collapsing onto the sidewalk.

Harvey Johnson opened the door of Ruben's house and actually stepped outside as he inspected the dead zombie lying on the sidewalk. Jack lowered the rifle, saying nothing. Telling the man what a fool he was would just be more sound to lure the undead.

"Jack? Are you there? Can you hear me?" The voice came from the radio.

He closed the door and hurried as fast as he could to the kitchen table. "Micky, I'm here. Where are you? Give me your location."

The reply was slow in coming. "There's no point," Micky said. "They opened the gate. They didn't wait."

"Who opened the gate, Micky? Slow down and tell me what happened."

"While I was talking to you, some of the others opened the gate and tried to drive out. There were too many zombies. They got in. They got inside. I'm trapped in here."

"In the radio room?"

"Yeah. It's just me. I don't know if anyone else survived. The screaming's stopped."

"Are there any windows?"

"Yes. I mean, no. It's a computer lab. The wall by the door is just one big window looking out into the hall. They're outside. I can see them. The window won't hold. Or the door won't. They're going to get in."

"Don't panic," Jack said. "Worst thing you can do is panic. Are you armed?"

"Yes. Yes, I've got a gun. One of the soldiers gave it to me before he went to help with the evacuation."

"And there's one door?" Jack asked. "Let them in through the door, then smash the glass and make your exit through the window. Do you know where there's some rope?"

"What, to hang myself?"

"Get to the roof, secure the roof access, and wait on the rooftop. Tell me where you are and I'll be on the road in five minutes. The rope's so you can climb down when I get there."

There was a long pause on the line. "I'm in a wheelchair, Jack. The door's breaking. Good luck."

Jack gripped the arms of his chair. He wanted to go into his bedroom and close the door, sit in the dark, and never emerge. He wanted to go outside, start walking, and never stop. He wanted to rip and tear, to shout and scream. He knew better than to do any of those, so he just sat in his chair, waiting for the rage to pass. Slowly, he became aware of movement in the corner of his eye. He returned to the window. Harvey was rolling the zombie's corpse down to the gate. Jack leaned back. Ten weeks of food. Based on how frequently the Johnsons raided a house, his neighbours wouldn't last much longer. Water depended on rain, and there wouldn't be as much of that in ten weeks. How long could he sit around, waiting for help to come?

It was easy to say leave, but to go where? The farm? He'd have to get across the Columbia River, but after that rumour about an evacuation, the roads had become a nightmare. Travel always spread viruses, and zombies were no exception. The evacuation must be long over by now. No, he'd go to the farm, but not yet. He had food here, and water, and a roof. He wasn't a drain on Conrad's limited resources. No, it was better that he stay put, at least for now.

Outside, he saw Harvey sprint for his house and slam the door closed. There was only one thing that could mean. Neither rushing, nor dawdling, Jack walked around the interior of his house. He picked up the shotgun by the front door, put up the ladder that led up to the crawl space, and pulled down the bars on the bedroom door behind which was his pantry and armoury. As he went through the kitchen, he downed the last of the coffee. No point saving it now. Finally, he returned to the table where he put his rifle back into place.

Ever since the first news from Manhattan, he'd wondered what he'd do if a horde stormed up the driveway. He was too old to run. The commune had a wall around it, but no gate across the entrance. He'd considered finding something to block the driveway, but a gate wasn't much of a deterrent without armed people standing behind it. He'd tried to recruit a few, but instead they'd left. All except the Johnsons. Since he was on his own, and since one wall was as good as another, he'd decided to make his stand in his home, though mostly on top of it. He'd have the high ground. When the bullets ran out, he'd just lie down and wait for the cold to take him.

He leaned forward, lining his rifle up on the drive, and saw he'd been wrong. Harvey hadn't been running from a horde. It was a car. A ridiculously impractical lime-green Kia that had no place on a farm, but which was perfect for a young lawyer trying to save the world. As fast as he could, he dashed outside, though he'd only reached the kerb by the time the car's passenger and driver had both got out. The driver, he didn't know. The passenger didn't look anything like a big-city champion of justice. Dressed in patched denim, with a baseball cap over her eyes, she looked just like she was a student again.

"You're alive!" his granddaughter, Dessie, said, almost skipping up the path towards him.

"Of course I am," he said, allowing her a brief hug. "What took you so long getting here? Did you forget someone's father took away my car?"

"He's dead, Gramps. Dad's dead," she said.

"Conrad? Oh." His shoulders slumped. "How?" he managed, his voice coming out in a hoarse whisper.

"The Brubeckers had been infected," Dessie said. "He was trying to save their boy."

"Of course he was," Jack said, forcing the emotions down. "I raised him right. He's a good man. And the boy?"

"Alive."

"Good. Good." He breathed out slowly. "We'll talk about it later. Are you staying, or are we leaving?"

"Leaving, I think," Dessie said. "There's supposed to be an evacuation to Vancouver Island. We thought we could all go."

"No," he said. "The coast is overrun. I heard it over the radio. Everyone was trying to get in on this evacuation. What's wrong with the farm?"

"There are zombies everywhere. Is it safe here? There are forty-one of us."

"Here? No. There's no water source. Not enough room, either. We'll head back across the border. I know the terrain in our state. I know where we can hide."

"You're taking charge, Gramps?"

He considered the question, but only for a moment. "Yes."

"Good. How long do you need to pack?"

"Twenty minutes," he said. "Who's this?"

He gestured to the woman standing by the car, a .357 Magnum in hand, and her eyes on the twitching curtains of number three.

"Grandpa, this is Henley," Dessie said, walking over to take the other woman's hand.

"It's nice to meet you, sir," Henley said.

"Sir? Hmph," he said, taking in the beanpole waif who'd be knocked over by a strong breeze. She wouldn't know what to do with a good meal. Maybe that was a good thing now that regular meals would be in short supply. "You're dating, are you?"

"Yes. Yes we are," Dessie said firmly.

"Family calls me Grandpa Jack, or Grandpa, not sir. Do you know what to do with that hand-cannon?"

"You betcha," Henley said.

"Then you'll know what to do with a rifle. Here." He handed her his. "Watch the road. Zombies are about today. Dessie, the pantry is already packed. You just need to bring it out. I'll be there in a moment, but there's something I need to handle first."

"What?" she asked, but he didn't reply. Instead, he headed down towards the Johnson house.

He stopped on the path leading up the drive. The door remained closed.

"I know you're in there," Jack said. "I can see your curtains twitching. Come on out. I'm done shouting." To emphasise his point, he said no more. He counted to five and decided that his civic duty had been met. As he turned around, the door opened.

"Hello, Jack," Harvey said, only his face and fingers of one hand visible.

"You can put the gun down, Harvey. If I wanted to shoot you, I'd have done it already." He paused, thinking through what he'd said. "No, I mean if I was *going* to shoot you, I'd have done it. We're leaving. You two as well. Pack your things. Food, clothing, and drinking water, if you've any left."

"We're fine here, thanks, Jack."

"You're not. You're already scavenging from our neighbours. I know how much was in Ruben's house, and you've already emptied numbers seven and four. The food here will be all gone in a couple of months. Less, the way you two eat."

"Help will come," Jane said, from behind her husband.

"And it's just arrived. You're coming with us. Don't make me drag you out of there. You've got twenty minutes."

Shaking his head at the impossible stubbornness of the old, he walked back up to his house.

"Eyes on the road, Henley," he said as he passed the car. She snapped to attention.

Inside his cottage, Dessie was loading a bag.

"You're doing that wrong," he said.

"Of course I am. There won't be enough room for everything."

"We'll have two cars, and the Johnsons don't have much to bring."

"Your friends are coming too?"

"They're not friends, and they're only neighbours in the geographic sense, but they're people, so we'll help. Why's she called Henley?"

"What do you mean? That's her name. She chose it."

"I guessed that," he said, and opened the gun locker. "And why do her pants have so many zips?"

"What? Oh. It's goth-skater chic. Very retro. All the old stuff is in again."

"She's a skater? That's no job for someone your age. It's no job for *anyone.*"

"No, she's a coder. Or she was."

"Hmph." He knew what a coder was. Vaguely. They were supposed to earn good money. "And she's obsessed with fashion, is she?"

"It's important to some people. Even now. Especially now, when we've lost so much. Sometimes our identity is all we have left."

"When your neighbours start eating each other's faces, I'd say—" But whatever it was would remain unspoken as he was interrupted by a gunshot. He hurried to the door, reaching it three steps behind Dessie.

"Zombie," Henley said. "Only one."

"Good shot," Jack said approvingly, and went back inside to finish packing. It didn't take long. In preparation for a siege, he'd already packed everything useful and had it ready to be hauled up to the roof. Everything else, the nicknacks, the mementos, the books, the ornaments, those could be left behind. Most of them.

He picked up a misshapen ashtray with chipped yellow paint. "Your dad made this for me. He was nine. It was supposed to have been a mug, but it went wrong, so he turned it into an ashtray. Learn and adapt, he said. I was very proud of him."

"I know. He knew," Dessie said. "He knew why you didn't want to stay on the farm. He didn't know why you wanted to live all the way out here, but he understood."

"I loved him, dearly. I… I'm not good at expressing it."

Dessie nodded but said nothing.

"We should hurry," he said.

"Is there anything else you want to take?" she asked, looking at the photos on the table next to the easy chair. "Oh. You kept this one."

"Which? Oh, yes. You, your sister, and that English girl, Kim."

"With Mom and Aunt Sue in the background."

"My girls," he said.

"You've got your radio set up. Did you hear anything about England?"

"Not really. They were moving people to the coast and seemed to have a handle on things. Of course, it's a smaller place. Easier to manage."

"Maybe they're doing okay."

"Maybe. We'll take that photo. Okay, anything else. No, we're set. How far away are the rest of you?"

"About twenty miles."

"Then we'd better hurry. I want to be across the river before nightfall."

Chapter 1 - Dead Letter Office
Gifford, Washington State, March 4th, Year One

A shattered skull, the otherwise intact skeleton, the handgun that had fallen into the pickup's footwell, it was obviously another suicide. Maggs Espoir picked up the note left on the passenger seat of the blue Ford. A year entombed with a decaying corpse had caused the ink to fade, the paper to yellow, and a pale green mould to claim the bottom third of the page. The few words still legible — *sorry, nineteen, carousel, love* — gave only a tantalising glimpse into the victim's final regrets. Carefully, she placed the note back on the seat, picked up the semiautomatic Smith and Wesson, and ejected the magazine. Five bullets remained. Five chances to say no to death, but maybe this victim knew their luck was played out. She slipped the rounds into her pocket; they were too precious to leave behind. The back seat held three thirty-gallon water barrels, all empty. The trunk held nothing but empty tote bags and a pair of children's ice skates.

"D'you find anything good?" Marshall Henderson called out. The eighteen-year-old was strolling across the highway with a shotgun slung over his shoulder as casually as if it were a hockey stick.

"Just a suicide from the early outbreak," Maggs said. "I think he came for water, but got bitten and decided that this was a good place to check out."

"Better than some, I guess," Marshall said, giving the car the briefest glance before turning to look west, taking in the rushing tumult of the Columbia River. He shrugged. "Kayleigh's drained the deer. We're ready to go unless you want to eat some here?"

Maggs had never had children of her own, but she had spent enough time around them to recognise the tone of a hungry teenager. In Marshall's defence, hunger had become a regular visitor long before they'd been forced across the border into the United States.

She checked her watch. "It's not even ten-thirty. You know the rules. No lunch before half eleven, and no dinner before five. Tell everyone to pack up, and we'll get moving."

She closed the trunk and spared a moment to look at the empty water containers in the back seat. Had someone been expecting him home? Had they sat up long enough for dusk to become dawn, hoping for his return? She knew well that nerve-fraying vigil, and from long before the outbreak. Whenever the storms raged, when all sensible souls were tucked up with a good book, it was her husband who'd ventured out into the frigid dark to keep the lights of civilisation burning bright. On those nights, at home, alone, her mind would play unwilling host to a gathering of her darkest fears. Though he'd returned, time and again, she'd known each parting could be the last. It had taken the end of civilisation for fear to become reality. Even now, after a year's separation, she refused to think he might be dead. No, not her Etienne.

She closed the driver's door and returned to her young team. Roy and Ricardo, the two former miners, were finishing securing the three dead deer to the roof of the fun-bus. They'd spotted the animals from the crest of a rise half a kilometre farther south. The five herbivores had been obliviously munching on the first shoots of spring until the engine noise had disturbed them. The animals had looked toward the now unfamiliar sight of an SUV and a camper van, but then resumed grazing, dismissing the vehicles' growl as unthreatening. That had been their first mistake. The second was assuming that the two-legs who emerged from their mobile steel cages could only move at a zombie's lumbering stagger. Ginger and Georgie had fired their crossbows in near unison. Only after two of the deer had fallen did the pack begin to bolt, but not before Roy had bagged a third.

"I bet we get bear for dinner," Kayleigh said, pointing at the blood dripping down the ancient van's windows.

"If we do, we'll find space for it," Georgie said, lovingly patting her old camper van, whose sunflower-patterned paintwork was now streaked red. The VW camper had originally come from France, and during the lifetime of De Gaulle. How it had ended up in Quebec was explained in the logbook's epic tale of love and inheritance, and more repairs than Theseus's ship. Georgette Barbazan had inherited the van after the outbreak from an aunt who, like Etienne and the dead driver of the abandoned car, had gone out one night for supplies and never returned.

"We'll stop for lunch at Kettle Falls," Maggs said. "If we can cross the Columbia River there, we could cross the border today. Imagine sleeping in Canada again."

Her young companions grinned at the idea, laughing and joking as they finished packing up. It did sound so simple. Cross the river, the border, the mountains, and then the industrial sprawl of the western hinterland before reaching the Fraser River. Even then, they would still need to find a boat to take them to Vancouver Island. They'd never been closer, or seemed so far away.

It was just over a year since the impossible news from New York had upended their lives. She and her husband, Etienne, had kept working as the world collapsed, ensuring a steady supply of electricity to Quebec and beyond. He kept venturing out into the increasingly dark and dangerous wilderness to repair the lines while she'd done what she could in the control room in Alma. Their once-quiet town had become as dangerous as any war zone, except there wasn't a soldier to be seen. Neighbours killed neighbours, whether they were infected or not, just to steal enough for a meal. When her husband hadn't returned, when the lights went out and there was nothing she could do to turn them back on, she'd fled, leaving him a note as to where to find her. Picking a destination had taken her all night. She'd needed somewhere remote, but close enough that she could reach it within a few hours. Somewhere with food and fences, and without people, and somewhere he would know.

The zoo at Saint-David-de-Falardeau had seemed to match her criteria. It certainly had fences, and it had food, if you didn't mind meat of a more exotic variety. How many people would have thought of going there for sanctuary? As it turned out, lots. Among them were the miners, Roy and Ricardo, and the mine's administrative assistant, Ginger Krasiński. They had been welcomed, and so had she. Fern, the zoo's chief zoologist and veterinarian, had already released the herbivores and put down the tigers and other carnivores, so meat was off the menu. To the zookeepers, the animals were co-workers, patients, and in some cases, friends. Nevertheless, that didn't stop Maggs thinking about giraffe steaks every time she had to eat a bowl of food-pellet slop. To some, living beyond their fences, even that seemed like paradise. As the risk of violent raids from their neighbours rose, the group decided to flee instead of fight.

Again, selecting a destination had been a challenge. They'd needed somewhere they could farm, somewhere remote, somewhere they could survive a long winter. For Maggs, that meant electricity. She'd drawn up a list of the hydroelectric dams she thought she could manage with help from the more engineering-minded of their group. Ear Falls on Lac Seul had been selected. Fern knew of the area as a refuge for caribou, while Gordon Thouvenot, the mine's union rep and foreman, had spent a few summers catching walleye in the vast lake's murky waters. Electricity, meat, fish; it had seemed a lot when they'd sat down for another gritty meal of pellet stew. The downside was that it was situated halfway between Lake Superior and Lake Winnipeg, so it could easily be reached by refugees heading north from Minnesota or from farther south. On balance, they'd decided the risk was worth it.

Along the way, they picked up Kayleigh Brauer, an agricultural student from Wichita who, along with three friends, had skipped classes and the country to get over a bad breakup. Kayleigh had picked Quebec City as a destination because it was the first flight available when they reached the airport. Whether it had been the right choice for her, it hadn't been for her friends who'd died during their escape from the dying city.

While Ear Falls was deserted, the nearby town of Red Lake was packed with survivors from across Canada, the border, and even from Mexico. The total number fluctuated, and there was never a truly accurate census, but by summer, seventeen thousand lived near or around Red Lake. Five hundred found a home at Ear Falls, including Maggs and her team.

Early one morning in July, Marshall had walked into the hydroelectric plant and started sweeping. She'd not noticed him for two days, but since he seemed happy to work and reluctant to complain, she'd said nothing until four roughs had arrived from Red Lake, looking for him. That was when his story came out, and it was a common enough one, even before the outbreak: a boy who thought he was a man, a bad crowd, an invented debt, a future of servitude. They'd sent the wannabe enforcers packing, put together a posse, gone north, and visited the rest of the gang to teach them what it meant to be human. The mayor of Red Lake hadn't liked that, nor had the deputy mayor, ostensibly running Ear Falls. But what else could they have done? If you didn't stand up for the weak, you had to bow down to the strong.

Despite that, and a hundred other minor incidents, life hadn't been too bad, largely because they all assumed there would be other groups scattered across the world. As soon as the zombies died, they would reconnect and rebuild. Another week, another month, another year, and it would all be over. But as the first hint of fall brought a crisp chill to a lazy dawn, plague had arrived in Red Lake. They didn't know where it came from, but it had spread fast. Within days, it seemed everyone there was infected. They'd closed the road linking the dam to the town. When they finally went north to see why no more than a handful of dying refugees had come their way, it was to find everyone dead or gone. Only those around Ear Falls had remained, though some didn't stay long. By harvest, only four hundred and ninety were left. A sudden storm ruined most of their crop, and more people vanished while the rest tried to salvage what little they could.

Winter came early and ferociously. The snow grew deeper. Tempers shortened. The mayor disappeared. Since he couldn't have fled, Maggs suspected a darker end for him, but had no proof. A ballot had been held to select a new leader. Fern was elected and she immediately created a council. That had been a mistake. Democracy truly had been their first step towards despotism. The first thaw had arrived as early as the winter, bringing the realisation that the zombies were dying. Again, they'd decided to leave, seeking better farmland a good distance from the plague city. Once again, people looked to Maggs for a destination. With plenty of gasoline and with the undead seeming to have died during the cold months, she'd suggested Vancouver Island. Within hours, everyone was speaking of it as their promised land, and so they'd departed, but not before she'd left a note for Etienne saying where they'd gone.

They'd barely travelled five hundred kilometres before the snows returned, trapping them for five days. After another two hundred grinding, sliding, freezing kilometres, they'd lost five of their coaches and had to stop to look for more. Despite the note she'd left for Etienne, she thought they should hunker down until the weather eased, and then find the nearest dam. Fern agreed. Unfortunately, she was no longer in power. Martin Genk, a pump-and-dump millionaire, had engineered a quiet coup, using the votes of Gilbert Brass, their militia captain, and Ezra Schmidt, their chief caterer and one-time mega-pastor, to deselect her as leader. As they controlled the militia, Ezra's semi-militant acolytes, the food and fuel stores, and had the democratic fiction of a legitimate vote, she and Fern were powerless to stop them. Instead, they had done their best to prevent the clowns from turning their convoy into a circus, but with mixed results.

Initially, aside from some obviously larger portions and less work for their new overlords, nothing had changed, including their destination. Now, eight weeks since they'd left Lac Seul behind, the tension was growing. Maggs was glad that she, Georgie, Marshall, Ginger, Ricardo, Roy, and Kayleigh were on scouting duty and didn't have to spend their days trapped in the camp.

Hats, their ghost-grey cat, and the eighth member of the scouting team, let out an irritated hiss.

"No! It's my blanket!" Marshall said as he tried to dislodge the cat. "Ow! He just slapped me!"

"Because it's *his* blanket, and always has been," Ricardo said. "You were just keeping it warm for him."

Maggs smiled. Perhaps things weren't as bad as they seemed. They had fresh meat. They were close to Canada and close to the Pacific. Spring had truly arrived, and though a day didn't go by without her seeing a zombie, the hours often did.

She kept the speed low. They'd gone through three tyres already this week and were down to their last two spares. The next time one blew, she'd look for a new car. There was no way that Georgie would ever relinquish her camper van, but this SUV was a relatively new addition to their fleet. Marshall had spotted it just after they'd crossed the border. It came with five thousand miles on the clock, and every Bluetooth accessory known to twenty-first-century gimmickry. Not that any of those worked. When they'd first turned on the car's digital control console, a petulant message appeared, demanding that the car be taken to the nearest dealer for a firmware update.

"The sign," Ricardo said, gesturing ahead.

The word *Survivors* had been painted over a road sign, with an arrow pointing east towards the forest, where another sign was attached to a tree.

"There's another sign on the ground," Marshall said as Maggs slowed.

"Look for a turning," Maggs said as they passed an upturned picnic table daubed with the same one word surrounded by painted hearts. It might have looked more welcoming if gravity hadn't dribbled the red paint downwards in an effect far too similar to blood. A hundred metres beyond that was a USPS office, bearing the same sign in faded paint, but on a building daubed with dozens of names.

Maggs stopped and threw open the door even as she scanned the names for her own.

"Wait," Ricardo said, jumping out even as he grabbed his masonry-pick from the footwell. With a sawed-off shotgun in one hand and the pick in the other, he marched over to the small postal outpost like an avalanche ready to fill a canyon.

"It's abandoned," Maggs said, though it was no use. Ricardo raised his foot and kicked the door open.

"I guess it's lunchtime," Roy said as he jumped out of the bus.

"Fine, yes," Maggs said. "Ginger and Georgie, see if you can get a bit closer to the river. See how swollen it is. Keep an eye out for signs of fishing or water collection."

It was an odd place to have a post office. There didn't seem to be a town nearby, or even a village. The only house in sight was an equally small cottage almost hidden behind rampant pines. But if it was a strange place to find a post office, it was a stranger one to find survivors, though there didn't seem to be anyone around.

"It's clear," Ricardo said, coming out of the door with a thoughtful look on his face. "Odd place. I'm going to check out the surroundings."

"Marshall, go with him. And don't go beyond shouting distance," she said before turning her attention to the names.

Rachel Wood, Marty Gower, Flip; there were more than she'd first realised, with some names partially hidden by later and larger additions. Inside was a very different story. Hundreds of stories, really. The wall was covered in scraps of paper, with names and short messages.

To Felix Hawton from Sophia Hawton. We tried to join the evacuation, but we couldn't get through the mountains. The people who haven't left are doing absolutely everything to protect what they have. It's chaos. We're heading south. We'll get work at a farm. Farmers will still need workers. When things get organised, we'll see you again. We love you, Sophia, Carla, and Kit.

Linda Renford, from Johnny. Linda, if you're reading this, then you had the same idea we had. Follow the river south, join the evacuation ferries at the mouth of the Columbia. There's so many people on the roads, they'll redirect the ships. I'm sure of it. Stay strong. I'll wait for you.

Queenie. We went to the cabin. Come look for us. L.

They bombed us. I knew they would. Whoever is reading this, it's an invasion. The zombies, the collapse, now the bombs, it's all been planned. Don't trust anyone who says they're from the government, they're just enemy agents. Hide. Stay inside. Don't trust anyone.

Joanne, your sister's place isn't safe. Zombies came. We survived, but they wrecked everything. We're heading into the mountains. Octavia.

Nicky, I love you. I'm sorry.

Maggs took out a phone and began recording while silently skimming through the messages. The notes nearest the door seemed to have been written close to the outbreak. A little further on, she found missives from after the bombs had fallen. Towards the back, the notes grew more spaced apart. It was difficult to tell which was most recent, but the one attached to the counter had been left in November.

Harvey, winter's coming. We're heading back across the border. You know where to find us if you can, and we're going to keep on assuming you will. To anyone else, it's coming up to Thanksgiving. We were trying to get to the border, but the snow just started falling. If we don't turn back now, we'll be trapped for the winter. We're heading back to Oregon. We'll try again in the new year. Who you are, who you were, and who was behind all this doesn't matter now. We've just got to survive, so I'll wish good luck to you, because I know you'd wish the same to us. Jack.

Maggs lingered on the last note for a few moments, reading it again before heading back outside. Meat sizzled on the electric grill running from the small generator. Ginger and Georgie were cleaning the van while Kayleigh dressed their three deer.

"What's the river like?" Maggs asked.

"Wet," Ginger said.

"There's a spot where you could collect water," Georgie said, "and there are a few ropes and buckets, but they haven't been moved in months. Maybe not since last year. What's in the post office?"

"Notes left by people who travelled this way," Maggs said. "The most recent I've found so far was in November by a group who picked this spot to turn around and head back to Oregon before winter truly set in. There's a few hundred notes, though, so there might be a more recent one. I took a video, so we can go through it later."

"Are you going to leave a note for Etienne?" Kayleigh asked.

"I… I suppose I should, yes," Maggs said, glancing again at the names daubed across the post office.

"I'll get the paint," Georgie said. As she went to add Etienne's name to the front of the post office, Maggs walked over to the SUV and retrieved her notebook. She'd been leaving notes for him ever since Lac Seul, though she was no longer sure he'd find them. In her dark moments, she dreaded that he was still in Alma, waiting for her to return. In her darkest moments, she tried not to think of him at all, out of fear of what nightmare scenarios her brain might conjure. But leaving the notes had become something their crew did, just like the letters she wrote to him most evenings.

My Dearest Etienne, since the Columbia River drains into the Pacific, we are finally close to the ocean. It's been almost two months since we left Lac Seul. I don't know if you found any of my other messages, or if you'll find this one. Other people have left notes here, so I will as well. We're still aiming for Vancouver Island, and I hope I'll see you there. To everyone else, hello. It's March, a year since the nuclear war. We've travelled from Ontario in the hope of reaching the better farming climate on the far side of the mountains. There are people still alive out there, in small groups and alone. Some are friendly. Some are not. We think the zombies are dying now, and that the cold weather kills them more quickly. Good luck, whoever you are, and keep heart. You're not alone. The worst is over. You will survive. Maggs.

Chapter 2 - The Difficulties of Making Friends
Kettle Falls

Maggs yawned as she put the SUV into drive. In the back, Marshall and Hats contentedly shared a charred strip of fat. Having a second portion of flash-fried venison had been a mistake. She certainly shouldn't have had a third. Her stomach wasn't used to being full, and was gurgling in protest at the unexpected labour while her brain was insisting it was nap time.

"We'll have a rest when we get to the border," she said.

"Want to bet you fall asleep first?" Ricardo asked.

"Is it that obvious? Then we'd better continue our education. Something lively, please."

Ricardo grinned and turned on the CD player. Today's accompaniment was Spanish guitar overlaid with an allegro drum beat and lyrics about day labour on a California farm. She wasn't sure whether it should be classified as country, rap, or classical, but she was enjoying it. Nor did she know whether the artist had been an award-winning success, or if this was an album sold from a guitar case. From the printed-at-home liner notes, she suspected the latter.

A week ago, while searching a drive-thru for forgotten condiments, they'd found a bag containing a dog lead, some chew toys, a blanket, a coil of rope, and the CD. There was no sign of the dog or its human companion, but no sign of recent violence, either. The lyrics were too fast to follow, so she let the music wash over her, letting her brain conjure images of hot southern summers, cool drinks, and warm nights. Yes, life was hard, but it wasn't over, so she listened to new songs, discovered new books, and tried her hand at new hobbies whenever she had the energy.

"Road sign," Ricardo said.

"Kettle Falls," Maggs said. "We're getting close."

The gas station immediately ahead was anything but inviting. The awning had collapsed onto the cab of a tyre-less van that had once been part of a barricade. A soot-stained husk of a school bus blocked the other lane, while razor wire had been dumped between the forest and the gas station.

"Danger!" Ricardo said, thumping the radio to kill the music. The driver-side wing mirror shattered.

"Ambush!" Marshall yelled.

From behind the gas station, a red tractor lurched onto the road, carrying a two-metre-high, four-metre-wide sheet-metal shield bolted to its front. The mobile barricade jounced into the gap between the school bus and the van, blocking the way ahead.

"Steady. It might just be a warning," Maggs said as she braked.

Behind her, Marshall gave an incoherent scream of fear and anger that was instantly lost beneath the roar of his revolver as he fired through the door.

Maggs spun her head left and right, trying to make sense of the chaos while clearing the ringing from her ears. People in muddy camouflage were moving towards them from both sides, three on the river's side, four from inland, plus whoever was behind the barricade.

Ricardo threw open his door and fired his shotgun one-handed, ripping an approaching hunter in half. Marshall had opened his door and was busily emptying his revolver in the general direction of the inland team.

With all chance of negotiating gone, Maggs grabbed the Glock from the door-tray, threw open the door, and jumped down into a shin-high drift of mud. She heard bullets hit metal, and cries of pain and anger, and ignored it all as she levelled the semi-automatic and fired at the advancing attackers. Three shots, and one dropped. She didn't know if that had been her bullet; it didn't matter. She found her next target, a woman in a grubby green parka fumbling with the bolt on an AR-15. Before she pulled the trigger, a puff of feathers erupted from the woman's coat as a crossbow bolt sprouted from her chest. Maggs glanced back at the funbus where Ginger and Georgie knelt on the roof. She couldn't see Kayleigh or Roy, but knew they'd be close. She'd lost sight of Ricardo, but she heard his shotgun roar above the Valkyrie's trumpet of handguns and screams. Damn kids! They thought they were invulnerable until it was irrevocably proven that they weren't, but it was too late to retreat. That only left attack.

"Don't. Stop. Don't. Think," she repeated between breaths as she ran forward. Her voice grew in volume, becoming a banshee's wail as she slogged through the sticky mud caught between the vehicle and the verge. A figure bedecked in Arctic white swung around the side of the boarded-up gas station with a rifle held at his hip. She kept on running. He looked down, shaking his rifle. Was it jammed? She fired twice as she sprinted straight for him. The third time she pulled the trigger, it was her turn to be betrayed by her gun. She didn't know if it was jammed or empty, or if any of her bullets had hit; she just kept running, kept screaming, kept pulling the trigger until she was close enough to leap.

She aimed for his shoulders, but he twisted, trying to stab at her with the rifle's barrel. He missed. Her hands clawed at his coat as, unbalanced, they slipped down, tumbling together into the swampy muck. His greasy hair swept across her face as she jabbed at his kidneys, but his thick coat dulled her blows. He swung a fist into the side of her head. It felt like she'd been hit by a truck. Her vision swam, her ears rang, her back and legs grew cold as he pushed her down, deeper into the mud. His fingers curled around her throat. She clawed at his hands, trying to break his grip while staring into eyes filled with fear and rage, and then with an oddly blank look of surprise. Something warm and wet sprayed across her face. The hands around her neck slackened. The body slumped on top of her before being hauled off. She looked up into Ricardo's worried eyes.

"Are you okay?" the young miner asked.

"I will be," she said, taking his offered hand. "Where are the rest of them?"

"They ran," he said as he pulled her up. He pointed his bloody masonry pick inland. A distant rifle shot sounded, but Roy and Kayleigh were making sure their assailants kept running.

Maggs rubbed her neck as she took in the carnage. After all that fire and fury, there were only four corpses left in the frosty mud, each surrounded by a steaming pool of blood. None were her people, though Georgie was wrapping a bandage around Ginger's arm. Marshall moved quickly among the corpses, gathering loot.

"Just the guns and ammo, Marshall," Maggs called. "Ricardo, grab whatever fuel is in the tractor."

She leaned against the abandoned school bus and breathed deeply. Never once in her life had she wanted to be a soldier, and the wrong side of fifty was definitely too late to start learning *that* trade. Kayleigh and Roy walked slowly back from the edge of the road, their eyes on the distant treeline.

"We counted nine of them still running," Kayleigh said. "At least two were injured. They went to ground in a cluster of houses over yonder."

"Okay, go help Marshall and Ricardo. Let's get out of here before they come back."

She ejected her magazine, confirming the worst. Her gun hadn't fired because she was out of bullets. She slid it back into her holster. Among the grey clouds, it was hard to discern, but there might have been a hint of smoke to the north.

"Do you want the knives as well?" Marshall asked, cutting through her contemplation. He carried a shotgun over one shoulder, a rifle over the other, and a pair of revolvers in his belt.

"No, we don't need them. But take those revolvers out of your pants before you trip and sing soprano the rest of your life! Give them here."

Sheepishly, he handed the revolvers to her. Both had wood-effect stocks, and one had an overlong barrel. Civilian guns, for sure. The long-barrelled weapon had a little crest on the grip's base. She had no idea what it meant, if it meant anything at all.

"Tell everyone we're moving out," she said.

"Yes, Maggs." He splashed his way through the mud, and she looked back up the road towards the town. Somewhere up there was a bridge that would have taken them to a road that, eventually, would have led them back to Canada. They'd have to find a different route.

Chapter 3 - Signs and Poor Tents
Sprague Lake

They stopped just before the USPS office to check they weren't being followed. Twenty kilometres later, they stopped again atop the crest of a hill where the Columbia was nothing but a shadow nearly lost among a distant forest. They silently stood, listening as much as watching, but aside from a warning chirruping in the treetops around them, there was nothing to be heard. The third stop was an hour later, so they could change their clothes and inspect the damage. It was only superficial, both to them and to the vehicles. Georgie was more upset about the bullet holes in her bus than Ginger was about the scrape to her arm.

"You'll get Fern to look at it when we get back," Maggs said. "Until then, wear that sling."

"Maggs, it's fine, really," Ginger said.

"No, it's not. We shouldn't be shooting at each other," she said, before catching herself. She shook her head. "No matter how careful we are, it's never careful enough. You better check on Marshall. Whatever he's found, I'm sure we don't need it."

She walked out along the road to stand by Hats, who was attempting to be aloof and carefree while also not straying too far from the safety of their steel carriages.

"You're not fooling anyone," Maggs said. "But I hope I am." She closed her eyes, focusing on the sound of the birds, trying to slow her breathing, but couldn't hold back the stuttering gasp. She could feel shock was about to overcome her, so she bent down, and picked the cat up. That first shot, which had taken out the wing mirror, might have been an accident, or a warning shot that came too close. They didn't know if this group were truly hostile. They might merely have been cautious. Then again, they might have been murderous brigands. There was certainly no way to know now. "Why do people always have to destroy one another?"

"I don't think a world run by cats would be any better," Roy said.

"Oh, you'd be surprised," she said. "They can be quite sociable among themselves. It's only around us that they act superior. They think it makes them look cool. Is everyone okay?"

"I think so. Marshall found a coin collection. Some of it's silver. Do you want me to hurry them up?"

"No. We might as well head back now. We could do with a rest, and definitely an alternate route to the border. I'll have to spend some time with the maps."

Roy nodded, clearly indifferent. At twenty-five, Ricardo was the oldest. Roy was a year younger, but had only been working at the mine for a year. He'd taken the job to bail out his parents' bakery after they had made the mistake of borrowing money from a 'friend'. The interest and threats had nearly broken them. Gordon had stepped in, arranging a visit from the union lawyer accompanied by the police. A patrol car sitting outside the loan shark's business for eight hours was enough to scare him away, but the damage had been done. His parents' love for the kitchen had been robbed from them, so Roy had stayed on at the mine while everyone in the family, collectively and individually, tried to work out their next steps. But then the outbreak had come.

Five days after Manhattan, Ricardo and Roy had driven from the mine to collect Roy's parents. They were both dead. Neither man had shared any other details of that trip, and their silence spoke volumes. In losing one bond, Roy had forged another, but that had nearly been upset when Ricardo and Ginger became an item. It wasn't until they stumbled upon Kayleigh that balance had been restored. Now, for Roy, this journey was life. He had no goals beyond a good meal shared with good company followed by somewhere safe to sleep. They were all like that, these young adults who had so much promise, so much life. It saddened her that their ambitions had been so quickly demolished. It saddened her more to realise how flimsy were the foundations her generation had provided.

"D'you want a coin?" Marshall asked, coming out with the others in tow. "It's a dollar. I think it's gold."

"It's a Sacagawea dollar," Georgie said. "And it was in a case all on its own. No explanation as to why it was special, so we think it's gold."

She put Hats down so she could take it. "Thank you." It was far too light to be gold, but it was in perfect condition. "It's great." She pocketed it. "Let's head back. It should be dinner time."

A good bed, a good meal, and good company, sprinkled with whatever entertainment they could make. And the burning need to never stop searching for Etienne. In her deepest, darkest moments, she knew she'd never find him, and so she would forever search. Yes, it was a simple life, and on days like today, even that seemed out of reach.

It was nearing four, car-time, when the intertwining pillars of smoke from the cooking fires welcomed them back to the old campground at Sprague Lake. Their current base was on the lake's northern shore, protected by a chest-high barrier of aluminium sheets, bolstered by the flatbed trucks that carried some of their communal equipment. Maggs drummed on the wheel while she waited for the guards to let them in, but soreness from the battle quickly bubbled into impatience. She hammered the horn.

"Still waist-high," Ricardo said, pointing at the low fence.

"Mr Brass has had another busy day, hasn't he?" Maggs said bitterly. Whenever they stopped, Brass's guards were supposed to erect a head-height barrier out of whatever local supplies could be found. The aluminium sheets they carried with them were only supposed to be a temporary stopgap until better materials were found.

"Look out your wing mirror," Ricardo said.

Reflexively, she looked, but of course, the mirror was gone, shot out during the ambush.

"I don't think a wall will help us much against people with guns," he said.

"A valid point, but don't say it to Brass or he'll stop paying even lip service to the concept of a guard. Ah, finally."

Tatiana Olegovka, six-six of muscle and rage, and sergeant of the guard, appeared on the other side of the barrier, and glared at Maggs with practiced irritation. Maggs resisted the urge to monosyllabically express herself; instead she smiled sweetly. Technically, the second in command of the guard was Reggie Laughton, but everyone thought of Tatiana as Brass's number two, though no one dared call her that to her face. She'd have said that Tatiana had a face only acne could love if it weren't for her improbable entanglement with Alexander. The bookish mathematician was so habitually lost in the past that Tatiana had to go looking for him before every meal. Fortunately, Tatiana had other things on her mind today and let them through with nothing more than a dismissive wave.

For the first week after leaving Lac Seul, their encampments had looked like the last night of a festival, with the mood to match. Of course, back then, they had all slept indoors. After the change in leadership, the mood had darkened. Now, with their nerves as frayed as their clothing, they resembled a refugee convoy desperately trying to reach a safe haven. In many ways, she supposed they were.

Most of the children were playing soccer, but using their hands as much as their feet, much to the chagrin of Marcel. He'd played professionally in Finland for three years, Sweden for two, and Spain for half a glorious season before an egregious high tackle had banished him to a retirement of coaching in the Canadian leagues.

People slept in their vehicles or in tents next to them. Laundry and bedding that had been hung to air were being taken back inside before the first dew fell. The wash block had as long a queue as when she'd left, with the more fastidious getting in a cold shower while there was still a little sun to help them dry. The air was thick with acrid smoke from too many individual campfires. Despite the odour, each fire was thronged with people sewing, stitching, reading, talking, or guarding their meagre possessions to prevent them from being stolen. Maggs didn't think there really was much theft, but the increasingly adversarial mood made it easier to blame each other than forgetfulness.

Maggs parked behind the ambulance where Chloe Barnett was guarding its closed doors. The nurse stood as they approached, though her smile faded as she saw the bullet damage.

"Is anyone hurt?" Chloe asked.

"Ginger was grazed, otherwise, no," Maggs said. "It was people, not zombies."

"So she won't turn, but she still might die of infection," Chloe said as she grabbed the emergency treatment kit. They must teach the 'nursing voice' in school, because Chloe had barely been out of training before the outbreak, yet she had it down pat.

"I'm fine, Chloe. Really," Ginger said, waving her away. "Roy bandaged it, see?"

"Then I'll grade his work," their nurse said. "Come with me, please."

"I guess I'll catch up with you later, Ric," Ginger said.

"Where's Fern?" Maggs asked as she followed Chloe and Ginger back to the folding desk that doubled as their minor-care ward.

"Seeing Harmony," Chloe said with a nod towards the ambulance. "What happened to you?"

"An ambush," Maggs said. "Ginger can fill you in on the details. I better pay homage to our lord and master."

The rest of her crew needed no orders. Roy and Ricardo were unstrapping the deer, counting the bullet holes the carcasses had received during the firefight. Kayleigh and Georgie had already left to collect fuel for tomorrow's mission. Marshall had gone to fetch water, but via the ball game still in progress. It was to Maggs alone that went the pleasure of reporting to their great and glorious leader.

At the zoo, Fern had been in charge. A lifetime of not being eaten by Siberian tigers had been deemed the closest experience anyone had to dealing with the undead. When they reached Lac Seul, they were absorbed into a much larger group run by a once-popular mayor who'd been out of his depth. Martin Genk was a very different proposition, a hollow vessel who would make sure that everyone had bread and water while he dined on cake and champagne.

The original campsite contained twelve four-person lodges and a thirteenth, larger hall-like room which could have provided space for thirty people to sleep indoors, but Martin had allocated it as his own private club house. He called it the community hall, but his 'movie nights' were strictly invite only.

For want of a throne, Martin Genk sprawled in an office chair, legs akimbo and gut out. Gilbert Brass, the self-styled captain of their defence force, occupied the sofa, also taken from the campsite office. Ezra Schmidt sat primly on the other side, trying his best to look ethereal. He ran the kitchens. In theory, he was in charge of water gathering, too. In practice, that was coordinated by Gordon because it was too important to be left to the charlatan. Maggs could have said the same about cooking, but there was an obvious reason the trio wanted one of their own to guard the stores, a reason visible in their waistlines.

"Ah, you're back, wonderful," Martin said, giving a once-perfect smile that showed his yellowing teeth. "We had a quorum, so I'm sure you don't mind that we started without you."

"You're having a council meeting without us? Fern wasn't informed."

"She was busy doing God's work, and that can never be interrupted," Ezra said.

Maggs looked for a chair. Theoretically, there was space on the sofa, but Brass was so notoriously handsy, he'd make a glove-maker weep. She pulled a folding chair from the rack and noisily set it up. "What did I miss?"

"Very little. Everything's great here," Martin said. "Why don't you update us on your progress?"

"We were ambushed outside Kettle Falls," Maggs said. "We killed four of them and chased the others away."

"Zombies?" Ezra asked.

"No," Maggs said with as much patience as her weary bones could manage. "It was people. Zombies don't set ambushes."

"That we know of," Ezra said. "The devil works in ways beyond our knowledge."

"No theology before dinner," Martin said as he made his way over to the wall on which he'd pinned a map. "Kettle Falls?" He muttered the name over and over as he searched for the location. "Ah. We needed that crossing. That was the road that took us to Diablo Falls and the Baker River Valley. You said there were dams there you could fix."

"Depending on the level of damage, yes," Maggs said. "But that was only ever our secondary route. The primary would have taken us farther north, and to the Fraser River. The Baker River Valley is deeper inland. It would make a great rest stop, but it's still too far from a port to be even a temporary base."

"How many hostiles did you face?" Brass asked.

"We counted thirteen running, but there were probably more."

"And you let them escape?" Ezra asked.

"Would you rather I'd shot them in the back?" Maggs said. "It's been a while since I went to church, but I remember Jesus being pretty big on the concept of mercy."

"Now, Maggs, no need to get worked up," Martin said sternly.

Maggs bit her tongue. "I think our best option is to cut eastwards and then go north. We know most of the route, so we won't lose much time, and it'll get us far away from these ambushers."

"You mean they might have followed you back?" Ezra asked.

"I seriously doubt it," Maggs said. "But they obviously have fuel, and our campfires are as good as beacons. The longer we stay in the area, the greater the chance they stumble across us, or we run into one of their scavenging parties. Since we killed four of them, they might want revenge."

"It was reckless of you to attack them in the first place," Brass said.

Her patience snapped loud enough to be heard in Montreal. "*They* attacked *us*. That's how an ambush works."

"Now, now," Martin said, in his best peacemaker voice. "I'm sure you did your best. We can't go east. People won't accept us going back on ourselves. They want to go to Vancouver Island. It seems obvious we'll have to go west." He turned back to the map, running his finger along roads until he found one more palatable than the others. "There's a crossing through the Cascades near Mount Rainier. That's our new goal. We'll come out near Seattle, and that's on the coast."

"Better than going to somewhere called Diablo Lake," Ezra said. "That name alone should dissuade any God-fearing folk."

Maggs walked over to the map, looking at the route Martin had suggested. "That'll take longer. A lot longer. And Seattle is on Puget Sound, not the Pacific, and about two hundred kilometres from Vancouver Island. We'll need far too much fuel to sail a boat from there."

"We are more likely to find fuel in a city as big as Seattle," Martin said. "But this is a democracy. Let's put it to a vote. Those in favour of going west?" He, Ezra, and Brass raised their hands. "Ah, we have a majority decision."

Maggs knew there was no point arguing. "Then we should leave tomorrow morning, all of us, before the ambushers have a chance to find us."

"You said they're a hundred kilometres away," Ezra said.

"They're on the Columbia River, and we need to cross it. I don't know which sections are navigable, but they must know the crossings and the reason we were trying to reach Kettle Falls. By now, they could have sailed down to the next bridge and set up another ambush. Either we go east and then north and around them, which is safest, or leave as soon as we can and just hope they aren't ahead of us."

"Did you see any boats?" Brass asked.

Martin waved that away. "We'll follow Maggs's advice and leave tomorrow. All of us. And I think that concludes tonight's business."

Maggs walked out, furious with the other council members, and just as furious with herself. What had she expected? Martin was a fool, but he wasn't stupid. As long as they were en route to Vancouver Island, there would be few objections to his travelling in comparative luxury. If they were to turn back, there might be protests, and he could forfeit his trappings of leadership. A solid roof and a larger portion of their meagre rations weren't much, but it was better than sleeping in a tent. Oh, and the companionship, of course. Three women were waiting outside. None had been coerced, but neither did any of them look particularly enthralled at the evening ahead.

Martin was a self-serving egotist. Ezra was a leech, a letch, and a lush. Brass was the real danger. He controlled the ammunition. His militia, fifty strong, was the only armed group other than her scouts, and he paid them to stay loyal. Brass knew he was too abrasive to be a leader, so he backed Martin, who kept Ezra and his diminishing band of believers around as a counterweight. They were freeloaders, but Martin was right about one thing: while they were still heading to Vancouver Island, there wasn't an appetite for revolution.

She stomped her way back to the ambulance where Chloe was again behind her desk, though this time with a paperback in her hands.

"Why would anyone want to be a leader? Why?" Maggs asked.

Chloe raised a hand, pointing at the ambulance.

Maggs nodded, quietly fuming until the door opened and Nana Otunde stepped out. The old nurse wasn't a tall woman, and on some, the shaved head would only make her look smaller. She had been an orphan, a refugee, an immigrant, a widow, and a victim more than once, yet she had lived her life refusing to be bound by labels, even though currently, according to her hat, she was a pirate.

"Ah, I thought I heard the dulcet tones of our gallant first mate," the older nurse said as she reached out a hand to help the seven-year-old Harmony down the steps. Someone had found the girl a pink princess dress to wear over her dungarees, but which had been further decorated with a ragged parrot stitched to her shoulder.

"Ahoy there, my pirate princess," Maggs said, taking a guess based on the skull and crossbones on Harmony's hat, and the eye-patch hanging around her neck.

"I'm the pirate *queen,*" Harmony said. "Did you find treasure today?"

"Actually, we did!" Maggs said, remembering the coin Marshall had given her. She took it out of her pocket. "Real treasure. Solid gold. Marshall's got more." She handed the girl the coin. "Hats is in the car, asleep as usual. Why don't you wake him up before he misses dinner?"

Harmony walked over to the SUV. She didn't run, and she wasn't walking very fast, but she did manage it unaided. Maggs shared a look with Nana, but the old nurse shook her head before forcing a weary smile.

"It's been a good day," Nana said softly, before following Harmony. Maggs climbed the steps to their mobile surgery. Fern was slumped in a chair, legs out, head back.

"Busy day?" Maggs asked.

Fern flopped a hand. "Why did humans learn to talk? Animals are so much easier."

"You had a lot of patients?"

With an effort, Fern pulled herself upright, running a hand through her short black hair. "Not really. The usual mix of minor injuries, depression, vitamin deficiency, and general exhaustion. We need hot showers and laundry, and at least a week of solid food. No one is getting enough calories. No one but our lords and masters. But above all, everyone needs work. Spring is here. It's time we were planting."

"I know. How's Harmony?"

"The pills are helping. I'd like to up the dose, but as it is, we'll run out in twenty days."

"Ginger told you about the ambush?"

"Yes. It sounds terrifying. How are you?"

"Just a little bruised. Martin wants us to go west tomorrow, towards Seattle. There'll be pharmacies and clinics there. Probably a pill distributor for the entire northwest. We'll find more meds."

"I hope so," Fern said. "With a good diet, and clean air, and the medication, Harmony should be able to live a normal life, but that isn't the same as a cure."

Chapter 4 - Orders from Above
Sprague Lake, March 5th

Her skin radiated more heat than a reactor. It wasn't so much a hot flash as a boiling waterfall, producing enough steam to power Toronto. Even if her skin hadn't prickled with damp, sleep was impossible in the SUV. Impossible for her, anyway. Harmony was having no bother, snoring away on the backseat in time with Hats's purring. That was youth for you, but give the girl another forty years, and she'd have nights where she could melt an iceberg. *Please* give her another forty years.

Maggs had never had children. It had been her one regret before the outbreak. Since the world had turned inside out, she'd thought of it as a blessing. Despite that, and all of a sudden, she'd acquired a tribe of her own. It was that, as much as the inherently poor design of her own body, which was keeping her awake.

Was Vancouver Island still the best choice? The climate would be a definite improvement. According to a guidebook she'd found, the competing weather systems created near tropical conditions on the mainland-facing shores. Yes, the book was biased, but it wouldn't outright lie, would it?

They'd lost fifty people since leaving the lake. From her team, Kumar and Alex had died from infection. Not the zombie virus, but the more traditional kind. Other people had disappeared, including some of the children, and all the expectant mothers. Not all of the fathers, though. Based on when it had happened, she was almost certain she knew where they'd gone: The International Peace Garden that straddled the border between Manitoba and North Dakota.

While scouting near Moose Mountain in Saskatchewan, they'd come across a group of twenty. At first, everything had been friendly. This group called themselves gardeners rather than survivors or looters. They'd said they were part of a large group straddling the old border at the Peace Garden, and they were actively looking for new members, especially those with knowledge of medicine or electrical generation. That attitude had changed when they'd learned that Maggs and her crew were just the scouting party for a much larger group.

Dr Pearson had been with them that day, and he'd offered the gardeners what medical assistance he could while the rest of them awkwardly chatted. It was then he must have enquired how many dependents a doctor could bring with him and still expect a hero's welcome. He'd disappeared a day later, taking nine pregnant women, five new mothers, and seven children. Three fathers, four guardians, and another two fathers-to-be had gone with him. The remaining fathers hadn't been asked, but none had seemed upset with the discovery their unborn children had vanished.

She'd not liked Pearson, who thought an expensive education automatically made him a polymath, but he was a good doctor. Long before he'd left, he had created a list of alternate medications for Harmony, and a dietary regime that was next to impossible to adhere to.

Other than Harmony, there were only nine children left, watched over by Marcel and Toby. The scarcity of youngsters had definitely been a factor in the camp's change of mood. Self-censorship had almost vanished, while aggression, intolerance, and selfishness were only increasing.

She flexed her feet. A memory of chair shopping with Etienne came back to her. He'd taken off his shoes before he'd tried out the armchairs and couldn't understand why no one else did the same. He was the real reason she was continuing to Vancouver Island. If she were to leave now, it would have to be with her team, Fern and her crew, and with Marcel and the other children. There were a few teenagers, just a bit younger than Marshall, that she should take, too. And there were a few older folk who wouldn't survive long in the gladiatorial nightmare that Martin, Brass, and Ezra would create if there wasn't a steadying hand. And there it was. The real reason she stayed. As much as she dreamed of finding Etienne waiting for her on Vancouver Island, she couldn't abandon these people. Most were lazy, rude, and ungrateful, but they were also tired, hungry, and scared. They didn't deserve to be left to the wolves.

She closed her eyes, conjuring an image of her husband, safe, and happy. It was always summertime in her fantasy. He stood on a wide-open plain, with an old-fashioned farmhouse behind him. Wind turbines rose high above maize that was nearly as tall as he was. But tonight, that image just deepened her sadness.

When the condensation on the window glistened by the first light of a false dawn, she opened the car door. The gust of cold air caused Harmony to grumble. Hats laid a paw on her cheek, gently pushing her head back down.

"It's okay, dear. You can sleep for another hour," she said, and received a 'close the door,' glare from the cat.

The curtains of the fun-bus were still drawn. At encampments like these, the couples took it in turn to sleep there, while the adults crammed into the shelter they rigged up behind the trailer. Fern, Nana, and she took turns in the SUV with Harmony. Gordon always slept in the ambulance, guarding their meds. Tonight, though, it looked like he wasn't guarding it alone. His companion was Evelyn Proctor, the ballerina-turned-lawyer who'd taken a very early retirement to conquer community theatre. They were both older than her, so why they were sneaking around like teenagers at a barn dance was beyond baffling. It was none of her business, so she walked on.

Marcel and Toby had pitched their tent in the doorway of the draughty cabin theoretically allocated to her and Fern; the children were inside. Everyone else was in a car, coach, or tent. Everyone except the three councillors and their favoured lieutenants. It had been the same at their previous resting spot. It needn't have been. She'd suggested they stay at Clear Lake, to the northeast, and on the outskirts of Spokane. There'd been more than enough room, and far better fishing. Martin had suggested Sprague Lake and put it to a council-vote. As usual, he'd won. He'd claimed its proximity to the highway junctions gave more options for the final leg of the journey, but he just wanted to exert his authority.

The lake water was far too blue to be healthy. She wasn't sure if it was a chemical spill or an algal bloom. Fern had reminded people to boil and filter it, of course, but she'd seen people bathing in the shallows. The sooner they left, the better. For once, she was glad to see Martin and Ezra walking towards her. If they were already awake, they could look forward to an early start.

"Good morning," she said brightly. "It seems like a clear day, at least to start with. Good driving weather."

"We were just discussing that," Martin said. "We think it's best to stay here until you find a better base."

"Stay here?"

"Yes, for now," Martin said.

"Here we are protected by the guiding light of the watchful angels," Ezra added.

"What about the ambushers?" Maggs asked. "What if they come here? What if they're sailing down the river now?"

"Captain Brass assures me that's unlikely," Martin said. "We have water, and enough food for today, thanks to those deer. Statistically, we're more likely to find trouble on the road, and we'll certainly waste fuel when the road is blocked. It's the only rational choice."

"And it is God's will," Ezra added.

A million things came to mind, most of them monosyllabic, but she kept those to herself. Instead, she simply shook her head and walked back to the SUV.

Chapter 5 - The Prodigal's Inheritance
Suntides Golf Course, Yakima

The sign for an RV site and golf course finally lanced the boil of irritation plaguing her since her morning confrontation with Martin. "We'll stop here, Ric. Just on the right," she said.

"Trouble?" Ricardo asked, hunching forward over the wheel.

"No, curiosity at an economic incongruity."

This would be the fourth stop of the day in their search for a new base for the convoy. Their first, an elementary school, had been littered with bones. At the second, a farm, the river behind the barn foamed blue, suggesting a chemical tank was leaking somewhere nearby. At the third, they'd not even had time to get out of their vehicles before a host of zombies trekked through a warehouse's broken doors.

Lunchtime was nearing, and so were the mountains. They were on the outskirts of Yakima, a place she was sure she'd heard of in a song. Frustratingly, she couldn't remember which one. Ricardo stopped on the drive leading into the site, angling the SUV so they could make a quick exit. The falling fortunes of the establishment were told in the three signs. The oldest was for the Suntides Golf Course, and though the green and gold paint only required a wash to look brand new, the back of the metal sign bubbled with rust. Next to it, and just as large, was a hand-carved wooden sign, now weathered and cracked, advertising vacation cabins for rent. The third, and most recent, was merely paint on wood, offering RV mooring spaces for low, *low* prices.

Kayleigh sniffed disapprovingly as she loaded her crossbow. "Smells bad. Are we going to stop here?"

"Maybe," Maggs said. "Are you coming, Hats?" The cat offered a dismissive sniff before curling up on the passenger seat.

Inside the un-gated grounds, and to the left of the ruler-straight driveway, were the cabins. She'd heard of optimistic marketing, but this was taking it a step beyond. Ten double-wides with loose sidings, broken steps, and cracked windows occupied pride-of-place close to the entrance, each separated by a knee-high white-picket fence. Beyond that were a row of smaller, and even more decrepit, trailers and caravans stretching off into the distance until the road took an abrupt turn to the left.

To the right was the parking lot, though that had been divided into two, with the half closest to the road now designated as RV pitches, and poorly screened behind widely spaced planters. The other half of the parking lot still served the golf course. The clubhouse now hosted a laundry, store, showers, and the least inviting bar-and-grill she'd ever seen.

"No defences," Ricardo said.

"Yeah, they could have built a wall out of the trailers," Ginger said.

"What is there to defend?" Marshall asked.

"It's too close to the town, and to the highway," Roy said. "Besides, a trailer has thin walls."

"But a golf course could be farmland, and a river is a water source," Kayleigh said.

"Roy, Kayleigh, Georgie, take a look at the trailer homes," Maggs said. "Count how many there are in case we don't find anywhere better than this, and see what state they're in. Everyone else, with me. We'll check out the clubhouse and the golf course."

"You want to get in a few holes?" Roy asked.

"I want to see if anyone ever *did* try to farm here," Maggs said. "We'll meet back here in thirty minutes. Usual rules apply."

They'd established the rules on the journey from the zoo to Lac Seul and refined them when they returned to the road this winter. A distant gunshot or scream meant fall back, regroup, and then go to help. Whoever entered a building first kept their focus on the ground, because zombies increasingly only crawled. Whoever entered second checked cupboards, doors, and every mound that might conceal a zed. But don't forget to look up, especially if there was a false ceiling, because they didn't want a repeat of the time Ricardo ended up wearing a zombie like a scarf. No chatter, no looting, no sightseeing, not until the job was done. Trust your nose, your ears, and your gut. If something felt wrong, it probably was. Despite a year of practice, following the rules still hadn't become instinctive, even for her.

She drew her tomahawk from the loop on her belt. It wasn't the best weapon for crushing a skull, but none were. A spear, pike, or lance was too unwieldy in confined environments. Swords required too much skill. Maces required too much strength. Machetes required too much height if they were to be hacked down on an upright zombie's head. For that matter, so did the tomahawk, but it came with a small spike atop the shaft, allowing her to thrust as well as swing, so it would do until she found something better, or until the zombies all finally died.

The sprawling extension had been painted an orange that didn't quite match the faux-brick facade of the original clubhouse. The front door was closed and covered with too many advertisements to see through. The lock had been broken, though the splinters were aged by a dozen storms. She turned the handle, and pushed the door inward, but it didn't move.

"Of course it's barricaded," she said, taking half a step back, and so was off balance when a weight hit the door. It swung outwards, and she was thrown to the ground as a zombie flew out, tumbling atop her.

The zombie's hand curled around her arm, its face inches from her own. The impact knocked the breath from her, and the last of the air from the creature's dead lungs, straight into her face. Gagging on the stench of decay, she shoved her other forearm up into the creature's throat, holding its snapping mouth back from her face.

The weight was suddenly removed as Ricardo hauled the zombie clear, hurling it to the ground. It turtled, legs and arms thrashing as it tried to right itself, until Georgie put a boot on its chest, and then a crossbow bolt in its brain.

"You okay?" Ricardo asked, hauling Maggs to her feet.

"Fine," she said, trying not to wince at the jolt in her shoulder from his ungentle chivalry. "Fine, thank you, but that's the second day in a row I've fallen. My back wants to file a complaint."

"It's clear," Marshall said from the doorway. "No movement."

"Here," Ginger said, holding out the tomahawk that Maggs had dropped when she fell.

"Thanks. It was my own fault. I was so busy trying to remember what to do, I forgot to actually do it."

"Well, I didn't hear anything," Ginger said. She meant it kindly, of course, in that way the annoyingly young often did. Maggs smiled.

"Not totally clear," Ricardo called out from inside the office. There was a thunk and crack of his masonry pick demolishing thin skin and weak bone.

Ginger headed inside. Maggs stretched her arm and cautiously followed her into a small store. The shelves were empty, but the aisles were full of plastic storage boxes stacked to waist-height and sometimes taller. She wiped the grime off the transparent lid of the nearest and saw a large bottle of syrup inside.

"Two zeds on the ground," Ricardo said.

"Three," Marshall said from behind a cash register in the middle of the store. "But I think they were already dead."

"Maybe more," Ricardo said. Flecks of bone fell from the tip of his masonry pick as he pointed it towards a pair of doors at the back. One was marked *Staff Only*. The other was covered in crumpled blinds as if something heavy had been shoved against the window.

"I've got this," Ricardo said. He pushed at the office door, but it didn't move. He stepped back and swung his masonry pick at the hinges, smashing them with one blow each, before quickly stepping aside so the door could topple outwards. A bookcase mostly blocked the entrance, but there was enough of a gap to peer through. "It's empty."

"This door's locked, too," Ginger said, pushing the staff door. "And it's metal so don't you try to knock it down."

"Find the back door," Maggs said. "You go with her, Ric. Marshall, go outside and listen for trouble. I'll take a look around here."

They had found something, that was clear from the boxes and the hasty barricades, but was any of it useful? The nearest plastic box contained a mix of bar and liquid soap, shower gel, and shampoo, all of different brands. The one next to it contained an assortment of canned food: coffee, chilli beans, microwaveable mac and cheese, vanilla frosting. Each box probably came from a different trailer.

She turned her attention to the office, pushing the bookcase far enough aside that she could squeeze in. Both Marshall and Ricardo were wrong. The office *wasn't* unoccupied. A body lay behind the desk. Possibly female, though she was basing that entirely on the cut of the jeans. The work-boots were a generic size nine, and the plaid shirt could have belonged to anyone. An engagement ring might have told her, but the fingers were gone. Taken by mice, no doubt, along with most of the facial features. As far as she could tell, the skull was intact. From the knife on the desk, next to a large family photograph, and an empty pill bottle, she'd slit her wrists just after taking enough codeine not to care. There was no whisky to wash it down, and no note left behind.

The office gave her the impression of new management. The photo on the desk was faded with time, but had been taken outside the entrance. Ten years ago? Longer? Was the woman some prodigal who'd found success in the big city, but returned home to take over a failing family business? Maybe. From the sales graph on the wall and the printouts of land values, she'd guess the idea was to improve sales before selling the entire site as a going concern.

Maggs looked through the door at the zombies who'd been on the other side. Perhaps there was no one left to whom she needed to write. That was the greatest tragedy of the undead plague, that it too often forced people into a choice between suicide, killing the ones they loved, or dying at their hands.

Maggs returned to the main office, checking the contents of the crates until a metallic clunk marked the opening of the metal door.

"We struck oil," Ginger said. "About three hundred litres."

"Cooking oil?"

"No, oil-oil. Gasoline, we think. Ric's checking it. And there's a generator. Unplugged but ready to be used."

"And no one took the gas?" Maggs asked.

"There's another door to the corridor. It was locked, too," Ginger said.

"Ah, I see. And elsewhere?"

"It's all empty. What did you find?"

"Food," Maggs said. "Some clothing. Soap. It was a family business. Looked to be seasonal, so it wouldn't have been very busy at the time of the outbreak. They gathered everything useful from inside the trailers. All but one of them were infected. The zombies trapped the last member of the family in that office."

"That's grim. What kind of food?"

"Cans, packets, and jars. Not much of anything in particular, but enough in total for everyone to get something. How was the fuel stored?"

"Individually, in twenty-litre containers. Should we create another stash?"

Maggs looked around at the crates. "It looks like someone's already done that for us. Make sure everything's secured and close up the doors."

She walked back outside, waving to Kayleigh, who was standing guard outside a trailer-home while Roy and Georgie searched it.

After Martin had taken over, and she had been relegated to scout duty, her team had begun leaving caches of fuel and food along the route. It was never much. Shared among four hundred and fifty, it wouldn't have stretched to much more than a mouthful. But for her crew it would keep hunger at bay until they found more. If divided out among Fern's team, the children, and the others they just couldn't leave behind, it wouldn't stretch to more than a meal. Even so, she'd kept leaving the hidden stashes. It was the only precaution against total collapse she could make, and the more she experienced of Martin's leadership, the more it seemed necessary.

Chapter 6 - What's in the Box?
Yakima County

Being knocked to the ground for the second time in twenty-four hours had melted the little enthusiasm for exploration she'd been able to feign. When they got a puncture, twenty kilometres northwest of the golf course, she felt the residue begin to bubble and steam. While Roy and Ricardo changed the tyre, Kayleigh and Ginger cheered them on, and Georgie and Marshall kept watch. Maggs focused on the now not-so-distant mountain peaks, trying to recall the calming breathing techniques she'd never properly mastered. *Breathe deep and slow, rest the mind, focus on a point, let it become—*

"It was a trap," Roy said.

"What was?" Maggs asked, dragging her mind back to the present.

Roy held out a metre-long piece of board embedded with rusty nails. "This was deliberate."

"Ginger, Kayleigh, let's check the road," Maggs said. "Georgie, Marshall, expect trouble. Ric and Roy, when you're finished, check this area, but be very careful. Look for tripwires or… well, whatever nightmares your imagination can come up with."

"Not traps again," Kayleigh said as they spread out along the road with Maggs in the middle, Kayleigh on the right, and Ginger on the left.

"At least it wasn't a tripwire," Ginger said. Their car before last, a roomy and ancient pickup whose only electronics had been in an equally archaic boombox fitted to its own bracket in the backseat, had taken two shotgun shells to the engine. The tripwire had been strung across the road between two street lights. If it had been strung a little lower and had caught on their tyres, the slugs would have torn through the cab. Instead, they'd caught on the grill, wrecking the car but leaving them unscathed.

"What were people thinking, leaving traps?" Kayleigh said.

"They weren't thinking," Maggs said, sweeping her eyes left and right. "Not clearly. But none of us were."

"I know we shouldn't judge anyone then by our standards now, but it still makes me want to yell," Kayleigh said.

"Movement," Ginger said, aiming her crossbow at the trees to the west-southwest. Maggs and Kayleigh froze, waiting.

"Deer," Ginger finally said, relaxing her arms a little. "It's too far away to shoot. If we're still, it might come closer."

"If we bring back more meat, Martin will just have another excuse not to leave," Maggs said.

"Caw, ca-caw!" Ginger called out. That produced a louder rustling from among the trees. "It's gone. At least tripwires make sense," she said as they continued their walk. "Zombies could trigger them. That nailed board was designed to stop a car. Who'd do that?"

"Exactly what I was wondering," Maggs said, "so keep alert."

After checking two hundred metres of road, they turned back. They'd found one more improvised stinger-trap on the road, and another five washed into the overgrown verge, all within a hundred metres of the first.

"Before winter, or since?" Ricardo asked as Roy wheeled the dead tyre into the grass.

"When they left their traps? Before," Ginger said. "These weren't designed to stop zombies."

Maggs looked around for somewhere an ambusher could lurk. Other than the trees, there was nowhere within rushing distance. There'd been a driveway snaking into the trees about a kilometre back, and a cluster of roadside homes another kilometre before that. Those were too far. A sign advertised gas and food ahead, though the place was currently hidden by the trees. "Some mysteries can't be answered," she said, as she took out the map.

"Are we stopping for lunch?" Marshall called down from the roof of the fun-bus.

"Not yet," Maggs said. "We're almost at the point where the Wapatox Canal and the Nachos River meet. That can't be more than two kilometres away."

"Oh, I could really go for some nachos," Kayleigh said. "With extra cheese. And pickles."

"On nachos? That's a war crime," Marshall called down.

"More importantly, we're only about ten kilometres from where the highway splits into the 410 and the 12, and both branches head through the mountains. The 410 would bring us closer to Seattle, so that's better, but if the pass is blocked, we've got an alternative. Ginger and Ric, can you paint a warning about traps on that road sign? When you're done, Georgie can drive you to catch up. Marshall, you can bring up the SUV. We'll start checking that the road is clear, and for about five kilometres, I think. When you catch up, we'll swap over, and we can begin on lunch."

Maggs, Kayleigh, and Roy began walking back up the road, quickly at first as they covered the ground they'd already checked.

"We could cross the mountains today," Kayleigh said, "and be in Seattle tomorrow."

"Maybe," Maggs said. "But the roads through the mountains could be tough. There aren't many passes. Four days would be more reasonable."

"Harmony needs her medicine," Kayleigh said.

"She's got enough for three weeks," Maggs said.

"What she really needs is a doctor," Kayleigh said.

"I know." Silence settled as they paced the road. There was a building at the edge of the gas station's lot whose windows were boarded, all save one. An ideal sniper's nest, once upon a time. When she glanced around, she saw Kayleigh and Roy were gesticulating to one another.

"What is it?" Maggs asked.

"Roy?" Kayleigh prompted.

"There's a doctor in Manitoba," Roy said.

"You mean Dr Pearson and the Peace Garden?" Maggs asked. She turned around and kept walking. This time, she was watching the filling station as much as the roadway.

"We've left fuel and food almost everywhere we've been," Roy said, "and there's all the gas and food at the golf course. I think there'd be enough for us to drive straight there, only stopping to sleep. We wouldn't even have to stop to hunt."

"There's something there," Maggs said, walking across the road to a wisp of glistening metal. "Here's your tripwire," she said, holding up one end of an already broken strand. She followed it into the verge and to an upturned wooden crate. When she saw that, she stepped back onto the road. "We'll wait for Ricardo."

"You think it's a bomb?" Kayleigh asked.

"Probably. And something homemade," Maggs said. "If we left, we'd have to bring Fern with us, and Nana, Chloe, and Gordon. Marcel, Toby, and the remaining kids, too. If we're bringing Gordon, that would mean Evelyn, and there are a few adults like Audrey who need medical care. I'd say forty people."

"We could take a coach," Roy said.

"A coach would need diesel, and we've been stashing gas. That supply we found at the golf course was gasoline. But you're right, we would need a coach. I don't know if Martin would simply let us all drive off. He's smart enough to realise that our departure would bring forward a power struggle between Ezra and Brass. Whoever wins, Martin is out. We'd have to sneak away, and for that, the fewer vehicles, the better."

"They wouldn't stop us," Kayleigh said.

"They might try," Maggs said. "They have too many guns and too little training. It wouldn't take much for shouts to turn into shots. People could get hurt. Some might die. As far as us leaving is concerned, hurt is worse because there's no way Fern would leave if there were injured people needing help." She waved at their two vehicles driving slowly up the road, getting them to stop what she hoped was a safe distance away. "Ric, I think we've found a bomb. Can you defuse it?"

"I can look," he said, jumping out of the fun-bus. After a brief examination, he shook his head. "I'm not even going to lift the box."

"What is it?" Ginger asked.

"No idea without looking," he said. "There's a wire leading to it, a weight holding it down, and those four poles keeping it in position. It might be empty. Or it might blow up the moment I try to see what's inside."

"Can we trigger it from a distance?" Maggs asked.

"Maybe," Ricardo said. "I guess we could try shooting it with a rifle. See if that does anything, but if it goes off, it could scatter shrapnel across the road, and we'd have to spend hours clearing it up or risk more burst tyres."

"Hmm. I wonder if that's the point," Roy said. "These weren't traps as such, but means of dissuading people from travelling this road, and through the mountains."

"That's going to make the next hundred kilometres a lot of fun," Georgie said.

"Can we ignore it?" Maggs asked.

"It hasn't blown up yet," Ricardo said. "But when the convoy comes this way, it'll be the most vibrations the road's known for a year."

"What about a wall of tyres?" Maggs asked. "A filling station might have some rotting away at the back."

"That should absorb the blast, yes," Ricardo said.

"Marshall, come down from the roof. There's no one around. We can leave the vehicles. Georgie, make sure Hats is locked inside. If he gets it into his head to investigate, he'll lose all of his nine lives at once. Everyone, keep your eyes open for more tripwires. Does everyone want to leave the convoy and head to the Peace Garden?"

"You told her?" Georgie asked Kayleigh.

"Technically, Roy did," Kayleigh said. "And it's not like we're going without her."

"If anyone wants to leave, or if you all want to leave, I won't try to stop you," Maggs said as they walked up the driveway into the gas station. There were no wires or any obstructions on the road. That didn't reassure her.

"We're a team," Ricardo said. "We stick together, and we'll follow you anywhere, but we won't follow Martin when we get to Vancouver Island."

"We're agreed on that," Maggs said.

"And there's Harmony," Ginger said. "She really needs a doctor."

"She's not the only one," Maggs said. "There's a stack of tyres over there, behind the bar. Be careful when you move them."

"Want me to check inside?" Marshall asked.

"No," she said, just before everyone else. "We'll assume it's all rigged, wired, and ready to blow."

They waited for Ricardo to give his approval before they began rolling tyres back to the road. It required far more coordination than she'd expected, so there was little chatter until they reached the roadside bomb.

"Ric, you're the expert, where do you want to put them?"

He wasn't an expert, but he had more experience than the rest of them combined. They stepped back, letting him stack them.

"Four trips should do it," Maggs said as they headed back to the bar. "Look, we don't know if there's anyone still left in the Peace Garden, or if Dr Pearson reached it, or if he'd be able to do more than he's already done by giving us that list of medications. Harmony has to be the priority. Finding her an adequate supply of medication should be step one, and that's going to be in Seattle if it's anywhere. Once we have the pills… I don't know. There is still a chance that there's a community on Vancouver Island with doctors who could really help her."

"And if there's not?" Georgie asked. "We can put up travelling with Martin and Ezra, but that's all we're doing right now. We're not going to let them actually make decisions about how we live."

"I know," Maggs said.

As Ricardo lifted another tyre from the stack by the back of the bar, a dull explosion ripped through the air. The ground shook, followed by the patter of shrapnel falling on the road and the gas station's lot.

Maggs slowly straightened from the crouch she'd automatically dropped into. "I guess we don't need any more tyres, eh?"

Inside the box, along with the explosive, there must have been every loose bolt, nail, and other small piece of scrap metal in the garage. There had been a thick steel plate which should have directed the blast outwards, onto the road, but it had merely been blasted halfway through a nearby pine. While the explosion had solved one problem, it had created another, and so they began clearing the debris from the road.

"This would have been so much easier with a magnet," Marshall said as he came to collect his lunch. He was the last to check in. "What are we having?"

"Mashed potatoes," Roy said.

"For real?"

"Instant mash from Idaho, courtesy of the golf course," Roy said. "With cheese and real herbs, apparently."

"As opposed to fake herbs," Ginger said.

"You'd be surprised what some restaurants got away with," Roy said.

"Don't tell me until after I've finished eating," she said.

Maggs tried to savour the now-unfamiliar taste of potatoes and cheese, but too soon, her spoon was rattling around an empty bowl. "We won't get through the mountains today. We'll finish up here, check the road for a few more kilometres, and then head back via the golf course. We'll search it again and make sure it's suitable for the convoy, and we'll tell them to leave tomorrow morning, first thing. They can have the food, but we'll take the gasoline with us until we can find somewhere safer to stash it."

"Can we take any more of these potatoes?" Marshall said.

"Absolutely," Maggs said. "Once we get to Seattle, we'll look for the pills. We'll find enough to keep Harmony safe, and on a higher dose. We'll also head to the coast. If there are people on Vancouver Island, they would have come through Seattle's port. I think it was a major one for the U.S. We'll be able to tell if it's been recently visited. That's when we can make our decision about staying or leaving. Does that sound reasonable?"

"Yeah, it'll be easier to leave when everyone is settling in," Ginger said. "Less chance of violence."

"We won't be the only ones leaving," Ricardo said.

"Just imagine it, everyone except Martin, Brass, and Ezra, all gone," Marshall said.

"And that's why we need to plan and prepare," Maggs said. "The little stashes we've left will keep starvation away for a few dozen. No more. We can't have this turning into the entire convoy turning around. And we can't have it turn into a shootout as Brass tries to stop people from leaving. We'll keep on making sure everyone has the best chance at survival, and then we'll disappear."

The reply was more thoughtful than enthusiastic, but from the tone, the loudest dissenting voice was her own. She knew she was only continuing onward in the hope there were so many survivors in the north that their four hundred and fifty would be but a drop that could disappear into their ocean. Everyone else's survival would become someone else's problem, and she could return to looking for her husband.

Chapter 7 - Desperate Minds Think Alike
Sprague Lake

Maggs found no distraction in driving as they returned to the golf club to collect the gasoline and then headed back to their lakeside camp. She hoped she was making the right choice but couldn't help fret that she was merely putting off a decision that had already been made. At least there was a sentry standing by the gate. The usually work-shy Reggie Laughton waved them through. Where Tatiana was a stickler for the rules, he was a lazy chancer who should be in handcuffs, not carrying them. As she drove inside, she was struck by the absence of people. The vehicles were all there, as were the tents, but the usual hubbub was missing. She stopped the SUV next to the ambulance. Nana was sitting on the back steps, holding Gordon's shotgun.

"It's trouble," Nana said. "You'd better be quick. Marcel wants to leave. Go on."

"Where's Harmony?"

Nana tapped on the door behind. "She's safe. Hurry now."

"Georgie, Marshall, Kayleigh, check Toby and Marcel's place. Watch the kids." And with that, she marched up the shallow hill. Beyond the thick row of pines that had shielded the big-tipping cabin-hirers from the spendthrift campers, she found a crowd gathered around the cabin Martin had claimed for himself. About two-thirds of their community were present, formed in a semicircle, looking inwards. As she pushed through them, she found a second line made up of Brass's guards, all looking outwards and with weapons ready.

"Put that sword down before you put someone's eye out," she said to Alexander as she pushed through the loose cordon of militia, mostly armed with shotgun or rifle. Beyond, she found Marcel and Toby squaring off against Brass and Martin. Her arrival had cut short the shouting match, drawing all eyes to her.

"There's only Reggie on gate duty," Maggs said loudly enough to carry beyond the militia. "We saw zombies today, and yesterday we were ambushed. We need a proper guard watching the road."

"So it *is* true," Marcel said. A restless murmur rose from the crowd while the guards shifted uneasily. "There *are* bandits nearby."

"About a hundred kilometres away, yes," Maggs said, half turning around so she could better address her real audience. "That's a hundred in a straight line. Direct distances are harder to gauge because we don't know what roads they'd use, or if they'd follow the river."

"Or if they'd follow us at all," Martin said, also pitching his voice to carry. "Why would they come looking for us? Maggs attacked them, and they defended themselves. Four of them are dead. They won't come looking for more trouble."

"*They* attacked *us*," Maggs said. "It was an ambush. We don't go around killing people, except in self-defence." The crowd was growing restless. Feet shuffled in the mud. Hands were put onto weapons. Among the population at large, those were mostly blades. Ammunition was scarce. For the last eight weeks, whatever bullets they'd found had been given to the militia. Only Maggs had been able to openly defy that order. This was exactly the type of one-sided confrontation she'd feared. From Brass's eager expression, it was precisely what he'd been hoping for.

"We found somewhere better than this," she said, speaking even louder. "Just below the mountains is an RV site with a golf course. It's far more spacious than here. And there's some food. Canned fruit and vegetables. Enough for a good meal for everyone."

"It's too late," Marcel said, his voice low, his eyes fixed on Brass.

"He's right," Toby said. "We're leaving. You can't keep us here. You can't force us to go with you. We should have never come west."

"Then leave," Martin said, and far too easily. "Go on. Leave now. Anyone who wants to."

"Not without gas," Toby said.

"That's ours," Brass said. "If you stay with us, you get protection, fuel, and food. If you leave, you get to take what you brought, and you didn't bring any gas."

"The Lord has provided," Ezra called out from the shelter of his cabin's doorway. "He will continue to provide, but only unto the righteous."

"Everything belongs to everyone," Marcel said. "Or do you think you are kings, because we are *not* your subjects."

"If you take our fuel, we won't be able to reach Vancouver Island," Martin said. "You would endanger every hard-working citizen here."

The murmur among the crowds grew louder, but Maggs couldn't tell which side they were on. Brass had his hand on his holster. If he fired, it would become a free-for-all. The militia would be swamped before they got off more than a few shots. It was impossible to know how many would die, except she'd bet Brass would shoot Toby and Marcel, and maybe even Martin. But Brass wasn't paying close enough attention to Marcel's hand, now gripping his long hunting knife. However it began, it would end in a massacre.

"Wait. There's an obvious solution," Maggs said. "How many people want to leave?"

"Twenty," Marcel said.

"Okay, there we go," she said. "Only twenty people. As Martin says, we *are* all free to go, but we don't want to imperil anyone who remains. I have a way of doing that. We found some gasoline today. Not much for four hundred and fifty, but it is enough to get twenty people back to Canada. It won't change what we have in our stores, so it won't make any difference to our journey. Deal?" she added, turning back to Marcel and Toby.

"Deal," Toby said even while Marcel was processing the proposal.

"There we go. Solved," Maggs said. "And you'll leave tonight, too. Before dinner." That got a worryingly loud murmur of approval from the crowd. "So, go on. Go. Leave now. Right now. Ricardo will bring the fuel to you, and make sure you leave. Go!"

She turned back to Martin but kept her voice loud enough to be heard by the mob. "And tomorrow, we'll continue west, to the campsite where there's food, and where there's a golf course we can all relax in. We'll get through the mountains the day after, and be in the outskirts of Seattle. Just imagine what treasures we might find there."

Martin looked at her, and the crowd, and seemed to finally understand that he was as likely to die as anyone else should the bullets start flying. "I do miss golf," he said. "I might get some practice in."

"Great," Maggs said with as much cheer as she could muster. "Everyone make sure you're packed. We're leaving at first light. I want to be at the campsite by lunchtime so our cooks have plenty of time to prepare our feast. And Tatiana, could we please have someone else standing watch? None of us is safe if we leave guard duty to Reggie."

Brass's eyes were full of disappointment. "It won't be so easy next time," he said, and turned around, heading back to his cabin.

From the deepest depths of her soul, Maggs dredged up a smile for Martin before weaving her way through the thinning crowd. "What did I miss?" she asked as she took Fern's arm, walking the doctor away. Gordon and Chloe fell into step behind them.

"Ezra gave a sermon where he made some ridiculous comment about how you being attacked yesterday was a sign from God about how the unbelievers will be tested," Fern said. "For him, that's pretty inventive, except he forgot that most people hadn't heard about your ambush. Word spread throughout the camp. The guards gave conflicting confirmations and denials. Martin tried hiding, and the whole thing turned into a showdown about ten minutes before you got back."

Maggs stopped and turned around. "Gordon, can you check that Marcel and Toby are taking *all* the kids with them and find out which other adults are going. Chloe, go with him, and make sure they have whatever medication they might need. Hurry."

"You're sending the children away?" Fern asked. "That makes no sense. The children will be safer with us."

"Will they?" Maggs asked. "Come on. It's too crowded here." She walked Fern between the tents and cars until she found a relatively isolated spot by the trailer carrying their reserve of spare tyres.

"This is no place for children, and it's only going to get worse," Maggs said. "I almost had a rebellion of my own today."

"No, really?"

"Well, no. Not exactly. Nothing like this, but the crew wanted to take Harmony to the Peace Garden. I've been weighing the pros and cons all afternoon. The people we met in Manitoba seemed nice. Normal, you know? It wasn't just that they didn't shoot at us, but they were friendly rather than wary. I know it's a low bar. We're hoping we can find more pills for Harmony in Seattle, and that increasing the dose will help her without producing any new side effects. But the pills won't remain efficacious forever. And what if that particular medication was banned in Washington State? You know how contrary American healthcare was. She needs a doctor. And she needs to be around people who will do what they can to save a child. That isn't here."

"You want to send Harmony away, too?" Fern asked.

"Yes, with Nana to the Peace Garden with Marcel, Toby, and the others. I think they'll have enough fuel to reach it. They'll certainly get close enough that Marcel could cycle the last bit. We know the route. Dr Pearson might be there. If he isn't, those people will take them in."

"You hope. Like you hope they're still alive."

"There is no alternative, not if we want to save all the children," Maggs said.

"It's so dangerous, travelling all that way, and just on a hope."

"I know. But the same can be said for staying here. Face it, Fern, we're hoping for a miracle, and have been since we left the zoo. Miracles don't exist. Marcel, Toby, and the other children are leaving. Harmony can go with them or stay with us. You're her doctor, you decide where she'll stand the greatest chance."

Conflicting emotions warred across Fern's face before settling into resigned defeat. "How did it come to this? I better tell Nana and Harmony, and make sure they're packed."

"Good. I'll speak with Marcel and Toby." Maggs looked around for her crew but only saw Marshall. "Where are the others?"

"Ginger went with Ric to get the fuel," Marshall said. "Roy went to keep watch on Marcel and the kids in case Brass went there."

"They'll need water. A lot," Maggs said. "Go fetch it."

She doubted it was a coincidence that Marcel had decided to leave on the same day her crew had approached her about the same thing. There was no point in asking. Not now. The trio of minivans in which the last of their children travelled were parked outside the small cabin. Marcel was busy loading luggage while Ricardo was strapping fuel cans to the roof. Roy was standing a little way back, watching Tatiana, who was watching them in turn. Georgie was helping Toby line up the children.

"Georgie, Marshall is fetching water. Go help him. Roy, help Georgie and Marshall."

"Something's going on," Roy said. "There were four guards here until Tatiana sent them away."

"Whatever it is, we'll deal with it, but we need the water first," she said. With one eye on Tatiana, she hurried over to the van where she cornered Marcel. "How many adults are going with you?"

"Four," Marcel said. "We need more. You should come with us." He glanced up at Ricardo, still tying fuel cans to the roof.

"I can't. *We* can't," she said. "If we all leave, everything will fall apart. The children could get hurt. We have to stay to make sure you get away. What's your plan?"

"We can fish. We'll farm. The children aren't safe here."

"Agreed, but that's not a plan. Nana's going with you. And Harmony. You're going to drive to the Peace Garden, where Doc Pearson went. Harmony has three weeks of medicine, and then she'll get really sick, really fast. She needs more. That means a city."

Marcel slowly nodded. "Do you think they'll be friendly?"

"Yes. They wanted us to join until they found out how many we were. Do you promise you'll go there?"

"I promise to try. It's a long way. If we run out of fuel, we'll have difficulty looking for more if it's just the five of us."

"Give me your map."

"I remember the route."

"Good. Give me the map, and get back to loading."

As the last of the children got aboard, Marshall, Roy, and Georgie arrived with the water, and Maggs finished annotating the map. She gave it to Marcel. "We've been leaving small caches of supplies. I've marked where. It's not much, and it's probably not enough, but it should get you close enough to cycle the rest of the distance. Good luck."

He held out his hand. "Thank you. Maybe we'll see you there one day."

"Maybe. Now go, before everything here turns ugly."

The crowd was growing. There wasn't much entertainment in the camp, and watching people pack was a change from watching them cook, but there was a simmering frustration in the air.

Fern arrived with Harmony and Nana, still carrying Gordon's shotgun over her shoulder.

"You do everything that Nana says," Maggs said to Harmony.

"Is Hats coming with us?" Harmony asked.

"Not yet. Soon," Maggs said.

"Make it soon," Nana said. "We'll see you in Manitoba."

Maggs simply nodded, and stepped back, turning her attention to the guards while her friends, her tribe, her family, got aboard. Without any ceremony, Toby turned on the engine and pulled away. For a moment, Tatiana remained in the road, blocking the way. As Maggs took a step towards her, the sergeant stepped aside, letting the cars pass. Ricardo was already at the gate, holding it open. Within minutes, the cars were gone. Soon after, their engines were lost to hearing. Maggs turned away, blinking back tears that were born of anger as much as regret.

Chapter 8 - A Day Without Harmony
Yakima County, March 6th

Maggs breakfasted early and alone, methodically making her way through the bag of honeyed almonds she'd been keeping for Harmony's birthday. She'd spent the night being conspicuous in a camp chair, fifty metres from the gate. No one had left, and no engines had been turned on. Whether because of her, or because they had no interest in chasing and bushwhacking Marcel and the children, she truly didn't know. Once the convoy rolled out, it would be impossible to stop a vehicle from heading off in pursuit. Brass's people were responsible for making sure no one was lost to a breakdown or otherwise left behind, so it would be easy for one or two of their vehicles to slip away. It had been a clear night, and Marcel knew the dangers. By now, he should be at least three hundred kilometres away. Far enough not to be caught, she hoped. And that was all she could do.

She put another almond in her mouth, sucking it like hard candy. When the sweet coating was just a memory, she chewed the nut into a fine paste which she let sit on her tongue before swallowing. After a night of second-guessing and repeated rehashing, she'd finally decided that Marcel had made the right choice to leave, and that she'd made the right choice not to. But she was acutely aware that her decision hadn't been to stay, but to not leave with Marcel so that he, and Harmony, could get away. Yes, a crisis had been averted, but she should have seen it coming. There would be another one soon, so how would she prevent it? At what point would she admit that she couldn't stop it, and so should leave, whether they had the supplies or not. By the time she reached the last almond, she had no good answer.

A sleepless night seemed to be contagious. Before the first hint of dawn banished the stars, the encampment filled with the sound of tents coming down and sleeping bags being rolled up. By first light, everyone was waiting to go, with occasional detours to the toilet, or just as far as the nearest tree. They were leaving, so it didn't matter, but the sudden breakdown in hygiene further reinforced her fears of what was to come.

When they left, it was with two additional vehicles in their scouting convoy. Ezra and two of his acolytes shadowed the SUV's bumper so close that they didn't dare go above fifteen kilometres an hour, meaning they were only a few minutes ahead of the main convoy. Tatiana, Alexander, and two other guards were behind the fun-bus, thankfully out of sight.

Maggs sat in the back, trying to sleep, but Hats, restless after a night without Harmony to cuddle, kept digging his claws into her lap.

"Bad cat! Bad," she muttered half-heartedly. Hats ignored her.

"I think that only works with dogs," Ginger said. She'd volunteered for driving duties, almost pushing Marshall into the fun-bus. Whether she wanted to escape the inevitable rehashing of the events of last night, or wanted to spend more time with Ricardo, Maggs wasn't sure and was too tired to ask.

"We had a dog once," Maggs said as she readjusted her pillow. "Eight years ago. A little terrier. Etienne found him by the roadside during a truly ferocious storm. Poor little thing was an inch away from death. Gaspode, we called him. Our cat at the time was an elderly lady who found Gaspode's exuberance a little too much to take. We had to make the top of the house her domain, and limit him to downstairs. That worked for a while, but when we were out, he wanted to play with Lady Beatrice. She took to escaping the house, and a cat flap works just as well for a dog, so he was able to follow. He got hit by a car. Lady Bea was sitting by his body when I got home. She'd managed to drag him to the kerb. It was very sad. Sorry. I didn't mean to bring you down. I just haven't had enough sleep."

"Tell me about it," Ginger said. "Things will be calmer tonight."

"They won't," Maggs said. "The children's presence was like a valve, shutting down the worst excesses of the group at large. Now they're gone, people will start to wonder what we're doing and why. Without them, we can't pretend we're a tribe. We're just a group of adults travelling together, and soon people will start to ask why they're listening to Martin. Come the first crisis, survival instincts will kick in. We'll have theft and violence and worse."

"We should have gone with them," Ginger said. Her tone told Maggs that she was really asking why they hadn't.

"There wasn't enough fuel. I don't think there's enough for them. Between what we found yesterday and what we left along the way, they should get to within a hundred kilometres of the Peace Garden. That's close enough for Marcel to cycle."

"It's close enough for him to run," Ginger said. "But he'll have to run alone. There aren't enough other adults for anyone to go with him. Lily's pregnant. That's why she went with Marcel."

"She is? I didn't know," Maggs said.

"*She* didn't know until she took a test a couple of days ago. She'd asked me to find one for her. And after, she didn't want anyone to know."

"Should I ask who the father is?"

"Absolutely not," Ginger said, glancing over at Ricardo sitting silently in the passenger seat. "I sort of guessed, but she wouldn't confirm it because she was worried about what I'd do. It's… It's not good."

"Oh. I see. But that's just what I mean. The presence of the children coated our travelling circus with a thin layer of civility. And it seems it was thinner than I realised. Now that they're gone, our bitter demons will burst through more often and more violently. That's not sustainable." She straightened in her seat. "But we couldn't have gone with them. We'd have doubled the fuel requirement, so halved the distance travelled. And if we had left, the camp would have fallen apart."

"When we leave, it will," Ricardo said.

Maggs mulled over the question, or perhaps statement, implicit in his comment. "Yes," she finally said.

"Zombie," Ginger said. It was stumbling through the woods to their left.

"Leave it," Maggs said. "Let Tatiana stop if she wants the trouble." She readjusted the pillow and tried to sleep.

By the time they reached the golf course, Ezra's hammering of his horn had grown so frequent that even Hats couldn't sleep.

"I counted sixteen deer," Ginger said as Maggs opened the door. Hats jumped out and hissed at the cars behind. "They must have heard our engines yesterday and come to investigate."

"We could use that trick for hunting," Ricardo said.

Maggs stood, stretched, and tried not to laugh as Hats copied her.

"Where's the food?" Ezra asked as he marched over to them, his jacket askew.

Maggs waved vaguely at the drive leading up to the golf course, but otherwise ignored him as she made her way over to the fun-bus. "Roy, there was coffee in the office. Kayleigh, I saw a hot-water heater. We'll set up the generator as soon as it arrives and give everyone a hot drink. Ginger, you and Ric are on mug duty. Marshall, guess what?"

"I'm on water duty, aren't I?"

"Only because you do such a good job at it. Take Georgie, and I'll see if the sergeant minds doing some work."

Bracing herself, she walked over to Tatiana and could hear Ezra following.

"I was talking to you," Ezra said.

Again, she ignored him. "Sergeant. There's coffee inside. Not much, but enough for everyone to have a mug each. It might help improve the mood, but we'll need water." She turned to address Ezra. "Unless the advanced unit of the catering team brought some?"

"You didn't ask us to," Ezra said.

Maggs turned back to Tatiana. "So we have to do it ourselves. If your people could help Marshall and Georgie fetch water, we should have enough by the time people arrive. After last night, it should help settle the mood."

Tatiana narrowed her eyes, her face assuming an expression written in a language Maggs couldn't read. "Jessop, D'Angelo, help them get water," she finally said. "Where is the food?"

"In the site office," Maggs said. "There are infected corpses in there."

Tatiana marched off with Alexander tagging along. Maggs turned to Ezra, but he was already hurrying after Tatiana. Letting the two of them fight it out, she walked back to the road to welcome everyone else.

It took half an hour for the first car to come into sight, during which time she'd spotted something moving in the ruins opposite. Definitely four-legged, and far more agile than a zombie, and also more reticent. Probably a raccoon, and maybe lunch unless it hurried away. She waved the coaches inside, where Alexander directed them into the parking lot.

When a second truck filled with guards stopped on the road, she let them take over, and headed up to the cooking station Roy had set up outside the office. Three long folding tables, all from inside, were full of dusty crockery awaiting a rinse. The hot-water heater lay on its side with the element exposed, but on the cooking station were three portable hotplates and a row of large pots. Next to the tables was a growing stack of crates containing food.

"Does the water heater not work?" she asked.

"The regulator burned out," Roy said. "The hot plates will do the job, just as soon as someone brings me a generator."

"And why is the food out here?"

"Tatiana's orders," Kayleigh said. "She wanted it where it could be seen."

"Interesting," Maggs said. There was no sign of her or of Ezra. "I'll find some volunteers to take over here. Grab some coffee. We'll have our break when we're at the top of the mountains."

"We're leaving?" Kayleigh asked.

Mindful of the refugees within earshot, she chose her words carefully. "This place will do for a night, but we want to be through the mountains tomorrow. We can't do that until we've found ourselves a traversable pass."

They were back on the road in fifteen minutes. Two minutes after that, she closed her eyes and tried to rid her mind of the infuriating buzz that always visited her after contact with their preacher. She'd just managed to drift to sleep when the SUV jolted to a halt.

"Trouble?" she asked, pulling herself up as she looked around.

"I don't know," Ginger said. She pointed ahead at a road sign which had been painted over with the words *Rejoice, Repent*.

"Looks old," Ricardo said.

"Not that old," Maggs said. "A month or two at most. Keep going. Slowly, please." She cracked the window, hoping a dose of fresh air would keep her alert as they entered the mountains.

The abandoned cars grew more numerous, and not just on the road. On the steeper sections, the crash barriers were often broken. Below, rusting wrecks hugged the stout trees growing on the downslope. As the road continued to snake upward, the cars grew more numerous, and more damaged. On the uphill-side of the deflated tyres, successive storms had gathered heaps of debris, increasingly dominated by broken window glass, glittering in the morning's strong sun.

She didn't want to think about what had happened to the passengers. It was unlikely that many had been offered a ride by a passing stranger. However, all of the fuel caps were open. After the tragedy, someone had come this way to gather fuel. It was likely to have been someone nearby, though there was no indication any survivors still lived around here; the increasingly sparse buildings were in a worse state than the cars.

The debris grew more densely scattered, the wrecked cars more numerous, the scrubby vegetation more sickly until the road abruptly vanished. In its place was a pond, about fifty metres long and twenty wide, with the slight breeze causing the algae-topped waters to lap against the pool's ragged banks.

"Reverse," Maggs said as she wound down the window. She leaned out. "Reverse, Georgie! The road's gone!"

"It's not nuclear, right?" Ginger asked. Everyone had their fears. For Ginger, it was the slow, lingering, untreatable agony of acute radiation poisoning. That was how her cousin had died, the last surviving member of her family. It was a fear that should have been easy to put to rest, but their one remaining Geiger counter had broken three weeks ago, and they'd yet to find a replacement.

"It's too small," Maggs said. "And it looks like some cars were able to get out of here, so there was probably no EMP. I think we're okay, but there's no reason to linger." She took out her map, talking aloud as a way of distracting Ginger, and as an alternative to looking at the bones gathering moss inside the abandoned cars. "We've not even crossed the Nile River. Hmm. Well, we knew there were two highways. We'll have to take the other one."

"That's more to the south, isn't it?" Ginger asked.

"It is. We'll come through the mountains much further from Seattle. It can't be helped, and we've only lost an hour."

The rest of the drive through the mountains was easy, though the mood remained tense as they focused on the vegetation, trying to decide if it was dying or unnaturally verdant. It wasn't until they stopped for their overdue coffee break that Maggs truly saw the view and understood what it meant. She looked down at the curling ridges and tree-coated slopes, seeing only a vast emptiness behind them, while ahead, she only saw danger. National boundaries and state lines had been consigned to history. This was their Rubicon. Once crossed, she truly didn't think they'd go back, and yet she found it increasingly difficult to see a future in what lay ahead.

"Let's finish up," she said.

"The coffee's no good?" Roy asked.

"No, it's great. I'm just running on empty," she said. "I... I..." She slowly turned around, looking back down the road before she thought to look up. The clouds were too dense, causing the sound to bounce off the mountain peaks and roll down the slopes. It was impossible to tell where it had come from, or which way it was going, but she knew that sound. A sound she thought had vanished last year. A sound which faded as swiftly as it had arrived, yet whose memory echoed around her head.

"A plane," she whispered, before raising her voice. "That was a plane!"

"What's the big deal?" Marshall said, as Kayleigh jumped for joy and Ginger took Ricardo's hands and attempted to make him dance.

"What do you mean? That was an aeroplane?" Georgie said.

"Yeah, I get that it means survivors. Fuel, too, I guess."

"But think about how many survivors," Maggs said. "They'd have to clear a runway, find the fuel, and repair a plane. Or maybe they've been constantly maintaining it since the outbreak. I..." She shook her head, not wanting to say it aloud, but Roy'd had the same thought.

"The evacuation zone!" he said. "Vancouver Island. If anyone kept a plane running, it's them."

Maggs nodded, then shook her head, not sure if she wanted to laugh or cry, but certainly not daring herself to speak.

"It might not be Vancouver Island," Marshall said.

"Dude, read the room," Ginger said.

"It doesn't matter *where* it came from," Georgie said. "Their community is so secure that they can spare people to maintain and run a plane. They can spare the fuel, too. This has to be a group at least as big as ours."

"Or it's one pilot who found a plane and just enough fuel to fly once," Marshall said.

"Don't be a donut," Roy said.

"I'm not. I'm just not sure why you're all acting as if that coffee was laced."

"You can explain it to him as we continue," Maggs said. "We've still got to find somewhere on the far side of the mountains to stay, and I'd really like to find it today. More now than ever."

She didn't trust herself to drive, so sat in the back, running through one scenario after another to explain the plane, and finding most of them positive. Even the sight of another road sign painted with the words *Rejoice, Repent* didn't phase her. She doubted they were the work of a pilot.

Near Morton, she saw another sign, this one by the road in rain-washed gold paint over slightly bleached green. *Shady Acres.*

"This might do," Maggs said. "Slow down." She looked back down the road. They were at a Y-junction with houses nearby, but only the driveways emerged from among the deep screens of trees. It was secluded, but not remote.

"There's no gate," Ricardo said.

"But there is a wall," Maggs said. "I think it's a retirement home."

Chapter 9 - Shady Acres
Morton

A wide driveway led between stands of cedar and spruce to a central roundabout planted with a floral calendar and surrounded by eleven houses. From the spreading sea of blue blooms, March had successfully invaded April and had recently opened a second front into the dark green leaves of February. The house numbers corresponded to the months, a little like a clock face, except for number six. The driveway occupied that position, while that house, smaller than the others, was off to one side, near the main entrance and partially concealing the nearly empty parking lot from view.

"Definitely a retirement commune," Maggs said, taking in the handrails and ramps leading up to each front door.

"A nice one," Kayleigh said. "My maw-maw would have loved a place like this."

"There are greenhouses around the back," Marshall called out from halfway down a path that led behind the houses and towards a row of benches, a brick-built barbecue and a half-finished pizza oven.

"Come back here and help Ric," Maggs said. "Roy and Kay, start with number five. Ric, check number seven and work your way around. Ginger and Georgie are in the parking lot. I'll have a look at the greenhouses. I need to stretch out the stiffness."

There weren't any barricades on the driveway, and only one set of windows looked to have been boarded up. The shared gardens told her this had been a close-knit community, so if the residents had stayed here for any length of time, they would have helped each other set up defences. Perhaps they'd not been physically able.

She picked her way along the path and took in the grounds. Benches were half-buried among the weeds beneath trees that would offer shade in summer and fruit in the fall. Raised vegetable beds had a similar style of construction to the pizza oven and brick barbecue. Perhaps they were the work of a resident. The greenhouses were twice the usual size. Inside were neat racks of tools, stacks of soil, and packets of seeds. It was very orderly, very professional, and definitely untouched since last year, and possibly not since the start of that pre-outbreak winter.

She went back around to the entrance where Georgie was sitting on a bench outside number six.

"There's an ancient Mustang under a tarp in the parking lot," Georgie said. "And a sit-on mower in a little tool shed. The lock was broken, and some tools were missing. But there's a water pump in there. I think they had their own well. Ginger and Roy went to take a look. What are the greenhouses like?"

"Bare," Maggs said. "The residents left before planting. Still, that's not an issue for us."

"It's a bit small," Georgie said. "You promised people they'd all sleep indoors."

"I know." She sat down on the bench, waiting for the others. "This will have to do"

"It'd do for us," Georgie said. "Somewhere like this would be ideal, for us, and for the kids."

"You're thinking about Nana and Harmony? Me, too. Somewhere like this would be ideal. *Like* this, but not here. Harmony still needs medicine and medical supervision. The children need adults to look after them. Honestly, they need more kids, too. And if we were to stay here, where would Martin go? More importantly, how far away would he go? That's if we could persuade him to leave."

"Yeah, I don't want him as a neighbour," Georgie said. "What are we doing now, Maggs? I mean, yesterday, the plan was to keep going to Seattle, but that was to get Harmony some pills. We don't need them anymore."

"We do need some. Harmony wasn't the only person with a chronic illness. As to what we're doing, I... I'm not sure. We couldn't have gone with Marcel, not without stirring up the kind of trouble some of us wouldn't have walked away from."

"I know. But we could walk away now. Right now. We could stay here and never go back."

"What about Fern?"

"Oh. Okay, yes. Then tonight, or tomorrow."

"We wouldn't catch up with Marcel," Maggs said. "I gave him the list of places we'd left our cache of fuel. We'd have to find more, and I don't know how long that would take. We wouldn't see him again until we got to the Peace Garden, so we don't have to leave immediately."

"So that's the plan? To follow them?"

"I don't know. Probably. Possibly. That plane changes everything. There must be a functioning community on Vancouver Island, or somewhere else nearby. They might have a medical facility. In which case, we need to make contact with them before trekking back across the continent. Oh, Kayleigh's found something." Grateful for the distraction, she stood up and waved to Kayleigh as she came out of number four. "What did you find?" she called out.

"A rifle case with no rifle, and a gun cabinet with no guns," Kayleigh said. "It's a weird house. The bedroom and bathroom have bars to hold them closed, but they're on the outside. I'm sure it's post-outbreak work, but it looks like a prison."

"Maybe the story of this place wasn't quite as bucolic as I imagined," Maggs said. "Can we stay here, do you think?"

"Sure. The house keys were left in the locks. Some kitchens still have food in them. It's musty and mouldy inside, but I've seen way worse. Are we staying?"

"For a night or two," Maggs said.

"Jackpot!" Marshall called out as he left number eleven. "Noodles, sugar, vitamins, soda, ketchup, and some mystery cans. Who wants a proper lunch?"

"Check with Roy before you open anything," Maggs said. "Has anyone else been through here?"

"Probably," Marshall said, pointing at number ten. "Someone slept there and didn't tidy up. The rest look neat."

"If someone stayed here, but didn't strip it of food, there might be food in other nearby homes. That'll give the populace something to do while they're here. Oh, and when we get back, not a word about the plane. Make sure everyone knows. We can tell Fern, Chloe, and Gordon, but no one else. Marshall?"

"Yeah, yeah, fine. It's not like I have anyone to tell."

Night had fallen by the time they reached the golf course. If the mood that morning had been subdued, tonight it was downright funereal. A crowd was waiting for them, though they looked more bored than agitated.

"Evening all," Maggs said, smiling as she got out of the car in the hope a display of positivity might dispel bad tidings. "We made it through the mountains."

"What's it like?" Yvette asked. A year ago, she'd been a top-of-the-class basketball captain with a music scholarship, and destined for the Sorbonne, CERN, or possibly even Stockholm. Now she was a kitchen drudge, unnoticed by everyone except Marshall who didn't realise how obvious his infatuation was.

"It's warmer on the other side," Maggs said. "Definitely warmer. Didn't see many zombies, or any people, but there are plenty of deer and moose."

"Not like here, then," André said, a thirty-year-old who'd written three books no one had read, and had spent his time in Lac Seul as Martin's shadow. Recently the two had been avoiding each other like the plague. "Nine turned up soon after you left. Another eleven came later on. We've been stuck inside all day."

"We couldn't go out to collect wood," Yvette said.

Maggs belatedly noticed the lack of campfires. "We'll leave at dawn," she said. "We found a nice little retirement commune. It's small, but bigger than this, and it's on the right side of the mountains. There are some supplies left behind. Nothing too spectacular, but enough for a bit of flavour. We'll leave at dawn, so make sure you're packed."

The crowd dispersed. André wasn't the only one unable to mask his disappointment. What had they expected? That she'd come back with civilisation towed behind her?

Five of the trailer-homes now had lights streaming from their windows, but she took a guess that Martin would be found inside the one where sound effects were escaping, too. There was no point putting it off. She went to clock in.

Martin was hosting one of his movie nights, along with Reggie, Ezra, and three of his acolytes. The women looked as bored with the movie as they were of the company, though the beer was probably helping. A dozen empty bottles were already scattered about the floor.

"Maggs! Welcome back," Martin said cheerfully. "You're just in time for the good part."

"What are you watching?" she asked.

"Saving Private Ryan," he said, pausing the screen. "Can you believe these girls have never seen it?"

"Ah, there was a time I'd not seen it, either," Maggs said.

"Then you must stay," Martin said, either not understanding or simply not listening.

"That's kind, but I'm bushed, Martin. We got through the mountains, and found a retirement community on the far side. It's a bigger plot than this, though there still won't be enough room for everyone indoors, but there's a wall around the property, and nice grounds. A bit more food, too, and plenty of deer and moose nearby. We might get a bit of hunting in."

"Oh, perfect. Everyone's been in a real mood today. Some fresh meat would cheer them up."

"They're packing up," Maggs said. "We'll set off at first light and should be there by lunchtime. I'll leave you to your movie."

"If you're sure," he said, even as he raised the remote. As Maggs turned around, she realised that Ezra hadn't spoken. His head lolled to one side, his eyes staring vacantly ahead while his mouth was fixed in a Joker grin. Saying nothing, she went to find Fern.

"I think Martin's high," Maggs said. "And Ezra is completely out of it."

"Possibly," Fern said as she packed away the last of her medical kit.

"It's Brass," Gordon said. "His people, when they search anywhere, hand him the pills they find. Reggie hands a lot of them to us, but there's a notable shortage of stimulants and tranquillisers. I think he's been playing dealer."

"Reggie or Brass?" Maggs asked.

"Either," Gordon said. "Both. I'd guess Brass is planning to get rid of the competition as soon as we're settled. Two disappearances on the same night would be suspicious. Two overdoses, not so much."

"I can't deal with that tonight," Maggs said. "There's something else, though. As we were crossing the mountains, we heard a plane. It was hidden by clouds, and the pass was surrounded by so many peaks, I couldn't tell which way it was heading, but it definitely was a plane."

"Did you tell Martin?"

"No. Though I could have recited the whole of Airplane and he wouldn't remember tomorrow. I don't want to say anything until we're actually through the mountains. I don't think Brass would like the idea of a group much larger than ours. Besides, it was just one plane. It could mean anything. Or it could mean nothing."

"Or it could mean everything," Gordon said.

Chapter 10 - Resting Beneath a Willow
Morton, March 7th

Maggs had gone to bed thinking of Etienne. As the temperature dropped, her thoughts turned to those solitary nights while he had been out repairing the transmission lines. Chocolate and fast food had been her lifeline during those lonely vigils, though chocolate had also been her go-to for surviving Monday mornings, Friday meetings, and frozen February weekends. There'd been book clubs and dinners with her friends, of course, but she'd still had to go back to an empty house. She knew that some people were quite happy being alone, and many others were unhappy but got on with life as best they could. Not her. She loved company, and especially that of her shining star. Their time apart had made their time together all the more precious. But now, after a year's separation, her memories of him were beginning to fade. When she conjured his face, it wasn't as sharp. His voice wasn't as warm. Memories of their adventures together weren't as comforting, instead only heightening her sense of loneliness and loss.

It was a relief when the greying sky heralded dawn's inevitable arrival. Packing didn't take long because most hadn't bothered to unload. Martin seemed to have a hangover, and there was no sign of Ezra. Brass marched around in his fatigues, barking random orders at the exhausted travellers like a dime-store Patton, but he left her and Gordon alone as they readied everyone for the road.

They left at five, at least according to her clock. She couldn't remember the last time she'd adjusted for longitude, but the next time would be when they put down roots. Maybe on Vancouver Island, but maybe near an airport. Trying not to get ahead of herself, she got behind the wheel and began retracing their route from yesterday.

She hated travelling in convoy, partly because the pace was much slower, and partly because Brass's people kept overtaking, then stopping in the road, forcing everyone else to come to a halt. Sometimes it was to kill a zombie. Other times, it was to hunt. Or so the militia said. Their childish display of power was no more productive than their attempts at hunting.

When they finally arrived at the retirement commune, the SUV was third in the convoy. Maggs drove straight inside, parking outside number six, though with enough space between the SUV and the house for Fern's ambulance.

"We're sleeping inside tonight," she said. "Ric, get Hats settled."

Brass, who'd been ahead of them and hadn't realised this was their destination, skidded up the driveway, around André's minivan, and nearly straight into the floral calendar.

"Is this it?" he yelled as he threw the door of his pickup open. "This is where you picked?"

"The parking lot is over there," she said, and then ignored him and turned to André. "Can you be parking warden? Thank you."

"We had more space last night," Brass said.

"Not all of us," Maggs said.

Leaving him to fume and André to direct traffic, she went to inspect the building she would call home for the night. Number six was the residence of the live-in warden and caretaker. This cottage was smaller but otherwise identical in style to the other eleven houses. Inside, the living space was shared with an office, while the chairs were set out in a style reminiscent of a therapist's, though with a well-worn armchair that could swivel to face the TV. By the window was an antique desk, perhaps a gift or inheritance from a resident. A wall-planner recorded medical appointments, birthdays, and vacations of the commune's occupants. The computer beneath the desk was ancient, while the paper files on the bookcase were extensive. There was only one photograph, a black and white picture of a young child and an older woman in front of a Model-T. Though the event recorded looked old, the paper and ink looked as new as the chrome frame. There was a story to be told there, she was sure, but like so many, it was now buried with the dead.

The swivel armchair looked so comfortable she didn't dare sit lest she never get up. The small couch looked less worn, while the occupants of the bookcase looked so well read, it was a miracle that the ink hadn't been worn out. Raising questions about the caretaker's grip on reality, he'd organised it alphabetically rather than thematically, with murder mysteries touching covers with epic fantasy. Grudgingly, she admitted he did have good taste, and there were a few she wouldn't mind reading herself.

"He or she?" she called out towards the bedroom, and the cascading sound of drawers opening and closing.

"What's that?" Georgie replied.

"The person who lived here. Was it a man?"

"Yes, someone old. About fifty, judging by his taste," Georgie replied.

"And what does that mean?" Maggs said.

All sound from the bedroom was replaced with the abyssal silence of a twenty-year-old who belatedly realised what she'd said. "Because it's so neat," Georgie said. "It's the sense of style that only comes with experience."

"Hmm. Fifty's not old, and don't you forget it. We'll use that bedroom as an exam room. Get it ready for Fern. The first patients will arrive soon."

Not that there would have been much illness after a day of driving, but there were still people who wanted to see a doctor. Some were neurotic. Some were chronic. Many were just lonely and scared and took comfort in the civilised ritual of a confidential chat with a professional.

Roy and Kayleigh were in the kitchen, setting up the burners to prepare their water.

"Where's Marshall?" Maggs asked.

"Mooning over Yvette," Roy said.

Kayleigh elbowed him. "Be nice!"

Maggs shook her head and left them to it. They knew what they were doing. So did the rest of their travelling tribe. Vehicles were being parked. Tents were going up. The latrine team was currently digging a pit. Martin stood outside a house, clearly torn between being seen, and going inside and to bed. There was no sign of Brass, or of Ezra, which she took to be a good sign. She waved to Fern, Gordon, and Chloe, sorting out which equipment should come inside tonight, and made her way to the gate.

Outside, the guards were unloading the aluminium sheets they'd use to block the driveway. The coaches were neatly parked on the roadside. A few of the wood-gatherers were already collecting dead branches for the cooking fires. Most were just milling about, exhausted, uncertain, and bored. She smiled and waved, and walked on, getting a feel for their temporary home.

From the frequency and proximity of the driveways, they were on the edge of a larger settlement. Beyond the rampant front yards, overflowing gutters had stained every wall. Window frames already bowed. Doors were frequently broken open. There were few cars in the driveways, but why would there be? When people heard of the evacuation, they would have gone north. Seeing people coming from the south, others would have taken to the mountains, only to become stuck in the deadly snarl-ups still blocking the roads.

One house, on a plot larger than most, had a moat of rusting barbed wire outside. Fire had swept through the attached garage and to the house, leaving the window frames blackened as if the building had been crying and its mascara had run. The first time they'd seen somewhere like that, they'd actually named the house, giving it an identity. After the fifth, they'd stopped. After the tenth, she'd stopped counting.

She reached a bridge crossing a swollen creek. Fifty metres upstream, on the riverbank, was a bench. Hoping that meant it was a good spot for fishing, she picked her way through the aspiring jungle towards it. The river surged to her left. To the right, beyond the narrow path, lay rampant undergrowth, but with hints that the bushes and trees had been diligently maintained not too many years ago. Behind that was a mossy fence. Perhaps the river had changed course since the boundary was defined, or perhaps the owner had wanted to share the spot with their neighbours. Thanks to a decade of strategic pruning, the bench remained shaded by a willow while having a majestic view of the river and the secluded forest behind. She could just picture the summer stream, slowly meandering towards the bridge, dotted with water boatmen dancing across the surface. Now, at the tail-end of a dark winter, the river frothed and foamed, swollen by the upstream thaw. Just beyond the bench, a landslip had taken a bite out of the riverbank, creating a shallow pool where the river's speed slowed.

"It's the perfect spot," she said, before hunting for a fallen branch she could use to make a trotline. After carrying it back to the bench, she drew her hunting knife and trimmed the branch. From the pocket of her padded vest, she took out an old tin of cinnamon candy that now contained a coil of fishing line and the best of her hooks. Kayleigh kept more with their cooking supplies, but she had enough for a test. As she tied the line, a flash of silver danced against the current. Yes, this would be a good spot. From the tin, she took out a piece of deer jerky. It hadn't been dried for nearly long enough, and was turning rancid. Hopefully the fish wouldn't be picky.

With her line set, she returned to the bench and took out her journal. Her most recent entry was two days old and not very long. As was often the case of late, she just wasn't sure where to start.

Dear Etienne, I'm sitting on a bench, beneath a willow tree, on the outskirts of Morton, just west of the Cascades, and in Washington State.

She paused. That had been the easy part. In search of inspiration, she turned to the bench and she saw the name carved into the frame.

The bench was placed on a riverbank, beneath a tree, in memory of Willow Debrook, who died fifteen years ago, aged twelve. Was she named after the tree, or was the tree planted in honour of her birth? I'm not sure, but this must have been a favourite spot of hers.

Leaves rustled behind her. She looked up, thinking it was a bird, but the rustling came again, louder. Slow, soft, and rhythmic. She swung around and saw a ragged dog standing on the edge of the path. It was a German Shepherd, and probably a pure-bred, though its coat had grown scraggly and lank, barely concealing the scrawny body beneath.

"Smelled the bait, did you?" she asked, keeping her tone friendly. With her left hand, she picked up the tin and flipped the lid open. Her right hand slipped to her revolver. She flicked the tin, sending the rancid meat flying towards the dog. It turned its head, not towards the offered tribute, but to the trees. Something else was moving in there. Not good. The dog turned its gaze back to her. Not good at all.

"Take what's offered. You won't like what's given," Maggs said in her firmest tone while her hand tightened on the revolver's grip.

The dog seemed to be weighing the two items on the menu for its dinner, but decided she was the tastier morsel. It tensed. She drew the revolver. A shot sounded from among the trees. The blast hit the dog square in the flanks as it leaped. It landed on the riverbank's edge, whining and paralysed as blood pulsed from the savage wound.

Ricardo stepped out of the trees, his shotgun now hanging loose in one hand.

"You were gone a long time," he said.

Maggs holstered her revolver and picked up her hunting knife. "I foolishly thought I might find a few minutes of peace to arrange my thoughts. Thank you." She walked over to the dog, pitifully moaning for aid. "Sleep now," she said, covering his eyes before stabbing the knife down into its neck. "And to think my biggest fear used to be having my chocolate stash stolen by Mel in accounts."

Ricardo crossed over to the dog and bent down. "My fear was the dark."

"Really? And you're a miner."

"Because I'm a miner. I know what absolute darkness is. When the safety beams cut out, when your flashlight fails, when all you have is your memory of where you are and which way is out, that's true darkness. You can't judge distance. You can't judge time. All you can hear is an ocean of rock threatening to crash down on your head."

"Did you never consider a different line of work?"

"Once you overcome the fear, once you accept that you, the rock, the air, you're all just atoms briefly arranged in an interesting pattern, once you realise that the only difference between you and the ground above your head is time, there's peace in the darkness. Mr Barker. On the collar. It says Mr Barker. Do you think that's the dog, or the owner?"

"The dog, I suppose."

"And now it's dinner."

Chapter 11 - Meeting the Neighbours
Lewis County, March 8th

Maggs was the first to wake. A chair indoors was a step-up from the front seat of a car, but she sorely needed a proper bed. They, and the associated privacy, were in short supply, and last night had been Roy and Kayleigh's turn. As quietly as she could, she rose, stepping around Georgie and Hats, curled together on the floor. She pulled the curtain back. Condensation obscured her view, but the light beyond was bright and natural.

"Is it morning?" Marshall groaned from the chair where he'd spent the night.

"Shh. It's still early. Sleep," Maggs said, picking up a fallen blanket and laying it atop him before going outside.

It had rained during the night, leaving the air crisp and fresh, but the sky was now clear, and full of angry chirruping at the invasion by wingless apes. Yes, spring was truly here, and it had come early. She should have been taking pleasure in that, and no small measure of relief. The blizzard months were over. The firestorm months of summer were still safely distant. Early spring should be a time to relax. Except it was also the time to plant. While their primary reason for leaving the lake was the mystery plague, they had selected Vancouver Island as their destination because of its better climate after a ruined harvest and a savage winter. They should be planting. She turned her gaze towards the greenhouses, but it fell on Martin, carrying his insincere smile towards her.

"Hoy there, Maggs," he called out, loud enough to be heard inside. "I've just checked in with the guards. Another quiet night. Nothing to report beyond a few owls. I wonder what they taste like."

"Wasn't it bad luck to kill an owl?" she asked.

"Worse luck to go hungry. Listen," he added walking a little closer and lowering his voice to a conspiratorial whisper. "How long will it take you to find a boat?"

"A boat? I... I couldn't say until we reach the coast. It would be nice to say we'll get there today, but two days is more likely. Since we won't find a ship docked at a pier, we'll have to look for a boatyard, and will probably have to search a few before we find something seaworthy. Then again, we might stumble across someone's yacht moored for the winter in their front yard."

"You think a week, then?" he asked.

"A week? At least. And then we need to find fuel. And that's before we've sailed a metre closer to Vancouver Island. At this rate, I honestly don't know if we'll ever get there."

Martin frowned. "We can't have defeatism. The boatyard would have fuel, yes? That's the plan. Find a boatyard, find a boat, *and* find diesel?"

"Well, yes. We'll need more than one boat, I think. Ferrying everyone two hundred kilometres aboard a yacht would take until fall."

"Good. We need fuel."

"Yes, I know."

"No, I mean we need it *now*. We're almost out of gas *and* diesel. I think we can manage another fifty kilometres, but we've next to nothing for the generators."

Maggs blinked slowly as she processed what he was saying. "How?" she finally managed. "We set off with enough to reach the coast with enough left over to power two generators until summer. I was there in that meeting when we did the calculations. What happened?"

"It must have been a leak. That's not important," he said far too casually. "Looking forward, it's imperative you find that boat and the fuel, okay?"

She stared at him, the questions piling up, but she knew she wouldn't get an honest answer, so didn't even bother trying. She turned on her heel and walked back to their small house.

"Up, everyone up," she said as she threw open the door. "We need to be on the road in ten minutes."

"Did we oversleep?" Ginger asked as she sat up.

"Nope. But we're wasting daylight."

"What's wrong?" Gordon asked, having followed her in from his roost in the ambulance, parked just outside.

"The fuel's gone. Martin claims a leak. I... I think he's known for a while."

"Is there any left?" Kayleigh asked.

"A little, and I'm not sure how much. Enough to travel a few kilometres. So today, we are going to find a better semi-permanent home. Somewhere everyone can sleep inside. Somewhere we can plant. And then finding fuel is our new priority, because we'll need it for so much."

"I bet he stole it," Marshall said. "Him and Brass. I bet they stashed it somewhere on the road."

"Maybe," Maggs said. "But they'd deny it, so asking is pointless."

"We could try Everett," Gordon said. "It's a city north of Seattle. The big Boeing factory was there, with the hangar so large it had its own cloud system. If there's fuel anywhere, it's there. And it's a good spot to look for that plane."

"Everett? Good. Yes," Maggs said. "But if it's north of Seattle, we won't get there today. Gordon, can you find out what happened with the fuel. I don't think there's anything we can do about it, but I'd like to know who's complicit, or who's that utterly incompetent." She clapped her hands together. "Come on, people. We're against a clock now."

"How so?" Georgie asked as she rolled up her sleeping bag.

"Because as soon as everyone else finds out about this, they'll explode," Maggs said.

Martin Genk wasn't an idiot. He was arrogant, bigoted, self-righteous, obnoxious, and chronically selfish, but he *had* risen to head up a multibillion-dollar company. Yes, he'd had the assistance of a seven-figure inheritance, a calculated marriage, and a strategic divorce, but he also knew how to manipulate a situation to his own advantage. That made Maggs wonder how long the fuel crisis had existed. Had he known of it before they'd crossed the mountains? Specifically, had he known of it when Marcel had announced his intention to leave? The mountains represented a psychological barrier as much as a physical one, but now they were through, the chance and desire for turning back would be that much less. Thus, by not revealing this crisis until now, his ability to maintain his grip on power would seem greater.

"Stop!" Ricardo said, breaking through her silent reverie.

"Zombies?" she asked, tapping on the brakes even as her eyes darted between the windows and mirrors.

"Smoke," he said.

About three kilometres ahead, a twisting tendril of grey gracefully rose above the trees.

"Is it a cooking fire?" Marshall asked, leaning forward between the seats. "No, it's too large."

"It could be an ambush," Ricardo said.

Maggs looked around again, inspecting the encroaching wilderness. "Whoever they are, they're going to be our neighbours, so we have to say hello, but we'll expect trouble. Marshall, tell the others."

While she waited for him to return, Maggs slipped her revolver into her coat pocket, putting a flashlight into the other to balance the weight. When they set off, she kept their speed as low as the SUV could manage so they could visually gauge each passing building for signs of settlement, or of danger.

"Broken door on that house," Ricardo said as they drove past a clapboard one-and-a-half-storey.

"They should have sealed up the door," Marshall said. "Everything inside will be ruined."

"Exactly," Ricardo said.

As the pillar of smoke flitted in and out of view, they saw other properties with shattered windows and broken doors. None appeared to have been recently looted, let alone occupied. The road told a different story; wrecked cars had been pushed to the verge, and the occasional fallen tree had been hauled aside.

"Who would clear the road, but not search the houses?" Marshall asked.

"Someone who's only just arrived," Maggs said. "Check the map for airfields."

She did her best to rein in her hopes as she leaned forward, looking for smoke. She saw it again, just beyond a new meadow that had once been a field. Probably grazing land before the outbreak, and it hadn't been ploughed yet this year. A track led up the side of the field, but was blocked with a metal gate, recently covered in wire mesh. She stopped next to it and got out.

"There's no lock on the gate," Ricardo said.

"What would be the point?" Maggs said. "Roy, Kayleigh, stay with the vehicles. Ginger and Georgie, I want you to follow but let yourself fall a little way behind. There's no point risking an ambush. Hats..." The cat was still asleep on the dashboard. "Make sure he doesn't run off. Best smiles everyone, let's go and say hello."

She lifted the latch and pushed the gate open. It dropped nearly a centimetre. After another few storms, it would need to be repositioned. Quick and recent work, she kept that thought foremost in her mind as she walked up the track.

"Boot prints," Ricardo said quietly.

There were a lot of them, going in both directions, at least three pairs of large feet, and two of medium-sized. There were no small prints indicating any children.

"We should have blasted the horn," Marshall said as they climbed towards the top of the shallow hill.

"Just keep smiling," Maggs said. At the peak of the shallow hill, the track branched. Below them was an old farmhouse, a newer barn, two very new RVs, and a muddy tractor. One branch of the track disappeared behind a square of low trees that was probably an orchard, and towards what might be chalets, or could just be sheds. Another branch disappeared into the new wilderness.

Three people were walking towards them from the house. At the back was a young woman in a very traditional farm dress and apron. At her side was an older man clad in mud-covered dungarees, and a younger, bearded man carrying an axe over his shoulder. There would be others nearby, watching, and she assumed at least one had a loaded gun aimed at them, so she raised a hand, waving a greeting.

"Hello! I'm Maggs, this is Ricardo and Marshall. The two sightseers back there are Georgie and Ginger." She waved behind her at the two women strolling up the track with all the urgency of a seal on a sunny rock. "We're from Quebec."

"Quebec, really?" the woman said.

"Hush, Meredith," the older man said. He looked about sixty. His face was taut and sun-damaged. His eyes were hidden behind a permanent squint while his left hand flexed as if he was ready to give a signal.

"Quebec, yes," Maggs said. "We've spent the last year travelling. We're looking for somewhere to stop for a few weeks before we try to get back across the border."

"There's no room here," the young man said.

"No, I'm sure. There are about four hundred and fifty of us," Maggs said, and ignored the surprise that revelation produced. "We're hoping to get closer to the coast, find a boat, and then sail north, back to Canada. Until then, we'd want to do a little hunting and light farming, though we'll be leaving our fields behind, of course, when we leave."

"I didn't catch your name," Ricardo said, taking a step forward. The young man with the axe took a corresponding step towards Ricardo.

"I'm Meredith, this is Paul, and that's Mike," Meredith said, stepping forward to put a cautioning hand on the arm of Paul, the younger of the two men.

"A pleasure to meet you all," Maggs said. "It looks like we'll be neighbours. Where should we avoid hunting? We don't want an accident."

"This is our land," Paul said. "We were promised forty acres."

"Quiet, boy," Mike snapped at the younger man before turning back to Maggs. "You stay on that side of the road. We'll stay on this side, then we won't have any trouble. Agreed?"

"Great. Perfect," Maggs said. "And is there anything you need, anything we can look for while we're out scavenging?"

"The Lord provides," Mike said.

"Yes, indeed," Maggs said. "Oh, do you have a plane?"

"A plane?" Paul said. "No."

"I thought I saw one earlier. I wondered if this was where it had come from."

"Haven't seen one since tribulation came upon us," Mike said.

"I must have been imagining things," Maggs said, deciding she'd had enough of the fruitless exchange. "We'll be seeing you around, I expect. Take care." She waved and headed back down the track.

"Well, that was—" Marshall began.

"Shh. Not here," Maggs said.

Chapter 12 - Mani, Pedi, Zombie
Alder

She waited until they were back at the road before speaking. "Let's get out of here."

"What are you thinking?" Marshall asked.

"That's just it, I'm still thinking," Maggs said. She took them north, then west, then north again, finally stopping outside a roadside diner and garage about four kilometres from the farm.

"This will do," she said as she pulled off the road. "Check inside, Ric. Marshall, climb up to the roof of the fun-bus. Watch for followers."

The garage had been looted a dozen times, and then trashed in frustration a dozen times more. Even so, there were useful items that could still be salvaged: windows, pipework, and sturdy timbers.

"Georgie said they weren't friendly," Roy said, cutting to the heart of the question Maggs was asking herself.

"They weren't *un*friendly," Marshall called out from the bus's roof.

"I don't think they've been there long," Maggs said as Ricardo came outside. "What does it look like inside? When was the last person here?"

"Before winter," he said. "There are some machines and tools, some good rope and chains. If we were staying in these parts, we'd take it."

"The RVs had Nevada plates," Ginger said.

"My bus has Quebec plates," Georgie said.

"Exactly," Ginger said.

"Why come up here?" Roy asked.

"Why leave Quebec?" Ginger said. "There's a hundred possible reasons. The weather, zombies, bandits. Or it could be they just want farmland."

"There's a lot we don't know," Maggs said. "They must have some diesel because they're running a tractor, and had enough fuel to drive here. They're only now ploughing a field, and they've not secured any nearby properties to preserve basic supplies. I think they arrived in the last week or two, and the most pressing question is whether we think they're dangerous."

Everyone looked at Ricardo.

He took his time before answering. "Them? No. Two RVs? Ten people. I didn't see any firearms. They're homesteading."

"But?" Ginger asked.

"They said they were promised forty acres," Ricardo said. "Promised by whom? What do you think, Maggs?"

"As to who made the promise? Not a clue," she said. "But as to my own question, they were uninviting before they knew how many we were. Maybe they have reason to be suspicious. We certainly do. But if I'd been in their place, I'd have invited us inside to get a better feel for how dangerous we were."

She went back to the car and sorted through their maps until she found one for the entirety of North America. "Their RVs came from Nevada, but their accents were... I'm not sure. For now, we'll say they came north to escape the blistering heat. And this is about as far north as you can get without crossing the border. They must have had a lot of fuel, and it sounds like they're part of another group, but they don't know anything about a plane. Well, if the plane didn't come from the south, then Vancouver Island still seems like its likely departure point. I guess we'll just continue on as before."

"Wherever we go, we'll be within a day's drive of them," Roy said.

"Marshall's right. They may not have been friendly, but they weren't hostile," Maggs said. "They probably don't have a doctor. That's our way in. Fern will learn more during an exam than we could chatting by the gate. Hopefully, we can trade with them. Even if we can't, we should learn what happened further south, and maybe further away than that. But we'll still need somewhere to sleep. Let's try westward."

As they got ready to leave, Maggs looked back in the direction of the farm, thinking of Meredith. She'd borne an expression Maggs had seen often enough before the outbreak, the look of someone who had reached the end of the road, figuratively and metaphorically. The expression of someone in need of help.

They were only one kilometre short of when they'd have to turn around when she saw the purple and white signage for the Laurel Hills Spa and Resort. They'd stopped often since leaving the farm, but hadn't found anything less ruined, more defensible, or freer of bones than the retirement commune.

"It's here or nowhere," Maggs said, and turned on her indicator light.

The wall's pink facade had cracked every few metres, revealing concrete beneath, and suggesting a new and cheap renovation that hadn't survived its first winter, but it was over two metres high. The open gateway led to a wide driveway that bisected a large meadow, gently sloping uphill. The grassland stretched for at least two acres on this side of the property, dotted with an even mix of bare-branched deciduous and lush evergreens, all around fifteen years old. Between the trees, benches and outdoor exercise equipment slowly drowned beneath the rising greenery.

At the top of the shallow hill was the spa complex itself, though it looked less like a hotel than a haunted mansion trying to outrun its starkly modern extensions. The front entrance had a porch supported by four giant columns. Behind and above were tall but narrow windows, while the newer additions had more windows than wall. Those on the ground floor were covered in vinyl posters showing overly muscled models posing beneath meaningless slogans. Upstairs, the windows sported reflective glass that made it impossible to see into, but she counted four storeys at the front, two at the rear.

Maggs stopped right outside the purple front doors. They got out of their vehicles, listening to silence return as the birds they'd disturbed settled back to their roosts.

"What does rejuvenate to regenerate mean?" Kayleigh asked, reading the slogan on a window to the left of the doors.

"About three hundred dollars a night," Maggs said. "It looks like it extends around the back quite a way, and if they have rooms, they must have had a restaurant, and washrooms. This could be it."

"It won't have enough bedrooms for all of us," Roy said.

"No, but we can double up, and repurpose the gym and the meeting rooms," Maggs said. "Everyone will get to sleep indoors, and that would be an improvement. Kayleigh, Roy, and Marshall follow the drive around to the parking lot. See if there's a pump or plant room, access to a septic tank, water storage, anything like that, but watch out for zombies."

"C'mon, scruff," Kayleigh said, pushing Marshall along the road.

Ricardo pulled his masonry pick from his belt and approached the front door. It was made of solid wood, offering no view inside, but the pile of leaves in the gap struck her as promising. The door was unlocked and swung open with barely a creak.

Inside, the lobby was dark. Concave mirrors would have reflected daylight before the windows were covered with posters of suspiciously sweat-free athletes. There was little furniture, except an empty supplement display stand and a purple-trimmed reception desk, atop which were five seed trays.

"The door back here's hiding a stairwell," Georgie said. "There's no elevator."

"I guess if you don't like steps, you don't come to a health resort," Ginger said.

"Pity the staff," Maggs said, as she dipped a finger into the seed tray, pushing through the dry soil. She couldn't find any seeds.

"Found a bullet," Ricardo said, pointing at a hole in the wall. "There's another one over there."

"I found a knife," Ginger said holding up a white-handled Bowie knife she'd found behind the reception desk.

"Any bodies?" Maggs asked as she walked over to the swing doors to the left of the hallway. They were sturdy and thick fire-doors with magnetic wall-locks that had disengaged. Each had a small head-height window through which she shone her light onto a broad and empty corridor.

"Nope. No bodies. No notes. No clues about who lived here," Ginger said.

There were four doors from the lobby. One double-set led to the right, another at the back of the entrance hall led to the stairwell. A single door opposite led into the staff area. All had swung closed, and all appeared to be locked. "Hang on," she said, having returned to the swing doors to the left of the entrance. "There's a wedge here." She kicked at the triangular sliver of metal, but the door still didn't move. "Check the other doors."

All except the single staff-door were wedged shut.

"Seems obvious which way to go," Ricardo said.

"Do you mean we should literally walk into a trap?" Ginger asked.

"That one, then," he said, waving his pick at the door to the left of the entrance.

"A door someone sealed?" Ginger asked. "That's worse."

"And we need to know how much worse," Maggs said. The doors didn't seem designed to swing into the corridor, but had no handle, so she had to pry them open, and then saw she was wrong. The doors were designed to swing both ways, but someone had drilled metal bolts into the floor to prevent them opening inwards.

"This is such a bad idea," Ginger said as she clipped her flashlight to the homemade bracket on her crossbow.

With her tomahawk in one hand and a light in the other, Maggs walked softly along the corridor, listening for danger, but only hearing the excited buzz of her tinnitus. The corridor's walls were lined with a plastic facade, similar to the lobby, except here it was a more welcoming butter-yellow fading to orange-sunset at the ceiling. The six doors, three on each side, were a more vibrant blood orange. She tried the first door and found a room that looked a little like a doctor's office, except for the posters extolling the supposed benefits of dealing supplements to your friends.

Above the doors at the corridor's end was a too-bright sign announcing the Hydration Chamber. The doors were closed but, unlike the first set, they hadn't been wedged shut.

"Do you think it's an indoor pool?" Ricardo said as he pushed the door open.

"It's a bar!" Ginger said, aiming her light at the beguiling list of healthy shakes and nutritious fruit blends.

"Or a greenhouse," Maggs said. The tables had been pushed together, close to the windows from which some of the opaque plastic film had been removed. Atop them were seed trays, filled with soil, but with no shoots, or even any labels.

"Dry," Maggs said, touching the soil. "This place is well-insulated. No damp."

"The bar's dry too," Ginger said, "but there's a row of optics hidden behind the counter. No taps, but they served hard liquor. They just didn't advertise it."

"This is the more public half of the place, then," Maggs said. "Here for walk-ins, or drive-ins, I should say."

"You think people would really drive here for a gut-busting grape delight, or tummy-tightening tayberry teaser?" Ginger asked, reading from the menu.

"Sometimes, on Sundays, Etienne and I would drive fifty kilometres just for pancakes," Maggs said, heading over to another set of closed fire-doors. "It's the restaurant, but I think it would have become a farm. There's more seed trays, and a handcart with some sacks of plant feed. Ah, I thought so," she said, peering into an open sack of feed. "It looks like the soil in the trays. There's about five empty bags here. Oh. They filled the trays with concentrated fertiliser instead of soil."

"Ah, so she wasn't a farmer," Ginger said. "That makes sense. She was probably one of the staff."

"The kitchen's back here," Ricardo said.

It was tidy, but the cupboards were empty. Washed dishes were left by the sink. Based on the single mug and plate, she'd guess at one person being here alone, in the end. But had she left, or had she died?

A door at the back of the restaurant led to a row of bathrooms. Nine individual cubicles, which didn't seem enough based on the size of the restaurant.

"We'd better check each," Maggs said. "And then we'll go upstairs." She checked her watch. "It's taking too much time."

"Why rush?" Ginger said. "If we're out of gas, we've only got one shot at moving, right? So, wherever we move to has to be perfect."

"Empty," Ricardo said, letting the first washroom door swing closed. "Looted, too."

"I think I heard Roy," Ginger said, turning back to the door.

"I'll check," Ricardo said, and headed back through the restaurant.

"Maybe that retirement place wouldn't be so bad," Maggs said, stifling a yawn. She'd been feeling tired all day. She could blame a lack of oxygen in this airless hotel, except she'd been feeling like this for at least a week, and was worrying it was a symptom of something deeper.

She turned the handle, stepped back, and froze as a corpse toppled forward. Undead arms curled around her neck. She screamed her panic away and thrust the tomahawk forward. The spike merely ripped away a strip of the rotten shirt and dried skin, barely slowing the creature's momentum. Maggs managed to stay on her feet as she staggered backwards, but the zombie now had a tight grip on her neck and came with her.

"Don't move!" Ginger said.

Maggs ignored her, doing the only thing she could think of, ducking down and twisting as she brought the tomahawk back. Off balance, the zombie stumbled, falling to a knee, but still maintained its death grip on her neck. Maggs was pulled forward even as she swung the tomahawk towards its head. She hit its shoulder. The bone cracked. One of its hands went limp. She attempted a roll. It became a sprawl, but dislodged the zombie's other hand, and left her two metres clear of the creature. Ginger fired. Her bolt neatly sliced through the zombie's skull.

"That's *three* times in a week," Ginger said as she offered her hand.

"Thank you," Maggs said as she got back up. She rubbed her neck as she walked back to the washroom door. "Okay, more attention this time. Ready?"

Ginger loaded her reloaded bow. "I am now."

Maggs opened the door again, this time stepping back, though it was now empty. Inside was a large blue barrel with a spigot she assumed had contained water, and an unopened pack of self-adhesive bandages on the floor.

"Got injured, came here to clean himself up, and then turned," Ginger said.

"Probably. Next one."

This time, she knocked on the door while keeping one hand on it, listening, but also feeling for vibrations. The doors were thick. By the time she reached the end of the corridor, she thought she understood why. "Look how close the bathrooms are to the kitchens," she said. "I bet you could hear the clattering of the pans if these doors weren't soundproof. And vice versa."

"Eww."

The last door wasn't for a bathroom, but a stock room.

"Ooh, now we're getting somewhere," Ginger said.

"Food?" Maggs asked, leaning against the wall outside, trying to slow her heartbeat.

"No. Cleaning stuff. But there's a lot of it. Hang on, this room goes back a long way. Oh. It's just… Well, see for yourself. It's a fake wall. It is, right?"

A board, on which hung three brooms and a mop, was leaning against a row of shelves. It was clear where it should fit, concealing a small alcove with dials and digital control panels on the wall, and a hatch in the floor.

"Definitely a fake wall," Maggs said. "And it must be post-outbreak. That control panel is for the internal air system. They shouldn't be covered."

"You've got to wonder what's down there," Ginger said.

"We don't have time to wonder," Maggs said, bending down. "Be ready."

The hatch swung upwards easily, revealing a dark hole. Maggs shone her light down a three-metre-long ladder and onto a square of purple carpet at the bottom. "Hello?" she called.

"Like it would be a good thing if anyone answered," Ginger said.

"Well, here goes." Maggs let the light dangle from its wrist strap as she reached for the first rung.

"You're not going down."

"Would you like to go first?" Maggs asked, but began descending before Ginger could answer. As soon as her head was below the floor, she wrapped an arm around the ladder, swinging the light about to take in the chamber. "It's a storeroom," she said, climbing the rest of the way down. "A bunker. A prepper's hideaway."

There were so many shelves. *And* they were full, stretching out for at least the length of the main building. She stepped aside to make space for Ginger. The rug was only a metre by two. The ends of six criss-cross yoga mats lay beneath it, so they were probably there to soften the fall of supplies lowered from above. The shelves between the foundation pillars were utilitarian steel. The rest were flat-packs of a mix of sizes and materials.

"I've got clothes over here," Ginger called out as she began to explore. "All one size, more or less. Same with the shoes. I bet it was the zombie in the bathroom."

Maggs made her way between racks of unboxed but unused cookware, and to a living space. Thick red velvet curtains had been hung from the ceiling, separating the individual areas: a kitchen, a living space, a bathroom, a bedroom. None were overly large, but with the curtains drawn back, it would still have been homely. The sofa was a futon with extra cushions atop a homemade frame, facing a small TV sitting on a bookcase filled with DVDs.

"It doesn't look that comfy," Ginger said, prodding the futon.

"I guess he was limited by what could fit down the hatch," Maggs said. "I think those chairs came from the bar."

"Chairs and a sofa," Ginger said. "Interesting. Seating for three."

"But with enough pans to feed an army and no indication anyone else lived down here. Go find Ric and the others. If all's well with them, check the bedrooms upstairs. I'll finish up down here. Tell them we'll meet in the lobby in thirty minutes."

As Ginger left, Maggs tried the lamp by the chair. It didn't work, but there was a cable running along the floor, and another from the mini-fridge in the kitchen space, but there was no mini-freezer to go with it. The cupboards contained a mundane collection of jars and tins, and even a few packets. She continued exploring, but the cellar wasn't as large as it first appeared, and after twenty minutes, she thought she'd seen enough. She made her way back to the ladder to find out what the others had learned.

Chapter 13 - A Month for One, a Meal for Many
The Laurel Hills Spa and Resort

Maggs was first to return to the lobby, though she'd barely had time to prop herself on the reception desk before the heavy door to the stairwell opened, and Roy and Kayleigh came out.

"Where are the others?" Maggs asked.

"Still searching," Roy said. "So far, it looks great up there. A few rooms are messed up. A few are untouched. There's about seventy in total, but if we include the meeting rooms here, plus the staff rooms at the very top, there's enough space for everyone."

"Ginger said you'd found a prepper's secret bunker," Kayleigh said.

"She's exaggerating," Maggs said. "It's a basement containing the air and heating systems, and the electrical conduits. Someone hid their supplies down there, and then hid the entrance. Later on, he probably got infected, and turned in one of the bathrooms, and then just waited there until we arrived. But we only found the one zombie. You?"

"No, none," Kayleigh said. She picked up one of the tubs Maggs had found in the basement. "But you found food."

"If you want to call it that," Maggs said. "It's some sort of nutritional mix. There are twenty large drums, split into four flavours. I think they then decanted them into smaller tubs with more interesting names, at different ratios, to come up with a supplement to sell. But assuming the ingredients on the drums can be trusted, it's fortifying and nutritional. There's a few weeks of normal food, too."

"Is there enough for lunch?" Roy asked.

"Go for it," Maggs said. "The hatch is in the storeroom just past the bathrooms. Go together, though. I'm not one hundred percent certain the hotel is clear."

Maggs headed back outside, where Hats was sitting in the car, looking forlorn and neglected in the way that only a well-loved cat can. The moment she let him out, he darted beneath the car and refused to budge.

"You're a mad little thing, aren't you?"

There wasn't much to see from the driveway. The spa was built atop a rise, and the top floor might offer a view, but from ground level, she could only see a handful of distant roofs between the beginning-to-bud trees. At the same time, they truly weren't that far from Seattle, Tacoma, and Puget Sound.

"Yes, this will do."

Half an hour later, Maggs was sat in the dining room, at the head of the table which had been properly set. Next to her, Hats was already devouring his second plate of tuna. In front of her was a bowl of fish, rice, and green beans.

"Told you we'd find some," Kayleigh said, handing Maggs a bottle of hot sauce.

"You're a treasure."

"How long will the food last?" Marshall asked between chews.

"About an hour if you continue eating like that," Roy said. "Remember to taste it."

"Remember to breathe," Kayleigh said. "The normal food is enough for a person for a few months. So, for everyone, it'll last for a meal."

"If Martin and Ezra don't steal it," Ginger said.

Kayleigh shrugged. "True. If the powder is what the contents say, then they could provide us all with enough calories for two weeks. I think we should aim to only use them as a vitamin supplement, maybe just for breakfast."

"There's a generator in the basement," Roy said. "I think we can turn the lights back on."

"And the air pumps," Georgie said. "The air in here is really stale. I don't think any of the windows open."

"Yep, shouldn't be a problem," Roy said. "There were two diesel cans in the pump room. We should be good for a few weeks."

"Good. I think people will like having lights again," Maggs said. "What about running water?"

"In theory, we can have that, too," Roy said. "On the far side of the parking lot, there's a service driveway, a few sheds and utility buildings, and a back gate. There were too many padlocks to open it, and it was too high to climb, but beyond I think I saw a river. I don't think that's where their water came from, but the pump room is in good condition. The generator shut off when the fuel ran dry, but it looks in working order. All we'd need to do is fill up the feeder tank. Hot water might be asking too much with the fuel we have."

"So there was power when the survivor died?" Georgie asked.

"Seems like it," Roy said. "How many rooms are there?"

"Eighty-six, I think," Georgie said. "That's including the suites and the staff bedrooms that share a bathroom."

"Between the bedrooms and the treatment rooms downstairs, everyone can sleep indoors," Maggs said. "If we can hunt and fish, we should have enough food for four weeks, by which time we should have some salad leaves and other bits growing. Good."

"And then what?" Marshall asked.

"Potatoes and corn, I suppose," Maggs said.

"No, like, we're not going to Seattle anymore, are we?" Marshall said. "We don't need to. Harmony's gone."

"We're going to Vancouver Island," Ricardo said.

"Then why don't we just go?" Marshall asked, pushing his bowl forward and his chair back.

"We can't leave Fern, Gordon, and Chloe behind," Ricardo said.

"And Yvette?" Kayleigh added.

"No, yes, we'll get them, too," Marshall said. "But we don't need to stay, do we? This food would last us for weeks. The diesel would get us to the coast."

"Not if you put it in my bus, it won't," Georgie said, but no one laughed.

"You want to know why we're staying, and not long after we decided we'd leave?" Maggs said. "First, I don't know that we *are* staying with this group. I don't know how we'd get our people away from the convoy, but I'm sure if we spent thirty minutes thinking about it, we'd find a way. Assuming Fern would agree to leave her patients behind, of course. But then what?"

"Manitoba," Marshall said.

"Vancouver Island first," Ricardo said.

"Yes, and what then? Old pills will keep Harmony alive for another year. Maybe two. Maybe ten. They won't last forever. What about the next time someone gets sick? All the old pills will stop working for everyone. We can power up a hydroelectric plant. We can salvage replacement parts, but we can't build new ones. We got this far thanks to the fuel we found along the way, but a day will come when we don't have any left. At that point, we're limited by how far we can travel by bicycle. Eventually, the roads will become utterly impassible, and then we'll be stuck on our farm. We have to think about these things, about what we do next, because it has implications for the rest of our lives."

Silence reigned, though only briefly.

"Okay, yeah, I get that, but what *do* we do next?" Marshall asked. "Manitoba or Vancouver Island?"

Maggs shook her head. "That's not the way to look at it. This isn't an either-or. We've crossed the entire continent and can pinpoint a few actively aggressive groups, and a few more that weren't hostile but weren't welcoming, either. And they were small groups. We've seen no functioning villages, let alone anything larger. The only community who are potentially comparable with our own is at the Peace Garden, but we never went there to see it for ourselves. We *hope* Doc Pearson went there and thrived, and that Nana and Harmony can reach it and find safety, but we don't *know*."

"Sounds like a reason to go after them," Marshall said.

"We need to find more people," Ginger said. "That's what you mean."

"In part, yes. But I also worry *we* are all there are. Us and the Peace Garden, all alone in the world."

"And the people who ambushed us," Roy said.

"And those unfriendly farmers we met earlier," Ginger added.

"And that plane," Georgie said.

"And the plane, yes," Maggs said. "Hopefully, the plane represents a large community. Maybe those farmers do, too, since they implied they were part of a larger group. But what if it's just one pilot, and another twenty farmers on a plot half a day's drive away? The people in the Peace Garden were worried about our numbers. They can't number more than a thousand. That's not enough to save civilisation. It's not really enough to save the species. Our group could be vital to saving both. But if we disappear, and let Brass, Ezra, and Martin fight it out among themselves, how many will we find still alive five years from now? How friendly will they be to us if we leave them to fight it out? Maybe I'm being too pessimistic. Maybe I'm being too optimistic. I just don't know. But it would be a tragedy if we were to do all we could, and for Harmony to live until she was eighty, or for you to reach ninety, Marshall, only to be the very last person alive."

"No way is he outliving me, the way he eats," Kayleigh said, and the tension broke a little.

"We'll look for that plane," Ricardo said.

"Yes," Maggs said. "And we'll look in ports and harbours, because large groups will have boats, and that's where they'd go. And we'll head to Vancouver Island because it's a logical place for survivors to have gone. Afterwards, and if we've found nothing and no one, we'll have to think again. Until then, we need to make sure this group has the best chance it can. And that means somewhere they can start farming. It's either here or the retirement commune."

"This place is bigger," Roy said.

"I just wish we knew more about the guy who lived here," Ginger said. "Where did he get infected? Where did he look for supplies? Why didn't he leave?"

"Wouldn't it be great if he kept a diary?" Maggs said. She reached into her bag and pulled out a notebook. "It was on his nightstand down in the basement. The first few pages are lists of supplies and in different inks, so I think he added and crossed them out as time went by. The first entry takes place on March 4th. What was that, twelve days after the outbreak? If you can cook up another portion, Roy, I'll read it aloud."

Chapter 14 - Diary of the Damned
The Laurel Hills Spa and Resort

March 4th

Zombies. I just knew it would happen. With all the radiation from the phones, the hormones in the food, and lead in the water, it was inevitable. Why'd the government get suddenly obsessed with giving us vaccines? Zombies, that's why. The government was behind this outbreak. Must have been. Well, I never had a vaccine and never got sick. No poison in the body, no poison in the mind. It saved me, I'm sure of it. Now we've just got to ride it out. It's been nearly two weeks. It's got to be over soon.

March 6th

Kelly and Paris left yesterday to see if they can get on the evacuation to Vancouver Island. Why's it going to be safer there? I told them it was safe here, with me. Charlie will come back. Just wait. They didn't listen. Now I'm alone, but that's good. I've got enough food for a year. Out there, out in the dead world, it's going to get real bad. Blood in the streets. People eating dogs. People eating people. No, stay put. That's safe. That's best.

It's weird. I can't sleep at night. I keep hearing things. I think it's the house. What was it Charlie called it? Creeping? I guess all new buildings are like that, and old buildings, and this one is both. I'm sleeping in the day. At night, I go up to the attic to watch for lights. There's a lot, but always in the distance. No one comes out here. Not yet.

What if they did? They'd find my stash, wouldn't they? I should hide it.

March 8th

Now try and rob me! I moved everything useful down to the basement and put up a false wall. Needs another coat of paint, but no one will ever spot it. I left some decoy boxes upstairs. If anyone comes, my supplies are safe. In another month, the zombies will die, but everything's going to be chaos for months after. I should have bought gold. Money's going to be worthless. That was probably their plan. Destroy the dollar, make everyone poor. Maybe it was China. Probably. That means the invasion's happening. It's probably begun. They won't find me, as long as I stay hidden. I can outlast them.

March 9th

I moved down to the basement. If someone comes looking for supplies, I don't want them to find me! I've been watching for planes, in case there's an invasion. There was a fighter jet, but I don't know whose it was. There weren't any large planes. Not yet.

What if Kelly and Paris come back? What if they get caught? I know they'll talk. They're not patriots; they'd sell me out. They know the new wall shouldn't be there. They know all this food is here. I've got to be careful. I've got to start going on patrol.

March 13th

I thought I'd got infected. I mean, I must have been infected, but something stopped it. Healthy body, healthy mind. You don't need to pump it full of chemicals to stay healthy. I bet that's how the Chinese made the zombies. They put something into the food. Doesn't matter. Survival of the fittest, and that's me!

I went out at dawn, on my patrol, checking the trees. Someone was there. I thought it was Paris or Kelly. Maybe it was. The thing was so covered in mud, I couldn't tell. I didn't even spot it at first. As I was creeping through the trees, the mud seemed to come alive. I lost my grip on the shotgun, so we went at it, there in the dirt. I won. But when I got back, I saw scratches on my arms. I thought my song had been sung, but I'm still here.

March 15th

If I'm protected from infection, then I could go get more supplies. I've been thinking about it. Lord knows there's not much else to do but think. The longer I wait, the fewer supplies there'll be. If there was a zombie in the woods, no one else can be hiding there, so my stash is probably safe.

I've not seen any planes overhead, or any helicopters. I don't think the Chinese are around here. Why would they be? They'll have gone further north.

March 17th

Yesterday, I was about to go out again when people came. I heard the engine while I was at the door. I hid and listened. There were maybe eight people clumping around upstairs. I had the shotgun ready in case they found the hidden wall, but after an hour, they left. They took the decoy food and left a real mess, but they didn't find my stash. The decoys worked. I tidied up a bit, and put out some more food, then I came back down here. I'm going to stay put today, but I'll need more water.

March 18th

I shouldn't have tidied up because they came back. They knew someone had been there yesterday. I heard them tearing up the place. Laughing. Like survival was some kind of joke. People like that don't deserve to live.

At first, I was terrified. But this is my place. I know the layout. Sound doesn't really carry here, except through the pipes. I couldn't tell what they were saying, but I knew where they were. I waited until I heard them all in the dining room and made my way upstairs. Three people, I thought. Ruining my home. I got the first in the back, while he stood on a table, dancing. He tumbled sideways, like a gymnast doing a cartwheel. The other two ran. I got one in the entrance lobby. He stopped to shoot back. He missed. I didn't. The other made it to his car. I think there was someone else in there. I couldn't tell. They drove off.

My first battle. Not bad. Two down. Two fled. And I've got another gun. The rest of their gear is junk. Sneakers, not boots. The kind for fashion, not even sport. Dumb. I took the bodies out to the trees near the wall in the north. I was going to bury them, but just moving them was exhausting. I guess it's the adrenaline wearing off. Tomorrow, I'll have to clean up.

March 20th

There's no sign of that car returning. I think, this time, those looters got the message. Hell, by now, they're probably dead. People like that don't stand a chance. But they won't be the last. I went to bury the bodies, but something had already found them. Wolves, I guess. I didn't know there were any around here. Deer wouldn't eat people, so what do I care?

I guess I was lucky. If they'd had their guns out, they probably would have got me. I don't want to end up dead. Injured wouldn't be much better. I've set up a few traps and ways of sealing the doors. If they get in, I can seal them into the dining room. I'll limit where they can get out, and I'll have the advantage. If there's too many, I could leave.

How?

I need more gas. I'll have to look for it. Not today.

I thought of painting warning signs by the road, saying there were zombies inside. That would keep people away. But what if the first people to see it are the army and they just burn the place down? I think they would. Especially if it's the Chinese army.

March 22nd

I tried hunting. There's nothing out there. Nothing except the wolves, and I didn't see them. I did see some birds skipping between the treetops, but a shotgun shell would blow them apart. I looked in a few houses nearby, but other people had already raided them. I guess laws don't mean anything anymore. I came back when I heard gunshots. I couldn't tell where they were from.

March 27th

Everything feels different. The weather is strange. The sky is weird. It's hard not to think about it. I tried reading, but I don't get why people still bothered after they invented TV, so I went out to look for a DVD player and some discs. When I got back, there was a car outside the spa. I moved round to the side of the building, but stayed in the cover of the trees. At first, I thought they were just ordinary survivors. The car was civilian, but they wore camouflage. They looked wrong, not friendly.

Survival of the fittest. That's what it comes to. What it always comes to. We got soft these last few years. But in the old days when we settled the West, they'd think nothing about killing someone for a warm place to sleep. They would kill me if they had the chance. I had to do it first.

I waited until they were both outside. I waited until they were at their car. I took out the woman by the door first. I got the kid by the trunk second. Survival of the fittest.

March 28th

They might have been Chinese spies. They did kinda look Chinese, and why else would they be wearing camouflage? Getting rid of the bodies was a priority. Digging graves is a real workout, but I didn't want to leave more bodies above ground. If I'd known how much effort digging was, I'd have tried to monetise it. All you need is some dirt and some shovels.

To the alpha go the spoils. There was a lot of food in their car. Junk food. Poison, really. But boy, did it taste good. They had gas, too, so I powered up the generator. And I had my DVD player. I hadn't found any proper movies to watch in that house, just some of those dumb British movies where everyone talks too much. But it had the guy who played Odin, so I just pretended the whole thing was him living on Earth in a disguise.

I think those two were Chinese deserters. What did they call enemy agents who were behind the lines waiting for an invasion? The secret column? Something like that. They didn't have a radio in their car. No weapons. And I don't think that kid was as young as I thought in the moment. I think the invasion has failed. They were stranded here. Well, they got what they deserved.

There's no TV signal. No radio signal, either. No one is broadcasting. Not yet. Soon they will. In another few weeks, it'll be over.

March 30th

If the invasion has failed, and the lack of any planes in the sky or explosions in the distance kinda confirms it, then maybe this won't be over in a few days. If things are so bad and the Chinese have just given up on conquering America, then I could be in for a long wait. What's worse, the government coming to help, or them not coming at all? Either way, I need more of a plan. This could last for months. I don't have enough food, water, or gasoline. I don't have enough movies, either.

I decided to go north, towards the cities where there was more stuff to be left behind. The roads are crazy. Abandoned cars everywhere. It's like everyone just gave up. I saw some zombies. One ran towards the car. Not fast. But it was definitely running. I hammered the gas. It's not worth stopping to fight them. Fast zombies? Those are the worst. I almost turned around, but I'd only have to go out again. It was better to get it over with.

I'd been driving for an hour when I saw the smoke. I guess the house is about ten miles from here. It's set back from the road, behind a patch of trees they used to sell for lumber. I think that's what saved them from the undead and the looters. It's a nice house, almost like a ranch. At the back is a homemade jungle-gym they made for their grandkids. That's why they stayed. Their kids and grandkids lived in Seattle. They figured this place was where they'd come. I didn't have the heart to tell them that no one was coming now.

Sally and Jim, that was their names. Jim had worked for the postal service. Retired five years ago. Sally worked three mornings a week at a school. They offered me coffee. I wouldn't normally accept, but I felt obliged. They hadn't seen any people for two weeks. They actually wanted *to see people. I suppose I understand that, in a way. I had to tell them about the people who'd attacked me.*

They invited me to stay. It was weird. That's when I knew something was wrong. I figured it out when I went to the bathroom. The cabinet was full of pills. I don't know what they were for, but these two were clearly dying. When the pills ran out, they'd be done for. They were waiting for someone to save them. But no one could. That's the harsh truth. There's no one coming to save us. We have to save ourselves. It was a mercy killing. Against fast zombies, they wouldn't stand a chance. They'd just be two more undead, out there trying to kill me. My way was better. Yes, merciful.

April 4th

I saw a convoy approaching the spa. I was outside, checking the perimeter. They were coming along the road. I shot at them. It wasn't a military convoy, just normal cars. Looters. I acted on instinct. I was in the long grass, outside, on the other side of the wall, so they couldn't see me. I thought they were going to turn into the spa, so I opened fire. Only two shots. Warning shots.

I regretted it as soon as I fired. The lead car sped up, and they drove past, but the one at the back stopped. Two people got out. They had rifles. They didn't know where I was, so they didn't fire, and neither did I. After twenty minutes, they drove off.

Opening fire was stupid. Reflexive. Automatic. I don't know what came over me. There were far too many to fight. Maybe they weren't coming to the spa, but now they know that someone is alive around here, and with something he wants to defend. I don't know what to do.

April 7th

I've got enough food to last six months. Jim and Sally must have visited the grocery store every day whether they needed to or not. I guess old people do that, don't they, just so they can talk to people? It's sad how some people ended up living.

I've got enough diesel to keep the power on, or I can use it to drive away. Where to go? Alaska makes more sense than Mexico. I looked at a map, and it's further than I thought. I guess I'm stuck here, for now.

April 12th

There's no pleasure in being proved right. Zombies came. At least thirty. I was outside, just getting ready to fetch more water, when I saw them. They were on the road. They were only walking, not running, but it's not worth the risk going out there. And there's no point trying to fight them. Not when I don't have much ammo. They're not dying. Not yet. So I've got to just sit and wait.

April 18th

Farming is the answer. What do plants need? Soil, nutrients, light, and water. The light is obvious, and I have to get water for me. As for nutrients, I've got the nutrition powders. If it's got what people need, and since all that comes from plants, it must have what they need, too. I went south. There's a hardware store, not far away. It had been looted, but where hasn't? I got the seed trays. And I got plant food. Sacks of the stuff. I wasn't sure it was worth it when there's dirt outside, but why not give my plants the best?

I didn't forget seeds, but there were none there. I guess, if someone took them, someone else is trying to farm. There could be other survivors around here. I need to be careful. What I have, they'll want.

April 20th
The zombies came back. There's more of them. These ones came from the south. It's not so bad being stuck inside. I've locked up the hotel, but I guess most of the potential looters are dead. It's only zombies I need to worry about. I suppose I could sleep upstairs, but I feel safer down here.

The food isn't lasting as long as I thought. I should have brought more back from Jim and Sally's.

April 22nd
The zombies are still there. I wish I had those seeds. I could watch my plants grow. Wow, I never knew the end of the world would be so boring. I need some more movies.

April 29th
There seem to be fewer zombies out there now. Soon, I'll be able to go out again. I'll go to Jim and Sally's. Get more food. Get more seeds. Water's going to be my major priority. I really need to shower, but I should give it a couple more days.

May 3rd
There are other people. And not far away. I saw their trucks as I was getting supplies from Jim and Sally's. It was my third trip there. I heard their engines. I pulled in behind a house, and just sat there, waiting. They didn't notice me. I guess I just looked like another abandoned car. They had three trucks. Civilian. Probably scavengers. I don't know where they were heading, but they're either escaping trouble or bringing it with them. I made that the last trip of the day. I've got seeds, and I've got some more food.

May 4th
I went outside to get more water. I got bit, again! It looks pretty bad. I've taken some pills. Now I've got to wait for it to heal.

Maggs turned the page. "That's it," she said.

"What a… he was a killer, a murderer," Georgie said.

"We should be careful about traps," Ricardo said.

"We haven't seen any yet, except those blocks on the doors," Ginger said.

"Whatever we think of him, he was honest in what he wrote," Maggs said. "More importantly, I think we can stay here. And if that's the plan, then some of us better head back to the group and get them moving."

"Today?" Ginger asked.

"Why delay?"

Chapter 15 - Planning a Massacre
The Laurel Hills Spa and Resort

"You really think we should move again?" Martin asked, turning his head to speak to the crowd as much as to Maggs. "I've told them about our fuel situation. We would be committing to this refuge until we find a new supply. We can't afford to waste what little we have relocating from one hovel to another."

When she, Georgie, and Marshall had returned to the retirement commune, they'd found a grim mood already simmering. Brass's entire team were deployed along the wall, giving the place a prison vibe where the inmates were on the verge of rioting. The return of the brightly painted fun-bus had temporarily broken the spell, causing people to mix and mingle around, and atop, the floral calendar, if only to find out why the SUV was missing.

Maggs took in the crowd, meeting one set of eyes after another. She saw despondency, despair, and exhaustion, but that was nothing new. There was something else, a restless anger looking for an outlet.

"I get it," she said. "We're finally so close we can almost taste the salt on the breeze, but we just don't have the fuel to get to the coast. We've got to stop. We'll need time to find more gas, find a boat, and to survey the island. Wherever we stop, it'll be for at least a few weeks, so it's time we thought about farming. This spa has more land than the greenhouses here. Inside, there are about eighty bedrooms and a few suites, so about half of us can share those. Everyone else can sleep in a meeting or treatment room, or one of the offices. We'll all be inside. The place has a backup generator, and enough diesel to run it for about ten days. We'll have lights at night, and power for TVs, and to charge whatever devices you want. Once we sort out the water supply, we'll have flushing toilets and cold showers. And once we find more fuel, we can have hot showers, too. Maybe even a sauna. Imagine getting all that grit out of our pores. It's not perfect, but it's a step up from here."

"I suppose we'll have to take your word for it. Again," Ezra said.

Maggs ignored him, just like he was ignoring the public mood. It had shifted with the mention of showers and the general availability of electricity. Those had become a luxury of late, one their leaders had mistakenly granted only to themselves.

"What about these farmers you said you'd found?" André asked. "You said they weren't friendly."

"They weren't," Maggs said. "They weren't hostile, either. I think they're just scared of outsiders, especially a group as large as ours. It's possible that they, or the group backing them, has spare fuel. I thought we'd ask Fern to visit them, offering a check-up. That should allow us to open a dialogue, and maybe to trade."

"Trade? What do we have?" Brass asked. "We have been reduced to little more than beggars. We need diesel. They have it. The solution is obvious."

Inwardly, Maggs smiled, though she was careful not to let it show on her face. "You would prefer a war? Who would fight it? Ask for volunteers, here and now. Go on, ask how many people here want to kill our neighbours when we can buy what we need with healthcare. We have a doctor. We can heal them. Why would you want to cause pain instead?"

"We're not murderers," Gordon called out. "We're not thieves. All we want is a quiet plot of our own to grow a few crops and help our neighbours rebuild. This spa sounds like where we could begin."

"Exactly," Maggs said. "It's a beginning, not the end. We can plan for the future once we're there. It's your choice, but the rest of my team is there, so I'll be leaving in half an hour. Come with me or stay."

Ignoring Brass, Martin, and the rest of the crowd, she headed back to the ambulance. Chloe was already packing away their gear.

"Marshall should be helping you with that," Maggs said. "Where is he?"

"Helping Yvette," Chloe said.

"Did he volunteer?"

"She asked."

"Oh. Interesting. I'll check the house."

There wasn't much to do. Kayleigh always packed their kitchen away after use. All personal possessions not critical to scouting, and not sentimental enough to be brought with them, were stored in small, labelled crates next to the door. Similarly, Gordon kept their medical supplies so organised that the entire clinic could be packed up in ten minutes. Maggs busied herself with tidying away the books and magazines, closing the drawers, and otherwise cleaning up in preparation for any other survivor who might come this way.

"Is this spa really as good as you make out?" Gordon asked, entering with a bag in each hand.

"I think I was underplaying it," Maggs said. "It's not perfect. Far from it, but it's probably the best place we've seen since we left the lake. I think we could stay there for a month, or that some could, while we arrange travel to the island."

"Good enough for me," Gordon said. "We need more space. More outdoor space, too. Things got tense today."

"Was it Ezra?"

"Brass. He was throwing his weight around, trying to recruit some more people. The teenagers, mostly."

"Did he have many takers?" she asked.

"Not really. Not yet. I had a word with a few of the more impressionable boys, pointing out that Brass was creating a pyramid scheme where the people at the bottom did the work for the people at the top. For now, they listened."

"Mr Thouvenot, may I borrow you for a moment?" Evelyn asked from outside.

"Of course, ma'am," Gordon said.

Maggs waited until he was gone before she rolled her eyes. Regardless of age, gender, or life experience, there was a fool in all of us, waiting for love to set her free. Who had said that to her? Etienne. Of course. And she felt a moment of shame and guilt that the association had taken her so long to make.

Maggs led the way as the convoy drove west, hoping to maximise fuel efficiency by setting a pace that would frustrate a golf cart. She retraced the route she'd taken on her way back from the spa, one that avoided going too close to their new neighbours. She didn't fear them, nor was she that bothered about scaring them with the sheer size of their convoy. Her main fear was that revealing their location might spur Brass into launching a raid, or even a takeover. She didn't know the man very well, except that he was the sort who had absolutely no intention of ever wielding a spade.

Putting that to the back of her mind, she kept her eyes on the skyline, hoping for a plane, or just another plume of smoke indicating a new farming community. With each kilometre, the chances diminished as a heavy bank of clouds settled overhead. The sky grew dark, and her mood deepened to match it, until she saw the lights ahead. The spa was lit up like a beacon, with electric light streaming from every window, and from the spotlights aimed at the front doors.

"Take the bus back to the parking lot, Georgie, and start directing traffic," she said as she jumped out. "Marshall, help Gordon with the medical gear. Don't leave anything in the ambulance." She turned to Ginger, standing in the doorway to the spa, Hats at her feet. "You look just like the owner," she said.

"Me or Hats?" Ginger said. "Sorry about the lights. Ric's fixing all the fuses."

"No, it's good. It's welcoming," Maggs said.

"The previous guy here did some rewiring," Ginger said. "We think it's one of his traps. He wanted to disorientate any interlopers by blasting them with light and darkness, and maybe with electrocution. Roy and Kayleigh are boiling water so everyone can have a drink and a wash. The strawberry shake mix tastes okay when it's warm."

"Great. Where's the clinic?"

"We thought we'd use the treatment rooms just off the lobby. We've claimed the top-floor staff-rooms as our domain. There are only seventeen rooms, a mix of singles and twins, and they share two bathrooms. They're small, but more than we're used to."

"Great. Go and keep watch on them. They're for us, the medical crew, and… and the sanitation team. No one else. Go on now. I'll handle things here."

The first of the vans pulled up. The occupants stumbled out, blinking in the bright light.

"Come on inside. It's dry," Maggs said as the rain began to fall. "Drive the van around to the back."

One by one, the cars, vans, trucks, and buses disgorged their passengers before the drivers took them on to the parking lot. It was only when the last of the vehicles pulled up that she noticed Brass and his command car were at the very rear, just ahead of Martin, and the minibuses of Ezra's faithful. They were all usually nearer the front. Was it a preventative measure in case people tried to flee, or was it a case of one keeping an eye on the other?

"This is certainly a sight," Martin said as he took in their new home, catching himself on the car's doorframe to maintain his balance.

Maggs bit her lip and went inside, and into a disordered frenzy of noisy congestion as everyone searched for a quiet corner to make their bed. She took a few steps towards the dining hall, but it wasn't her job to organise the chaos. Feeling no guilt at all, she went upstairs to inspect their new digs.

The staff sleeping quarters were small, each room barely larger than a single bed, except where it was large enough to contain two. There were two shower rooms and two separate toilets, one each at opposite ends of the L-shaped attic. In the centre, opposite the stairwell door, was a lounge area with a few sofas, chairs, a small fridge, a microwave, and a coffee machine, which Roy was currently inspecting while Kayleigh and Marshall unpacked their own portable kitchen.

Maggs collapsed onto a sofa. "I'm bushed. Tell me that coffee machine works."

"It does," Roy said, "but there are no pods. There are some teabags. Nettle and mint."

"Well, that's better than water. Speaking of which, how are we fixed?"

"We haven't tested the water that was left here," Kayleigh said as she plugged in a hotplate. "Based on that diary, we can't trust that he filtered and boiled it, so I think we should keep that for flushing the toilets. Fetching more should be the priority."

"But it won't be, will it?" Marshall said, dropping the bag he'd been emptying.

"Careful with that!" Roy said. "It's our spices. You don't want to eat deer without a little coriander."

"Yeah, sorry," Marshall said.

"What's up?" Maggs asked. She assumed the answer might be five-seven with blonde hair and a penchant for fluffy coats, but there hadn't been time for Marshall to speak with Yvette since the young woman had arrived at the spa.

"How long are we going to put up with this?" Marshall asked, slumping onto the sofa next to her.

"I thought we went through it earlier," Maggs said. "We're looking for other survivors, and for fuel and supplies, here and on the islands. I'd say a month or so, and that's if we don't find anything or anyone more promising than those farmers we found this morning."

"No. I mean Brass and Martin. And Ezra. I get what we have to do. Save humanity and all that. But we don't need them."

"You won't find anyone up here disagreeing with you," Kayleigh said.

"Shh," Maggs said, motioning towards the rooms given over to the sanitation crew. All were hardworking, and responsible enough to know cleanliness was next to deadliness, but they were a group unto themselves. "I thought we went through this weeks ago. It doesn't matter who calls themselves the leader as long as we're heading for the same goal."

"Yeah. But we're not. Not now. Not if we're staying here," he said, with the righteous vehemence of a young man who'd spent all afternoon listening to an idea echo around his head. "We should just get rid of them."

Perhaps it was tiredness. Perhaps it was just that she agreed with him. "Get rid of? You mean kill them. Why don't we kill them? That's what you're really asking. It's not like there are any laws anymore."

"Yeah, it's wrong, I know."

"Is it wrong?" Maggs said. "There are entire civilisations built on the notion that anything is justified if it's done for the greater good. But let's not be coy. It would be pre-emptive murder of those three, and at least some of their followers, plus whoever is on guard duty. Twenty people, maybe? It could be more. It would have to be at night, so we'd have to kill anyone they were sleeping with, and that'll bring the number up."

"I didn't mean—" Marshall began.

Maggs laid a hand on his knee and cut him off. "It would be knife work, and for all of us. We'd have to time it carefully because one scream would give us away. Of course, if something did go wrong, if even one person hesitated, or slipped, if one victim screamed, it would turn into a pitched battle in the dark. It would be utter chaos with no one knowing which shadow was a friend and which had to be killed. There wouldn't be many people alive come dawn."

"We should find Ric," Kayleigh said, taking Marshall's hand before giving Maggs a worried look.

Maggs watched them go, Marshall's question playing in her head.

Chapter 16 - Evidence of a Brief but Glorious Past
Thurston County, March 9th

It was half two when Maggs got out of bed and went to sit by the window. It was said that civilisation was only three meals away from collapse. How true that was. It had been easy to be appalled at the diary-writing survivor who'd occupied the spa before them. He'd found murder so easy, or it had seemed so in his private writings. But he had been alone, fearing invasion and his own brutal death. Yes, he was easy to condemn, but was she in any position to judge? After a long evening of self-reflection, she wasn't so sure.

Marshall's suggestion had thrown her. He was a sweet kid. A little goofy at times, always a little nerdy, and desperate for you to share in this week's obsession. If Ricardo or Ginger had suggested they kill Martin, she'd not have been surprised. Even Georgie. But Marshall? No. Obviously, he was frustrated. In part it was because he was learning how the world *really* worked a little sooner than he otherwise might. But there was something deeper going on, and not just with him.

Her own reply had been just as surprising. Since the outbreak, she had killed four people for certain, not counting zombies or what random gunfire might have done. All four deaths had been in the middle of battle. Even after the first, she'd felt nothing. No self-recrimination, no regret, no remorse. But how much regret had a Viking felt? If she felt anything, it was only surprise at how easily her emotions had shifted. Her ability to love, to empathise, to grieve hadn't been diminished. In fact, those emotions often seemed more powerful, more raw. But her tolerance for incompetence, laziness, and for the sheer insanity of chauvinism, theism, and the other petty bigotries had evaporated.

If there was no fear of the law stopping her, and no moral qualms, why not just bring an end to the incompetents living in the suites below? Poison would be the answer, not blades. Something slipped into the choicest morsels found while scavenging. Or simply borrow the ending from the book Brass seemed to be reading and arrange an overdose. Why not? Because once they were dead, someone else would have to step up, and she didn't want to lead this group, that's why not. She didn't want to lead anyone.

She wiped her hand across the window. A cone of light marked where one of the guards was on watch by the gate. Were they still a guard, or had they become wardens? Soon, what she wanted might not matter.

As dawn arrived, Maggs woke her team. While the sun was still getting its boots on, and long before Martin and Ezra dragged themselves back into the realm of the conscious, they were on the road. Maggs delegated Marshall to drive; he needed the practice. She sat in the back with her map, marking down strips of farmland and impassable roads, until the nutrient shake she'd had for breakfast began to make itself known.

"Ah, perfect timing," she said after a few minutes more. "Pull in here. Yes, this will do."

It had been a farm. Mixed arable and grazing, judging by the fields close to the road. The sprouting vegetation was more uniform than most wild meadows, making her wonder if it had been a winter cover-crop left un-harvested and which had then self-seeded. The house itself was the real reason the spot appealed over its neighbours. A jumble of farm equipment, lumber, and junk, topped with barbed wire, ran around the farmhouse. Someone had tried to live here after the outbreak, though there was no sign of them now.

"Ric, take Marshall and check out the house," Maggs said as she got out. "Roy, have a look at that field. See if you can identify the crop, and if not, bring some back. Kayleigh, do you have any paper?"

By the time her conversation with nature had run its course, Marshall and Ricardo were back from the farmhouse.

"How is it?" she asked as Kayleigh offered her a bottle of what they were calling sanitising gel. It was made of overproof rum mixed with gelatine and scented with rosemary and pine oil to dissuade anyone from stealing it to drink. She had no idea how effective it was as a disinfectant, but she felt better knowing she'd tried.

"There's a vegetable patch behind the house!" Marshall said, as excited as a cat with a new box. "And there's something growing in it."

"What?" Kayleigh asked.

Marshall shrugged. "Dunno. It's just green leaves."

"Any sign of people?" Maggs asked, waving her hands in the air to dry.

"There are a couple of nearly clear fields," Marshall said. "They're not huge. I think they worked them by hand."

"No people. No sign of disorder," Ricardo said. "Eight to ten inhabitants. Probably left in December. There's some Christmas decorations up."

"Weird time to leave," Georgie said.

"Maybe they realised they wouldn't survive winter," Ginger said.

"And left before they were snowed in?" Maggs said. "Maybe."

"Yeah, but you're missing the good part. They left their food behind," Marshall said.

"What kind of food?" Maggs asked.

"Canned and jarred. Looks like it was done last year." Marshall took a can out of his bag. It was about twenty-five centimetres tall and with a fifteen-centimetre diameter, but with only a handwritten sticker as a label. "Artichokes in salt water," he said. "No date, nothing else."

"May I see?" Roy asked, and looked at the can. "This is from a commercial machine. We used to get our tomatoes in cans like this, one pallet a week."

"You went through a *lot* of tomatoes," Kayleigh said.

"Not nearly enough, sadly," Roy said.

Marshall took out a glass jar. It was half as tall as the can.

"Those I've seen before," Maggs said. "That's one of the standard home-canning sizes. Mrs Jepson tried to set up a canning club a few years ago, back when that homesteading reality show was all the rage. Interesting. Very interesting. What do you make of the crop in that field, Roy?"

"A soup, I think, but beer is a possibility. It's barley, left to seed. They must have planted it last fall and aimed to harvest it this spring. That would tally with an early December departure."

"A bit more investigation, and we'll work it out," Maggs said. "But not right now. Let's continue searching the area, and then return in a few hours. And if that happens to be lunchtime, wouldn't that be a happy coincidence?"

They continued north, driving slowly, marking down fields, stopping at the better-preserved farmhouses. None had been occupied within the last six months, and few had any useful items from before the outbreak. At first, she assumed the missing farmers had looted the properties, but after the sixth house without a single bar of soap, bottle of bleach, or clean pair of underwear, she began to wonder. It wasn't that the amount missing was so great, just that the looting had been so thorough. Back at the zoo, they'd quickly realised that, when scavenging, it was better to make one trip to a large town to claim everything they needed. Fuel was too scarce, and the world too dangerous, to make frequent small trips. Equally, they couldn't waste fuel by bringing back everything they *might* need. Instead, they'd noted down where to find caches of light bulbs, solar panels, and other useful items they hadn't had an immediate use for during last year's long winter.

More vehicles had been abandoned on the roadside than she'd seen on the far side of the mountains. Cars equalled people, and those became zombies, and some of these must have been infected. Trapped together between a wintry landscape and a congested road, it would have been a constant battle to escape. The numerous bleached bones told her many had lost that battle. But there were no active zombies on the road, or trapped in the wrecks. The open fuel caps suggested that survivors had been this way. So did the wall.

Towering five metres high, it marked the end of the road. As they got nearer, she saw that it also marked a T-junction, with the wall having been built along the sidewalk, for about half a kilometre in either direction. Immediately in front of the road down which they'd travelled, a message had been painted atop an old billboard, '*Welcome Home*'. Beneath the sign was a rustic mural of a summertime farm scene. It had been painted in the optimistic space-age style of the 1950s, but it was definitely a post-outbreak piece of work.

Opposite the mural, and across the road from the wall were the remains of a gas station whose roadside signage was bent and bullet-flecked but still standing.

"I think they used it as a range marker," Maggs said as she stretched her legs, taking in the neat pile of logs where the forecourt had been. Beyond the old gas station, and behind it, the trees had been removed for a depth of fifty metres, and for as far as the wall was long. The felled trees had been trimmed and stacked, presumably waiting to be used in construction or as firewood. The un-split logs would have offered cover to an attacking force, except that the undead didn't seek cover, and none of the bullet holes looked recent. There were no bodies or bullet casings. A battle might have been fought here, but long enough ago for the victors to clear up.

At first, she thought there'd been no other houses outside the wall. It was odd because on the road behind them, they'd been growing so close to one another, she was sure they'd entered a suburb. Then she spotted the patch of concrete, and then another, on which the piles of lumber stood. The houses had been completely dismantled, down to their foundations. Yes, definitely a killing ground, just like a castle of old.

The base of the wall had been braced in a trench, dug into the sidewalk. Cement had been added afterwards, making it impossible to tell how deep the excavation had been. She stepped closer, peering through an empty screw-hole and into the fortress. Immediately behind the wall was a bric-a-brac jumble of wood, but beyond that was a bare yard, with only a few bean poles rising from the exposed soil. Behind that was a nondescript one-storey, but with a new wooden balcony-platform added to the rooftop.

"It *is* a castle," Maggs said. "They built an actual castle. Or maybe a fort. Makes sense, I suppose. That doesn't explain the cars."

"What cars?" Ginger asked.

"Exactly. We've been dodging them all morning, but there are none in sight," Maggs said. "Most of the defensive walls we've seen were built with cars. Not here. It's uniform metal sheets. Look. They're identical. Two metres by one, with the same four bolt holes in each corner and the centre. I've seen this before somewhere."

"It's industrial decking for temporary road repairs," Ricardo said.

"I thought I recognised it," Maggs said. "There must be a storage depot around here somewhere. Fetching them would have taken time. Putting them up would have taken more time, or a lot of people."

"I guess that makes sense," Ginger said. "If you lived here, and you saw people fleeing north, and others heading south, and everyone else looting the grocery stores, you might decide the safest thing to do was to stick with your neighbours and protect what was yours."

"That *is* what the government said we were to do," Georgie said.

"Do you mean to tell me that there were some people who actually did what they were told?" Maggs said. "I swear, this world never stops surprising me."

Chapter 17 - Behind the Walls
Yelm, Thurston County

They followed the wall until it took a ninety-degree turn onto a much smaller road. Just beyond the corner, a two-metre-high triangular metal wedge jutted out over the sidewalk.

"There's a fence behind it," Marshall said, after jumping up and down a few times to see over the wedge. "This is a gate, right?"

"Something like that," Roy said. He tried pulling at the gap where the two sides met, but to no avail. Ricardo tried pushing but quickly gave up with a chagrinned shrug.

"I can see cogs," Roy said, peering between the sheets. "And a large chain. There must be a lever or other mechanism to open it."

"Hey, where are you going?" Marshall called out. He was addressing Kayleigh, who was already halfway up a ladder pinned to the wall beside the closed entrance.

"Inside," Kayleigh replied, without pausing in her climb. Roy made to follow her, but Maggs laid a hand on his arm.

"Trust cuts both ways," she said quietly.

"Oh, ya, it's an entrance alright," Kayleigh said when she reached the top and peered over what Maggs was now thinking of as battlements. "It's empty. Wait. No, that's a… It's too small to be a dog. Oh, it's gone. Hold up, I'll climb down and open it."

The moment she disappeared from view, Roy took another step towards the ladder.

"Patience," Maggs said. "That cuts both ways, too."

With a grinding of metal gears and a clatter of chains, the wedge-shaped gate swung apart until each half was at ninety degrees to the wall. Behind was a stout roller-gate that screeched open.

"Come and see this. You'll love it, Roy," Kayleigh called out, though she was still out of sight.

Just inside the wall was a neatly painted wooden structure bearing the inscription '*Speak Friend, and Enter*' above, for reasons that made no sense to Maggs, a picture of a melon. Inside the shed were levers and wheels attached to an imposing set of chains and gears.

"It's all mechanical," Kayleigh said.

"It reminds me of an old sluice gate we saw at a weir in France," Maggs said. "Right down to the cutouts from magazines. There, it was mountains. Here, it's lakes. Someone spent a lot of time in this little booth dreaming of being somewhere else."

Beyond the booth, and flush with the wall, was a roller gate that Kayleigh had drawn back a metre. Inside, sawn logs were stacked along the base of the wall, probably for storage as much as for reinforcement. A ladder led up to an observation platform just below the wall's top, and to which was lashed a storm-battered chair.

Beyond the wall, the house's driveway had been widened, post-outbreak, with the entire front yard now covered in blacktop. The old double-wide garage at the top of the drive had been converted into an inspection post. The garage doors and the rear-wall had been replaced with chain-link gates. Inside the old garage were racks of tools, a single table, and a couple of plastic recliners. Otherwise, it was empty. Beyond the rear gate, the new driveway continued across what had been the back yard. This new access road was enclosed on both sides by steel-reinforced pine fences.

"This is impressive," Marshall said as they walked down the new access road and out into the compound proper.

"No, getting a dam operational is impressive," Georgie said. "This is something else."

They had come out on a smaller, less worn road, hinting that this particular neighbourhood was only a few years old. All the fences between the properties had been removed, as had the lawn. The front yards had been combined and dug over, forming neat little plots with narrow drainage ditches between them. Between the houses, new extensions linked the properties, turning previously detached homes into terraces. The windows, and sometimes the walls, had obviously been salvaged from outside the wall, creating an almost medieval hodgepodge of architecture. But the joins were well sealed, the roofs looked sound, and each of these new terrace-blocks had been immaculately painted.

Garages had gained new windows, too, while the old driveways now played host to glass greenhouses. Tractors and other agricultural gear were parked along the road's left-hand lane, but the right-hand lane had been left clear. Black plastic pipes ran along the sidewalk, with offshoots heading to each greenhouse.

Maggs bent to inspect it. "It's a covered electrical conduit," she said, dusting down her knees. "Why don't you take a look inside? Two teams, entering at either end of the terrace. Just a quick look. If there are bodies, leave immediately. This might be another Red Lake situation."

Curiosity was instantly replaced with caution at the reminder of the plague. Maggs didn't go inside, instead turning her attention to the vehicles parked along the roadside. She walked past five tractors before she reached one that wasn't strictly agricultural: an RV with cinderblocks instead of tyres. A sign painted on the door itself said it was now a library. A smell of damp and a thin trickle of water escaped as she opened the door. The interior had been stripped down, the fittings replaced with shelves, and those were laden with books. Fiction as well as non-fiction, and just as many for adults as for children.

Farther up the road were another three tractors, a much larger excavator, and then a small crane. Where were the cars? They weren't outside the houses, and they wouldn't have been left in the garages after the new greenhouses blocked access.

She walked over to another of the new terraces, picking her way across a strip of tilled and bare earth. The new addition was one storey high, and about fifty metres long. A curtain was drawn across the nearest window, so she made her way along to the next. The room beyond was narrow, containing a desk, two armchairs, two sets of bunk beds, some shelves that were half full, a cupboard, and a curtain covering what was probably a door leading into a corridor. There were no dishes on the desk, clothes on the floor, or any other indication of a hurried departure. In fact, nothing to indicate recent occupancy. The beds had mattresses and pillows, but no sheets. Whatever had caused the occupants to leave, they'd once had a much larger population than this block was zoned for. They'd built extensions. They'd built bedrooms with bunk beds. And they'd made a very thorough job of it.

The perimeter wall must have come first, defining the boundaries of their castle. An excess of people had come afterwards, and rather than being sent away, they had been invited in. Houses outside the wall had been dismantled and rebuilt inside as shared-facility single-storey apartments. Shared rooms, too, at least for some. But that would mean less land for farming within the wall, and more mouths to feed. Where were the fields? The tractors suggested they had them, and within low-speed driving range. She walked back to the road. There was little mud on the tractor's tyres, so they'd been cleaned after use. Where was the fuel store?

What was it she'd said to her team, that it was unlikely they'd just stumble across enough diesel to reach Vancouver Island? Perhaps they just had.

"Fancy a feast tonight?" Roy called, walking towards her with an unlabelled metal can in his hand. He turned the can on its side, holding the top out for her to see, though she had to get closer before she could read it.

"Tomatoes? And that can looks the same as those we found at the farm."

"Right down to the handwriting," Roy said. "If they shared the same commercial canning factory, what else did they share? There's a generator in the mudroom. No fuel for it."

"They must have had a lot of diesel to power all these tractors," Maggs said. "How much food was in the house?"

"Kayleigh is still doing a count," Roy said. "There's an entire room given over to food. Not just a pantry, an entire room filled with tomatoes, artichokes, potatoes, jars of pickled cabbage and dried mushrooms, and that's just what I've grabbed for lunch. There's more. A lot more. It's a home, not a storehouse. About fifteen people lived there, with about four months of food."

"Only fifteen? It seems so large."

"There's space for about thirty more, just counting bunk beds. But get this, there are two bunks per room, but looking at the brackets on some of the walls, and how most of the bunk rooms have four small closets, not two, I think they could have held twice as many at one point. Maybe they got hit by the plague, too."

"Maybe. Or maybe this is where those farmers rode out the early days before they went to take over that farm. Did you see any bodies? Any notes, or signs of violence, or anything that'd tell us why they left?"

"Only this."

He held out a square of paper. *"Flip, Back in three days. M. PS, you were right! Ask Laurie."*

"Oh. That's not very illuminating."

"Nope. The beds were made, except the ones that were stripped," he said. "There are clothes, tools, and cleaning supplies. The only things definitely missing were the guns. There's a gun locker by the door, but it's empty."

"No cars, and no guns." She looked again at the note. "And they thought they were coming back. When do you think they left?"

"After harvest. That's all I can say so far. It's probably around the same time those people left that farm."

"Yes. The groups must be linked," Maggs said. "Gather the others. I want to see how big this compound is."

Chapter 18 - Last Advent
Yelm

The compound wasn't a square, but an irregular polygon much deeper than it had initially appeared. By the time they reached the centre, she guessed its maximum length to be over a kilometre, leading her to revise upwards both how many people had once sought sanctuary here and how much nearby farmland they must have cultivated. The compound was a castle, a place of safety to which workers could return after a day's labour in the fields, a refuge to retreat to when the undead attacked.

The community's heart was to the west of centre, where four larger, taller, and older, homes stared at one another over a narrow crossroads. Around the house in the northeast, a new fence had gone up, made of the same metal sheets as the outer wall. Judging by the bright and cheery drawings covering the house's windows, that building had become a school. Another house had red crosses painted on the outside. Part of the road had been given over to a basketball court. The rest was full of picnic tables. The other gardens held storage sheds, a herb garden, an array of solar panels, and two small wind turbines.

"That's not much power for such a big place," Maggs said. "Say five hundred watts per panel, twenty panels... Okay, yes, I can see why they were only running power to the greenhouses."

"What about the wind turbines?" Marshall asked.

"They might generate a kilowatt," she said, looking up at a turbine which wasn't even taller than the rooftops. "They're the sort you might have at an off-grid cabin. So are the solar panels. They're for remote places where an irregular supply is better than none. Every house should have a set-up like this if they wanted to maintain their pre-outbreak energy usage. Not that they would need to, but it's not much power for such a big settlement."

"We saw a generator at the house we went into," Marshall said.

"Yes, good point. Everyone have a look around. I guess one of these buildings will be their town hall. If a note was left anywhere, it'll be there. We want to know when they left, and why."

"Can I get started on lunch?" Roy asked. "With all these ingredients, I can do it right, but that'll take time."

"Absolutely. But bring our vehicles inside first. We'll definitely have some supplies to take back. Marshall can help you."

"Oh, I think Kayleigh would prefer to help cook, and everyone else would *definitely* prefer she helped instead of me," Marshall said.

"No woman wants a man who can't cook, Marshall," Roy said, putting his arm around the younger man's shoulders. "Time for you to have a few lessons."

Maggs smiled as the group dispersed. The prospect of a good meal, and many good meals to come, had finally dispelled the sour mood fermenting since yesterday. She walked over to the solar panels, following the wires into a concrete block house. The exterior had been painted mauve, but there was no disguising the fireproof walls. That precaution, along with the fire extinguishers by the entrance, spoke of someone unfamiliar, or uncomfortable, with the six domestic storage batteries sitting in the middle of the room. The entire system had been turned off at the breaker-box, with a large, clearly labelled lever pulled down into the off-position. Behind that, with a vent leading up into the roof, was a gasoline-powered generator. It had been drained.

She went back outside and over to a smaller concrete shed. It was a purpose-built fuel store, filled with shelves of fuel cans. Most were empty, but she found nineteen with at least something in them. A good number, though not enough to get to the island. And they were labelled as gasoline, while the empty cans were labelled as diesel. This couldn't be their main fuel store, wherever that was.

Whoever had set up the fortress was a mechanical engineer, not an electrician. It wasn't that electricity had been an afterthought, but its generation wasn't an immediate priority. After all, there was a gas station just outside. The wall had come first, then the refugees, and then the zombies. Those not fighting had built extensions, turned garages into bedrooms, and put up the greenhouses. When the zombies died, they'd gone out to farm and find fuel, starting nearby with the vehicles abandoned on the highway. It must have been late in the year when they'd begun to think about electrical generation. Solar and wind were an obvious choice. But to salvage panels or turbines would have required time and fuel otherwise needed for the harvest. They'd compromised with an experimental set-up that would have squeezed a few more growing-weeks out of the cold months, a proof of concept to power the freezers, and to make sure the children didn't freeze. This year, they'd planned to roll out power to the homes, too.

Or had they? They must have been connected to that abandoned farm. There were no fields inside the wall. And the houses had space for more than had recently lived inside them. They were already dispersing people. They would have aimed to continue it this year. That was the priority. Small farming communities with a central hub where the tractors could be stored and the canning could take place. Maybe small, scattered farms was an idea they could borrow as a way of removing Martin's influence, and Brass and Ezra's stolen authority. If they were to stay in the region, it was more beguiling than being trapped close enough to hear each other snore. That being said, where had these people gone?

Now she was closer to the school building, she saw the paintings had been drawn directly onto sturdy window-boards. They were mostly scenes of yellow suns and white snows. The work of pre-teens, she supposed. But then school would have been for the younger children, providing childcare as much as education. Older children would have been busy in the kitchens and fields, getting hands-on tuition in the work that was to become their life.

The gate into the playground was latched but not locked. It was a small school, but those few children who'd survived appeared to have had a pleasant and sheltered time. A tree was surrounded with handmade targets for ball throwing, with baskets tied to the lower branches. Wooden cutouts of unicorns stampeded away from the gate, and towards a spaceship big enough for a dozen children to plot mischief in.

The door from the playground into the house was unlocked and softly creaked as it swung inwards, into a boot room. The air smelled of damp. The floor was dusty. The carpet had been removed. On the wall were pegs, each with a name, above a rack for shoes, currently filled with rain boots.

It would have been a utility room, back when this was a house. The washer and dryer had been removed. The sink hadn't, but it didn't look to have been used in many a moon. She shone her light along the window frame. Damp and mould had taken grip. Leaving her light on, she pushed on the door into the house, but it caught on something. Letting her light dangle by the strap, she put her shoulder to the door, forcing it open with a bang. She shone her light down a hallway decorated with colourful alphabets, regional birds, Spanish phrases, and occupied by a small corpse that was trying to stand.

It was a child, barely a metre tall, in a ripped purple parka with a fur-lined hood that hid most of her face but not her broken teeth. She lurched forward, tripping on her own feet, one bare, one still wearing a slipper. As the girl fell to the floor, Maggs took another step back. Her hands dropped to her belt, even as her mind recoiled at the sight. Not a child. Not again. She dragged her revolver free. The undead child began a rolling crawl. A second zombie staggered out of the open doorway behind and tripped over his prone classmate.

This second zombie was a boy, maybe a little taller, a little older, but still just a child. His grey sweatpants were stained black and green with decay, while his pelican-patterned t-shirt was ripped across the chest. Maggs steadied her aim. The boy jerkily rose, his head bucking back and forth. She pulled the trigger. The bullet roared from the chamber, missing the boy by a finger's breadth before thumping into and through the wall behind. The boy turned his head, his face seemingly bearing an expression of confusion. For a fraction of a second that stretched to eternity, she thought she'd been wrong, that this child wasn't infected, that he was still human. The boy's face twisted back towards her. No, there were no emotions, no life, behind those eyes. It had reflexively followed the sound of the passing bullet, that was all. She fired again, and he toppled like a marionette whose strings had been severed.

The girl was still crawling towards Maggs but making slow progress. Maggs clenched her teeth, holding back a scream as she lowered her aim and fired down.

"Maggs?" Ricardo called from behind her.

"Zombies," Maggs said. "Kids." She grabbed her light, dangling from its strap around her wrist, and shone it on the open doorway. "I think we're okay, but—" Somewhere inside the building, wood cracked. A heavy weight hit the floor. Another undead child stepped through the doorway at the corridor's end.

"I've got this," Ricardo said.

"We'll do it together."

"One is easier. One in the corridor," he said, pushing her back. She couldn't see the child now, just Ricardo, standing like a rock firm enough to anchor the world. Then he lunged, and something lightly hit the floor.

"What's happening?" Ginger asked from just outside.

"Zombie children," Maggs said. She went outside. "What are the other buildings like?"

"Empty," Kayleigh said.

From the open doorway came a grunt of exertion, the smash of bone, the thud of another corpse hitting the floor.

"Georgie, you're Ricardo's backup. Kayleigh, check the gates are all closed so they can't get any further than the playground, then go to the road to wait for Roy and Marshall. Tell them what's going on. Ginger, you're with me. There's another door at the side. We're going inside, and we'll clear the place, room by room. The walls are thin, so blades only. Okay?"

Ginger nodded, grim-faced, but this wouldn't be the first time she'd helped Maggs with the darkest of duties.

The side door led into the kitchen. A large wall-poster listed the children's names, their favourite foods, and in a few cases, allergies. Half of the fitted units had been removed, and a second cooking range had been installed in their place. Pans and pots were on the draining board. Bright green plates were stacked on the cook's table in the middle of the room next to a long row of plastic cups, ready for the distribution of a break-time snack. She crossed to the door and pushed it ajar. It stuck halfway and she had to squeeze into the neighbouring room, a classroom for kindergarteners, judging by the size of the tables.

From the hallway came a steady crack and thump as Ricardo performed his executioner's work, but from somewhere much closer came the rattle of plastic. A small cupboard beneath an algae-coated terrarium shuddered. Maggs motioned for Ginger to open the door as she raised her tomahawk. She aimed the light at what she thought was likely to be head-height.

"Now."

Ginger opened the door. Inside, tangled in a jumble of skipping ropes and bunting were two boys, neither older than eight, wearing red dungarees and matching green t-shirts. Their mouths snapped in unison as their trapped hands tried to tug themselves free. Maggs brought her axe down, but the blade tangled with the bunting. She pulled her arm back and hacked at the bunting, freeing the two brothers, and then swung again and again, giving them peace.

Chapter 19 - New Life in a Dead World
Yelm

After she'd checked each room twice, and was satisfied that all the undead children had been found, they closed the doors on the school, and gathered outside in the road.

"Is everyone okay?" Maggs asked, receiving a chorus of muted nods, and exhausted shrugs.

"We should burn it down," Marshall said.

"A fire would spread. We can't risk losing all the supplies," Roy said.

"I can't," Kayleigh said, shaking her head back and forth. "I just can't. Not anymore. I..." Her lips moved, but she couldn't find the words to express the everyday torture that existence had become.

Roy reached out to put his arm around her, but she shook him off, turned her back, and walked to the fence, staring at the desolate playground while her shoulders quietly shook.

"Leave her," Maggs said softly. "She just needs time. We all do."

"How'd it happen?" Georgie asked.

"I don't know. What I saw..." Maggs closed her eyes as the faces came back to her. When she found the words, they came in a rush. "There was an Advent calendar in one of the classrooms. The tenth door was the last to be opened. After... After everyone else left, the children must have remained behind."

"There were two adults in there. Both shot," Ricardo said. "One bullet each, through the head."

"Suicide?" Marshall asked.

"I didn't see any guns."

"There must have been more adults here. Parents. Certainly more guardians," Maggs said. "And that note implied they didn't think they would be gone long. So, they must have left in early December, and the children were infected on the tenth or eleventh. There was crockery drying in the kitchen, and their outdoor boots were lined up in their little cubbies. It was after lunch, I think."

"You can't get infected from food," Marshall said. "You can't, right? It has to be a zombie bite."

"Don't speculate," Ricardo said.

"Ric's right," Maggs said. "There's too much we don't know. Even if the cars are missing because they drove them away, where did they keep them? Where's the fuel store? Where are the farms? We need to search more houses. And we need some new clothes. Lunch can wait. Let's keep looking around."

Maggs looked at the tiling as she ran a damp cloth over her face; she didn't want to look in the mirror. The bathroom had been remodelled, and by a professional. The toilet had been removed, as had the bath, with four shower cubicles installed in their place. She supposed cubicles was the right word even though they were separated by plastic curtains rather than anything more solid. As the sinks matched, she guessed they'd come from the ensuite and the downstairs toilet. Both of those rooms had been stripped out and converted into bedrooms. The toilets were in a block of their own, part of the new extension that connected the two older properties. Like the shower block, the toilets had stalls, though those partitions were of sturdier stuff. Both new facilities had been expertly tilled, and it had been a labour of love, rather than one of profit margin. Here, the colours began with sunflower yellow at the floor changing to frothing white, then sea green, then blue. A beach on a summer's day, she thought. Why not? If they were trapped inside with the undead outside, why not make their homes a work of art? What else was there to do?

No water came out of the taps. Instead, they were making do with sealed jugs found in the pantry. The water had been stored with the food, and Hats had given his lapping approval, so it was most likely an emergency supply.

She pressed the lever to raise the plug and watched the dark water drain. That part of the plumbing still seemed to work. Only then did she look in the mirror, stalwartly avoiding her own eyes as she continued her inspection for bites. She dressed in clothes they'd found in a plastic storage box, along with a sprig of lavender. It wasn't her favourite scent, reminding her too much of the foster home in which she'd grown up. Lavender soap had been the cheapest at the time, and so it was all they'd had for her entire adolescence. But laundered clothes that didn't smell of damp were a rarity. She put the stained clothes into a garbage bag, taken from the house's well-stocked supply closet, and made her way downstairs and outside.

They'd taken it in turns to change and to stand watch, while Roy and Marshall had finished preparing lunch. Ricardo was setting the table. Georgie was stacking the food they would take back to the spa. Kayleigh was outside on the porch.

"Georgie, tell the boys we're ready to eat," Maggs said, and went outside.

"Sorry, am I needed?" Kayleigh asked.

"Only to eat." Maggs guided her back down into the swing-seat and sat next to her. "It's hard now, but you will get through it."

"I won't forget it."

"No. I wish, after all we'd been through, that I could say that the worst is over, but existence is a roller coaster, never anything except ups and downs, the more joy we have, the more pronounced the pain. That doesn't mean there won't be joy again. You need to be strong now." Maggs paused, but no secret could be kept forever. "Does Roy know?"

Kayleigh jumped as she spun around to stare at Maggs. "How do… What do you mean?"

"I might not have had children, but I'm not blind. You need to tell him. And then you need to tell everyone else so we can all be excited about the good news."

"Good? How can it be good? Who would want to bring new life into this world?"

"What do you think we're doing all this for? It's not for ourselves, is it? We could have driven off weeks ago. We're doing it because new life gives us all hope. A future that brings purpose to the past. All the friends we've lost, they died so a child could be born. So we *will* get excited, you *will* get a baby shower with the silliest of games, and the next… seven and a half months?"

"I think so."

"They *will* be full of name suggestions and unwanted advice that's more terrifying than helpful. You're going to have make everyone a godparent by the way, otherwise we won't hear the end of it. Okay?"

Kayleigh nodded. "Thanks, Maggs."

"We will get through this, believe me. Now, why don't you have a word with Roy?"

It was an odd meal, planned in peace, postponed by horror, finished in haste. Smashed potatoes, sautéed vegetables in a chilli sauce, and old-world tinned hot dogs that were so salty she almost didn't finish them. The pièce de résistance was canned strawberries, at which only Hats turned up his nose.

"We've some news," Roy said after the last strawberry had been eaten.

"I'm pregnant," Kayleigh said.

As Maggs had expected, the mood changed in an instant. The infected children weren't forgotten, but they were no longer utmost in their minds. Full, and happier, the meal wound to an end.

"It's a shame we have to go back," Marshall said.

"It is, but we must," Maggs said. "So let's take them back some food. Roy, take some extra for us as well. And can you check the gasoline stored in that shed? If it's still usable, bring it. Bring *all* of it."

"You're changing your mind about staying?" Marshall asked.

"No, not exactly. Not yet. We still don't know where that plane came from, and we don't know what happened here. Yesterday, I said we have a responsibility to keep our people alive. Well, we've just found enough food to keep them fed until harvest, and maybe beyond. Our duty is almost done. I've the beginnings of a plan, and one that doesn't require any more violence. It might not come to anything. If it does, we need to give Ezra and Brass a chance to leave with whoever wants to follow. If it doesn't pan out, then I want us to keep our options open. For now, that means we need a supply of fuel, and we need to keep it secret."

Chapter 20 - When No One's Watching the Watchmen
The Laurel Hills Spa and Resort

The skies turned yellow as they made their way back to the spa. Grape-sized raindrops splattered on the windscreen while a penetrating wind began whistling through the SUV's dented doors. It was the perfect weather for a good book and a hot drink, and Maggs now had both: *Murder at Lunopolis*, and a box of hot chocolate sachets, both from the kitchen of the house where they'd found the clothes. But as the rain grew heavier, her mood darkened to match the sky. Her shoulders tensed. Her hands grew tight on the steering wheel. Her vision narrowed to the road ahead while the faces of the undead children filled her mind. They were only banished when the lights from the top floors of the spa came into view. As bright as any lighthouse, they seemed to offer just as stark a warning, as did the RV parked outside the gates. It was their vehicle. Rather, it was the RV used by the guards when they were on nightshift. But it should have been on the inside of the barrier, not fifty metres down the road.

Maggs slowed as they neared, rolling to a stop just before it, peering ahead for signs of danger, disaster, or any other reason why the RV appeared to be under quarantine. Maybe that's what had happened, someone had been bitten. It was the only logical explanation she could come up with.

"Wait here," she said, reaching for the door handle. A brace of illogical, and far more terrifying, explanations came to her. "But be ready for trouble." She threw open the door and took two steps towards the RV before changing direction and heading for the gate. She called out, but couldn't hear her own words, let alone a reply. She pulled the gate open and saw no one on the other side, nor anywhere for a guard to shelter from the storm. Concern was still winning over annoyance as she turned around and saw the RV's cab. The lights were on. Reggie was inside, smiling as he watched her.

Reginald K Laughton had been a basketball star in his college days but had dropped every opportunity since. Twenty years later, he was on probation as a night-time security guard at an Ottawa mall. The night of the outbreak, he'd stolen a delivery truck and driven north, probably his only notable move since he walked off the court. Tatiana might have been a cold-hearted robot, but at least she was efficient. Reggie was simply a parasite.

On any other day, she'd have just walked away. Not today. She let the wind whip her fury into rage as she stormed towards the RV. She was sick and tired of the man's petty abuse of small privileges. Him and people like him, through inaction as much as by their deeds, had made this crisis so much worse, and he was doing it still. She wouldn't stand for it. Not today.

And then she saw that he wasn't alone. She stopped. Rage disappeared, replaced with simple determination because Yvette was standing behind him, arms defensively crossed, and Maggs could see far, far too much skin for such a cold day.

Maggs threw open the RV's door, and was almost knocked back by the blast of heat. She hurled herself up the steps, drawing her revolver even as she scanned the cabin to see who might else be there, but it just appeared to be Reggie and Yvette. Thankfully, she was still dressed, though only wearing a crop top and shorts barely adequate for summer.

"Hey, this is militia only," Reggie said, as he lurched out of his chair. Maggs used her free hand to push Yvette behind her before she raised her revolver.

"Woah, what is this?" Reggie stammered.

"Go to the bus, Yvette," Maggs said, aiming the barrel between Reggie's eyes.

"What are you doing?" Reggie asked, but there was no confusion in his eyes, only fear.

"She's seventeen. *Seventeen*! You tell me what you're doing. Go on. Tell me."

"I'm training her. She's a new recruit."

"Where's her gun, Reggie? Where's her weapons? Why've you got this place hotter than a sauna? Why are you drinking, if you're on guard duty? Why's the RV outside the gate? Where are the other guards? Don't bother lying. I know the answer. You're disgusting."

There were heavy footsteps behind her. "Maggs?" Ricardo asked. She didn't look around, just stared into Reggie's eyes, trying to think of a reason not to pull the trigger. There was one reason, of course. One above all.

"You're on notice," she said, and turned on her heel. Ricardo stepped aside as she left. Yvette was outside, shivering.

"I'm sorry, Maggs," she said.

"None of that. None at all. Ever," she said, taking her arm and marching her over to the bus. As she saw them coming, Ginger ran over, crossbow raised.

"Yvette's joining our merry band," Maggs said. "She needs some clothes. Take care of her."

As Ginger helped Yvette onto the bus, Maggs turned back around. Ricardo had followed her to the vehicles. There was no sign of Reggie in the RV's cab.

"Did you kill him?" Maggs asked.

"Did you want me to?"

Maggs took a breath, uncertain what words the exhalation would carry. "No. Not here and now, no." She finally holstered her revolver. "But there might be trouble later."

"Later, or sooner, it's overdue."

She had nothing to say to that, so she headed back to the car. Marshall had got out, and was looking at the bus with a mix of anger and sadness. Perhaps there had been a deeper reason why he'd been so ready to suggest bloody violence last night.

The rain had cut visibility, but not so much that she couldn't see the uneven heaps of turf and soil marring the wild meadow on either side of the driveway. A result of farming, she hoped. She pulled in outside the entrance.

"Marshall, get the cars parked, and get more fuel. Ric, tell Roy to take the food to the dining room, not the kitchen. Make sure people see what, and how much, we brought back. Tell Georgie to get Yvette upstairs and sorted out. I'll deal with Martin and whatever else we have going on here."

She opened the door and briefly looked for Hats, but he'd disappeared into the nest of blankets. "Wise choice."

The entrance lobby was filthy, and so were the survivors huddled there. By the desk were a pair of wheelbarrows filled with shovels, and a good amount of dirt.

"What's going on?" she demanded of the room at large.

"We're waiting for the rain to stop," Alexander said, standing up, and then having to push his way through the crowd so he could be seen. "Ezra ordered them to dig. But it's futile in the rain."

She took another look at the mud-encrusted labourers, and realised they were all members of Ezra's congregation. Not his acolytes, the heavies who might as well be called a gang, but the lost and broken survivors who clung to his perversion of religion as their only tether to a saner time.

"He had a vision. Farming is one of the new commandments," June said, though without much conviction.

"So he's Moses now, is he?" Maggs asked. "If you want a commandment, cleanliness is next to godliness, so clean these tools, clean the floor, and then clean yourselves. We found a compound abandoned in December. There's enough food to last us for months. There's going to be a feast tonight."

"Did I not say God would provide?" Ezra said. Maggs hadn't noticed him lurking at the back, huddled in a very warm, and clean, coat. "Our prayers were answered with a vision. Our work was rewarded with this gift."

She took a long, slow breath. "Alexander. Reggie has taken an RV outside the wall. He's alone, and he's drunk. The gate is unguarded. You're a guard. Do something about it. As for the rest of you, I'll be back here in twenty minutes, and if this lobby isn't clean, none of you will be getting dinner."

She stormed off, wanting to head straight to Fern so she could vent, but decided to get the encounter with Martin out of the way first.

Martin and Brass were in the glass-walled overspill room behind the restaurant. Most of the panels over the windows had been removed, offering a spectacular view of rain hammering against the window. They'd found armchairs and now lounged in front of the view, sharing a bottle of red wine.

"Ah, Maggs," Martin said, with barely a glance. "Welcome back. The weather is always against us. Dark, dreary, a portent of times to come."

"The weather doesn't pay us any mind, never has, never will. What's going on here? The gate's unguarded, and Ezra's people are huddled in the entrance lobby like a bunch of muddy school kids."

"Unguarded?" Brass said, straightening in his chair. "Reggie should be on duty."

"He's there, but he wasn't on guard. He thought he had leave to rape Yvette. She's seventeen, Brass."

"I… I think there must be a misunderstanding," Martin said.

"She has joined our militia," Brass said.

Maggs clenched her fists, and found her right was already around the grip of her revolver. "She's under my protection," Maggs said. "I will not tolerate the abuse of children from anyone. Ever."

"Of course not," Martin said, getting up. "We'll have a full investigation. I promise. Now, how was your day? Did you find more gasoline?"

"What? We... we found a fortress compound which had been abandoned in December, but we don't know why it was deserted."

"A fortress? It's a military establishment?" Martin asked.

"No, just a few streets around which they built a wall. There's a little electricity, and water, though we've not properly investigated that. There might have been a thousand people there, with enough food to survive until spring, but they just upped and vanished during Advent. It's worrying. And I don't need to come back and find the fundamentals of civilisation being thrown by the wayside."

"No, of course, and we'll look into this," Martin said. "I'll look into it. Personally. That would be enough food to last us until winter."

"I suppose so. There were zombies there. We found about fifty so far, all children."

"Ah, I see."

"That explains what happened to the missing occupants," Brass said.

Maggs shook her head. "No. They left their greenhouses ready for crops. It looks like they left for a few days, but never came back. This isn't good."

"No, indeed," Martin said. "Why don't you wash and change, you've given us a lot to think about."

Maggs looked down at her rain-soaked but clean clothes, then at Martin, and at Brass who had turned his back and was pouring another glass of wine. Not trusting herself to say anything more, she left.

Gordon was reading a hefty paperback outside the offices that had become their examination rooms.

"New clothes," he said as she sat down next to him. "Bad day?"

"Pretty bad. Zombie kids," Maggs said. "What happened here? It's all gone to hell."

"Brass, Martin, and Ezra went for each other's throats this morning. Ezra decided that he would take care of farming. If he controls the farming, he controls the food. Not that he said it aloud, but that was his motivation."

"I heard he was giving out commandments," she said.

"He's losing support. I think only Angelica and Simon are left from his congregation before the outbreak. Lottie took a job with the wood-collection crew to avoid him, and she used to be one of his most vocal supporters. Two of his acolytes went with her. I wouldn't be surprised if the others don't follow."

"Ah, so he's doubling down on the rhetoric in the hope he doesn't lose even more support? Madness. Sheer madness. It's like twelfth-century France on a micro scale. Brass and Martin seemed pally a few minutes ago. I guess, if Ezra's support is collapsing, that only leaves Brass as a power player."

"And he doesn't need Martin. It's only a matter of time before Brass makes a play for the top job," Gordon said.

"And then we get the pitched battle I wanted to avoid. It's a mess."

"Yep. Fern and I missed most of it. We went to see the Connollys."

"Who?"

"Our new neighbours, the farmers that you met yesterday. They weren't happy to see us, and didn't want the services of a doctor. I can't tell if they're deep into old-time religion, or if they're just scared of strangers. They did ask if we had a dentist. Otherwise, we didn't learn much more than you did."

"We can try them again in a week or two, but bring them some gifts," Maggs said. "I found Yvette in the RV, parked in front of the gate, with Reggie. There were no other guards in sight, or hearing." She laid a hand on his arm as he made to stand up. "I got there before anything happened, I think, and we should be sure of our facts before *we* do anything." She sighed. "Advice I should have heeded myself before I spoke with Martin."

"What did he say?"

"That he'd look into it. For whatever good that'll do."

"Reggie's a barely sentient boil with bad breath, and you know what you do with a boil?"

"I know," Maggs said. "Beating him to a pulp won't change anything, and it certainly won't change him. I was thinking of holding a trial, but if Ezra, Brass, and Martin are battling it out for a non-existent throne, this would just become another front. Yvette would be the only loser. I don't know what we're going to do. Rather, I know what we might end up having to do, but it's not something to undertake lightly. Oh, speaking of that, do you have any bullets? I used up all mine at the compound."

"I think I've a few in my box," he said.

She followed him into the office, and while he looked for ammo, she recapped what else they'd seen during the day.

With her revolver reloaded, and four spare rounds in her pocket, she went back to the lobby. It was still being cleaned. Ezra had vanished, along with about half of his congregation, but those who remained were working hard and seemed to be cheerful enough. She offered a few words of praise and thanks, and went to the restaurant. Roy and Kayleigh had wedged open the door to the kitchen, and were sitting at a table where they could watch the cooks. She pulled up a chair.

"We were just discussing baby names," Roy said. "I like Striker."

"Veto," Kayleigh said.

"Vito? Now there's a good name," Roy said.

Maggs smiled and let herself escape into a few minutes of light-hearted normality before the next crisis arrived.

Chapter 21 - Red and Blue
The Laurel Hills Spa and Resort, March 10th

For once, she slept long, not waking until her narrow bed was bathed in a formless grey light. She'd forgotten to draw the curtains.

"You really think you're a dog, don't you?" she said, as she threw aside the sliver of the blanket that Hats hadn't claimed. The cat opened a judgemental eye, blinked once, and closed it again. "Or a human."

She'd intended to go to bed early, but she'd had to make sure the cooks prepared everything they'd been given. Then, over dinner, people had asked questions about what she'd found in the compound. After one of the worst days of her life, she could find no platitudes, so she had given them the unadulterated truth. It was all they'd wanted to hear. She'd sensed that her audience, of about two hundred at its peak, had finally realised that the utopia which they'd been promised would forever remain out of reach.

After the crowd had finally dispersed, she'd spoken with Yvette. Brass had pressured the teens into joining the militia through a mix of promised bribes and generational guilt, seemingly oblivious to the hypocrisy of preaching to others about the responsibility and duty of adults. Reggie had undertaken their initial training, beginning with gate duty. Initially, there'd been four other trainee guards, but he'd sent them away before he'd moved the RV. Thankfully, it hadn't gone much further. Not this time.

She got up and walked to the window. Outside, a trio of birds took it in turns to swoop down for the not-early-enough worm. It would be a bright day. Maybe even a warm one. She could almost hear the vegetation stretching in preparation for a busy morning's photosynthesis.

What if it *had* gone further? What if, next time, it did. With someone like Reggie, it would. She'd dealt with a lot of Reggies. Too many, truth be told. She couldn't fire him, and she couldn't involve the police. Martin wouldn't do anything. Nor would Brass. That left her with the responsibility. If her gun had been loaded, would she have shot him? Yesterday, after having to deal with all those poor children, yes. Next time? She didn't want there to be a next time.

"How did it get so bad? How did I let it?" She turned to the room's only other occupant, but the cat was keeping his own counsel.

A few early risers already occupied the dining room, taking advantage of the coffee she'd brought back from the compound. On Fern's instructions, it was only one cup per person, and a cup, not a mug, and certainly not one of the branded bottle-beakers in which the spa had served their shakes. Maggs smiled and waved her good mornings, while Hats zigzagged between the tables, gracing his presence on those he knew would pay him his lordly tribute. Maggs headed straight to the window-table where Fern was staring into her cup as if the answers to the universe were to be found in its depths.

"When you stare into the abyss, the abyss cries out for cream and sugar," Maggs said.

"Hmm?" Fern said, blinking as she slowly sat back, briefly straightening her shoulders before they slumped again.

"I know that look. Who is it?"

"Audrey," Fern said. "She had a seizure as she was getting into bed. She fell and cut her head. She lost a lot of blood. I don't think she had a concussion, but Gordon and I took it in turns to sit up with her. Before we could stitch the wound, we had to cut away a chunk of her hair. It was a good thing she was unconscious, I suppose."

"Are we out of anaesthetic?"

"Everything except the topical creams. But she'd have hated to see what we were doing to her hair. You know how she is about it. There'll be hell to pay when she sees a mirror."

Maggs smiled. "But she's okay?"

Fern took out a neatly torn square of paper. "That was her original medication. I've written down two others that I think might work. What she's taking right now just isn't powerful enough. I tried upping the dose, but it was affecting her balance. She could barely stand. We need to try something new and hope the side-effects don't make it worse."

"I'll make this a priority. Is there anything else I can look for?"

"A pharmacologist?" Fern leaned back and sighed, loudly enough to get a few quickly averted glances from the other diners. "Failing that, since we're staying here, we'll have to bring in every pill bottle you can find. And then..." She didn't finish the sentence but finished her cup and stood. "I'll see you later."

It was a situation they'd been in before. Prior to the outbreak, Sally Nolan had been on a cocktail of immune suppressants following a kidney transplant. Every two weeks, she'd visited the doctor for a suite of tests and the careful recalibration of her medication. It being winter, she'd had a month's supply in case of emergencies. Maggs had arrived at the zoo just as that month had ended. Despite scavenging pharmacies and homes, they'd only found three of her listed medications. They *had* found a pharmacopeia. Between them, Fern and Nana had come up with substitutions that they thought would work. They hadn't. Sally Nolan had died.

She finished her coffee and took the empty cups back to the counter. The only option for breakfast was a watered-down version of what hadn't been eaten last night. She wasn't hungry enough to attempt it. Leaving Hats to continue his morning ritual of regal begging, she went outside.

The air was fresh, brisk rather than bracing. The sun was up, but the farmers were all absent. Work smarter, not harder: that coffee-mug mantra was one of Martin's favourite exhortations. She'd always preferred 'work smarter *or* work harder', but here there was no evidence of either. The heaped soil and turf from yesterday's ill-planned adventure in farming had become a mudslide, encroaching on the drive. Something had to be done about that.

"And by whom, if not you?" she asked the world at large. For once, the universe answered. She heard an engine.

Was it a plane? She scanned the sky, seeing nothing but a few birds and a solitary wisp of cloud. As the sound grew nearer, she realised it was a car's engine, and one approaching the gate. Had someone already left this morning? Wondering what new devilment Martin and Brass had cooked up, she marched down the drive. Tatiana was standing atop the roof of the RV, now back inside the gate, wearing an unfamiliar expression of puzzlement. Her guards stood behind the aluminium sheets blocking the driveway, alternately looking outside and up to their sergeant.

"What is it?" Maggs asked.

"A police car," Tatiana said.

"Do they have a warrant? Never mind," she added quickly. "Open up. Let's be friendly."

Parked about twenty metres back from the entrance was a sheriff's car. The driver was still behind the wheel, but the passenger had got out. He wore a badge on his belt, a tucked-in plaid-shirt, and an honest-to-goodness Stetson on his head.

"Howdy," he said, as Maggs walked down to meet him.

"*Bonjour*," she felt obliged to reply. "I'm Maggs Espoir. Welcome."

"Sheriff Constant Dalton, once out of Nevada, and now I'm up here. Please, *please*, just call me Dalton. We got word you were in these parts from the Connolly homestead. Thought we'd come say hello and see what help we could offer."

"Could we offer you some coffee in exchange?" Maggs asked.

"That would be mighty fine," he said.

"Drive on up, I'll meet you at the top," she said. "Come on, Sergeant, clear the road for the sheriff," she said, and began walking up the driveway before any of the guards could offer an objection.

She was only a third of the way up when the car overtook her. The sheriff tipped his hat. Dalton's sun-weathered face was clean-shaven, allowing him to show off a winsome smile. His boots were made for hiking, not horse riding, but his hat looked battered enough to be something he wore for more than just style. He looked as if he were in his late forties, but carrying it as if he knew he was still in his prime. Clean and presentable was a rare trait in their changed world, as was anyone claiming to be an agent of a higher authority. According to the shield painted on the bodywork, it was a sheriff's car from Clark County, which she knew was in Nevada from many a Las Vegas-adjacent murder mystery.

By the time she reached the house, the car had stopped, and Martin and Brass had crawled out from beneath their rocks to greet their visitors.

"Come this way," Martin said. "We'll get you some breakfast."

"That's mighty kind. Come on, Sydney," Dalton said as he and his companion, a younger man of about twenty-five who looked more bored than excited, trailed after him.

Maggs walked up the steps after them, but by the time she got to the dining room, Dalton was inside, and two of Brass's guards were at the door, preventing anyone from entering.

"Out of the way, Reggie," Maggs said.

"No entry to anyone. The boss's orders." Reggie grinned.

"Your clock's ticking down, Reggie," Maggs said, and turned around. Now wasn't the time for confrontation, not when they had guests. She went back outside, joining the growing crowd waiting for news, her crew among them.

"They wouldn't let me in to hear what he was saying," Maggs said.

"Do you want me to try?" Fern asked.

"Let me," Ricardo said, his lip curling into an eager smile.

"No, let's not play that game. We'll try a different one. Ric, why don't you fetch Hats? I'm sure he's in the kitchen, begging for scraps. Use the outside door."

He nodded, and with Ginger in tow, made his way through the crowd.

"Who are they, do you know?" Fern asked.

"Not really. They came via the Connolly farm. That's how they knew where to find us. He said his name is Constant Dalton, he's a sheriff, and from Nevada, as is the car. He looked clean-shaven, freshly showered, and recently laundered. The clothes were repaired, but with no obvious stains. Rugged, I think is the word for him. A little weather-worn, but it suits him. Mid-forties, I think, so still young. Outdoorsy rather than athletic. He reminded me of Timothy Olyphant, but that's probably the hat. The accent is definitely southern. The type that's described as warm molasses, you know?"

"It sounds like you'd like to know it better, eh?" Fern said.

"What? Oh, get your mind out of the gutter. He knows the farmers, so he must be part of a larger group, and he implied that he's acting in some official capacity."

"You mean he's the law in these here parts?" Fern said, barely stifling a giggle.

"That'd imply some higher authority to give him the badge," Gordon said, coming to her aid without even a hint of a smile on his face.

Speculating on who that authority might be kept them entertained while they waited for the sheriff to re-emerge. After eight minutes, about the length of time it took to politely drink a small cup of weak coffee, the doors opened and the sheriff and his assistant came out, with Martin, Brass, and Ezra just behind.

Maggs grabbed Fern's arm and pushed her way to the front.

"This is Fern, our doctor," Maggs said.

"Pleasure to meet you, ma'am," Dalton said, raising a hand to his hat. "We are short on medical personnel in this region, so we'll have work to keep you busy. I hope you don't mind. You'll be compensated, of course."

"I'll help anyone who's sick, of course," Fern said.

"Thank you. And you're the chief scout, Mrs Espoir?"

"Among *many* other things," Maggs said. "And it's Maggs, please."

Dalton smiled. "I'll give you the warning I gave to them. Steer clear of Seattle. It's radioactive. When we sent a survey team there, our dosimeters went sky high."

"How is that possible, so long after the explosions?" Georgie asked.

"We only have theories, and none are good," Dalton said as he headed back to his car. The crowd followed. "Either it's a spill, or a particularly nasty type of Soviet-era bomb. Whatever the cause, keep an eye on your Geiger counter when you go north, but don't go that far north."

"What about the coast?" Maggs asked.

"I saw the ocean for the first time a few weeks back," Dalton said. "That was due west of here. Can't say there's much there worth visiting. But boy, is the ocean something else. Some folks say the desert is bleak, but an open blue expanse as empty as the sky? No, ma'am, I'll leave that to those who like chasing whales."

"We were looking for a boat so we could reach Vancouver Island," Maggs said.

"Ah, of course. Mr Genk mentioned that. Well, I'm sorry to say I can't offer any guidance. We gave up trying to reach Puget Sound, at least around the cities. Between the radiation and the devastation from the bombs, it just wasn't worth the risk or effort when farming is such a priority. I don't want to dissuade you from trying, but like I said, keep watch on your radiation levels."

"We don't have a Geiger counter," Maggs said. "Not one that still works."

"Then don't go north at all, not yet," he said, walking around to the trunk. "I'll find you some radiation detection gear. I'd give you mine, but we travel light, to save on fuel, and I've only my own set with me. Mapping dangerous zones is about a quarter of my job. I'll get you a copy of our maps, too, so you don't stray into a death zone. I can give you this, though." He popped the trunk and took out two large fuel cans. "That's about thirty gallons of diesel. We'll bring more the next time we visit. We've plenty of fuel. Everything else is as scarce as prudence at a roulette table."

"When will you visit next?" Fern asked.

"I'd say a week. Maybe sooner. I'll add you to my rounds, so either I or Sydney here should swing by twice a week just to keep you abreast of the news, pick up your shopping lists, and any excess you have to trade."

"Shopping list? Wait, Maggs, the list of pills," Fern said.

Maggs took out the list of medicines and handed it to Fern, who gave it to Dalton.

"Can you look for those?" Fern asked.

"Medicine? Of course. This a priority?"

"Yes. Please," Fern said.

"Then the Clark County Sheriff's department will provide." He looked again at the list. "Give me a couple of days, would that be okay?"

"Yes. Perfect."

He raised a hand to his hat. "Saddle up, Sydney. We've got ourselves an old-fashioned mercy mission." He tipped his hat back and smiled, looking ten years younger. "It sure makes a pleasant change being able to do my old job again. Take care, y'all."

Maggs joined the crowd in waving the sheriff off.

"*Very* warm molasses," Fern said. "So warm, some might even say it was hot."

"Oh, stop."

As the car trundled through the gate Maggs let her hand fall and turned to Martin, who had already taken two steps back towards the door. "What did he say, Martin? What did he tell you?"

The crowd's quiet conversation ceased as all eyes turned towards Martin, but it was Ezra who answered.

"Rejoice! We are not alone," the off-brand preacher announced. "Our prayers have been answered. God has sent us a sign." He raised his hands high.

Instead of an amen, he received a single cough.

"What did he say?" Gordon asked.

"It's interesting," Martin began.

"There are other survivors," Brass cut in, more accurately judging the mood. "They're moving north where the farming will be better and the zombies fewer. They're taking over small farms, like the one near here. We're the largest group of survivors he's found, and he'd like us to become a regional hub."

"And they have fuel to spare," Martin said. "So that's one crisis solved. The sun's up, and we have work to do."

"The Lord's work," Ezra said. "We will reap what we sow, so first we must plant."

"I don't think that piece of scripture means what you think it does," Maggs said.

"Where are you heading today, Maggs?" Martin asked.

She turned to look at him again, weighing her answer. The mood in the crowd was wrong for a confrontation. "We'll head back to the compound, search the remaining homes, find out what happened in these parts in December, and bring back more food."

"You're right," Martin said. "We do need to know what happened here in December. Captain Brass can go to the compound and bring back food. You should look somewhere else."

"Not the coast, though," Brass said. "We're not going to Vancouver Island anymore, and we don't need any scouts. That's something to think about, isn't it?"

Maybe the crowd's mood was wrong, but hers wasn't. She stepped forward, her hand falling to her tomahawk.

"Everyone not doing anything else, you're now farmers," Gordon announced loudly as he stepped in front of her. "Grab some tools and follow me. I'll show you how it's done."

Maggs turned away. The time was coming. It just wasn't now.

Chapter 22 - The Open Road
Olympia

Maggs watched as Tatiana carefully poured gasoline into the SUV's tank.

"Four litres," the sergeant said. "That is enough."

"If we make fifty kilometres today, we'll be lucky," Georgie said.

"And you'll be walking back if you drive that far," Tatiana said. "Go twenty kilometres and turn back." She held up the now-empty can to her nose and sniffed. Her face crinkled in a scowl. "Twenty, I hope."

"You can spare more. The sheriff just topped us up," Marshall said.

"That is diesel. You want me to pour some into your tank? Fine. I'll get it."

"Tatiana, please," Kayleigh said. "We'll get more gas in a few days so we don't need to scrimp on it now. Give us twice as much, and we can reach the coast."

"What for? To make glow-in-the-dark sandcastles? I don't know why you are going out anyway. We should preserve the fuel. Promises mean nothing, and that's all the sheriff has given us."

"It's more than Martin or Brass has given us," Marshall said.

"This is fine," Maggs said. "We'll make it work. Thank you, Tatiana."

As Tatiana walked away, Ginger breathed out. "If zombies could talk, that's what they'd sound like."

"She's just trying to do her job," Maggs said. "I don't like her, but she is conscientious, unlike a lot of Brass's staff. Are we all set? Right, saddle up."

"You'll be wanting a cowboy hat next," Kayleigh said.

Maggs turned to glare at her and saw Yvette quietly cowering behind. "Yvette, you can come with us, or you can help Fern here. It's up to you."

Yvette looked like she'd been given the choice between swimming with sharks or running with wolves.

"She'll stay with us," Georgie said quickly. "Where are we heading?"

"The first stop must be to get some more gas from… from wherever we can find it," Roy said, editing himself in time while looking over at Yvette.

"No," Maggs said. "The sheriff said he'll bring more fuel. We'll leave the coast until he does, and until he brings us a Geiger counter. We *will* look out for fuel, but we must find out what happened here in December.

One direction is as good as another, so we'll head west and see where we end up."

"Did you overhear anything?" Roy asked as he drove them away. He'd swapped with Marshall for the morning, hoping for a few minutes respite from baby-naming.

"He mentioned a bunker. That's where they survived, in a military bunker," Ricardo said.

"In Nevada?" Maggs asked.

"No. Colorado."

"It must be Cheyenne Mountain," Roy said. "There was a documentary about it a few years ago."

As he recapped what he could remember about the documentary on Cheyenne Mountain, Maggs closed her eyes. Her reaction to the sheriff was unsettling. It wasn't that she'd not met attractive men during the last year, or before, but something about this morning's encounter felt different. Fern and Kayleigh had spotted it, too. Now, she felt guilty. Yes, she'd been thinking of Etienne less and less, and dreaming of him even more infrequently. Yes, it was natural. Yes, he'd want her to live her life, to be happy and fulfilled. That didn't stop the guilt. Worse, though, was the sadness that came with it, borne of the realisation that her subconscious was accepting the inevitable, that Etienne was dead.

"What do you think, Maggs?" Roy asked, throwing a lifeline down into her pit of lonely despair.

"Sorry, dear, what was the question?"

"We were just talking about what this means. The return of police, the military, the government."

"A *U.S.* government," Ricardo said.

"Well, we are *in* the United States," Maggs said. "Do you know how big the bunker was?"

"The documentary just said thousands," Roy said. "And they had supplies to last for five years. There's a town nearby, and other bases. If they brought the civilians inside tens of thousands could have survived."

"Then it wouldn't have been a sheriff from Las Vegas who came to say hello, eh?" Ricardo said.

"Fair point."

"He did say they're short on medical staff," Maggs said. "Though he said they didn't have any in the region, rather than none at all. Oh, it's difficult working out what it might mean when we have so little information. We'll need to interrogate Dalton when he next visits."

"But they're setting up farms," Roy said. "More than one, and not right next to each other. That has to mean a fairly large group."

"True," Maggs said. "Brass said they were short of food, but I wonder if that means fresh food rather than rations. Either way, it all seems like good news, and we are sorely overdue for some."

"If we stay, we'll become farmers, feeding the soldiers," Ricardo said.

"There are worse ways to make a living," Maggs said. "And he did say Fern would be compensated. That implies payment."

"And taxes," Ricardo said.

"It's better than slavery," Maggs said. "That's the real alternative. A strongman with an army, taking everything at the point of the sword. That's what Brass would give us. Ezra would be the same, just overlaid with promises of eternal plenty after you work yourself to death. And let's not pretend there aren't others who'd prefer being king of a dungheap over a day spreading manure on a field. No, I'll take taxes over dictatorship any day."

"Let's hope we don't get both," Roy said. "Now there's a sight." He slowed the car to a halt. A moose had stepped out onto the road, fifty metres ahead. "Shall I get the rifle?"

"No," Ricardo said. "We don't need the food."

"Agreed," Maggs said, happy to watch the creature, who was curious, but not scared. After a moment, a second, much smaller, moose emerged from the trees, crossing the road after its parent.

"Early in the year, isn't it?" Roy said.

"I'm not sure," Maggs said. "We should ask Fern. We're near the Olympia National Park, so perhaps that's where they came from." As the moose disappeared into the foliage, her eyes focused on the words on the road sign behind them.

"Olympia Regional Airport," she said. "Perfect. Let's go there. In all the excitement about the sheriff, I forgot about that plane."

An hour later, the bloom of optimism had been drowned in mud. Maggs swore as the chain slipped from her fingers and splashed into the ankle-deep flood water for the second time. The roads to the south of Olympia were atrocious. Not just blocked by abandoned vehicles, but sometimes still barricaded, frequently cracked, and often flooded. Here, two miles from the airport, they'd hit the trifecta. If it hadn't been for that road-sign marking their approach, she'd have been sorely tempted to turn around. She reached down into the murk, found the chain, and cursed her chilled fingers as she attached it to the back of the delivery van.

"Got it," she said and slogged through the shallow pool to the marginally drier ground where Ginger and Kayleigh were ready by the winch. The motor whirred, the chain grew taut, and the delivery van finally began to move.

It was empty. The back was missing a door, and every parcel inside had been opened. Most of the contents had been washed away by the new stream that cut across the road. The handful of forever-plastic trinkets which still littered the cabin suggested that the van's driver hadn't emptied the pre-outbreak load before attempting to drive south. The bullet holes in the door suggested why they'd stopped here, though there was no body in the cab, so perhaps the driver had escaped the ambush.

Metal screeched, water sloshed, and submerged treasures crunched as they dragged the van clear enough to pass through.

"That'll do," Maggs said, waving for Ginger to stop the winch, and went to undo the chain.

"Roy!" Kayleigh called out. "Finish up!"

"People definitely came this way," Marshall said as the others returned from their inspection of the nearby abandoned vehicles.

"On foot," Ricardo said.

"Or bicycle," Marshall said.

"Or flying carpet," Georgie said. Yvette was trailing behind Georgie, a tyre-iron awkwardly held as if she was ready to ward off evil, not fight it. Maggs knew that look. The poor girl was all alone, but surrounded by strangers, uncertain what to say or do, and terrified the wrong word would break the spell and have her cast adrift. "But they took everything useful. Shot the zombies, too."

"What's the plan?" Ginger asked.

"The plan? See what the airport is like and find a map of other airports in the area. Head back, eat, sleep, wake up tomorrow." Maggs turned to Yvette. "A few days ago, we thought we heard a plane overhead. We didn't see it because of the clouds, and maybe it was just thunder, but it might have been a plane."

"It definitely *was* a plane," Georgie said.

"From Vancouver Island," Marshall said.

"Maybe, we don't know," Maggs said. "But we hope it's from Vancouver Island. If there's one plane, maybe there's more, and an airport is the best place to look."

"Maybe it's Sheriff Dalton's plane," Georgie said.

"We'll have to ask," Maggs said. "Okay, let's get moving."

"No, hang on, that's not what I meant," Ginger said. "I meant what's the plan with Martin, Ezra, and Brass. Are we going to continue letting them live like lords?"

Maggs looked at their faces and considered her response. "No, but I think that will sort itself out. A sheriff won't want someone like Brass maintaining his own private army. The military government, or whatever it is, in Cheyenne Mountain won't let our leaders be parasites. But to do something ourselves, to oust them, would mean violence. I don't want to see people die."

"No one would mourn those three," Ginger said.

"Okay, no, but a stray bullet can kill anyone," Maggs said. "I don't want to see any innocent people die. A few days ago, or even a few hours ago, I'd have said a confrontation was inevitable, if not essential, but there might be a better way. A U.S. government that wants to create farms here, buying their produce, paying doctors, providing police, is a far better option for everyone than us just muddling along. This could be the community we were hoping for, the chance to rebuild civilisation."

"American civilisation," Ricardo said.

"Canada was in North America, too," Kayleigh said.

"Whatever gets built is going to be different to what went before," Maggs said. "But this is a chance for real civilisation. Schools, hospitals, laws. Despite the mud. Despite yesterday. Despite *everything* that happened yesterday, I think we can be hopeful."

Chapter 23 - J.R.R. Lubbock
Olympia

A wall of cars surrounded the airport. A good many bore a cartoon print of the insufferable chauffeur the U-Drive haulage company had employed as its latest, and final, mascot. Other cars must have been requisitioned from the lot or the road. In the southern corner, they were stacked like bricks beneath the sentinel shadow of a portable crane. Farther along, they'd simply been upturned. Where the post-crash remains of a 747's wing had struck them, they had been scattered across the nearby road like nine pins. Roy stopped the car just before the debris made the road impassable, and where the gap in the defences offered an easy route inside.

As Maggs got out, a bird cawed a warning, and a small flock took flight from atop the cars, relocating to the terminal building.

"Not all flights have been grounded, then," Roy said.

"It's a bit soon for you to start with the dad-jokes," Maggs said, carefully picking her way between the twisted wreckage and beneath the gently swaying wing. The grass sections of the airfield were overgrown, except for a few patches where chemical leaks from the jet had permanently poisoned the soil. Pieces of the plane were everywhere, and covering enough of the runway that even a helicopter would have difficulty finding somewhere to set down.

"The plane didn't come from here," Marshall said. "Where's the next one?"

"Good question," Maggs said. "Ric, can you check the main fuel tanks and the diesel tank for service vehicles. It'll be behind one of the hangars. I'll look in the terminal for a map of the regional landing fields. I'd say we'll need an hour and then we can head on to the next place."

Ricardo nodded. "Roy, Marshall, I need a word."

"That sounds ominous," Maggs said.

"Everything he says sounds ominous," Marshall said. "Hats, come on, it's time for guy talk." He took out a metal tin and offered the cat a morsel. As fast as a flash, Hats shot over to claim his snack.

"That trick works on Roy, too," Kayleigh said.

The wall's presence suggested the airport had become more than just a temporary transit point, but a hub for local survivors. The spilled and soiled luggage inside the terminal confirmed it.

"The evacuation was real," Kayleigh whispered.

"Or these people thought it was," Maggs said.

"Do you mean it wasn't?" Yvette asked.

"Careful," Georgie said, grabbing Yvette's arm as the young woman slipped on a mould-green towel. "Pretend you've come home from a night shift to find your house full of your roommate's passed-out friends."

"I... I lived with my parents," Yvette said.

"Ah, and they weren't the partying type? Nudge with your toes, and be ready to spring back and swing down. And turn on a light."

"I don't have a light," Yvette said.

"Here," Kayleigh said unclipping one of the bicycle-lights she had on her belt. "We'll find you another, and a spare. You can never have too many lights."

Maggs took another small step through the debris of clothing and toiletries, suitcases and backpacks, but there were also weapons. Tools, mostly. Hand axes, hammers, machetes, and hunting knives. The first-choice weapons would have been kept close to hand. These were the last-minute additions to a bag already filled with clothing and a few keepsakes. She nudged a water bottle. It sloshed as it rolled erratically across the floor.

"Everyone sheltering here would have fled after the plane crashed," Maggs said. "The panic would have been dreadful."

"Someone went through these bags," Georgie said. "After the fires went out. After the evacuation was over."

"Maybe a looter from the compound," Kayleigh said.

Maggs shone her light upwards, looking for signage. "There, that door looks official. We want the tower. That's where we'll find a directory, and map, of all the airports within flight range. You asked a question, Yvette. Was the evacuation real? Back in Quebec, when the CBC was still broadcasting, they announced an evacuation to Nova Scotia and to Vancouver Island. We've seen evidence that people heard those announcements and acted on the news, but we've seen no proof that the evacuations worked. Maybe they were so successful that no one wanted to leave their evacuation zone, or they were swamped with so many desperate people, those zones collapsed. Either way, we've got to find out."

The windowless double-doors were unlocked but partly blocked by a drift of rotting fabric on both sides. She put her elbow to them, pushing aside the debris, and releasing a fug of decay from the dark chamber beyond.

"We need gas masks," she said, giving the door another push. Somewhere in the gloom beyond, nails scratched on concrete.

"Zombie," Ginger said, sending the beam across the chamber: an overgrown corridor that led deeper into the building. Ahead, not five metres away, a masked bandit sat atop a security station, angrily glaring at the interlopers.

Maggs relaxed. "It's fine. It's just a trash panda."

The raccoon's glare doubled, before it bounded out of sight.

"She's so cute," Ginger said.

"That explains so much about you and Ricardo," Georgie said.

"The airport must have been bursting before the plane crashed," Kayleigh said as they made their way through the bag-lined corridors. Desperation screamed from the messages scrawled on the walls. Smoke, and the damp dripping from the air vents, had made most illegible.

"So many people," Yvette said. "Where did they go?"

"Home," Ginger said firmly. "Where else could they have gone?"

Maggs stepped over a stuffed rabbit. They'd died. That was the real answer, and they all knew it, but by not voicing it aloud, it was possible to cling to the fantasy that somehow, the desperate refugees had survived. One corridor led to another, and each was like the last, just another avenue in this above-ground tomb on the edge of another necropolis.

Finally, they reached the tower. It was the first space they'd seen that wasn't full of bags. That wasn't to say that people hadn't lived there.

"There's a camping stove here," Ginger said, picking it up. "But no propane cylinder."

"I think someone slept over here," Kayleigh said from near the windows overlooking the runway.

"Um… Maggs, I think you should see this," Yvette said.

In the northern corner, beneath a smoke-blackened window, was a workstation clear of clutter except for a leather folder. Taped to the front was a curling strip of paper with the slightly faded inscription: *To any survivor who makes it this far*.

Maggs opened it. "Well, well."

"Is it about the evacuation?" Georgie asked.

"I'm not sure," Maggs said as she began to read.

I almost made it onto the evacuation. Like I almost went to college. Like I almost got a promotion. Like I almost made it to my father's funeral. There are no runners-up in life. No consolation prizes for those of us languishing in this hellhole. But my wife and two boys made it onto the boat. Right now, they're alive, and I'll hold on to that.

Let me start again. My name is John Ronald Reuel Lubbock. My folks were big Tolkien fans, so it could have been worse. In high school, I was Big Mac, and in basic, Hamburgler, and that could have been worse, too. For the last five years, I've answered to Dad, and that's one nickname you just can't beat. Now, I'm just Ronnie, just another survivor, just like you.

I guess you're reading this because you came here hoping for a plane. Sorry. We did our best. It wasn't enough. We lived just a few miles away. I worked for Benton Aerospace. You won't have heard of it, but if you ever saw a guy on a plane escorting a blue case that had a seat all to itself, that was one of our delivery guys. And before you get all excited and conspiracy-minded, no, it wasn't alien samples from Area-51. Lord knows how that rumour started. It was probably an HB21-4L rotating bolt, because those were supposed to break if not installed correctly, and even on billion-dollar projects, there's always someone who doesn't remember it's righty-tighty. The point is, we did a lot of work through the airport, and I knew the staff. I knew some of the pilots, too. When the outbreak hit, I came here to see if they had more news than was coming in off the TV. All they'd been told was that flights were grounded, and they should stand by.

A lot of staff didn't turn up for work, but a lot of civilians did, wanting to buy the last ticket out of Dodge. That's how I became a security guard. I can't say it was entirely altruistic. I cut a deal with Paulie, an executive who'd been a fighter jock back in the day. He had his own plane, a thirteen-seat scenery-skipper. I said I'd help him keep the airport open for as long as we could, but as soon as it failed, me and my family would join him and his on a flight up to a little place I knew in Alaska. Yeah, things didn't pan out that way.

Orders came through all right, on the radio, on the TV, and sometimes by plane, and they all contradicted each other. A million people thought they were in charge, and none of them was the president.

We got a few military flights, and a few civilians coming up from California, but then the Air Force started shooting the planes down. It was chaos; there's no other word for it. I'd moved my family into the airport so they'd be nearby if we decided to flee, but after the military started shooting down jets, it didn't seem such a smart choice to take to the air.

But then we got news of an evacuation. Our role, the airport's role, was to transport people to Vancouver Island. From there, they'd be flown to a safe zone in the Pacific. Some said that was Hawaii. Some said Guam. Australia got more than a few mentions. But those were rumours, and the destination didn't matter, just as long as it was somewhere safe. No one knew who'd organised it, and that didn't matter, either. We were too eager to take the lifeline to bother with questions. We sent plane after plane. The old, the young, the healthy, anyone who was here. We were pushing people on to planes, and pulling others away when they were full. And to think I thought it was chaotic before.

People arrived from all over the country. The police had tried to organise checkpoints and roadblocks, but there were too many cars. Too many guns. I heard shots night and day, and couldn't tell you if the target was zombies, looters, or people being robbed.

If more people had helped each other, rather than just helping themselves, it would have worked. We could have survived. But isn't that the story of every disaster? I could say more, but most of it was rumour, and none of it matters. You can see what happened. A plane crashed. It flew out of Houston. The pilot said they were landing and then cut comms. There was no Air Force plane to shoot it down, not that a plane crashing on the town would have been any better. That was it for the runway. Maybe we could have saved the people if it wasn't for what climbed out of the burning wreckage. Zombies. And they were ablaze.

The worst times in life are when you realise your mission has failed, you have to abandon the civilians, and get your unit out. This time, my unit was my family. My wife was working as a medic. I grabbed her, my kids, and Paulie's family, put them into the back of an ambulance, and got them the hell out of there. There was no sign of Paulie. I had to leave him behind. I know he'd understand. He'd want me to save his family, just like I'd want him to save mine. I switched on the siren and headed straight for the coast, to the ferries that were the other way people were getting to the island. It shouldn't have worked, but people still remembered what an ambulance was for, and what the sirens meant. I got through the checkpoints. I got inside, and almost onto the docks.

It was night. No ferries were expected until nearer dawn. We huddled together on the pier, trying to keep each other warm, holding the kids so they could sleep. Just a few more hours, and we'd be safe. Dawn came. The ferry arrived. Our prayers had been answered. As it was slowly, oh so slowly, approaching the pier, the screaming began. Seconds later, the gunfire followed.

Some of us, the old folks who decided they'd lived long enough and the youngsters who thought they could do more, formed up. The ferry docked. Our families got aboard. And we held the line. Few of us were armed with anything more than clubs, but when the mob started running towards us, someone opened fire. It was a massacre, with hundreds down before anyone remembered that zombies don't run. Behind us, the ferry blasted its horn, letting us know it was leaving, and that only encouraged the desperate refugees and the zombies that were among them.

I can't describe that battle. I can't even remember it clearly. I fired until my weapon was dry, and then picked up a bat and swung like the scouts were watching. The next time I heard the ferry, the horn wasn't nearly as loud. I turned around. The ship was about sixty yards out into the water and picking up speed. My family was safe from the mob. I wasn't. There wasn't a line anymore. There wasn't any gunfire. It was just a brawl, except sometimes dead people got back up. Seeing no other escape, I ran to the end of the pier, and jumped. As my head breached the surface, I was kicked in the face. It wasn't intentional. Other people were jumping into the water, falling, being pushed. People, and the undead. I swam away.

After about twenty yards, I began to tread water. I could see the ferry's lights, and I could see people swimming towards it. They'd never reach it. Nor would I. My family was safe, and out of my hands. I had to look to my own survival, and I wouldn't last long if I stayed in the water. I set out for the opposite pier. Get ashore. Get dry. Get warm. I repeated it over and over as I put one arm in front of the other, doing my best not to swallow any of that putrid water.

It seemed like forever, but it can't have been more than ten minutes before a shape loomed out of the darkness ahead of me. A seawall. I pulled my way along until I found a ladder. I hung there for a few minutes, catching my breath. The ferry was out of sight. Most of the emergency lights on the other piers had gone out. I couldn't see much, but I could still hear the screams. I pulled myself up the ladder and onto the shore. The wind cut through my sodden clothes like a knife. Weighed down, I couldn't jog more than a few steps. I slouched along, probably looking like one of the undead. I was far from alone. People ran. Zombies followed. Horns blared. Guns fired. Cars crashed. People screamed. I just kept moving. Somehow, I made it out of the harbour. Maybe the zombies thought I was one of them. I don't know, and I'm not going to put it to the test.

The next thing I remember was being outside a hobby store. The door was locked, but intact. Same with the windows. I guess glitter and yarn isn't high up anyone's apocalyptic shopping list. I got in around the back and managed to block the door with a stock cage. I went straight to the office, stripped, and dried myself with loose bundles of yarn.

Things people don't keep in craft stores: matches, weapons, clothes. There were a few modelling knives and scissors, but nothing you could fight a zombie with. I did hack apart every chair in the office, wrapping myself in the material, while I waited for my clothes to dry. A fire was out. I did find some soda and cookies in a desk, so I drank, I ate. And then I fell asleep.

When I woke, the sun was up. My clothes weren't dry, but there was no point staying in the store. There were supplies at the airport, and at home. I hadn't been back home since we'd moved to the airport, and I figured it would have been looted, but who'd want to take my clothes? And I'd hidden a small stash beneath my workshop. Some food, a gun, and gold, not that money was going to be worth anything. The rest wouldn't amount to much, but it would last me long enough. I knew something that all these others didn't. I knew where the planes would still be landing: Bowerman.

I finished the cookies, got dressed, and took the one remaining can of off-brand cherry cola, and made my way out, into Tacoma. It was worse than I'd expected. There were fires everywhere. Screaming. Shooting. Living people were barely recognisable from the zombies they were fighting. I kept moving. That was key. Just keep moving. But the city seemed to have grown. The suburbs never seemed to end. Whenever I saw a large group, I took a different route. I stuck to walking at first. I figured I needed to conserve energy. I saw a couple fighting a cluster of zombies. I moved towards them, intending to help, though I had nothing but a broken broom handle as a weapon. One of them shot at me. I guess they thought I was undead. I left them to it and fled.

Soon after that, I found the bicycle. It was just lying in the street. I'd say that was providence made manifest, except the handlebars were covered in blood. It worked, though, and that was all I needed to get here. That was yesterday.

The wreckage is still smoking, but the fire didn't spread. I guess all that rain and snow must have helped. The wall is broken, and the airport has already been abandoned. The supplies we put aside are gone, and so are the spare trucks from when we'd considered creating a convoy and heading straight for the mountains. Paulie's personal stash was still in the office, in his desk, so I had something to eat. I reckon that answers the question of what happened to him. I wouldn't call jerky and nuts a meal, but it is oh so good to have my stomach full again.

There's a zombie out on the runway. It's not safe here. There are supplies in the luggage left behind by the people we helped, and by those we couldn't. Warm clothes and food, and probably weapons. It's tempting to stay and gather my strength, but I don't know for how long Bowerman will remain operational. My first stop will be home, to get my gun and clothes. And then I'm going south. I'll get on a plane, and I'll rejoin my family.

Paulie, if you're reading this, I'll treat your family as my own. I'll keep them safe. To anyone else, good luck, and never forget your humanity. Ronnie.

"Is that it?" Marshall asked.

"He could hardly continue after he left," Georgie said.

"There is more," Maggs said. "But I think it's a different writer. No, two different writers."

April 9th. We only came here because we were told there'd be walls and defences. Special weapons had been delivered to the region. The Pacific Northwest was a fortress. The army was waiting. It was another lie, just like that lie about an army being sent to California, about our allies coming to help. They hung us out to dry. Again. The evacuation failed before it began. Now we're stuck a continent away from home, with little to eat, and nowhere to go. No special weapons, no walls, no help, just death. Everywhere we go, there's death. L.G.

June 18th. I thought the zombies would be gone by now. That's why I came here. I mean, I came to the airport because I thought a clear runway would tell me whether any planes were still operating. If this was just an American problem, then others would have come here by now. Maybe to help, maybe to invade. Either way, they'd want a runway. But this one's a ruin. It's the fourth I've visited.

I saw this book, and those two entries, so figured I'd add one of my own. There were seventeen of us, friends, neighbours, strangers, who drove up to Olympia National Park. There's thirty-two of us now. It's tough, but it could be worse. We can hunt and fish, and we think there are others living out there. But when people get sick, there's nothing we can do. There were, once, thirty-nine of us.

I came to see how the cities were, and they're as bad as we feared, so I'm going to head back to the forest. I think this is the end for humanity. I think this plague is worldwide. Maybe it'll be safe to venture out in a year or two, but why would we want to? I'm sorry that I can't say anything more uplifting, but this is a bleak world we've inherited.

November 15th. It's Ronnie, again. I returned! How about that? I didn't make it to Bowerman, but I got close enough to see all the zombies surrounding it, and see the planes take off, and the boats leave.

What happened next has been the longest, and strangest, six months of my life. It would take days to write even a summary, and I don't have time. I'll stick to the important things, and I'll start with the bad news. The evacuation collapsed. We've not heard anything from Hawaii or Guam, let alone anywhere even further away. What the plague didn't destroy, the nuclear bombs did. Wher-

ever the refugees went, they're too busy saving themselves to come save us, so we've got to help one another.

We were trying to get up to Seattle. That was our mission. When I saw the note from the group in the National Forest, I wanted to change our destination, but the weather is worsening, and the roads are a mess. We're already a week behind schedule and we're running low on supplies and fuel. I'm sorry, but we have to turn back. We'll return in the spring.

I found refuge in Oregon. The craziest old coot you could ever imagine pulled survivors together. He's more stubborn than a mule and determined we won't be the last generation. If you want to find us, head to the bridge over the Columbia in Longview. We'll leave the next set of directions there. But wait until the weather improves, if you can. We're about to hunker down for the winter. You should do the same. Next year will be easier. Next year, we'll meet. Stay strong. Together, we'll survive.

"That's all," Maggs said, turning the page. "That's the last entry."

"Only three groups made it here," Ginger said.

"Two groups and one person," Georgie said.

"The evacuation failed," Ginger said. "That plane didn't come from Vancouver Island."

"It might have," Georgie said. "If people were left behind here, they must have been left behind there, too."

"But we've got a lead on where two groups might be," Maggs said. "That is good news. I suppose we should be careful how much we read into this account, or into how the forest-dweller visited four other airports since we don't know which ones. But there were survivors in Oregon, and others up in the National Forest. I would say, all in all, that this is the second piece of very good news we've had today. Ginger, you and Kayleigh go find the boys. The weather's nice. We should eat outside. Georgie and Yvette, you're on guard duty while I add a note of our own."

Dear Etienne, and whoever else might read this. It is March 10th, a year after the outbreak. We travelled here from Quebec, and we're looking for farmland. We just made contact with a group from Cheyenne Mountain. They have fuel to spare, though they're looking for farmland, too. I suppose everyone's thoughts are on the next harvest. Stay strong. You're not alone. Maggs.

Chapter 24 - The Fall of Alexander
The Laurel Hills Spa and Resort

There was no fuel left at the airport and no supplies. Nothing but a toxic fug of unidentifiable chemicals that made her nose flare and eyes water. It was no place to have lunch, so, as they often did when they stopped in towns, they went looking for a park.

Just to the west of the airport, they found one. Specifically, a trampoline park, according to the sign, but Maggs assumed there would be some outdoor space tucked away behind it. She pulled into the empty parking lot, enjoying that she could park askew, and had barely closed the door before Marshall was running towards the entrance. Roy jumped out of the fun-bus before it had even stopped, sprinting after him. Hats, not wanting to miss out on the adventure, zoomed across the leaf-strewn blacktop, overtaking them both.

"Trampolines, it is," Maggs said.

Unsurprisingly, the venue was barely touched since the outbreak. While Roy set up his stove, and Kayleigh and Yvette quested for forgotten vending machines, the rest of them bounced away without care, worry, or attention to any of the many warning signs.

Maggs had been graced with many new experiences during the last year, most of which she'd have been glad to forgo. Of the few positive ones, parks were near the top of the list. She'd rarely visited them during more normal times, viewing them as a refuge for young children, like they'd been for her. Growing up in room-temperature foster care, parks had provided an escape on dry days. After she'd turned eighteen, she'd felt increasingly as if she was invading the safe space of the next generation of lonely children. A little older still, and the sight of couples her own age with their newborns blended her emotions into an unpleasantly bitter mix, so she and Etienne had embraced the wilderness.

Despite their increasingly unkempt appearance, parks and playgrounds had become a reminder of the better aspects of human nature. There had been a time, and not long ago, when people had collectively decided to allocate a portion of their earnings to fund a shared space for others to enjoy peace and tranquility. It was a reminder that the vast majority of people, the world over, had dreamed of a utopia for all, not just for the moneyed few. Plus, swings were fun. Trampolines on the other hand, seemed to make her seasick. She managed to get down without breaking a bone and went to help Roy with the cooking.

They spent the rest of the afternoon inching through Olympia's suburban sprawl, searching house after house for forgotten pills. They found few, and little else to salvage. She put it down to their proximity to the fortress-compound as much as to the hordes of refugees trapped after the evacuation collapsed. They did find zombies. Three that were still active, and many more who appeared to have merely died. Sometimes two, sometimes ten. Once it was twenty-nine. Ensuring they were dead slowed their progress, but also gave them more time to search for medication, and time to ponder how much they'd learned in one single day.

As a result, she was still feeling relatively upbeat as they returned to the spa. Once again, the closed gate cast a shadow over her mood. This time, the RV was parked inside. She could see its roof above the aluminium sheets, but there was no one keeping watch atop it.

"This is taking forever," Marshall said as the gates remained solidly closed.

"It's retribution after yesterday," Maggs said, though even as that thought came to her, she wondered if it might be something more. If Brass were to oust Martin, he would do it while she was away.

"Pass me a crowbar," she said.

"I'll do it," Marshall said, reaching into the back for their tools. Before he found it, the gate swung outwards. Brass himself stood by the RV, with two guards at his side, both armed with shotguns, as were the two who'd opened the gate.

"This doesn't look good," Maggs murmured. She opened the window and leaned her head out. "What's happened? What's wrong?"

"Nothing to concern you," Brass said. "Get in or move on, you're blocking the exit."

She leaned her head back in and drummed the steering wheel. If it were a coup, he'd be inside, enjoying his seat of power, wouldn't he? The guards looked agitated rather than threatening.

"Ambush?" Ricardo asked.

"I don't think so, but only because if that had been their plan, they'd have started shooting already. Let's just hope I'm not wrong. Buckle up." She slammed her foot on the gas, and tore up the muddy driveway, braking to a dirt-spraying stop just shy of the entrance. She jumped out nearly as fast as Ricardo, who had his sawed-off shotgun ready.

"Want us to go inside?" Marshall asked.

"We all will, together," Maggs said, looking at the empty fields. It was heading towards five, so the workers should still be knee-deep in mud. It looked like they had been, for most of the day. About half of the meadow between the house and the road had been tilled, with the excess soil and turf taken down to the wall where it now formed something of a ramp on the inner side. "Yvette, carry the pills, please, and stay behind Georgie. Everyone keep alert."

As she went inside, she kept a hand on the hilt of her revolver and her head on a swivel, looking for danger. Instead, she saw Evelyn sitting behind the reception desk, drawing plans for a vegetable garden with pencil and ruler.

"Oh, you're back. Good," she said, sounding relieved. "You better go straight to see Fern and Gordon. There was an accident. A zombie attack."

"Here?"

"No, when they went to the compound to collect food."

"Where is everyone else?"

"Martin called for an early dinner. I think as a distraction," she said. "Everyone's eating."

"Marshall, Yvette, Georgie, move the cars," Maggs said. "I'll take the pills. You four, go see what's happening in the kitchens. That's always a good place for gossip."

Maggs found Tatiana in the waiting area outside the clinic, her hands gripped so tightly on her chair's arms that it was a miracle they hadn't broken. The moment Maggs walked through the door, the sergeant rocketed to her feet. They locked eyes, and Maggs only saw impotent terror in the woman's eyes. The sergeant slumped back down into her chair, her eyes on the closed door of the exam room opposite her chair. Guessing what personal hell Tatiana was going through, Maggs knocked on the door of the room Fern used as an office.

Fern opened the door, giving a resigned smile. "Maggs, welcome back. Come in."

Maggs followed her inside, placing the bags on the table as Fern closed the door. "We found pills, it's all from domestic supplies, and all we could find. About half are statins, osteoarthritis medicines, and anti-inflammatories. There's some opiates, too, surprisingly. The rest, I'm not sure." She took a seat and lowered her voice. "Is it Alexander?"

"It is. He was bitten at the compound while searching the houses. It's been about three hours now. Gordon is with him."

Maggs nodded. "But he's… I mean, he doesn't do that sort of work." She glanced towards the door and pitched her voice even lower. "She won't let him."

"Brass took command of the expedition and ordered Tatiana to stay here," Fern said.

"Why? That's crazy. It would make more sense to send Tatiana alone. That woman's a tank."

"I don't know. Either he wanted to assert his authority, or he wanted to make sure he could steal some of the food for himself."

"Huh." Maggs ran the theories around her head. Both seemed plausible. "How bad is it?"

"There were two wounds. A bite on the forearm and a swipe across the neck. Both would be serious without worrying about the undead. He lost a lot of blood. I've dosed him with antibiotics, rules be damned."

"He's not immune, then?"

"You said it yourself. She doesn't let him do this type of work."

Maggs nodded. Tatiana had admitted to having been a bodyguard and roadie for some minor musicians, but her tattoos spoke of a much more storied past. She had rage in her veins and pain in her soul, but only Alexander in her heart. Alexander was bookish and quiet, and could only hit five-six if he had something to stand on. They couldn't be more different. Maggs had witnessed enough relationships implode to know that opposites didn't attract, but appearances were only skin deep, and too few people never looked beyond the surface. He'd designed their portable defensive walls, rigged up the ploughs when they were driving through snow, and converted them into rams to deal with the post-thaw roadblocks. He shouldn't be in the guard, but kept far from danger, except he refused to ever stray far from Tatiana's side. She made sure he had the least dangerous duties, and since he never shirked, none of the others had reason to complain, not that they would dare.

"I saw Brass at the gate," Maggs said.

"He's keeping away from Tatiana," Fern said. "Wouldn't you?"

"Good point. Where's Chloe?"

"Supervising dinner preparations. We should have eaten by now."

"I'll check in on Alexander, and then see Martin. You stay here, inside this room. One way or another, this is going to come to a head."

"I think it already has," Fern said.

Alexander wasn't asleep, but playing chess with Gordon. Though Maggs's familiarity with the game was still at the stage where she called the canon-fodder prawns, it appeared as if the young man was winning. A clean bandage was on his arm, another on his neck.

"What a day I've had," Maggs said. "But it sounds like you've had even more of an adventure, Alex. There were more zombies in the compound?"

"Five adults, ranging from twenty-five to fifty years old," Alexander said, not taking his eyes off the board. "They were trapped in a house five east and four west from the school. The windows and doors had sealed from the outside, so sound didn't travel in either direction."

"Five adults. That makes a little more sense. It did seem strange that there were so many infected children and so few people to protect them."

"There were six additional corpses," Alexander said. "Four had been torn apart. Another two were probably infected, but already dead."

"Strange," Maggs said.

Alexander massacred one of Gordon's knights with a bishop. "Can I see Tatiana now?"

"In a moment," Maggs said. "I'm just trying to picture the circumstances that brought such an end. Something bad happened in December, but I don't know what."

"Did you find any clues on your travels today?" Gordon asked.

"Not specifically. We found two more abandoned homes with Christmas decorations still up, and a third without decorations but which might have been abandoned around the same time. They were all on the outskirts of Olympia, and close enough that they must have known of each other's existence. That was out of about forty homes. The airport was interesting in a different way." She described the letters they'd found. "So there were other survivors in these parts until fall. I'd like to keep looking for them. We need to know whether that danger could recur."

"There were seventeen graves," Alexander said.

"At the compound? I must have missed them. Seventeen?"

"Marked from April through to December 3rd," Alexander said. "If it had been plague, there would be a mass grave at the beginning, and a heap of bodies left unburied."

"And the kids wouldn't have stayed," Gordon said.

"I'll search some more tomorrow," Maggs said. "I saw the farm is well underway."

"I'd call it gardening, not farming," Gordon said. "But Ezra's a fool who wouldn't know which part of a cherry you plant, so I took charge. We'll finish out front tomorrow, and have the rest cleared within a week. Maybe sooner, now we know what we're doing."

"We'll need more land," Alexander said.

"The three houses abandoned in December would make good farms," Maggs said. "They each had a few acres. But there was a forty-acre plot between them that they might have shared."

"How many people could live there?" Alexander asked.

"They had about ten to fifteen in each group. There are plenty more houses around there, but assuming they survived on what they grew, twenty is reasonable."

"We need farming homesteads," Alexander said.

"Agreed," Gordon said. "It seems like we're putting down roots, and around here, we'll have to spread out some."

"You'll get no arguments from me," Maggs said. She stood and crossed to the door, opening it as Chloe came into the corridor with two trays laden with food. Vegetable stew dominated, swimming in a yellow sauce that filled the corridor with a once familiar smell.

"Mustard!" Maggs said. "I'm going to grab some before it's gone."

"There's plenty to go around," Chloe said. "Rationing is over, it seems. By order of the council."

Leaving Tatiana and Alexander to eat together, and Gordon to stand watch from outside, Maggs went to the restaurant, which rang with satiated chattering. She hung back, watching as person after person went to get their fill, and often went back for seconds. The dining room was packed, and the tables in the bar were filling up, even though some had already chosen to go outside. Everyone seemed relaxed. For now. She looked around for Martin, and saw him coming towards her.

"You said that rationing was over," she said by way of greeting.

"I'm about to," he said, before turning his back on her so he could climb up a set of portable steps one of the kitchen staff had been carrying. "Attention, please," he said, turning this way and that, so he could be seen on either side of the doorway. "Hello."

"Martin, what's going on?" Maggs asked.

"I'm about to explain," he said before raising his voice again. "There's some good news, everyone. Rationing is over."

That got a crumb-spraying cheer from the usual suspects.

"That's not the good news," Martin said. "Captain Brass completed an assessment of the compound earlier today. The conditions are better than we were led to believe. There's electricity, plumbing, and enough houses for everyone to have a room to themselves. The food stores alone will last us until fall. You know the numbers. We need half an acre per person. Well, this fortress's walls encompass a square kilometre. That's two hundred and fifty acres, or more than we need. Obviously, we're going to move there. The former inhabitants managed to produce a surplus, and we can do the same. The captain will need two weeks to ensure it's properly secure. I'm sure you all heard about today's accident. Unfortunately, our scouts, in their *excitement*, missed an obvious danger. Once the compound *is* secure, then we'll move. All of us. We didn't know this was the promised land, but that's just what it has proved to be. Eat up. Eat your fill. There's no point taking it with us or leaving it behind."

"Martin," Maggs began as he jumped down and pushed his way into the crowd. "Martin!" But he had already hurried from the room.

Chapter 25 - For Love
The Laurel Hills Spa and Resort

Maggs tried to will herself to sleep by recounting Greek myths. Wasn't there one where a greedy king willingly moved into a dragon's den because it was full of gold? Or was that one of the German fairy tales? Either way, it was a tale with a truly Grimm ending. She couldn't help think that, if they moved to the fortress-compound, some equally vile fate awaited them. Radiation, volcanoes, disease, raiders: there were many reasons why the fortress-survivors might have abandoned their hard-grown supplies. Each was worse than the last, but none was horrific enough to explain why the children had been left to the worst possible fate. It was madness to move without knowing why.

Equally, it was madness to kick their heels here for two weeks. Martin might have said it was so Brass could make sure the compound was safe, but that was a lie. Why not move together and have everyone join in the unpleasant task of clearing those homes? Yes, they'd have to find bicycles to transport most people, but it wasn't that far away. They could have everyone moved in within forty-eight hours. Sooner, if she shared her secret stash of gasoline or if they found the compound's own fuel supply. No, the delay was so Brass could secure the food and whatever other supplies he could find.

Yes, that was the reason, because Martin was many things, but he wasn't stupid. He knew the numbers. Half an acre per person per year for vegetables, supplemented by hunting, fishing, and seasonal foraging was the minimum the books agreed they needed. The fortress-compound might be situated on a two-hundred-and-fifty-acre plot, though she'd have said two hundred acres at most, but more than half of that was buildings and roads. Between the back yards and the greenhouses, she'd be surprised if there were seventy acres of tillable soil. Even then, the estimate of half an acre per person had come from books, not from their own experience. No, their experience of farming had been an utter disaster. While in Ear Falls, their community had primarily been hunters and fisherfolk, electrical engineers, and the guards watching the roads that came from the south. They'd been relying on Red Lake for farming, until the plague came.

Yes, it probably made sense to move some people to the compound. But like its previous inhabitants had found, they'd need to farm elsewhere, too. They would have to split into a dozen smaller communities, sharing the compound's canned food until harvest. Martin knew it because he wasn't stupid. Brass knew it, too, and he was the real threat now. So they would keep people here for two weeks, while Brass secured the food and fuel whose stewardship truly granted power.

Martin might not be stupid, but he was short-sighted. It was inevitable they would split into small farming communities who would share the canned food and then share their harvests. The canned food would have to be shared with Dalton's people, too. It wasn't as if they could keep it a secret. Brass's militia were barely organised thugs, while Dalton could call on the U.S. military. If the sheriff wanted to take the food, he could, so better to offer it freely. Offer space on their farms, too, for refugees from the south. Be open, honest, kind, and welcoming, and you'd get the same in return. But that required empathy, a concept which both Brass and Martin thought a weakness. And then there was Ezra. He thought empathy was a sin.

She sighed and pulled back the covers. Hats lazily hissed before returning to his dreams of chasing legless mice. She sat on the edge of the bed, her head in her hands. Dreams. They had been her downfall. She'd dreamed of finding Etienne again, long after all hope of that was lost. When Martin used his position on the council to replace Fern, they should have left. Or when they'd met the scouting group from the Peace Garden. Or when her team had told her they were unhappy. Or every evening they'd returned to the camp and seen how the mood had deteriorated just that little bit more. Instead, she'd stayed, and allowed those three to take what they wanted. Why? To avoid violence? Say that to poor Yvette. Say it to the next girl. Say it to the women who were already trading their dignity for better food.

"Enough," she whispered. She stood and stretched. She couldn't change the past, but she could make the future one she'd be happy living in. They had that gasoline. That was their advantage. She'd take over the fortress compound herself, and do it this morning. And she'd send word to Dalton via the Connollys that she was doing so, and that there was enough food for a thousand farmers there. Room, too. And then what? It could be weeks before Dalton returned. How would she avoid a pitched battle with Brass's guards? Who would support her if there was a fifty-fifty chance they'd be dead by lunchtime?

She stood and stretched, trying to get some more oxygen into her brain. With heat rising from so many sleeping, and satiated, people below them, there'd been no need to draw the curtains to conserve heat. Not that the triple-thick pane needed much help in keeping the night chill outside.

Her eyes were drawn to the lights around the gate. There were more than usual, weaving in eldritch patterns as the guards moved around. It must be shift-change. A light detached itself and began moving towards the house. Moving fast. Another followed. A third disappeared off into the grounds. The other beams were coalescing around the wall, pointing outwards. It was too far away to see what they were looking for until the searchlight atop the RV came on. A cone of stark light pierced the veil beyond the gate, illuminating the road and a horror she'd not seen since the darkest days of last year. A heaving mass of the undead had reached the wall. She couldn't make out their exact numbers, let alone their features, but there were hundreds. Another light disappeared from the wall. Dead or fled didn't matter. They would all be doomed soon.

Cursing the paucity of radios, she tugged on her boots and a sweater. There was no time to dress properly. She grabbed her belt with its tomahawk and holster, and wished she'd found better weapons.

They'd left a battery-powered lantern on in the hallway, but it's previously comforting glow now turned every shadow into a lurking zombie. They don't lurk, she told herself as she threw open the door to the next room: Ricardo and Ginger's.

"Zombies. Hundreds. At the gate," she said as the couple hurriedly sat up. "Get your weapons. Get dressed. We might need to flee, or we might be besieged. Ric, organise things here. I want everyone up and ready to help, but no one should run blindly into the night. Got it?"

"What are you going to do?" Ginger asked.

"Run blindly into the night," Maggs said, and headed for the stairs.

Fight, flee, siege: those were their three options now, and they weren't prepared for any of them. She reached the entrance hall at the same time as Gordon, Alexander, and Tatiana came running from the clinic, armed.

"We heard shooting," Gordon said. "Do you know what's happening?"

"Zombies at the front gate. Hundreds," Maggs said.

Tatiana threw open the front door and began running, with Alexander only a few paces behind.

"At least he's okay," Maggs said. "Gordon, gather people here. Organise them so we don't end up killing one another. Ricardo's pulling together a strike team. Send some of them to the back gate to check we're not completely surrounded. The rest of his team can come down to the front, but keep everyone else in reserve until we know what's happening. If it's as bad as I fear, it'll be a siege."

"Understood. Be careful," he said.

She nodded and ran after the two young guards. She didn't try to catch up or even match their pace. Instead, she slowed to a walk, trying to make sense of what lay ahead. Now she was outside, she could hear screams. Shouts. A single loud gunshot. Why weren't more people shooting? Was it already over? One of the approaching lights reached Tatiana, then seemed to dance in the air, turning a figure of eight before falling to the ground, rising up again, before turning around, and heading back towards the gate.

Nearer still and she could hear the gate's hinges screech in protest at the weight pressing against them. Another shot rang out, barely louder than the chaotic screams and cries for help. Behind it all was the sound of feet dragging along the muddy roadway, of dry flesh pushing and heaving, and of chains and hinges straining under the pressure.

"Over there!" Tatiana called, pushing and pulling the guards into a line. "Where are the guns? Where are the guns?"

A shotgun blast came in reply, but from Alexander. He'd climbed up the heap of turf dumped to the right of the gate and was now firing obliquely into whatever lay outside. Maggs opted for the better vantage point of the RV. She clambered up the external ladder. As she reached the top, she saw Tatiana firing over the gate, and into a greater mass of the undead than she'd seen since August.

The light was focused on the road, about thirty metres back from the gate. Under its glare, hundreds of rotting ghouls pushed each other towards them. The sentry who should have been operating the light had deserted their post. Maggs began directing the beam herself, shinning it along the road, trying to find the rear of the advancing column, but there was no end in sight.

Finally, more gunfire shattered the night, this time from the left of the gate where two guards were firing over the wall, but aiming directly forwards, not towards the road. Maggs spun the light back, trying to assess the extent of the threat. As the zombies neared, they were flowing left and right along the wall, drawn by the gunfire. There just wasn't enough of it to keep them at bay. Where were the rest of the guns? Brass had insisted on keeping the lion's share of the bullets ostensibly because his guards would have most need of them, but where were they?

The gunfire ceased as Alexander and his two colleagues ran out of ammo. She refocused the light on the gate, and then climbed back down, running over to Tatiana who'd gathered the dozen remaining guards into a single line, ten metres back from the gate.

"Why is no one shooting?" Maggs asked.

"No ammo," Tatiana said. "Brass took it with him."

"He left?"

"No, he is in bed," Tatiana said with stoic placidity.

"They're spilling along the wall," Maggs said. "They'll get inside the grounds. We have to pick a spot to fight them. It's got to be here."

"I know. That is why we are waiting. Lex will tell us when to let them in."

Alexander, no longer firing, stood atop the berm of loose turf, peering out at the road.

"Maggs, Gordon says the back gate is clear, but he wants to know what's going on."

She spun around. It was Yvette, looking breathless.

"Hundreds of zombies," she said. "We've got to fight them here. Brass has all the ammo in his room. Tell Gordon we need the ammo, and we need reliable people to come join the fight. Go."

Yvette nodded and ran back up the hill.

"She is doing well?" Tatiana asked calmly.

"What? Yes, I think so."

"I heard what happened. I told Brass that is not who we are. It won't happen again." She raised her voice. "Get ready!"

Maggs glanced at Alexander who was holding his shotgun above his head.

"Wait!" Tatiana called, turning to the gate, before turning away, smiling. Maggs heard it: engines, approaching fast. Two of the vans were hurtling down the driveway towards the wall. She wasn't sure they'd stop, but the vans swerved, spraying soil as they came to a rest on either side of the gate.

"Now we are ready," Tatiana said. The vans created walls, a funnel. It would have been the perfect killing field if they'd had ammo. Even as the drivers jumped out of the cab, Tatiana strolled up to the gate as if she was taking the evening air.

"For love!" she called out. She pulled back the bolt, jumping back as the gate bent inwards. The gate was supposed to open outwards, but without the central bolts to distribute the weight, the pressure on the hinges grew. As Tatiana walked backwards, and with a pop louder than the shotgun's blast, the left-hand gate fell forwards. The zombies immediately pushing on it followed, toppling to the ground. With the pressure now released, those behind surged forward, tripping on the fallen undead, collapsing themselves. Bone snapped as more zombies pushed their way into the gap.

"They're going to kill themselves," someone said. It was wishful thinking. A few died, yes, but others crawled on, while some regained their feet, staggering towards the line of guards armed with little more than tools.

"For love!" Tatiana called again, as she finally drew her pair of long-handled sickles. It was an odd battle cry, but Maggs could think of no better.

"For Etienne," she said softly, moving forward on Tatiana's right. Alexander appeared on the left, a broadsword in his hands. She hoped that the movie prop replica was as deadly as it looked, then forgot about everything except the creature ahead of her.

The man was about sixty, with a badger-beard tinted with mud and dried blood. His jeans were patched with leather at both knees and one thigh, and his thick black belt had the most intricate Celtic carving. If he didn't work with leather, someone who loved him did. Who *had* loved him, and not that long ago.

Maggs raised her hand. She didn't remember when she'd drawn her revolver, and didn't consciously order her arm to raise. As the leatherworker took another step, she squeezed the trigger. The sharp report sounded as loud as the gavel on Judgement Day, but the zombie's fall was lost beneath the surging crush of the bodies behind.

Maggs shifted aim and fired again. Eight more bullets. Seven. In her peripheral vision, she could see the surge push against the vans, and see their sides begin to rock. Six. The other gate collapsed, and the rush intensified; a wave of falling tripping zombies cascaded towards them. Five, four, and the revolver was empty. There was no time to reload. She slotted the gun back into her holster and shifted her tomahawk to her right hand.

An owl hung around the choker of the undead woman already reaching out towards her. Her arm was a tapestry of wildlife, a story of mice, owls, and deer, a story whose ending wasn't supposed to be on this dark roadway. Maggs swung the tomahawk down and wrenched it free. Her shoulder generated a protesting scream, and she let her mouth release it as she swung again. She was too short for this, too old, too tired, and the zombies were too many. A hand grasped around her ankle. She swung low, smashing through an orange beanie into a head she could not see.

"Step back!" Tatiana called out, and Maggs was glad to obey the instruction without asking whether it had been for her. The zombies followed them, a sea of ghoulish faces and grasping arms. She swung again, the blade severing a finger as it knocked a hand out of the way, but that did nothing to slow the advance. They would have to retreat, and take their chances with a siege. But she knew what those chances were. They would be out of water within two days, assuming the doors held. No, retreat wasn't an option. It never was with the undead. So she'd attack.

She screamed and raised the tomahawk. Before she could charge forward, the zombie's head exploded. Cold, wet fluid sprayed over her. Reflexively, she spat, stepping back as she wiped her hand across her mouth. A gunshot sounded, and another. A hand grabbed her shoulder. She spun around, saw Ricardo, and barely stopped her swing in time.

"Go," he said, pulling her backwards so he could take her place. She didn't argue. Panting, she limped back a few metres, able to once again take in more than the walking death immediately ahead of her.

Their defensive line was now two deep and ten long, swinging and hewing while others, on the van's roofs and atop the heaped mounds of cut turf by the wall, fired into the undead. By the RV, Ginger and Georgie were handing out ammunition. Chloe and Fern were already tending the wounded. About forty were present at the gate, and there was no sign of Brass, Martin, or Ezra.

Yvette ran over. "Is there a message for Gordon? Should he send more down?"

"Is the back gate secure?"

"Yes. There's no zombies there, none at all."

"Small mercies. Have two teams patrol the inside of the wall between here and the back gate to make sure there aren't any other breaches. We need another twenty people here. Keep the rest in reserve for now."

Yvette ran off, and Maggs turned back to the battle. Would twenty be enough?

Lionel Greaves, an accountant who'd escaped Toronto two years ago and was now standing in the second rank, was tugged from his feet, disappearing into the melee. Maggs ran forward, looking to drag him free, but couldn't make out which hands were his in the gloom. Instead, she took his position in the line and waited until it was her turn to attack.

Chapter 26 - The Cost of Victory
The Laurel Hills Spa and Resort, March 11th

Wearily, Maggs took in the carnage in front of her. She didn't dare look behind to count the cost, not yet. For this minute, just for this minute, it was enough to know that ahead, finally, was stillness.

"It'll be dawn soon," Ricardo said breathlessly as he flicked brain and bone from his pick.

"It's not even been an hour," Maggs said. "Go rest. And maybe wash. If more come, we'll need your strength. And Ric," she added, "thank you."

He opened his mouth to protest, but then shrugged, shook his head, and walked off. Maggs returned her eyes to the open grave that stretched in front of her, beyond the gate and down the road to the very limit of the RV's spotlight. It had been a close-run thing. Ric had saved her life twice that she knew of.

Alexander had returned to his perch on the wall, his shotgun now reloaded, his eyes once again on the road. Tatiana sat on the dirt, just behind him, her eyes watching the spa. If it hadn't been for those two, and for Ricardo, Roy, and Ginger, they might not have held the line even with the ammo. Without them, *or* the bullets, the spa would be besieged by now. Besieged was simply another way of saying trapped. No, that wasn't worth thinking about.

In some ways, the worst of it had been over the moment the bullets had arrived. The zombies had quickly fallen, creating an impediment to those behind. The walls had then become the danger point. She'd stood atop the turf and dirt berm, hacking and stabbing with no greater thought than that she couldn't stop. The end had arrived as unexpectedly as the assault's beginning. One moment, she was swinging her axe, and the next, there were simply no more targets. She'd stepped back, looking for an enemy, an opponent, and had only seen the twisted limbs and broken skulls of the twice-dead. She'd returned to the gate, to watch the shadows at the very limit of the spotlight's glare, waiting for the nightmare to begin anew.

"You're to drink this, please," Yvette said.

Maggs blinked, looking at a mug Yvette was holding out. Slowly, she looked up and around, finally taking in the other defenders. A few stood like her, watching the darkness, but most were now gathered around the RV which had become their temporary aid station.

"Thank you." Maggs took a sip and winced at the unexpected flavour. "This isn't water."

"It's mostly water, but with some of the watermelon mix. It's got electrolytes and glucose. Chloe said it would be better for everyone to have this."

"Why, what did we do to upset her?" Maggs asked.

Yvette looked towards their nurse, moving between the injured, before she got the joke. She smiled. "It's not that bad, is it?"

"No, it's… it's just surprising," Maggs said. She took a deep cold breath, filling her lungs. "It's not over yet. We need more water. And we'll need bleach. And towels. Clothes, too. And food, I suppose. I think it's over, but we'll stay down here tonight to keep watch. Tell Gordon that half of those in the spa can sleep, but half should remain ready and swap them over in a few hours. Got that?"

Yvette nodded earnestly, and ran back up the hill. Give people a purpose, and they would often surprise you. She finished the rest of the oddly flavoured water, and went to check on the wounded.

Everyone had an injury, herself included. Cuts, bites, a palette of bruises, a few minor breaks, and more than one bullet wound from a ricochet or stray. Fern and Chloe moved from one patient to the next, cleaning and bandaging, while Georgie stood close by, trying not to make it too obvious she was a precaution against infection. So far, only one person had turned: Chantelle Dubois, part of the wood-collection crew, who'd quit Ezra's congregation before they'd left Ear Falls. Fourteen others had died. More would follow.

"Was anyone here on guard duty tonight?" she asked, pitching her voice to carry.

Hans Stern, a professional saxophonist and part-time astrophysicist, raised a bandaged hand, causing his blanket to fall off. Maggs picked it up and wrapped it around his shoulders.

"What happened?" she asked.

"They just appeared," Hans said. "One minute, it was all quiet. The next, they were there on the road, marching towards us like… like… like nothing I've ever seen."

"They just appeared?"

"There was a sound first. One in the distance. A car alarm, maybe. I'm not sure. I don't even know if it was just my imagination. I sent Trey to check the parking lot and the back gate. Wait, is he okay? Did they get in around the back?"

"He's fine, and they didn't. They only attacked here. What happened to the bullets?"

"The captain took most of the ammo away, to keep it safe."

"What about radios? Aren't you supposed to have radios?"

"We did. We do. No one answered."

"Rest," Maggs said. "You did well. Thank you. Truly."

She left the injured and joined Ginger and Ricardo, standing closer to the pile of dead.

"There are about sixty dead zombies inside, another fifty around the gate, and about two hundred outside," Ginger said.

"Is that all?" Maggs asked.

"Maybe three hundred outside," Ginger said. "I'll count them properly in the morning. It's still a lot."

"It is. It just seemed like there were more."

"Where's Kayleigh?" Ginger asked.

"I sent her and Roy to support Gordon. I thought that would keep them both safe."

"Good," Ginger said. "It's a mess. A real mess."

"I know. It'll take us a couple of days to clear this."

"I meant Brass," Ginger said. "He was drunk when we went to get the bullets. He tried to threaten us, but fell over mid-rant. It was pathetic."

"We'll deal with him later," Maggs said. "But he *will* be dealt with."

"The bodies look fresh," Ricardo said. "They're not a year old."

Tiredness was slowing her brain, making it hard to quickly readjust to the change of topic, but now she looked at the dead, she was sure he was right. These weren't recently turned, but nor had they been wandering the countryside since the outbreak. Maybe three months since they were infected. What had happened here in December?

"Maggs, trouble's approaching," Ginger said.

Coming down the path were Brass, Reggie, and four of the missing militia, with Martin trailing along at the back. Reggie had a split lip, a black eye, and a limp. She wondered when he'd got it. She wondered how. She couldn't remember the last time she'd seen him.

"Seal the gate," Brass said. "Get it shut."

"No," Tatiana said, slowly getting to her feet.

Brass stopped near the RV, his entourage stopping behind him, uncertain which way to look. Tatiana walked towards him, brushing dirt from her bloody clothes. Alexander was at her side, his shotgun not quite pointing forward, but certainly not pointing at the ground. Except for those who were too injured to stand, the bloody, battered, but victorious defenders turned to face Brass and his cowardly followers.

"We need to have the gate shut, *Sergeant*," Brass said.

"You should have been here. You weren't," Tatiana said. "The ammunition should have been here. It wasn't. Leaders lead, but you nearly killed us all. We no longer listen to you."

"That's sedition!" Brass spluttered.

"It's not," Tatiana said. "We still follow the council and the collective will of the people. We won't follow you."

"If we were to follow *your* example, we'd all be dead," Alexander said.

"If you won't obey orders, that *is* mutiny," Brass said.

"I always thought a mutiny implies rebellion," Maggs said. "But the people here, the people who fought and died, they did their duty. *You* are the one who is negligent. You squirrelled away the ammunition, imperilling everyone. There will have to be a trial. You're responsible for the death of too many good people."

"Oh, it's you," Brass said, taking a step forward towards Maggs. "Of course it is. The little snake. The viper who led us here. This is your latest move, is it? Well, it—"

Maggs didn't consciously think of drawing her revolver. One moment it was in her holster, the next it was raised, her arm extended, as she marched forward until the barrel was less than a metre from Brass's forehead.

"*Everyone* almost died because of you," she said. "Remove his weapons and place him under arrest."

"By order of the council?" Tatiana asked.

"Yes," Fern called out. "I vote for his removal. What about you, Martin? Can you feel which way the wind is blowing?"

Martin, who'd said nothing so far and was clearly an unwilling member of the delegation, looked at the bloody, battered, and furious mob. "Yes," he said. "I vote for his removal."

"Three votes is a majority," Tatiana said, walking over to Brass. She reached for his pistol. Maggs and her gun seemingly forgotten, Brass reached down to stop Tatiana. Without changing her posture, her left hand jabbed out, a quick punch to his solar plexus, followed by a quick sweep with her right leg. He fell backwards, sprawling in an undignified heap, leaving his sidearm in Tatiana's hand.

The sergeant turned to Maggs. "Now what?"

"Lock him in his room. Make sure there are no weapons there. We'll deal with him in daylight."

"We'll do it," Ginger said, stepping forward. "What about these four?"

Maggs looked at Reggie. The others, she didn't really know, for good or ill, but Reggie was a blight as bad as Brass. One battle at a time, though. "That will be for the new captain of the guard to decide," she said. "For now, just take Brass into custody."

"We'll hold a trial," Martin said, trying to recapture some authority. "There will be a trial and an investigation. Yes."

"That can wait until morning," Maggs said. "Rest while you can, everyone. The night isn't over yet."

She walked away, not intending to go anywhere in particular, and found her feet taking her to the turf berm Alexander had claimed as his firing post.

"You should get rid of him," Tatiana said, joining her.

"Brass? Yes, and we will. But we'll do it properly."

"And that fool who thinks talking to himself is the same as talking to God."

"We will," Maggs said. "First, we need a new guard captain. There'll have to be a vote, and I'm going to nominate you. I don't think there'll be any other candidates, so congratulations on your promotion."

"Me? But I don't like you."

"I know. The rest of the militia will follow you. If you are in charge, we won't end up with a massacre, revolt, or executions. We may not be friends, but that doesn't mean we have to be enemies."

Tatiana shrugged and began to walk away. After a few steps, she turned around. "I don't *dis*like you," she said.

"I know."

Chapter 27 - The Peaceful Transfer of Power
The Laurel Hills Spa and Resort

As dawn arrived, the joy of survival, and the satisfaction of ousting Brass, were replaced with simple exhaustion as she surveyed the extent of what they'd survived. The bodies were densest around the gate where they formed a metre-high dam of broken limbs and fractured bodies. Before the wall lay a viscous pool of diseased blood, flecked with bone and rags, and an upturned green ball-cap still somehow floating atop the graveyard mire. The rising sun reflected off a pair of eyeglasses laying askew on the overgrown verge. Who they'd belonged to was impossible to tell, nor by what dark miracle they'd stayed on a zombie's head after infection.

"Seventeen dead, so far," Fern said, joining her at the top of the berm overlooking the road. She held out a bottle of their homemade cleaning gel.

"A sight like this makes you want to drink it, not wash with it," Maggs said.

"That's a surefire way to make it eighteen," Fern said. She pulled out a small flask. "This one is for internal use."

Maggs raised the flask to the sky, then took a sip. "Reminds me of August."

"It's not as bad," Fern said. "But there are fewer of us now." She took the flask back, made to put it into her pocket, but then took a sip herself. "On days like today, I start to wonder if the old religions were right. The gods are at war, and we're just the pieces in their endless games. Audrey died."

"No? I'm sorry."

"Me, too. She never complained, despite the pain. When there wasn't pain, there was always discomfort, but she could still maintain a serene acceptance of her fate and find a few words to brighten your day."

"Was it another fit?"

"She was here on the line," Fern said.

"She was? I didn't realise," Maggs said, turning to look at the medical station set up around the RV. Most of the injured were now awake, and a few were standing silently together, just taking a moment to acknowledge that they were alive. "How did it happen?"

"Blood loss, I suppose, though it could be written as suicide. Someone as sick as her, in a battle like that, she was bound to get hurt. Her last words to me were '*Pick your battles carefully, because one of them will be the last,*' and she was smiling, so I suppose it was a better end for her than it might have been. I'm going to keep everyone who was here under observation today, in case anyone else turns. Those who don't want to sleep can help deal with these bodies."

"There's a willow tree in the western corner," Maggs said. "I think that would be a nice place to spend eternity. The graves can be dug there."

"For our people, yes," Fern said. "There's too many zombies to bury them inside the walls. We'll need the land for farming."

"Yes," Maggs said, turning to look back at the partially tilled soil. "Maybe there's somewhere along the road we could bury them. I'll organise it after breakfast. Speaking of which." She raised a hand, waving to Gordon as he approached.

"Is it time?" Fern asked.

"More or less," Gordon said as he looked out over the dead. "That's a Seahawks jacket, an Orcas cap, and what I think is a Seawolves beanie. All teams local to the state. Or the clothes are. Fan-wear is always among the last clothes remaining in a store. Maybe we've got the answer to what happened in December. They all look recently turned."

"Maybe," Maggs said, looking around again at the bodies. "That's something else to look into after breakfast."

Exhausted eyes followed Maggs, Fern, and Gordon as they made their way into the dining hall, and over to the table where Ezra and Martin were already waiting, sitting quietly under Tatiana's judgemental glare. Alexander sat behind her, beneath a window, menacingly sharpening his sword.

Maggs nodded a greeting to Tatiana, giving Martin's styled hair and Ezra's freshly pressed shirt a slow once-over before sitting down. On cue, Ginger and Kayleigh came out of the kitchen, each holding a tray with bowls of their breakfast.

"Just the coffee for me, please," Maggs said.

"You need to eat," Ginger said.

"And I will, but later," Maggs said.

"Give that portion to Lex," Tatiana said. "He forgot lunch yesterday."

Ginger tutted as she placed a cup of coffee in front of Maggs, and then handed out the other bowls before taking the spare over to Alexander where she then stayed, ready for the spectacle about to begin.

Maggs sipped her coffee while the others ate. Fern, slowly as always. Gordon, like someone was about to snatch his food away. Tatiana, cautiously as if she were debating whose food she could most easily steal. Martin ate like it was his last meal. Ezra, though, looked smug, throwing occasional glances towards the doors where a cluster of his more thuggish followers had gathered. Maggs made sure to meet his eyes before nodding to Ginger. She tapped Alexander's arm. The two of them went to stand right in front of the acolytes, facing them. Alexander held his sword. Ginger had drawn a hunting knife. The time for subtlety was over. Maggs stood.

"Good morning, everyone," she said, and waited a beat for voices to subside. "From now on, all council meetings will take place in public, and you will all have the opportunity to give your input. Our first order of business is to approve Tatiana as captain of our militia with a seat on the council. Are there any objections from members of the council?"

"I should be saying that," Martin said.

"You object?" Tatiana asked.

"No, I didn't say that."

"Any objections from the floor?" Maggs asked.

"Who'd be that crazy?" someone said, though Maggs couldn't see who.

"Thank you. Then with no objections, it'll be put to a vote from the council. Those in favour?"

She and Fern raised their hands. All eyes went to Martin and Ezra. Martin, realising that running with the herd was the only way to avoid being trampled, raised his hand. Ezra, did not, but it didn't matter.

"Three for, the motion is passed. Congratulations, Captain, welcome to the council, and thank you for volunteering to serve. I would also like to extend the thanks of everyone for all you did last night. We're all in your debt."

Tatiana merely nodded before reaching for her spoon.

"The next matter is appointing someone to head up our farming efforts. As he's already doing the job, I propose we make Gordon's position official, and with a seat on the council."

"You're stuffing the council!" Ezra said, belatedly realising the plan.

"If we have a position for food consumption, we should have one for food production?" Fern said.

"Are there objections to that from the floor?" Maggs asked.

There weren't. No one wanted to interrupt the show.

"Those in favour?" Maggs said. This time, Tatiana and Fern added their hands to her own, while far more than half of the crowd raised a hand, too.

Maggs didn't bother looking at Ezra or Martin. "By majority vote, Gordon is on the council. Thank you, Gordon."

"This is a travesty," Ezra said.

"Your objection has been noted," Maggs said. "But now we move on to grimmer news. Captain?"

Maggs sat and took a sip of her coffee while Tatiana stood. "Seventeen are dead. We have ten rifle rounds, fifteen shotgun cartridges, and twenty-three handgun bullets. If there is another attack, we will be overwhelmed. Today, we must prepare." She sat.

Short and sweet, Maggs thought, hastily swallowing her mouthful of coffee and hurriedly standing before Ezra or Martin had a chance to jump in. "Thank you, Captain. Would we be better moving to the compound? They have walls already built."

This time, Tatiana didn't stand. "Lex says the perimeter is too large for us to defend. And how would we get there? Bicycle? We are here, so here we stay."

Maggs waited a beat in case she wanted to say anything else. "Okay, thank you. We should prepare for a siege, so expect to work hard today. Anyone who was working with Gordon on the farms yesterday should report to him. Some will help improve our defences, the others will begin planting. Everyone else should see Tatiana. There will be another update this evening, but we've a long day ahead of us, so eat up."

She sat, and took another sip of her coffee, waiting for Ezra or Martin to say something. Ezra stared at her. She smiled sweetly back. He shook his head, stood, and left the room. His acolytes followed, though not all of them left as eagerly as they might. Martin took the opposite approach, and buried his head in his bowl, eating methodically, and avoiding all eye-contact.

"I need to get back to my patients," Fern said.

"I'll walk out with you," Maggs said, accompanying her friend through the crowd.

"That was the easy part," Fern said softly when they reached the lobby.

"I know. We need someone in the kitchens. I was thinking Roy and Kayleigh."

"Chloe and Alexander," Fern said. "Food needs to come under medical supervision from now on. Alexander never misses anything, and that will show Tatiana that you really do trust her. It was the easy part, but it was done well."

"My first coup," Maggs said. "And not a shot fired."

She knew her history; the counterrevolution would be worse, but she would allow herself just a few minutes to enjoy the victory. She didn't even get one. As soon as she stepped outside, she saw Marshall, sprinting up the driveway towards her.

"More zombies?" she asked.

"No. It's the sheriff!"

Chapter 28 - An Engineer's Assessment
The Laurel Hills Spa and Resort

Red and blue lights flashed in the distance, marking where the sheriff had left his car, and the point where the bodies made the road impassable. Dalton, his driver, Sydney, and a new companion stood atop the berm to the left of the gate, where they'd made their entrance. Maggs made her way over to where they, along with Ricardo and Roy, were taking in the carnage.

"Morning, Mrs Espoir. Maggs, I'm sorry," Dalton said. "And I'm sorry we didn't arrive a little sooner to help you with your troubles."

"Hello, Dalton," Maggs said. "The help would have been appreciated, but we held the line. You're back sooner than I expected."

He lifted up a square black case. "Clark County promised, and we delivered. It's the medication you requested."

"Oh. Thank you. That's... that's very kind. Thank you. Sorry, it's just that Audrey died last night. The patient the drugs were for. She was in the fight."

"Ain't that a kick in the ribs?" Dalton said. "I am sorry. Truly. Whatever we can do to help, we will."

"I'm sorry for your loss." The speaker was the man next to Dalton. He was wiry verging on wispy, dressed in a voluminous fishing gilet, and baggy trousers that didn't drag only because he'd secured the material around the ankle with neatly tied string. His beard was closely trimmed, a style common enough when shaving water was a luxury. Clean, but scruffy at the same time. A walking, talking scarecrow. Definitely an engineer, she thought.

"Thank you. I'm Maggs." She let the unspoken question hang in the air.

"This is Brewster," Dalton said.

"Mr Brewster, welcome," Maggs said. "I'm sorry we can't offer you much in the way of hospitality."

"Did you lose many?" Brewster asked.

"Seventeen, so far," Maggs said.

"You've been through the fire," Brewster said. "You passed the first test, but there's another coming, there always is. And it's just Brewster."

"He's with the Army Corps of Engineers," Dalton added, as if he was the man's personal subtitle generator. "We were just hearing what happened."

"And I'm still getting my head around it," Maggs said.

"You need a second and third line of defence," Brewster said. "A trench outside wouldn't go amiss. How does your control room allocate reinforcements?"

Maggs blinked as her brain tried to find the right gear to keep up. "We had a… a change in leadership this morning," she said. "We have a new captain of our militia. I think those are questions for her."

"Where is she?" Brewster asked.

"I last saw her in the dining room. Roy can take you."

"Obliged," Brewster said.

"Fetch the fuel, Sydney," Dalton said. "And no smoking around it, please."

Sydney shrugged and walked back towards the road, fishing a pack of cigarettes from his tunic.

"Ric, can you get people moving?" Maggs asked. "We'll need to bury our dead and clear the driveway. We're going to create a cemetery under the willow tree over in that corner. That's for our people. For these? I think pile them together. We'll have to dig a mass grave somewhere along the road, but clearing the gate must be our priority."

Ricardo sketched a salute. "Don't pretend you didn't hear her," he said as he turned to the survivors. Everyone able had gathered close to listen in, except for three who'd gone to beg a smoke from Sydney.

As everyone went about their work, Maggs found herself alone with Dalton. "Thank you for the medicine, truly," she said.

"It was really no trouble. One of our farming groups, near Mount Rainier, were out looking for tractors, and found a barn full of medicine. It looked like someone had emptied a dispensary. We won't be short of medicine in the future. When the doc's squared everything away here, maybe she could take a look. We might as well move it all here where she can do some good with it."

"Of course. Maybe in a couple of days?"

"I was thinking next week but sooner is always better. I just wish *I'd* arrived sooner."

"Audrey laid down her life for others," Maggs said. "Her death is a lesson, and so is her life. Your arrival with the medicine is another. It means more than I can say to have proof there's someone else out here we can rely on. It's been a rough journey. Because we were such a large group, the survivors we met were not welcoming. I think they were scared we'd just steal their supplies. It's understandable, after the outbreak, but it's so disappointing, too. There shouldn't be any need for such fear when there's more than enough to go around."

"Exactly. I was hoping... well, maybe this isn't the right time."

"Go on, tell me."

"Well, I hoped your doctor could visit the other communities and start doing whatever she can to keep people healthy, and to show them that things are improving. It's like you said, there's a lot of fear. I think it'll take until harvest, if not until next spring, before it begins to dissipate, but sending a doctor to visit will help."

"Yes, of course. In fact, Fern went to see the Connollys yesterday for that very reason. Wow, it was only yesterday. They were suspicious of her. We might need an escort for any future trips."

"That won't be a problem. We'll make a day of it. I'll show you the sights, what few there are left." He turned back to the corpses. Ricardo was leading a team using weight bars from the gym to roll the bodies out into the road. "You said you had a change of leadership?"

"It should have happened long ago. Last night was the straw that sucked the lake dry. Our previous militia captain had the ammunition locked away in his room. We almost got overrun."

"But now you're in charge?"

"No, we have a council. I want this to be democratic, not a dictatorship. We're all here by choice. I think it took me a while longer than most to make it *my* choice."

"Ah. Yep, I get that," he said, turning to look at the dead. "I've often thought of just driving away. Find a little house with a clear stream. Chop wood, hunt, fish. It's beguiling, until something like this happens. We can't make it on our own, that's the truth of it."

"Does it happen often? A mob like this?"

"Up here? This is the largest I've seen. Further south, it's far worse. I think the monsters like the desert."

"Ah. Up at the lake, where we spent the winter, they seemed to die off. Maybe cold kills them in a way that hotter conditions don't."

"Could well be. That's something to pitch to the scientists. I'm sure one'll come up with the next convoy. Speaking of which, it's due in a week or two," he added as Sydney arrived with a diesel canister.

"And bring them the other one. We can spare it," Dalton said.

Sydney sighed, shrugged, and shuffled back down the slope, only pausing to light another cigarette.

"What's your plan now?" Dalton asked.

"Well, to build up the defences here. That's our priority. And then start farming. I think we'll have to split this group up, so we'll need to claim some nearby farms. I've seen a few in our travels, all within cycling distance. I mean, we're grateful for the fuel, but we don't want to rely on it. We'll need to explore, too, and find out where these zombies came from."

"Indoors somewhere," Dalton said. "There could easily be more."

"Yes, but we've found a lot of homesteads abandoned around December. I don't know why, but after last night, I'm thinking they were overwhelmed by the undead. It must have been a massive number. We need to assess how big a danger we're in and whether this part of America is safe for anyone. And if we *can* stay, then we need to identify sources of electricity. That's another reason to keep our groups close. It'll make transmission so much easier."

"We can send up an engineer."

"I know what to look for. I used to work for Hydro du Lac. My husband and I..." she trailed off, turning her eyes towards the blue sky.

"He didn't make it?"

"We were separated. I want... I *wanted* to believe he was still alive. I suppose I can still believe it if I choose, but I need to accept I'll never see him again, and that's hard."

"My wife asked for a divorce two weeks before the outbreak," Dalton said. "It was out of the blue, at least to me. She went to stay with her sister a hundred miles away. When the chicken hit the fan, I went to look for her, but their place was deserted. I've talked the stars asleep working out what I'd say to her if we were to meet again. It's hard. No doubt about it. One of the hardest parts of all this."

"It is, yes," Maggs said. "The kids don't get it."

"They're young."

"And half are in love, or think they are."

"They'll learn."

Together, they watched the workers begin their labour, digging graves, moving corpses, or bringing out materials to strengthen the wall.

"You said you worked for an energy company. Do you reckon you could build a power plant?"

"I could build a water wheel, or a domestic battery system. I could turn on a hydroelectric plant, if it's been powered down, and I could advise on how to repair it, if it's not too damaged. I think, with help, I could build a turbine, but not a new dam, simply because we don't have the concrete, or the people to pour it. Generating electricity is never the difficult part. It's always the transmission."

"So, we should look for something we can repair, and that might not be here?"

"It certainly won't be here, but it doesn't need to be. Small farms won't need much power. But nearby, we'll need a grain mill, a metal works, and canning facilities. A gunpowder mill, too, depending on how many bullets they had in your bunker."

"Not as many as you'd have expected," he said. "We're hunting for those, too, because they're just not equipped to fight too many more pitched battles down south."

"Is it true you lived in a bunker at Cheyenne Mountain?"

"Not me, I was picked up in the summer. But there is a bunker, yes. And it's a great life if you like three warm showers a week, freeze-dried rations, and obeying military law."

"That sounds like heaven," Maggs said. "It sounds like you have a legal system, then?"

"The military code and the old laws, when they're applicable. Punishments are a little biblical for my tastes, but there's too few of us to maintain much of a jail."

"How many are you?"

"Around five thousand military personnel and twenty thousand civilians. That's at the complex. There's another fifty thousand known survivors scattered between here and there. That's only an estimate, and it's a long time since I last got a report. There's rumours there might be more survivors out east. Hundreds of thousands of them, but I don't trust rumours."

"That's far more than I thought. More than I dared hope."

"Don't get too excited. Few of the soldiers were front-line combat troops. There *were* more, right at the beginning, but the CO let people leave to forestall a mutiny. They took a lot of the supplies with them. Word is that we're good for another twelve months, but we really need a farming base to survive next year, and it won't be down there."

"Because of the zombies. Tell me, do you have planes?"

"Me? No, I've not heard of anyone flying one since last year. Why?"

"Oh, I saw one a few days ago. Or heard it. That wasn't you, then?"
"Nope. That is something, though."
"We've got to have a trial for our former captain. We're going to make it as fair as possible. Will you have a problem with that?"
"What do you mean?"
"You're a cop, and we're mostly Canadians."
"Ah. No. But I can find you a judge. There's one at a farm not too far away. When we drop off the fuel to her group, I'll bring her along. Next week be okay, when I come to borrow your doc?"
"Perfect."
"I'll bring ammo, too. I wish I had some to spare, but we're waiting on resupply."

Twenty minutes later, Maggs stood in the road with Tatiana and Gordon, watching the sheriff drive away.
"Brewster is definitely in the top ten of the oddest folks I've ever met," Gordon said.
"I liked him," Tatiana said. "He was direct."
"What did he suggest?" Maggs asked.
"Multiple walls," Tatiana said. "Use felled trunks outside to slow their approach. Dig pits outside and fill them with wooden spears. Even after the ammo comes, use it sparingly until we can reload our own cartridges. He said he'd bring cameras and radios."
"What do we need cameras for?" Maggs asked.
"To put in the forest. Wildlife cameras with motion detection software, wirelessly linked to a control room. Someone on watch can warn the guards of approaching danger, or alert the hunters."
"Good. Yes. They'll be back next week," Maggs said.
"We'll probably have this cleared by then," Gordon said. "It'd be quicker if we found an excavator. Didn't you say there were some up at the compound?"
"Yes. I think so. And he did leave us some diesel, but not much. I think we should hold off on going back there until we have a more detailed list of everything we need."
"Bullets," Tatiana said.
"We won't find them there," Maggs said. "I assume none were found yesterday?"
"No."

"And we didn't find any. Or any guns. What worries me most is where those zombies came from. Obviously, it was nearby, and inside. Probably, it's connected with what happened in December. We need to be cautious while exploring, but we also need to know what happened."

"Are you going out again?" Gordon asked.

"I think so. I think we have to. All we really know so far is that the fortress people left in December, but thought they'd be back in a few days. We'll head back towards Olympia, where we were yesterday. If those zombies followed us back from somewhere along that road, we'll see evidence of it. And we'll look for more farms that were abandoned. Someone must have left a note, somewhere."

Chapter 29 - When the Well Seems Dry
Thurston County

After the battle had exhausted her body and the coup had exhausted her mind, the arrival of the sheriff had been like a shot of adrenaline that made her want to dance along the path that led to the parking lot.

"I feel bad about all those jokes I made about the government," Kayleigh said.

"Especially the U.S. government," Maggs said. "Come back, trickle-down economics, electoral colleges, and filibusters, all is forgiven."

"Philip who?" Marshall asked.

Maggs's laughter died when she realised that he wasn't joking, and no one else was even smiling. "It doesn't matter. Hopefully, it never will again."

On a day that had begun with so much tragedy, it was unrealistic for the good mood to last long. This one evaporated when they reached the car park. Waiting next to their SUV was Ezra with three of his more trollish acolytes. In his hands was a metal fuel can.

"You should clean these vehicles," Ginger said.

"Oh, but I thought you were running the vehicle pool now," Ezra said. "And as my parting gift to you, here is the gasoline. All that remains." He let the can drop to the ground. It clanged, obviously empty. Ezra smiled as if at some great victory.

"We're completely out?" Maggs asked.

"So it would appear," he said with genuine glee. "Would you like to pray for a miracle that would turn diesel into gasoline?" The laughter from his supporters sounded genuine, but she couldn't see the joke.

"We could take one of the delivery vans," Roy said.

"Oh, of course, use up the diesel, too," Ezra said. "But then there'll be none left for the generator. Oh, how wonderful it will be to face the next legion of hell in the dark."

Maggs looked around. "You can knock it off. There's no audience here, Ezra."

"Oh, there's always an audience. Above, and below, the past and the future. They're watching. They're always watching. So, what will it be, Maggs, darkness or a miracle?"

"You've wrapped yourself so deep in your own conspiracies, you're practically incoherent," Maggs said. "But I take it your miracle would be you telling us where you stashed the missing gas?"

"I have had a revelation," he said. "But the truth is only for the faithful. Our church is open to everyone. All you have to do is kneel down and pray with us." He gestured at the dirt.

"Oh, go shake a tree and see if any sense falls out. Some people take comfort in religion, so there's room for a holy man in our community, but this doomsayer schtick you're trying doesn't suit you, or us, or the times. We've enough darkness and portents without you conjuring more. Help us, leave, or face the consequences."

"But the consequences are upon you," he said. "You were warned, but you are in the thrall of a dark power. Vanity is guiding you now, leading you to your own, inevitable, hell."

Ricardo took a step forward, raising his masonry pick.

"Ah, of course, violence, the last resort of the simpleminded," Ezra said.

"The incompetent," Ricardo said slowly. "The quote is that violence is the last resort of the incompetent. And it's not from *your* good book, so I don't see it applies here."

"Roy, how far can we go with what we have in our tanks?" Maggs asked.

"About five kilometres. More if we travel light."

"Good enough," Maggs said. "Ezra, this is your last chance. Maybe you should spend the morning in prayer and see if you get another revelation. Whatever dreams you, Brass, and Martin had are over. There's an American government, with American police, American soldiers, and American laws. And in case you hadn't noticed, we're *in* America. They're in charge now, not you. We, here, are going to work with them to save lives, and to rebuild. You can help, or you can leave."

Ezra simply smiled. "Your arrogance will be your downfall." He marched off, leaving Maggs nonplussed.

"What did that mean?" Marshall asked.

"Nothing. He had his little script worked out, and was determined to see it through until the end. Roy, how far away is our fuel stash?"

"A couple of minutes. It's near the septic tank access point."

"Fetch some. Ginger and Georgie, go with him. Make sure you're not being watched."

"What fuel stash?" Yvette whispered to Kayleigh as the three walked off towards the low storage shed.

"We found a little a few days ago, after the announcement that the gasoline was running out," Maggs said. "We didn't tell anyone, because I was worried something like this would happen."

"Yeah, I still don't get what this all is," Marshall said.

"A desperate gamble by Ezra to remain relevant," Maggs said. "By which I really mean for him to avoid having to do any real work."

"We should be careful," Yvette said. "Ezra's dangerous."

"He's a charlatan," Maggs said. "A bully, just like Martin and Brass. I should have stood up to them before, and I regret that I didn't. I'm sorry, Yvette."

"It's not your fault," she said.

"It is. Mine and everyone else's. But we'll make sure this is a real new beginning for us all."

"Do you want some of us to stay behind to watch him?" Ricardo asked. "He will try something."

"I know. But we have to let it play out. A judge will be visiting us in a week or so for Brass's trial. Either that's the future we want, with judges and laws, or we can kill them all now. One path's hard. The other seems easy, but if we choose it now, then we'll choose it again and again until we've become the tyrants we hate."

She went to inspect the tyres, half expecting Ezra to have left them another surprise. They seemed intact. Nevertheless, she knew she'd only witnessed the first act of a man who thought he was going to walk off after a curtain call.

"Which way?" Ricardo asked as they finally pulled onto the highway.

"North, to Olympia," Maggs said. "But drive slowly and keep an eye out for zombies."

"We went to Olympia yesterday. Hey, get down!" Marshall said, as Hats clambered from his lap to his shoulder, before leaping into the back and onto the maps Maggs had been trying to examine.

"Exactly," she said, as she lifted the cat onto the spare seat. "Those zombies came from somewhere. We might spot where they were trapped, and that would be the best place to learn what happened here."

"And if we see nothing, it means this area's safe," Marshall said.

"Are you that keen to go camping?" Ricardo asked.

"Nowhere is truly ever going to be safe," Maggs said. "We got complacent. We can't make that mistake again. I'd like to take another look at the farms we saw yesterday, but this time with a view on defence."

The first of the farms was only a ten-minute drive away. While Georgie and Kayleigh searched inside for a diary or journal, Maggs took photographs, Roy took measurements, and Ginger taught Yvette how to stand guard. She sent Marshall and Ricardo to inspect the fields and look for a stream. After an hour, they were done.

"What do you want us to look at next?" Georgie asked.

"Somewhere else, I think," Maggs said.

"You don't like this place?" Roy asked. "I think it could work."

"Me, too," Maggs said. "My gut's telling me that we should spend longer here, but I can't think of anything else we need to see. The stream is a bit far from the house if there were a siege, but maybe we can dig a well when we put up some walls. How many people could live here?"

"Twenty," Roy said. "More, if we convert the barn."

"Not stay here," Maggs said. "Actually live, like we might have done last year. Everyone should have a space of their own, and there should be storerooms for clothing and tools, hobby space, and privacy."

"Twelve," Kayleigh said.

"But you'd need more than that to work this land, wouldn't you?" Ginger asked.

"Good point. We need two estimates, one based on comfort and the other based on farm size. This is going to require a lot more planning than I'd realised."

As they drove, she marked down the abandoned farmsteads which had obviously been searched, those which were clearly ruins, and the handful that would warrant further inspection now they were putting down roots. At their sixth stop, and their third abandoned farmstead, she asked Yvette to take photographs while she stood guard and took a moment to reflect on the morning.

If they still had newspapers, the battle would be the headline, with Brass's arrest barely making it above the fold. Dalton's revelations would be relegated to a few columns near the horoscope, but they would have the longest-lasting impact. They'd just joined the Cheyenne Mountain community. It hadn't been planned, but for anyone living between here and the military complex, it was inevitable. Twenty-five thousand at the bunker, fifty thousand more between there and here, and hundreds of thousands more in the east. It was less than point-one percent of the country's original population, but it was enough.

They had twelve months until the food supplies ran out. The sooner food could be provided, the longer those supplies would last, providing a margin this winter and maybe next winter, too. The task was enormous. If half an acre was needed per person, and there were two hundred fifty acres in a square kilometre, they'd need two hundred square kilometres of farmland. That was just to feed the people between here and Cheyenne Mountain, but they would have the farmers. Yes, the task was enormous, but so were the possibilities. A real society, with real doctors, and a real chance of bringing back some of the better aspects of the old world.

"Don't get ahead of yourself," she said to herself.

This was going to be very different from her dreams of Vancouver Island, but it was also going to be a life much more similar to her old one. Yes, the possibilities were endless, assuming there weren't any more zombie attacks.

"The gun-locker was right by the front door, and it was empty," Roy said as the crew gathered after they'd finished a brief search. "There could be some hidden ammo stash beneath the floor, but I can't see why."

"They must have taken it with them," Marshall said. "I would have."

"It's a nice place," Kayleigh said. "A family place. There's a cottage just down that driveway. You can't see it from here. I think twenty people could live here. Fifteen if we give people more space."

"We'll have to build a wall around the property," Maggs said. "And that will have to be done first, so we'll need to bring materials with us, which means finding them. Maybe we need a specialised team to do the prep work, moving from one farm to the next, leaving others to do the farming."

"Like us?" Georgie asked, with a slight frown.

"No. But someone. Sorry, don't mind me, I'm just thinking aloud."

With her mind fixed as much on the future as the present, and not at all on the past, they continued on.

Chapter 30 - December's Treasure
Olympia

"It's another fortress," Ricardo said, his clipped tone snapping her back to the present. They were in Olympia's suburbs, hemmed in on a highway where a channel, two vehicles wide, had been cleared through the stalled traffic. The abandoned wrecks had been used like bricks to build a wall on either side of the road, bumper-to-bumper and on top of each other, sometimes four cars high. It was a formidable barricade, but nothing in the nondescript commercial properties beyond the jumble of rusting autos appeared worth defending.

The car-wall ended at a junction with clear roads to the left and right. Immediately ahead was another wall, this one three metres high, and made of sheet metal panels. Just outside was a billboard. The top right corner was painted white, as if someone had been covering over the old sign but enough of it remained that she could read: *Ocean Paradise Mall, Redevelopment Soon.*

"No bodies," Marshall said as they got out.

"No bullets," Ricardo said.

"A pair of goldfinches," Maggs said, pointing up at a twisted street-lamp, before pointing north along the highway. "That front loader must have been used to build the wall. From the jumble of cars behind it, that's where they abandoned the job."

"The sheet-metal wall looks similar to fortress-compound," Ginger said.

"Yes, so let's remember what we found there as we explore," Maggs said.

"You want to go inside?" Ginger asked.

"No, but we have to," Maggs said.

"What happened in December?" Ricardo said.

"Exactly," Maggs said. "Plus, we need walls and could dismantle these."

"Assuming they're not keeping something inside," Roy said.

"Assuming that, yes," Maggs said. "But if they are, we need to know about it before we settle some farmers just a few kilometres down that road."

The entrance was directly across from the car-wall channel they'd approached by. Unlike the first fortress-compound, there was no wedge jutting into the road, just a sliding gate made of the same metal panels as the wall.

"Found it," Roy said after a few minutes of inspection. He heaved on a large rusting cogwheel that definitely hadn't been built for the purpose. A loud clang came from inside, then a clatter and a creak, as if the whole wall might fall. Ricardo added his strength to Roy's. Dusty gears began to grind, metal teeth bit into their chains, and the gate slid sideways across the entrance.

"It's stiff, but it's too similar to the fortress for it to be a coincidence," Roy said, stepping back when there was a gap wide enough for a person to walk through. "Give me a minute, and we'll get it properly open."

"That's wide enough. We can leave the cars here," Maggs said.

"We'll have to," Ginger said as she peered through the gap. "There's nowhere to park."

The parking lot was as busy as Christmas Eve, with nearly every spot taken. Between the mud-splattered four-wheel drives were vans of every colour, yellow school buses, and five coaches, parked askew directly outside the old mall.

"You want me to close the gate?" Marshall asked.

"No, we might want a quick exit," Maggs said, walking to the nearest pickup. The fuel tank's cap was closed, so was the neighbouring van's.

"This one's unlocked," Marshall called from the next row. "The keys are on the seat."

"See if there's fuel in the tank," Maggs said as she tried the door of a twenty-year-old people carrier held together by pro-dog decals. It was unlocked, and the keys were in the ignition. The engine coughed into life. The fuel needle swung up to a quarter of a tank left. She switched it off.

"I've got fuel," she announced.

"Me, too," Ginger said. "A full tank."

"Half for me," Marshall called, switching off the spluttering engine.

"Dead battery for me," Kayleigh said.

Maggs closed the car door and made her way back to the open channel left in the lot, waiting for the others to join her. Most of the tyres were a little flat, and the windows were covered in grit, pollen, and leaves, but otherwise, these cars were ready to be driven away. As best she could tell, the wall itself was finished, but like the sign outside, it needed a little decorating. There were no real ramparts to speak of, just a couple of scaffolding platforms that might have been left over from construction.

As far as she could tell, the wall only ringed one plot, previously containing a warehouse for Congo, the insurgent Chinese next-day-delivery company, a branch of Howdy's grocery store, and a two-storey mall whose signage had nearly as many gaps as named stores.

"There's a place in there called Python Home Defence," Kayleigh said, pointing towards the mall. "Didn't they make guns?"

"Did they? Well, those will be gone," Maggs said. "I think we should try the grocery store first."

"The food will be gone, too," Marshall said.

"I know. And that's why we look there first."

Whether originally from a province, territory, or from a U.S. state, they'd all experienced and witnessed very similar horrors in the days just after Manhattan. As the first reports from New York were propagating, grocery stores had been raided by the employees who'd arrived to open them. Dawn brought the next wave of looters, who would have been customers twenty-four hours before. With more stock on the shelves than could fit in a car, things were relatively peaceful at first.

By mid-morning, the shelves were beginning to look bare, and the mob mentality had set in. Carts were filled with whatever could be grabbed, regardless of need. Civility was replaced with aggression as the luckier few protected their haul. By midday, traffic had blocked the entrances, fists had been replaced with tyre irons, and then with guns.

The remaining stock disappeared overnight, usually with the contents of the cash registers, often leaving only a few bodies behind. With the grocery stores empty, the looters had spread out, targeting restaurants, offices, and their own neighbours, and often before the first local zombie had been sighted.

"No bodies," Kayleigh said as they reached the small grocery store's entrance.

"No glass," Marshall countered, pointing his axe at the ragged plastic and rotting wood covering the defunct sliding doors.

"But someone swept it up," Yvette said.

Ricardo pushed at the wooden frame concealing the doorway. It fell inwards, in one complete unit.

"Well, that's disappointing," Ginger said as she stepped onto it and inside.

The shelves were empty. Many had been dismantled. Possibly to be used in some part of the wall's construction, but perhaps even before the outbreak. A few signs still hung from the rafters, but the most common included the words *Closing Down*. Marshall climbed onto the counter of the nearest cash register. "I can't see anything."

"Want to check the back?" Roy asked.

"No, what would be the point?" Maggs said. "But there is a reason they built that wall. Something here is worth protecting. We'll see if it's inside the fulfilment centre."

Chapter 31 - The Fulfilment of Nobody's Wishes
Olympia

Outside the fulfilment centre, a doll's outstretched arm reached up between a small forest of ambitious weeds that had found root in the pile of discarded packaging.

"All she's missing is a torch," Ginger said as she attempted to kick a path through the mulch of cardboard and abandoned homeware.

"I could give her a lamp," Georgie said, picking up a mermaid-themed desk light with a broken tail. "Wasn't there a famous Lady of the Lamp somewhere?"

"Florence Nightingale," Yvette whispered, softly enough that she could deny she'd ever spoken.

The employee door was ajar, but whatever detritus had kept it from closing also prevented Marshall from moving it more than a few centimetres. He stepped back and shrugged. "Ric?"

Ricardo put his shoulder to the door. Inside, something cracked.

"I hope that wasn't you," Ginger said.

"I hope it wasn't a body," Maggs said, but as she shone her light into the shadowy loading area, it only illuminated the decaying carcass of capitalism.

"What a waste," Ginger said.

"What a smell," Kayleigh said. "I'm going to wait outside."

Roy nodded and turned to face the parking lot.

"We'll be as quick as we can," Maggs said.

The trail of colourful packaging, unwanted trinkets, and rotting cardboard continued through the loading area and onto the warehouse floor.

"Be quick, fan out, check the shelves. Take photos," Maggs said. "But watch for zombies."

She made her way over to a nonet of packing robots, all of which wore either a hat, a scarf, or both. The floor was littered with more clothes than a changing room on a Saturday afternoon. No doubt looters had been hoping to find a crate of cookies, camping gear, or weapons. Not wanting to leave empty-handed, they'd settled for what they could easily find among the towering shelves. Settled for and then discarded, since clothes could be found in any home, and these cheap strips of artificial fabric offered little protection against the cold and none against the real threat of those early months.

"They didn't label the shelves," Marshall said, coming over to join her. "It's like random stuff in each of the trays."

"It was all done with wifi, barcodes, and RFID," Maggs said, kicking a pile of crop-tops away from the base of the robot. "Well, that's frustrating."

"What are you looking for?"

"Information on the battery, but this just has a warning not to have one of these fall on you." She looked around again. "Batteries, Marshall. That's what we'll need. One per farm this winter to keep the freezers working. Actually, two, so there's one as a backup. We'll need freezers and enough lights that people can read or sew, clean, and do the other indoor tasks after dark. Batteries, solar panels, and wind turbines if we can manage them. I wonder if this outfit sold them."

"Where do you want me to start looking?" he asked.

"Nowhere yet," she said. "We'll have to come back and catalogue it properly. Maybe bring a generator and see if we can access their stock list. There will be useful things here, but we don't have time to search now. Gather everyone. I think we're almost done."

Back outside, the mall's loading bay doors looked as if they'd been rammed from both sides. They were twisted, and dented, but expanding foam had been sprayed around the edges and gaps.

"It looks like an explosion at a marshmallow factory," Roy said as he tried the side door, where more foam had been run around the edges, but whatever seal it had created had already been broken. "Shall we?" he asked, pushing the door inward.

"It smells worse than the fulfilment centre," Kayleigh said.

"You can stand guard outside, Kay," Maggs said.

"No, we'll stick together," Kayleigh said.

"Hang on," Roy said, having taken a few paces inside. He took out his flashlight, turned it on, and shone it ahead. "There's a body," he said. "A man, I think. His head's intact. Looks like two bandages on his left leg. He's got a homemade spear next to him, and a hunting knife on his belt."

Maggs shone her own light around the loading space, but there was no last testament written on the wall, no warnings or prayers, and no other bodies. A door behind the loading bay led into a small office-space whose wall had a depressingly cheery New Year's resolution bar-chart for each of the warehouse employees. At the top of the board was the grand prize: five days paid leave.

Maggs felt a lump in her throat. She'd tried to run an office like that. If given the choice, no one would go to work. Well, no one except complete lunatics like her husband. But it was where everyone spent half their waking hours, so why not make it as fun as efficiency and safety would allow. Reward good performance with the thing everyone truly wanted, an opportunity to enjoy the money their hard work had earned.

"Another body," Ricardo said. He'd opened the larger swing doors that led towards the rear of the stores. "Zombie, I'd guess." The corpse was twisted into a foetal position, with the back of its skull missing. A gun lay nearby.

Marshall picked up the pistol. "It's empty."

"Expect more inside," Maggs said. "We don't want a fight, though. Nothing here is worth it."

The corridor was broad enough for two delivery cages to pass, with studs in the floor marking where false walls could be installed. To the right was the building's outer wall. To the left was a featureless grey wall occasionally broken by a windowless door with a sign marking who, if anyone, occupied the unit beyond. The first three had no name. The fourth was for Game Hive, then Yarn Barn, Beyond Scent, and then Dandy Candy, who'd added their own yellow and red sign to the door.

"Please?" Marshall whispered.

One store was as good as another, she supposed. "Ric, here. Roy, try Beyond Scent." Georgie, Yvette, and Kayleigh followed Roy back to the previous store.

Ricardo ran his light around the frame. There was no foam, which was probably a good sign. He pulled the latch up and turned it sideways. The ratcheting click of the lock echoed. The door swung inwards, before sticking at thirty degrees.

"Wait here," he said, before slipping inside. Ginger stepped forward with her crossbow half-raised, ready to go to his aid.

"Clear," Ricardo said.

"After you," Ginger said, and followed Marshall inside. Maggs lingered in the corridor, trying to piece together the contradiction of the tall walls, a parking lot full of ready-to-be-driven vehicles, and a fulfilment centre littered with trash. Her thoughts were derailed by the sound of cardboard being ripped apart followed by a deeply satisfied sigh.

She slid inside, into a stock room with six rows of shelves, about a shoulder's width apart. In the space between the shelves were bed rolls, sleeping bags, blankets, and pillows. Six people had slept here. Five of them had left bags behind. Lanterns were placed on the lower shelves, suggesting whoever had slept in there had done a little late-night reading. Not all the shelves were empty. Marshall had torn a box open and was cramming his mouth with red worms.

"Cherry," he said when his mouth had sufficient room for words. "Sour cherry worms."

"Don't eat them all now," Maggs said. It looked like a fifth of the stock remained. That was an interesting detail. She bent down to check the contents of the nearest bag, a hiking-quality backpack. Clothes dominated, but there was also a naval fiction paperback, a wash-bag with two bars of soap and a ziplock bag half-filled with toilet paper. A water bottle was almost full of some liquid or other. She opened the cap. Very definitely not water. Rum, maybe. At the bottom of the bag was some canned food. She didn't notice a label until she lifted it up to the light. On the can's side was a sticker on which someone had written *artichokes*.

"Maggs!" Ginger hissed from the doorway leading into the store, waving her over.

The shopfront seemed cavernous now that it was empty of stock. The layout was identical to the branch in Saguenay that she'd visited when stocking up on aniseed fudge to take to Etienne's uncle Bertrand in the nursing home. The garish two-metre-tall rabbit looked forbidding now that its basket was empty of chocolate.

"Here," Ricardo whispered, his voice softer than usual.

Wincing at the crunch and crackle of discarded wrappers, Maggs made her way across the shop floor to the entrance. The glass doors had been covered with cardboard. Ricardo had peeled away a corner. He stepped aside so she could see out, onto what had been a food court. She played her light towards the tumbledown ruins of a cookie kiosk, illuminating a sea of bodies, lying atop each other, too many to count. She played her light back towards the other side but stopped when the shadows began moving out of sequence with her light. An arm. A shoulder. A head. One body, and then the next. The whole mass of death slowly began to undulate. The rustle of cloth became a cautioning whisper. Shoes began sliding on the bare floor. Flesh rubbed against decaying flesh as the trapped horde slowly woke.

Maggs backed up and pointed to the door. Ricardo nodded but waited until she was leaving before he followed her.

"There's—" Marshall began before Maggs cut him off.

"Shh! Zombies. Go."

Marshall stuffed another box into his bag and followed her out through the door and along the corridor to where Georgie looked suddenly alert.

"Zombies," Maggs whispered.

Georgie nodded, and ducked inside, before returning with Yvette, Roy, and Kayleigh.

"A horde. We're leaving," Maggs said, and motioned down the corridor before turning to check the others were just behind her. From inside the mall, the sound rose, an ocean willing to become a tsunami. Maggs bit her lip, not daring to breathe until they were outside.

As they left the walled tomb, they paused only long enough to seal the gates. Once in the relative safety of their transport, they drove away. Maggs waited until she saw the first overgrown field before she stopped.

"Marshall, climb to the roof," Maggs said. "See if they've followed us."

"How many do you think there were?" Kayleigh asked.

"Five hundred," Ricardo said. "Could be more."

"How?" Roy asked.

"Six people were asleep in the back of the candy store," Maggs said. "In one bag, there were cans of food, just like we found at the compound. I didn't check the other bags."

"So they came from the fortress?" Marshall asked.

"I don't know. Maybe," Maggs said. "But maybe not. We found some of that canned food in other homesteads, so I think the compound people might have traded with other people nearby."

"Um... Someone was sleeping in the candle store, too," Yvette said, holding up a slim book. "They left a journal. Sort of. It's not very long."

"Read it," Marshall called down.

Yvette thrust the book at Maggs as if it was suddenly red hot.

Hi, Micheal, I said I'd keep a diary of our little adventure, so here it is. First, and most important to you, we found candy. Yes, candy. In a candy store. It's just next door to where I'm bedding down. Are you jealous? You shouldn't be. Guess what happened. Old Mrs Lewis ate an entire bag of liquorice and was sick all night! Yes, even grown-ups get sick when they eat too much candy. I've got some bags of it for you when I get home.

I'm sleeping in a candle store, and writing this by candlelight as I wait for everyone else to wake up. The candles help with the smell. Oh, how I wish I could have a bath. They did give us water when we arrived. Enough to wash our hands and faces, though I'm sure some people didn't bother, and I bet you can guess who! But there are no showers. It's really not like home. I suppose it's like they said, we're here to do a job, so we will, and then we'll come home. We got a hot meal, though it wasn't anything like Tiff's cooking. All very processed. And no, there were no hot dogs! Ah, I hear people moving around. Time to get up, and earn our reward.

What a day! I'm utterly exhausted, and I can't say I have any interesting stories for you. The work is hard, and repetitive, and very, very boring. Now we know what we're doing, it's actually easy to put those sheets together. Building up a wall out of cars is harder, but Jenny's organised that sort of work before. Everyone is safe and well, and definitely in need of a shower!

Finally, a bit of adventure, and some I would happily have gone without. We saw five zombies today. I think the heavy engines from the excavators and cranes drew them in. We're all safe, that's the key thing. Jodi broke her arm, but that was while trying to play acrobat atop the part of the wall we'd finished. It's not too serious, just a little fracture that'll heal in a few weeks, but she's out of action. She's going to stay here with us. I know we've only been at it a few days, but I can't see it taking much longer.

It's night now, about eight. Maybe later. I would have written more earlier, but I left the book here, and only just came back to it. What a day. We finished the wall. The car wall will take longer. I'm still not clear why they want it. I suppose it'll be more obvious when the work is finished. Anyway, the good news is that we won't all be needed for that part. It's a case of too many people, not enough space. Remember how it was in the kitchens at Thanksgiving? Yep, like that but more so. I'll be with the group coming back first, so I'll see you soon.

Maggs turned the page, but there were no further entries. "That's all she wrote." She scanned through the handful of lines again. "Or he. It was winter. They went from somewhere to the mall to work, leaving at least one child behind. And they had food canned since the outbreak. Yes, I'd say this was the people from the fortress-compound."

"What happened to them?" Marshall asked.

"They got infected," Maggs said. "Or some did. There were a few gaps in the parking lot. There might have been some who escaped."

"What do you want to do?" Ginger asked.

"I want to give them peace," Maggs said. "But we can't. We don't have the ammo. We'll have to inform Sheriff Dalton. Maybe this is something we can leave to the soldiers. At least we know they're trapped inside."

"For now," Kayleigh said.

Chapter 32 - The Mystery of the Missing Minister
The Laurel Hills Spa and Resort

Maggs wrung the washcloth into the bowl. The water was only slightly grey. The room was only slightly chilly. Her knees were only slightly sore, and that was more from climbing up to the very top floor of the spa than from the day's efforts. All in all, not a bad way to end a day.

They'd stopped at six properties on the way back, another two of which had been occupied until Christmas, and three of which had been abandoned some time before. All told, she thought they had found enough farmland now. On paper, anyway. But each farm would need a strong wall, and a way to call for help if they were surrounded. Which also meant there would have to be people ready to go to their aid. Maybe that would be the soldiers. Maybe not.

What was missing from both of the recently occupied farms were firearms and ammunition. Both had obvious gun cabinets, one by the front door, one in a boot room. But if these farmers had gone to the mall, where they seemed to be willing workers, what had happened to their guns? She'd not seen any, though they hadn't really looked. She stared down into the murky water.

"Mirror, mirror," she murmured. It was the wrong question. Why hadn't there been any sign of a battle in the mall?

Knuckles rapped against the door. "Maggs. Sorry, it's me, Yvette. Gordon sent me to get you."

"Just a minute, dear," Maggs said, grabbing a towel. "How urgent is it?"

"I'm not sure. I was just told you were needed. It's council business."

She hurriedly dressed, and followed Yvette downstairs to the kitchens. Roy and Kayleigh were overseeing the cooks. Gordon and Tatiana were standing close to the serving hatch. Before she could be given any more unwanted responsibilities, Yvette vanished.

"What's wrong?" Maggs asked.

"Ezra's gone," Gordon said.

"Ezra, Reggie, Sloan, and Ira," Tatiana said. "I changed the guard schedule. The new handover is at four. Ira and Sloan were guarding the back gate this afternoon. They're gone. So is a van and all the diesel that wasn't in the generator."

"There could be others missing," Gordon said. "It's hard to tell. We'll need to do a headcount at dinner."

"Okay. How do we know Ezra and Reggie are gone?"

"Their gear's missing," Tatiana said.

Maggs waited, as she often did when speaking with their taciturn captain, in case any more details were forthcoming. As usual, they weren't. "Reggie wasn't one of Ezra's acolytes," she said.

"No. He was Brass's goon," Gordon said. "Whatever fate befell Brass, Reggie must have figured the axe could fall on him, too."

"True enough. And Brass?" she asked.

"Still in his room. Lex was watching him this afternoon," Tatiana said.

"What about Martin?" Maggs asked.

"I had him pushing a wheelbarrow," Gordon said. "I pointed out that people liked to see their leaders get their hands dirty, and that he wanted to be liked if he wanted to remain our leader. He took the hint. I'm going to have another word with him, but I think he'll be happy as a figurehead."

"So it's just Ezra and some other undesirables who've gone?" Maggs asked, her mood beginning to brighten.

"With all our diesel," Gordon said. "I think we've got enough for tonight, but the generator will be empty tomorrow. We'd just got some pipes rigged to the stream, but there'll be no power for the pump."

"That won't be a problem," Maggs said, picking her words with care since Tatiana was present. "We found a little gasoline. It's not much, but it'll last us until Dalton gets back. Tomorrow, we'll make our last trip to the fortress, and pick up their gas-powered generator and maybe the solar panels. I want to have another look around there, anyway. After that, no more excursions for a while. Everyone can have a hot shower, and we might as well splurge on getting the sauna running."

"What about the fields? We need some more farmland," Gordon said.

"I take it you haven't heard about our day, yet?" Maggs said. "We found the people from the fortress-compound, trapped in a mall in Olympia, undead. Their vehicles are parked outside the mall. There's fuel in the tanks. It's a lot of vehicles. Cars and trucks, gas and diesel. If we were still aiming to get to Vancouver Island, I'd say fuel is not a problem."

"If it is guarded by a thousand zombies, it is a *big* problem," Tatiana said.

"Sorry, let me rephrase that. I mean it *is* a problem, but of a different sort. Hopefully, we can get the soldiers to help us clear it out, and we can find a way of doing it while keeping the zombies trapped. But for now, we should play it safe. Except for one trip to the compound, there should be no more driving. Anyone who leaves, goes by bike. And we should thoroughly search everywhere nearby, deal with any zombies lurking in basements, but avoid anywhere they might be in large numbers. I suppose we should warn the Connollys, too. Dalton mentioned at least one more farm nearby. I don't think he told me precisely where. Maybe the Connollys know. This is a policy we'll have to revise day by day, but it is only a week of confinement. I think we'll manage."

"I bet Ezra's gone to the compound," Gordon said. "He's probably stealing our food as we speak."

"I could check," Tatiana said. "It's still light. We could collect the generator now."

"He's got one van, yes? There were no drivable cars at the fortress. He can take as much as he can carry, and we won't be any worse off. But if we go after him, we're doing it with axes and knives, and for all we know, he's got a few guns. If anyone kept a few bullets aside, it would be him. No, let him go. Hopefully, he'll go far enough away that he can't come back."

"And if he stays nearby, and goes back to the fortress day after day, until there is none left?" Tatiana asked.

"Well, there are only four of them," Gordon said.

"For now. We don't want to die for food," Tatiana said.

"No," Maggs said. "Okay, so what would you like to do?"

"Me?"

"You're the guard captain, and those food supplies are something we need to guard."

Tatiana met Maggs's gaze, unblinking. Time stretched, but Maggs didn't dare look away. Finally, after twenty seconds that seemed to have stretched longer than the lifespan of the universe, Tatiana spoke. "Send fifty volunteers to claim it. They can begin planting seeds."

"Is that safe?" Maggs asked.

"Is here? Alexander should lead them. He will know what to do."

"It's not a bad idea," Gordon said. "We'd need a permanent presence at the fortress before Dalton, or the Connollys claim it."

"We'll have to share that food," Maggs said. "It's not ours. None of this is. And it's not Dalton's either. It's no ones, so it's everyone's, and it's not worth fighting over."

"Agreed," Tatiana said, surprising Maggs. "I shall tell Alexander to pack."

The evening meal was vegetable stew. Maggs was already tiring of it, but she ate half her bowl before she stood.

"Hello," she said. "Good evening." She had to wait as some of those out in the corridor left the line, and came inside to listen. "Good evening," she said again when she thought everyone who was interested had come within earshot. The ladle clanged as another portion of dinner was served. In the distance, she heard laughter from the rear of the bar. Government business wasn't everyone's top priority.

"Ezra's run away," she said, deciding to treat the meeting as a news report and so begin with what the public would be most interested in rather than what was most in the public interest. "He stole the diesel and took at least three others with him. We asked for everyone's names at dinner so we could find out exactly who else is missing." Not wanting to shout over the crowd, she paused until the hubbub had subsided.

"This morning, as we were trying to leave, Ezra confronted me and my team. He announced there was no gasoline left, and intimated that he'd hidden it, and would tell us where it was if we knelt before him. I mean *literally* knelt, like he was a feudal bishop."

Where there'd been confusion before, particularly among the handful of souls who had thought him a conduit for their prayers, now there was anger. Again, Maggs waited for silence.

"He's gone. We're not going to look for him. We think we've found the occupants of the fortress-compound. They're zombies, trapped inside a mall in Olympia. They *are* trapped there, but until the sheriff comes back with some ammo, we can't do anything about them."

"Was that where the zombies from last night came from?" André asked.

"Not there, because they were sealed in, but maybe from somewhere like that, and near there," Maggs said. "We're not going to look. Not until we've got the ammo. For now, we're going to hunker down, and finish work on the defences. We did find some gasoline. It'll replace the diesel Ezra stole as soon as we pick up a gasoline generator to burn it. Alexander is going to take a team to the fortress tomorrow to find one. Tonight, we're going to restrict power to the lights, so we don't run out before dawn. But tomorrow afternoon, we'll have enough to get the pumps working. We'll have showers again. Cold showers," she added quickly, but still got a cheer. "Cold showers, but the days are warming up, so that's not so bad. Alexander will be staying at the compound with fifty volunteers in case Ezra thinks he can steal any of those supplies for himself. While there, they can begin planting. If anyone wants to volunteer for that, speak to Alexander."

"After he's eaten," Tatiana added loudly.

Chapter 33 - The End of a Friendship
The Laurel Hills Spa and Resort, March 12th

Maggs woke feeling like she had a bundle of warring kittens in her stomach. She fought her way free of the tangle of blankets and reached for the bedside lamp, switching it on so she could read the time. Twelve-thirty. She grunted in frustration. Hats offered a muted miaow of annoyance at his nap being disturbed by the light. After a brief twitch of his whiskers, he decided she could face her demons alone and went back to sleep. In his defence, at least thirty percent of her problem was too much sugar. After dinner, Marshall had shared out the remaining candy. If the announcement of Ezra's betrayal hadn't galvanised public opinion in favour of the new administration, that had.

"If Marie Antoinette had actually handed out cake, the revolution would never have happened," she murmured. Hats didn't even open an eye. Their revolution was over. And it had been peaceful, except for those killed by the undead. Perhaps their sacrifice had been enough to remind everyone of the precarious reality of their situation. Or perhaps she'd been judging them all unfairly. It was truly depressing to think she could have achieved the same outcome if she'd acted a few days, or weeks, sooner.

She sat up, turned off the lamp, and waited for her eyes to adjust before walking over to the small table by the smaller window. The journal was still there, open to a blank page. Her attempt to write a letter for Etienne had been confounded by a Himalayan-sized mental block. There was so much she wanted to tell him, but she actually wanted to *talk* to him, not write words in a book he'd never see. Writing the letters had brought her great comfort over the last year, but no longer.

"Oh, Etienne. I'm sorry. Life goes on, doesn't it? It has to. Even for me."

Outside, a few white beams moved slowly across the driveway as the guards went about their patrols. A few lights went out. A few more came on. The searchlight remained off, so she took that to mean it was shift-change.

She picked up her pen, and put it down again. There wasn't enough light to write. Besides, she worried anything she wrote would seem like a goodbye, only cementing her fears as facts.

Another two lights went out, and now there was only one at the gate. No, now there were five, but two pairs were red. Two pairs of red lights, one slightly further away than the other. Tail lights. Cars. She'd not heard an engine, but she couldn't hear anything from outside. There was no way to open the window.

"And what would you do if you could?" She made her way back to the bed, and turned the lamp back on before grabbing her clothes from the back of the chair. Had Ezra returned for Martin and Brass? Was that why Reggie had gone with the boxed-wine preacher? If they wanted to leave, she'd let them, but Tatiana absolutely wouldn't. If Ezra had found ammunition, it would be a bloodbath.

She looked again at the window. She'd not heard any gunshots, but she'd not heard the engines, either. All she could hear was the soft hiss of the central air system. She grabbed her tomahawk and stepped outside. The corridor smelled faintly of cherry blossom, no doubt from one of the candles found at the undead mall. Kayleigh was probably up, then. Or was it Yvette? Either way, better to let them sleep than mix them up in this latest, but hopefully last, spasm of a dying regime.

She was halfway down the stairs when she regretted not waking Ricardo. She'd have to make do with Tatiana, except shouldn't she already be outside? Had it been a terrible mistake to trust her? At the bottom of the stairs, she paused, trying to assemble her thoughts into a more coherent pattern.

"You're stalling."

She opened the door to the lobby. The only light came from an electric lantern on the reception desk; they still hadn't got around to replacing the bulbs in the overhead lights. Maggs relaxed as she saw Fern struggling with the front door.

"Is it Martin?" Maggs asked.

Fern turned, her face a sickly violet under the dim light reflecting off the lobby's purple panels. "I don't know. The door's locked," the doctor said. "I thought I heard an engine. Maybe a gunshot. I'm not sure."

"Definitely an engine," Maggs said, coming over to try the door herself. "I saw red taillights out my window. Hopefully this means Brass has made his escape."

"Tatiana was at the gate," Fern said. "She might be hurt."

"I'll wake Ricardo," Maggs said. "I'll wake everyone. We'll... I don't know."

Fern kicked the door again, though this time without much force. "Let them go. It's not worth chasing them. This will set us back, but it solves…" She coughed. "It solves a bigger problem. We don't need a trial, now."

Maggs nodded and leaned against the counter. The air down here tasted faintly of cherry blossom, too. "We'll head up to the compound at first light, grab all the food we can, and make sure they haven't set up camp there."

"We don't have…" Fern coughed, doubling over as she tried to clear her throat. "Excuse me. Sorry, it's the doctors' curse. You always pick things up from your patients. It's why I preferred…" Her words were lost beneath a racking hack. Maggs took her arm.

"Come and sit down," Maggs said. Fern's face, already ghostly under the reflected purple sheen, was looking dangerously pale. She helped her friend into a muddy chair by the door.

"I'm… I'm… I'm…," Fern muttered between racking coughs.

"I'll get Chloe," Maggs said, as the doctor gasped for air. Even as Maggs stood, Fern's last breath caught, her eyes went wide, and she slid sideways. Maggs managed to catch her before she hit the floor. Vacillating between running for help and staying at Fern's side, she tried to do both. "Help!" she bellowed as she checked Fern's airway. It wasn't blocked, but her face already felt strangely cold. "Chloe! Help!"

She couldn't find a pulse. Maggs checked again, before dredging up her training from so long ago. She straddled Fern, placed her left hand on her breastbone, interlocked her hands, and pushed. Five centimetres. Five centimetres. Five centimetres. The number spun around her mind. That was how deep you had to push, but how deep was that? And now she was finding it hard to keep track of how many she'd done. Hopefully enough. She pinched Fern's nose, and breathed into her mouth. Once. Twice.

"Help!" she called, before beginning the chest compressions again. "I'm sorry, Fern. I'm sorry," she said.

Fern's head jerked up, before banging back to the floor.

"Fern! Don't move. Please, don't move. You'll be okay."

The vet's head rocked back and forth. Her mouth opened. Her hands reached out, grabbing at Maggs's arms.

"Fern!" Maggs said, realisation hitting like an avalanche as she shook her arm free, scrabbling back over the muddy floor, until her shoulders hit the reception desk. "Not you, Fern. Not you!"

Fern thrashed, legs kicking, arms reaching. Her head slammed against the floor as she tried to stand and attack at the same time.

Maggs was frozen in place, not wanting to do what had to be done next. "Why?" she said. "Why?"

Fern rolled to her knees, unwinding like a spring, rising in a macabre pirouette to face Maggs.

"No," Maggs said, as she ran around the reception desk. "Fern, it's me." But it was hopeless appealing to a humanity that was now missing, and suicide to do anything but pick up her tomahawk from where she'd laid it on the desk.

As Fern lunged forward, Maggs batted her hands away with the flat of the blade before swinging the axe around, obliterating her friend's lower jaw. Blood and teeth arced to the left as Fern spun sideways, but she didn't fall. Gobbets of bloody flesh and shattered bone dangled from her chin, dripping to the floor as Fern attacked again. Maggs swung low, ducking down beneath those grasping hands. The blade crushed Fern's knee. The zombie toppled. Maggs straightened, rushing forward, bringing the axe down two-handed, onto the centre of Fern's forehead. For the second time in as many minutes, her friend died, leaving nothing but a still-familiar husk, oozing red-orange blood across the floor.

Chapter 34 - Pack a Bag
The Laurel Hills Spa and Resort

As silence replaced the pounding drumbeat of blood in her ears, the questions roving through her mind coalesced around *how*. The answer seemed obvious. A patient had been infected. She knew what she had to do. Her eyes fell on her axe, still embedded in her friend's skull. Yes, she knew what she had to do. Fighting back tears, she braced a foot on Fern's neck, and pulled her axe free, wincing at the sucking wrench peppered with the harsh grinding of bone.

"I'm sorry, Fern. It was my fault we came here. I should have done something sooner. Far sooner."

But the words meant nothing to her twice-dead friend. She picked up the lantern from the reception desk, raised her axe, and walked over to the doors leading to the treatment rooms in which they'd set up their clinic. She couldn't hear any sound from beyond, but she couldn't hear any sound anywhere, except for the gentle buzz of the air-circulation system. She pushed the door open with her foot, ready to swing, but the corridor was deserted. The ceiling lights were off, and no light glinted from beneath any of the doors. She put the lantern on one of the chairs, and opened the door to the first exam room. It was empty. So was the second. The third wasn't. A body lay on one of the treatment tables, their arm dangling limp over the side.

Maggs pushed the door as wide open as it would go, hoping that it wouldn't swing closed and block the lantern light. She raised the tomahawk, ready to swing, but the body let out a snuffling snore and rolled to one side. The blanket buffeted and ballooned before settling down. From beneath came another snore. Zombies didn't snore. Her eyes caught sight of the white sneakers with rainbow laces. Chloe.

She was about to call out, to wake the nurse, but caught herself in time. There were three other rooms. She let the door swing closed and moved on to the rooms opposite, but each was empty. Her heart pounding louder than ever, she returned to the one occupied room.

"Chloe?" Maggs whispered and wondered why she was keeping her voice low. "Chloe!"

"Wah? What?" Chloe moaned, pulling the blanket away from her face.

"Chloe, wake up. Now!" Maggs said, as she turned back to face the corridor.

"Maggs? What is it? Who's sick?" the young nurse asked.

"Fern. She turned. She was infected. I had to kill her."

"What?" Chloe asked, swinging her legs off the treatment table. "Dead? Fern?"

"Yes. Infected. Who was she treating? Where's the patient?"

"What patient, Maggs? What happened?"

"That's what I'm trying to figure out. Focus, Chloe. Fern was infected. Someone infected her. Who was she treating tonight?"

"No one," Chloe said. "There hasn't been a patient since Reese sliced his hand open on a shovel this afternoon."

"Someone's infected," Maggs said. "There's another zombie in the building. We need to find it before one becomes a dozen."

"Fern's gone?" Chloe said, her voice catching.

"Yes. She's gone. We're still here. Steady yourself, now's not the time for tears. Why are you sleeping down here?"

"Oh, Georgie… It doesn't matter. I just wanted some quiet."

"Where are your weapons?"

"Upstairs."

"I can't hear any screaming, so that's a good thing," Maggs said. "Then again, no one heard me shout out. You didn't, did you?"

"No. If I had…"

"It doesn't matter," Maggs said, speaking to herself as much as Chloe. "We're going to the top floor. We'll wake Roy and Ric and the others, and then we're going room-by-room. We'll check each one, waking people as we go. But we'll ask them to stay in their rooms, with the doors locked. Everyone milling around isn't going to help right now. Follow me."

Halfway up the stairwell, she thought she heard screaming but couldn't tell if it came from above or below, or from inside her own mind. When she opened the door at the top of the stairs, she knew exactly where the screaming was coming from: everywhere. Shouts of fear and pain, and calls for help hung as heavy in the air as the iron tang of spilled blood. A figure in peach and tan PJs staggered out of a doorway halfway along the corridor, bent, and threw up.

"Ginger?"

Ginger waved away a hand as Ricardo followed her out of the room. At any other time, she might have mentioned his bright yellow shorts, but they, like his legs, were covered in blood. He shifted Ginger's crossbow into the hand with the masonry pick, and pulled the door closed.

"Roy and Kayleigh turned," he said simply. "All three are dead."

Maggs closed her eyes, but only for a heartbeat. Now wasn't the time. "Fern turned, downstairs," she said. "Check each room. Clear the floor."

Ricardo held the crossbow out to Ginger. She stiffened as a scream came from farther down the corridor.

"Get armed," Ricardo said, and jogged off towards danger.

Before Maggs could stop her, Chloe had crossed to the door of the room she shared with Georgie.

"Wait!" Maggs said, but Chloe had opened the door. Inside was a chaotic jumble of clothes and gear, but there was no sign of Georgie.

"Grab a weapon," Maggs said. Chloe took one of the crossbows. Outside in the corridor, she saw Marshall almost fly out of a room, hitting the wall opposite. He was covered in blood, but he still had an axe in his hand.

"Marshall, are you okay?"

His eyes came into focus. "It's clear," he said, straightening his shoulders, before turning his back and moving on. Maggs went to the next room.

Still in their night attire, Glen and Eric, two Michigander actuaries who, last year, had been enjoying an extended Valentine's vacation in Quebec, lay curled and twisted in their sheets, now drenched with blood. Glen was already dead. As she opened the door, Eric, now undead, began thrashing, but the sheets hampered his movement. With each twist or turn, the sheets grew tighter around them both. A jet of blood pulsed from the exposed artery in Glen's neck, splashing against the wall. Maggs swung, but Eric's hand finally ripped through the sheet, and Maggs's axe slammed down on Glen's chest, breaking bone and spraying blood from the corpse. She screamed. Eric reached out. She dragged the blade free and swung again. This time, her aim was true.

Before she could catch her breath, a scream came from outside. She pulled her axe clear, turned, and saw Chloe in the doorway, her eyes wide.

"Look at me, Chloe!" Maggs said. "Look at me! Load that crossbow. Then get your go-bag. Get Georgie's too, and Marshall's, and mine, and go wait by the door to the stairwell, okay? You wait there. Get the bags. Go to the stairs. Go on."

Maggs moved on to the next room as Gordon came out of the one opposite. The old miner was dripping with blood. Everyone was.

"It's clear," he said. "Don't open the door. That was my room."

Maggs nodded. The screaming had subsided into sobs, but the corridor was slowly filling with the survivors. And they were all looking to her.

"Get weapons, and get your go-bags," she said. "If you don't have one, take one from the dead. We'll cry later. We'll mourn later. We'll figure out what's going on *later*. Right now, we need to get out of here alive. Go on, weapons and go-bags. You've got three minutes."

Hats was sitting atop the bags Chloe had brought to the doorway, looking as confused and terrified as the rest of them. Ricardo and Ginger joined them by the door to the stairwell.

"Where's Georgie?" Ginger asked.

"I don't know," Chloe said. "We had a… a fight. It was stupid. I went downstairs to sleep. I don't know where she is. Her shoes are gone."

"We'll find her," Maggs said. "Chloe, you're the doc. Bandage wounds. Do what you can. Yvette. Good, you're alive. You help Chloe."

"Here, Chloe," Ricardo said, fishing a compact Beretta out of his bag. "In case."

Chloe nodded her thanks.

"Do you have any more of those?" Maggs asked.

"Just that one. I kept it, in case."

Maggs nodded, not needing to ask which specific case, since it was all around them. "One floor at a time. Clear the rooms. Gather any bottles of drinking water. Leave everything else."

"I'll lead," Ricardo said.

Chapter 35 - The Scent of Springtime
The Laurel Hills Spa and Resort

Already knowing what they'd find on the floor below, she followed Ricardo and Ginger down the stairs. There were twelve people behind her, the only survivors of the sanitation, medical, and scouting crews. They were people who'd volunteered for unpleasant work. She trusted them. The next floor down had been claimed by Martin, Ezra, and Brass, and their cronies. She held little hope they'd put up much of a fight.

Ricardo paused at the landing to brace himself.

Gordon pushed past Maggs. "Me next," he said, his face as bleak as granite. She knew he'd been sharing with Evelyn and trying to keep it quiet. Why they'd wanted to maintain the secrecy was a mystery, though her fate wasn't; it was written in red all over his clothes.

Ricardo pushed the door open. Ginger was just behind him, and then Gordon. They set the pace, and it suddenly became a sprint. The stairwell opened onto a short landing with a closed supply closet immediately opposite. Ricardo and Ginger immediately went right, towards the cluster of zombies blocking the corridor.

"Go left, Gordon," Maggs said as she dumped her bag by the utility cupboard. Ricardo moved back and forth, hacking, cleaving, hewing. Ginger, braced against the wall, seemed able to judge his movements. Her crossbow twanged. Bodies crumpled. It was over in seconds. Beyond was a barricade of tables and other furniture, with Dimitri and André standing on the far side.

"Dump your bags here," Maggs said to the people filling up the hallway. "Marshall, guard the stairwell. Everyone else, we have to check each room. Every last one."

She jogged down the corridor, glancing inside the open doors only long enough to see the blood. The last door before the corridor became a T-junction leading to the suites was closed. She tried the handle, and found it locked. With the keycard system defunct, the rooms could only be locked from inside, so someone or something was still in there. She slammed the axe down on the lock. Two blows, and it broke. Around her, the sound of screaming was joined by calls to hold on, and of metal crushing flesh and bone. She hacked down, letting the blade bite deep into the laminated wood. The veneer cracked, the grey insulating foam beneath crumbled. She hurled her shoulder into the door, and it moved, but only an inch, and then shoved back.

"Oh, no." She threw herself at the door again. This time it flew open, the zombie behind it, off-balance, fell to the floor. Maggs ran forward, swinging the tomahawk down. Her first blow was on target, but it didn't have enough force, only peeling a slice from the face of Eloise, the opinionated nineteen-year-old who was allergic to shellfish, grapefruit, and hard work. Maggs raised the axe again, automatically extending her left arm as a counterbalance, which put it too close to Eloise. Her undead fingers curled around Maggs's arm with an iron grip that kept squeezing. Maggs tried to tug her hand free, but that only pulled Eloise upward. Now half-crouched, the zombie scratched at Maggs's leg. Her mouth bit down, even as Maggs again tugged her hand back. Eloise's teeth ripped clear two inches of skin before Maggs thumped the tomahawk's pommel down onto Eloise's forehead. Maggs pushed herself upright, tugging her hand free, spinning the zombie around before bringing the axe down one last time, onto the back of the young woman's skull.

"Damn it, Eloise!" she said, looking at her hand. Blood was already dripping down to her fingers. She staggered back to the doorway, belatedly remembering to look for other danger in the room; few people slept alone, but there was no one, only two feet, lying motionless on the far side of the bed.

She took a few steps forward to see who was on the other side of the bed. A sound came from behind the bathroom door. Unlike in the staff quarters, these were proper hotel rooms, fully equipped with insanely lavish baths and showers. Without functioning plumbing, they'd been reallocated as sleeping space, and there had definitely been a sound from behind the door.

Wincing as she used her injured hand to try the door, she felt weariness beginning to overtake her. "All right, here we go," she said.

"Who's there?" came a reply from inside the bathroom. A male voice she couldn't place.

"It's Maggs. I just killed Eloise. Come out. It's over."

She backed away, tempted to sit on the bed, but it was coated in blood. Lying on the far side was Mary-Anne. Probably. Too much of her face was missing to be absolutely certain. The bathroom door opened. Francois, the twenty-year-old from Trois-Rivières, who was constantly harping on about his trip to Paris last year, peeked out.

"Grab your go-bag, and let's move," Maggs said. "The whole building is like this room."

"What? What happened?" he asked.

"Zombies," she said. "Move, or be left behind."

She walked out into the corridor. Once again, the battle seemed to be winding down. She headed back to the stairwell where Chloe was already bandaging wounds.

"What happened to your hand?" Yvette asked.

"A bite," Maggs said. "Find me a bandage."

The bleach came first, and then the bandage, but oh, did that bleach sting.

"Maggs." Ginger came running up. "It's Brass. He's dead."

"Good," Maggs said, and didn't feel a moment's regret. "Martin?"

"He's gone. We're missing a few others."

"Right. So it was Martin who joined Ezra."

"They were behind this?"

"Probably. Get everyone lined up. Everyone must be armed. And find —" She stopped herself. She'd been about to ask for Roy, but he was dead. She couldn't think of him now, nor of Kayleigh, and certainly not of the baby. "Get everyone ready."

She leaned against the wall, trying to ignore the pain as she willed her brain to turn the disaster into a problem that had a solution. Most people slept on the ground floor, in the meeting rooms, the sauna, the coffee-lounge, and in the suite of offices with their view of the bins. Some of the kitchen staff slept in the basement, and those who wanted to be first in line for breakfast unrolled a sleeping mat in the restaurant. In other words, few slept alone, so the ground floor would be far worse than up here.

"Marshall, has anyone tried to come upstairs?"

"No. No one," he said.

Yes, the ground floor would be far worse.

She looked around to see Gordon watching her, regret and rage battling for control of his face. "We need to get outside," she said. "Regroup in the parking lot, then just a small team goes back in to pull out the survivors. There'll be some in washrooms, closets, places like that where they can't do anything but stay put. And then we burn the house down."

"Martin fled," Gordon said. "He was suspiciously quiet last night."

"I know. But we'll talk about that later." She turned back to the growing group by the door. "Yvette, you stay with Chloe. Marshall, you watch them both, and watch any sick people with them, anyone who's been bitten. You okay with that?"

"Sure."

"Really?" she asked, grabbing his arm, looking him in the eyes. She didn't want to spell out what he would have to do. She didn't need to. All youth and innocence had vanished from his face. He understood.

"Gordon, bring up the rear, make sure no one is left behind. Okay. We're going downstairs and outside to the parking lot. I'll lead the way."

"No," Ricardo said as he pushed past her. Wordlessly, Maggs followed him down the steps, forcing herself to concentrate, rather than think, to listen rather than regret.

The entrance lobby was empty except for Fern's corpse. Their small band of survivors staggered out of the stairwell, as bloody and weary as any zombie who had ever arisen. She motioned for them to be quiet. Ricardo stepped back from the front door.

"It's blocked. We need to break it down."

"Shh," Maggs said. There wasn't much noise coming from the rest of the building. The doors had muffled most of the sound, but she was sure there weren't any more screams. "Two hundred people slept down here. That could mean two hundred zombies. No noise. We'll try the back door. The fallback point is the stairwell."

She didn't wait for Ricardo, but led the way, axe raised, past the corridor with the bathrooms, and the stockroom with its ladder down to the basement. And there it was, the back door. Escape. Safety. Unless it was blocked. Before that worry had time to settle, the door swung inward. Outside, illuminated by the night-time emergency lights, covered in blood, stood Georgie.

"No," Maggs whispered, even as she drew back the tomahawk, ready to strike.

"It's me!" Georgie said. "Maggs, it's me."

Chapter 36 - Leaving it All Behind
The Laurel Hills Spa and Resort

"Were you bitten?" Maggs asked.

"Bitten?" Georgie asked. "What do you mean?"

"Everyone inside has turned into zombies. Everyone except us," Maggs said. "Whose blood is that?"

Georgie pointed to the ground, just outside. A body lay there, a knife embedded in his neck. His face was hidden beneath a gas mask, but Maggs caught the glint of a silver badge on his belt. She bent down to pull the respirator free, and saw a face she recognised: Sydney, Sheriff Dalton's deputy.

"There are soldiers at the front entrance, and at the gate," Georgie said.

Chloe pushed her way through the crowd but stopped short at the sight of the blood.

"Hey," Georgie said. "Look, I'm sorry."

"Me, too," Chloe said.

"Later," Maggs said. "What did you see, Georgie?"

"People. Armed. Maybe ten to fifteen of them. Five went inside earlier, but came out again about ten minutes later. The others stayed on guard, outside. They've sealed up the front doors. Our guards are dead. I found Lonnie's body."

Maggs looked again at the blood coating her. "Did you see Dalton?"

"No, but I saw Brewster," Georgie said.

Maggs looked at the cracked foam, barely dried, sprayed around the door. She'd seen that before. She breathed deeply. The smell of cherry blossom was finally beginning to fade. "Shh," she hissed at the increasingly agitated crowd. "Georgie, did you go to the parking lot?"

"No. The two other soldiers who were here headed in that direction. That's why I thought I should try to get inside."

"Gordon, you heard that?"

"I did. Ten to fifteen of them in total, at least two around the back."

"New plan," Maggs said. "Clear the parking lot, get out through the rear gate, using the gasoline we've got stashed. What do you think?"

Gordon walked over to the corpse and took the sidearm from Sydney's holster. After a moment's hesitation, he handed it to Georgie. "Guard the door. Don't let anyone get close. If we hear shooting, we'll come running. If *you* hear shooting, take to the woods. Ric, Ginger, with me. I'll need a runner."

"I'll do it," Yvette said.

"No, I—" Gordon began.

"I can do it," Yvette said. "I really can. I'm good at running."

"Alright." Gordon nodded to Maggs, and led the others away.

Maggs turned to Georgie. "Bring that body inside. Close the door, but don't let it lock. When Yvette comes and tells you it's safe, lead everyone to the parking lot. As soon as you can, as soon as Gordon says it's clear, drive away. I'll be there or I won't, but you don't wait."

"Where are you going?"

A muffled scream came from somewhere deep inside the building. With such thick doors, it had to be close.

"Don't wait, Georgie. Please. There's no time to explain. Just make sure they're safe."

Georgie grimaced, but nodded. Maggs made her way along the small group of survivors, getting them to line up on either side of the corridor. At the end, she found Marshall, with Hats at his feet, both of them with their hackles up, staring towards the horror still unfolding behind the walls.

"Pick Hats up," she whispered. "I don't want him following me."

"Where are you going?" Marshall asked.

She shook her head. There was no time to waste on explanations. She kept walking. Another sound came from somewhere inside the building. Not a scream, a faint knocking with a rhythmic pattern, like a signal being tapped on pipes, but it ended before she could decipher a meaning. There was nothing she could do for the handful of people still alive. There was so little time, and she didn't know how much. The scent of cherry blossom was still strong here. She had to know.

She walked to the end of the corridor where the false wall had been installed, and to the hatch leading down into the basement. There was a body by the hatch. Mario, the fry-cook from Brooklyn, who had been a decent chef when he'd had the ingredients. Appallingly short temper, though. His throat had been cut.

The hatch was open, but there were no lights on below. Some of the kitchen crew had slept down there. She shone her light down the ladder. There was no movement. No sound. She had to know. She scrambled down the ladder, dropping the last three rungs, ignoring the hard slap of her feet on concrete as she spun the light around the chamber. No movement. No zombies. But there were bodies.

Orlando, Josephine, and Sara were all dead, shot, but by crossbow. The bolts still protruded from their chests. All three were dressed for the outdoors, and there were five bags in a pile near the ladder. Sara wasn't a member of the kitchen crew, but had been one of Ezra's work-shy acolytes. She glanced at one of the packed bags, but she didn't need to look inside to know what it contained. The basement had been their food store, after all.

This minor betrayal no longer mattered. She made her way through the shelves to the air pump. There, she found what she'd been expecting. What she'd been dreading. An orange pressurised canister, taped into place, with more tape around the seal and a pipe leading from the nozzle into the air pump. They hadn't attempted to hide it, or even take away the tools. Those lay where they'd been placed. Presumably to collect later. She knew what it was. She knew who. Not how this had been created, and not why. This was a war crime. Worse. A peace crime. A true crime against humanity, what little of it was left. As her anger turned to rage, it was fuelled by a clink of metal behind her.

She spun around, shining her light onto a face she had grown to loathe: Martin. Her tomahawk was already raised, and she was ready to swing.

"Maggs, please, no," he said. "It's me! It's just me."

She stopped her arm, bringing it back, but she didn't lower her axe.

"What are you doing down here?" she asked.

"Hiding. They came down with crossbows," he said, his words almost a whimper. "Special Forces, they must have been. They had respirators and body armour. Who are they?"

She finally lowered the hatchet. "We're leaving. Follow me, or don't, but don't say another word. Silence is our only protection."

She walked back to the ladder, pausing only to pick up one of the bags. She didn't check to see if he followed.

When she reached the back door, the corridor was empty except for Georgie, and for Sydney's corpse. The door was closed, and Georgie had her ear pressed against it. She waved Maggs into silence. Maggs stopped moving, waiting until Georgie stepped back.

"I think we're okay," Georgie said. "They were walking about."

There wasn't time to ask for details. "Did everyone get to the parking lot safe?"

"Yes, but there were three by the back gate. We have to hurry. I brought gasoline."

Maggs looked down at the can standing next to the door, then back along the corridor, and beyond Martin who had a bag on his back and another in his hands. The building was far from silent, though she couldn't be certain that any of the sounds came from the living. Nevertheless, there could be survivors still. If they did survive the undead, they'd be murdered by Dalton's people. She couldn't save them. She wasn't sure she could save anyone, but she had to try, even if that meant turning a nightmare into a burning hell for anyone trapped inside. She grabbed the fuel can. "Matches?"

Georgie held out a box and gestured towards Martin. "Is he coming with us?"

"If he can keep up." Maggs splashed some gas on the walls, then lit a match, letting the book catch before dropping it. A blossom of flame crinkled the cheap paint. "Lead the way," she said, and didn't check to see if Martin was following. Georgie moved slowly at first. When she began to run, so did Maggs, struggling through the long grass, the muddy path, and to the SUV. The trunk was open. She fell into the back, letting hands pull her properly aboard.

"Wait for Ginger," she heard Yvette say as Maggs tried to sit more upright. Martin was aboard, also crammed into the trunk. Georgie hadn't got into the SUV. She guessed she'd gone for her bus. A moment later, an engine came on, and then another.

"Here we go," Marshall said. The SUV began to move.

There were ten passengers crammed into the car. But between their heads, she saw Marshall behind the wheel. Everyone else was trying to look out, but she hung her head. She'd seen enough. The car jerked forward, stopped, moved again. She closed her eyes. The car bounced and rocked, swinging left then right, and then accelerated.

"We're through the gate," Yvette said.

Maggs opened her eyes. She'd thought they'd already reached the highway. The car swerved left. She closed her eyes again, but this time only briefly. A plaintive miaow caused her to look up. Hats had clambered across the seats and looked as worried as the rest of them.

"Oh, come here." She pulled the cat onto her lap and buried her face in his fur so that no one would see her tears.

Fern. They'd not got along at first. Not after Maggs had explained exactly why she'd thought a zoo would be a good spot to hide from the undead. Fern had strong views that some animals were never food for people. But they'd grown to respect one another's abilities, and at some point, they'd become each other's confidantes. Roy was similar. She'd not trusted him at first, seeing him as just another who didn't think the brain was a muscle. He was kind and sweet, a poet at heart, responsible beyond his years. She'd loved Kayleigh from the first moment they'd met. Despite everything that the woman had been through, she'd thrown herself into helping without complaint. And there was the baby, of course.

"Which way, Maggs?" Marshall called out.

She blinked away the tears, and slowly pulled herself up, then forward a little. Those in the back seat eased out of the way so she could see a fraction more of the windscreen. "Do you have a compass?"

"Yes," Yvette called.

"Keep going the way we're going," she said.

"It's a T-junction," Marshall said, now slowing the SUV.

"Are we in the lead?"

"Yes."

"Go south," she said.

"Left," Yvette said. "It's more southish."

Maggs leaned back. "Pick south over north and west over east. Only stop at the top of a hill, but don't stop yet. Reset the odometer. We need to be at least thirty kilometres away."

"Got it," Marshall said before lowering his voice, though not low enough. "What's the odometer?"

Maggs looked over at Martin. For once, he had nothing to say. Her eyes fell on the two bags he'd brought with him, and then the one she'd picked up in the cellar. That could wait. She forced her eyes to scan the rest of the trunk's contents. It was just their expedition gear. Chains, ropes, blankets, a spare tyre, a ten-gallon water jug that was half empty, and a few spare tools. It wasn't much compared with what they'd found, and nothing at all compared with what they were leaving behind.

Chapter 37 - The End of Democracy
Lewis County

"Is this okay, Maggs?" Marshall asked as he pulled to a halt. She couldn't see far beyond the windows, but he'd already stopped.

"Perfect," she said. "Everyone, use a tree. I don't know when we'll next stop. But don't go far. We can't afford modesty right now. If anyone wants to take their chances alone, now's the time to leave. Otherwise, we'll be rolling again in ten minutes."

Marshall pressed the trunk release. A gust of fresh spring air swept through the car. Maggs got out and took the bag she'd brought with her. She waved at the van just behind, which Catherine was driving.

"It's a ten-minute break. Engines and lights off, I want to check for pursuit. Anyone can leave if they want. Pass the word down the line. Marshall!"

"He's busy, Maggs," Yvette said.

"Ah, when he's free, tell him to climb up to the roof of the van, to watch for lights following us."

"I'll do it," Yvette said.

"Thank you." She dropped the bag where she was standing, closed her eyes, and bowed her head.

"You alright?" Gordon asked.

She dragged her chin upwards, and realised she'd been about to fall asleep on her feet. "Utterly spent," she said. "I'm too tired to even throw up."

"You burned the place down?"

"I started a fire. I didn't wait to see if it caught. On the slim chance they came to rob us, I figured they might be too busy stealing our food to follow us. But it's a slim chance. Very slim. Were the cars guarded?"

"Not really. There were three of them near the back gate. Two with gas masks, one without. Armed, of course." He reached into his coat pocket and took out a pistol, offering it to her.

"No, you'd make better use of it."

"Hey, Maggs, is there a plan?" Ginger asked, coming over to join them.

"Continue driving south and west," Maggs said. "When dawn arrives, we'll find somewhere to stop. We'll rest there and take stock."

Chloe joined their group. "There's fifty-seven of us crammed into six vehicles. Everyone's got a few cuts and scrapes. Infection is going to be a real issue. Both kinds."

"We don't need to worry about anyone turning. Trust me. Yvette, do you see anything from up there?"

"No. Nothing. There might be a glow on the horizon. I think that's the spa."

"Then we're still too close. Ginger, swap with Yvette for a minute, and then we'll leave. We've all got to be strong, just for a few hours more, just until dawn."

Maggs returned to the SUV's trunk for the next part of the ride, bringing the backpack with her. Martin returned there, too.

"You didn't want to take a proper seat?" he asked as they pulled away.

"And that question sums up why you're a terrible leader," she said. "I should have challenged you long ago, and I'll regret to the end that I didn't. Why didn't you walk away just now? You could have."

"I was chosen to lead these people, and I will," he said.

"Really?" She opened the bag she'd picked up in the cellar and began rummaging through it. "Clothes. Two tubs of nutrient powder, strawberry flavour. Matches. A flashlight. Wrench. Water bottle. A can of strawberries from the compound. Fishing line and hooks. Some kitchen knives, a small saucepan, and a mug." She put the bag down. "There's a few more things, but I think we *all* get the idea." She paused for Martin to realise that everyone in the car was listening. "There were five bags in the basement, Martin. Five bags, four bodies, and you. What are in those two bags you have?"

"I don't know. I saw you pick one up and thought I should do the same."

"Really?" She reached over and picked up the nearest. For a second, Martin tugged back. She growled, like she'd sometimes had to do with her old cat, Boots, when he refused to climb out of her work shoes. Hats hissed. Martin let go. Maggs passed it forward to those in the backseat. "And the other one."

This time, she held out her hand, making him hand it over. She passed it forward before sitting back. "When did you go down to the basement, Martin?" she asked.

"When I heard the screaming, the same as everyone else."

"You said you saw the people who killed everyone in the basement," Maggs said. "You were there before the attack happened. I'm not going to criticise you for hiding. Against superior numbers, what else could you do? But you were there before the attack. You and the others were planning to leave during the night."

"Oh, give it a rest. I was hiding. What does it matter?"

"There's some clothes, some food, and there's a gun in here," Francois said.

"A gun? Pass it to Yvette."

"Um… I'd rather you didn't," Yvette said.

"Just make sure the safety is on and you'll be fine," Maggs said.

"That's not my bag," Martin said.

"You were leaving," Maggs said. "You and those other four were taking food with you. Was the plan to meet up with Ezra? Or were you cutting out on your own?"

"I don't know what you're talking about."

"Want me to stop?" Marshall asked.

"No, keep going," Maggs said. "Martin, this is the one time you could come clean and no one would care. It doesn't matter now."

"Exactly. It doesn't matter."

"You think you know what's going on, what just happened, but you don't," she said. "Ah, what's the point?" She closed her eyes. She didn't find sleep, and certainly didn't find peace. There wasn't even time to properly wallow in sorrow before they stopped again.

"You better see this, Maggs," Marshall said as he popped the trunk. She got out and walked around to the front of the car. Below, dark peaks jutted from uneven ground, glinting and glistening in the moonlight like stars fallen to earth.

It took a minute for her eyes to adjust to the gloom. "Are they abandoned cars?"

"Thousands," Yvette whispered. "I think that's the interstate. We'll never get through."

"Show me a map," Maggs said.

Marshall went to fetch one while the other vehicles parked up and the drivers and a few passengers got out. Marshall laid the map on the hood of the SUV, where it was almost too high for Maggs to view.

"Hold the light higher please, Yvette."

"Trouble?" Gordon asked.

"I'm not sure," Maggs said. "This is Interstate Five, and we must be south of Centralia. The Columbia River is in the south. Puget Sound is in the north, the Cascades are in the east. Those act like walls, and we must assume Dalton will search inside them, and hope he doesn't look beyond. So if we cross the interstate, we'll be safer. And if we can cross the Columbia, we'll be even safer still. There'll be too many urban ruins for him to follow us."

"So it *was* Dalton?" Gordon asked.

"I don't know," Maggs said. "We can talk about that later. For now, we've just got to get somewhere safe. If such a place exists."

As they were forging a trail through the mechanical graveyard atop the old interstate, two tyres were punctured by the broken debris, hidden beneath the ashy mud. The second time they stopped to change a tyre, dogs appeared. Their group was too large for the hounds to dare approach too close, but they lurked among the burned-out wrecks, eagerly plotting their next dinner. Even more exhausted than before, their clothes filthy as well as bloody, they finally escaped the highway.

With the skies beginning to grey, they crossed the Newaukum River. Maggs decided they'd travelled far enough. Just beyond the bridge, a large farmhouse with an even larger barn looked promising, in that it hadn't been barricaded or burned down.

"Here, pull in here," she said, dredging up a last joule of energy. Wearily, she climbed out, counting the other vehicles as they pulled in beside the SUV. "Ric, Ginger, check the house. Gordon, Marshall, the barn."

One by one, the vehicles emptied. Everyone stretched. No one strayed far, even after Gordon waved the all-clear.

"It's been a long day, a long night," Maggs said, raising her hands for everyone's attention. "There's a lot to talk about, and a lot to do. We'll stay here for a few hours, get our breath, and then go on."

"Go where?" Catherine asked.

"Across the Columbia River, into Oregon. West would take us to the ocean. Northwest leads to the national park, where we would effectively be trapped. There could be some survivors there, but that only means any obvious sources of food and fuel will be gone. Northeast is, eventually, Canada, but Seattle is first, and it's radioactive."

"According to Dalton," Martin said. "Your friend, the sheriff, was behind this, wasn't he? That's what everyone's saying."

Maggs mentally stamped down on her rising rage as an alternative to stamping down on Martin's face. "First, before anything else, we need to decide who is in charge. There has to be one person. One boss. No democracy. No votes. Just one person who undertakes the responsibility of making the decisions."

"Obviously, that's you," Ricardo said.

"Seconded," Gordon added quickly. "Let's put it to a vote. Those for?"

Most hands went up, some more eagerly than others.

Gordon turned to face Martin. "Anyone against?" he asked, a violent undercurrent in his tone.

"I abstain," Martin said.

"There you are, Maggs," Gordon said, "we've democratically voted to become a dictatorship."

"Okay, thank you. I will listen to what you say. I will ask for advice. But indecision could kill us. If anyone wants to leave, you're free to do so. As I was saying. North and west are out. East, back through the mountains, is the most attractive idea, but that's the region that Dalton patrols. We know of at least one farm that's part of his group and he hinted at more. Further east, there's that group that ambushed us before we crossed the mountains. They could be linked to Dalton. That leaves south as the safest of a bunch of bad options. We also need to consider our fuel supply. It won't last long. If we backtrack, we could end up running out back at the spa."

"How much fuel do we have?" André asked.

"I'm not sure," Maggs said. "I'll check that shortly."

"Was it Dalton?" Chloe asked.

"I think so, yes," Maggs said. "His driver, Sydney, was on guard outside the back door, and Georgie saw Brewster in their main group. You counted about fifteen of them?"

"About that, yes," Georgie said. "But it was dark. There could have been hundreds in the shadows."

"I saw the lights from two vehicles, and there were three guards at the back gate," Maggs said. "Fifteen sounds about right. Yes, we should assume this was Dalton. As for the how, they gassed us. They plugged a cylinder into the air circulation system, and then sprayed insulating foam around the outside doors to create a seal. They turned the zombie-virus into a poison gas."

"They aerosolised it?" Gordon asked.

"Yes, that's the word I was looking for. I guess they turned it into a pneumonic form. I'm no expert, but I'm not going to waste time trying to find some other explanation for the evidence. They aerosolised the zombie virus, so they have a lab, and people who know how to do that."

"The people who created the virus in the first place," Marshall said. "I bet it's them."

"It must be," Yvette said.

"Maybe, yes," Maggs said. "This must be what happened here in December to the people at the fortress compound. Dalton persuaded them to go to that mall, where he could more easily seal them in and infect them. *Murder* them, leaving the immune to be killed by their undead friends."

"How?" Marshall asked. "How do you get so many people to move?"

"You tell them you're the government, out of Cheyenne Mountain," Ginger said. "And that you've got an army that needs a secure redoubt to set up a new centre of government for the region."

"And then you pay them with fuel," Maggs said. "Or the promise of fuel, and the promise of rebuilding. Hope, really. That was their currency. It's depressing. There was a community here until recently. A thriving group of survivors. And Dalton killed them." She raised a hand for silence. "We'll have plenty of time to talk about it. Remember this. First, we can't trust anything Dalton told us. Second, they don't have many people. There were about fifteen at the spa. They clearly felt a group our size was a threat."

"The zombies that attacked us the other night. That was them, wasn't it?" Ginger said.

"I think so," Maggs said. "It seems too coincidental for that not to be the case. It must have been another group, like we found at the mall, that they unleashed. They probably wanted to make sure we had no ammo left before the main assault. And it gave Brewster the perfect opportunity to survey the place to see whether their gas could work there, or if we'd need encouragement to move."

"And if they'd asked us to move, we'd have done it, just like the people at the compound," Marshall said.

"Yes. There is no bright spot to this dismal business," Maggs said. "We've lost our friends. Our family. Revenge is impossible, so we must survive. That's the only way that we can make that sacrifice, that loss, mean anything. It's time to rest. Please try to sleep. If you can't, don't go out of sight of the building. You can keep your own water bottles, but hand in any other drinking water or food to… to Yvette."

"Me?"

"She's our new quartermaster. I'll talk with you afterwards, dear. We'll set out again in a few hours. That's all."

The air filled with questions, but she pretended they weren't for her. She took Yvette's arm and walked her over to the SUV.

"I can't be a quartermaster. I don't even know what that is," Yvette said.

"Keeping track of our supplies," Maggs said.

"Well, yes, I know the word. I mean I don't know how to do it."

"You can write and count? That's all you need. Kayleigh and Roy would have done it. I don't want to give the job to Ric, Ginger, Georgie, or Marshall because they have other jobs and know how to do them well. It has to be someone I trust. Do a stock take of what we have. We need to know how many meals we can make."

"I can do that."

"Good. Ask if you need help. Say if anyone's causing trouble."

Yvette hurried away. Feeling suddenly spent, Maggs made a pretence of inspecting their vehicles. Battered and muddy, they needed a wash. And so did she. Blood caked her clothes. There was so much, and she didn't remember whose it was. So many had died, and so quickly. Tatiana and Alex must have died while on duty. She could just picture Dalton driving up, professing some danger. Maybe pretending someone was sick, needing a doctor. They'd used crossbows inside, and that was worse than if they'd used guns. She doubted there were many soldiers in the world who trained with a crossbow. For the attack to be so quick, so nearly complete, they had to have done it before many times. The foam around the door. The inspection beforehand. The lies, so easily told. It was just so professional. So evil. Why?

Fern. Roy and Kayleigh, and their baby. She made it around the back of the van where she was out of sight, before she was unable to hold back the tears.

Chapter 38 - The Right Love at the Right Time
Lewis County, March 13th

It was dark when she woke from her second sleep of the day. She rose from the bed that Gordon had insisted she take and walked to the window, careful not to wake Yvette, Georgie, or Chloe, whom she'd insisted share the room. The rose-patterned curtains felt soft to the touch as she carefully drew them back far enough to see outside. The moon was high, and she guessed it was around two in the morning. It was so hard to tell without a watch, but hers was back in the spa. That was one more thing to add to their long list of items to find.

She'd woken from her first nap when the sun was just past its zenith. Call it noon, lunchtime, or whatever else you wanted, it had been time for departure, except Gordon had vanished. He'd left no word of where he was going, but Yvette had seen him wander off down the road. Since there was absolutely no way she'd leave him behind, she'd sent Ricardo and Ginger to look for him. Meanwhile, there was plenty that had to be done before nightfall, wherever they spent it. She'd asked Georgie to organise making a net out of whatever cord could be found, a team to gather more wood, and another to find every sealable container still in the house and boil enough river water to fill them.

It was two hours before Ginger, Ricardo, and Gordon returned. All three carried hefty bags filled with clothes and soap from nearby. She'd asked no questions, but announced they'd stay put for another day. Everyone went to the river to wash, and then to the fire to warm after they'd changed. By the evening, they'd caught enough fish to each get a mouthful of protein with their two bites of stewed vegetables. Herbs and spices had been added to the list of needed supplies.

Fifty-seven survivors. Six overpacked vehicles. Five loaded guns. The compact Beretta Ricardo had given to Chloe, and two nine-millimetres and two shotguns they'd taken from Dalton's men. Another eight firearms had been declared but remained unloaded. They only had forty-four rounds. But even if they'd had more, she wouldn't have shared the bullets out. Not yet. Today, shock and anger would turn to depression, and she wasn't sure how deep that would cut. They had three crossbows and fourteen bolts. They could make more of both, as soon as they found a small workshop, a hardware store, and, ideally, a craft shop that specialised in scale models. Until then, they'd reserve those for hunting.

Outside, she could see Gordon sitting on the bench by the budding apple tree between the house and the barn. As quietly as she could, she made her way downstairs and out to join him.

"Room for one more?" she asked as he turned to see who approached.

"Be my guest," he said.

"I wondered where Hats had got to," she said, nodding to the cat, curled up on Gordon's lap.

"He was lurking on the porch," Gordon said. "I don't think he can sleep, either."

She stretched out her legs, looking out at the moonlit meadow. "You can't head off like that again," she said.

"I won't. I'm sorry."

"We're not leaving anyone behind. If you wander off, others will do the same. We'll have to look for them. That puts everyone in danger."

"I know."

"Good. Then the talking-to is over. How are you doing?"

"As well as anyone," he said.

"That bad?"

He looked away and began to suck in a bracing lungful of nighttime air, but his breath caught. He swallowed. "You'd think loss would get easier with age," he said. "We've had enough practice."

"Not like this," Maggs said. "Even the outbreak doesn't compare."

"I suppose not. Back at the mine, when Tomas Herrick announced he was cutting south to get back to his family, and half the crew said they'd leave with him, I thought they'd be back in a week. I thought it would all be over by then." He sighed. "Haven't thought about them in a while. I guess, if the zeds didn't get them, the bombs did. So many people dead, and it never gets easier."

"No. We just get better at hiding it."

It was peaceful beneath the stars, and not so cold, now she had a fur-lined parka to wear, but her exposed ankles were feeling the chill.

"I think I loved her," Gordon said.

"Evelyn?"

"Hmm. I didn't think I'd love again. My first marriage was a complete train wreck. Three years, and we fought two days out of seven. We'd have fought the other five days if we'd not been working so hard we were barely in the same house. In the end, we were barely in the same bed. We married too soon. That was our mistake."

"But your second marriage lasted," she said.

"Joan was the love of my life. Or I thought she was. How did you know that he was the one?"

"Etienne?"

"Yes. You talk about him in a way that's straight out of the sagas. I've never known love like that. Or I didn't think I had. It's why the kids look up to you, especially Ginger and Ricardo. They've read about your kind of love. They've seen it in movies. It's what they all think love is, but I can't say I've known more than a handful who've ever got to live it."

Maggs fixed her stare at Orion, but she was the first to blink. "We were comfortable being together in silence. That's how I knew it would work. It was… ten days after I first met him. Maybe eleven. We wanted to be together, but it was too expensive to go out. Too cold, too, and we were exhausted. We got fries and poutine, and went back to my place. We were too tired to talk. He picked up a book and started reading. I did the same. We ate, and we read, mostly in silence, and we were both happy. That's when I knew."

"I should have tried that before tying the knot with Diane," Gordon said. "But I was twenty-three. All my friends were married. I thought getting hitched was what you had to do. Finish school, get a job, get married, have kids, work, retire, die. As if that's a life. Life is everything else. It's love. It's joy."

Maggs tugged at her trousers, trying to materialise an extra few inches of cloth. Whichever Victorian had invented socks that left the ankles exposed to the elements was a sadist. "It's pain, loss, and regret, too," she said.

"Isn't that the truth? Joan was amazing. We liked most of the same things, and we put up with the rest. Looking back, I think we were both happy. There were rough patches, but by and large, I had no regrets."

"It was cancer, wasn't it?"

"Four years ago. Long and lingering. In the end…" He stopped, leaned forward, bracing his hands on the bench. "Yes, in the end, I did actually feel relief."

"That her pain had stopped? It doesn't mean you loved her any less. Nor does you falling for Evelyn."

"No. I know. But at the wake, I felt a fraud surrounded by so much grief, and I was just glad it was over."

"And I bet you sobbed yourself to sleep many a night after that."

"Yes. And it was usually the nights."

"It usually is."

"But Evelyn… with her, I felt something different. I truly don't think I've ever experienced it before. I can't describe it, and that's how I know it was love."

"It burns quick, the candle that burns the brightest," Maggs said. "Ah, I don't know why people think I have the answers. I don't. Never have. I'm just an old gossip who can't stop reading. All love is different. There isn't true love, or one love, or any of that nonsense. There's just the right love, for the right person, at the right time. You found yours, at least twice. And there's no point in me saying you should be grateful for it. Not here and now when we've lost so much. Just remember some of your sadness is because we've lost absolutely everything at the same moment we thought we'd found salvation."

"Damn that man," Gordon said.

"Damn him indeed," Maggs said.

They sat in silence as the cold slowly crept up her legs.

"Why did he do it?" Gordon asked. "That's what I can't get my head around."

"Ultimately, evil," Maggs said. "However you want to define it, this is evil made manifest. It's not even a new horror. There wouldn't have had to be a ban on biological weapons if there weren't people eager to use them. How is a better question, but what I really want to know is the when and where of it all."

"I don't follow."

"Well, Dalton lied to us, but the most effective lies are those based in truth. He said they came from a military bunker. They used an aerosolised version of the zombie virus. The virus was unleashed on Manhattan, and no one was ready for it. The guy who was stuck in the spa before us, who built that false wall, worried about the attack being a prelude to invasion. If there was some foreign government behind it, where was the invasion? I think, or I wonder, whether the original virus was created by the Americans, and it got loose in Manhattan by accident."

"And Dalton's part of the group that created it? That makes as much sense as anything."

"But it doesn't help us. However it was created, and by who, Dalton decided to take it one step further, to make it even more deadly. There's no rationalising people like that."

"I suppose not. Are we moving on today?"

"I think so. We'll leave early. No breakfast. We'll drive slow, for about two hours, bringing us to within cycling distance of the river. Our goal is to find somewhere we can stay for a few days. So a village, I suppose. Somewhere with clothes and beds, and a stream. I doubt we'll get lucky with supplies again, so we'll fish and hunt. I'll scout the river, find a bridge across it, and somewhere on the other side we can camp. Then we'll look for fuel. A lot of it. Enough to get us to the border with Manitoba."

"The Peace Garden? I thought that might be our final destination."

"I don't know about final, but we need to warn them about Dalton."

Chapter 39 - The Slow Road to Nowhere
Lewis County

As dawn neared, the others came outside to silently greet the new day. When it was light enough for her to see her shadow, they left.

Away from the interstate, they navigated by compass, time, and mileage, but the frequent backtracking and delays while they cleared a partially blocked road made it difficult to keep track of direction and distance. By the ninth stop of the day, with the Columbia River nowhere in sight, anger was turning to frustration.

As Ricardo's team cleared the storm-dropped pines from across the one-lane track, Maggs waited by Georgie's camper, where Marshall was standing watch on the roof.

"See anything?" she asked.

"A really weird squirrel," he said.

"Why weird?"

"I think he's eating a leaf."

"Try to keep your eyes on the road," she said. Not that it would matter. Due to the dense trees and curving road, they could only see for fifty metres behind. Yesterday's stay at the farm had eliminated any lead they'd had. Between the tyre tracks and sawdust, they were leaving a trail a toddler could follow. Their best hope now was that Dalton wasn't pursuing them. If he were any normal foe, she would assume he would want to complete his murderous job and get revenge for the guards they'd killed. But no normal person would have done what he did.

She'd prefer it if she could lose herself in work, but Ginger had overruled her. Ginger was collecting water from a stream back beyond the last bend. Ricardo was removing the four giant pines that shouldn't have been left to grow so close to a road, even one as out of the way as this. And the two of them, and their teams, were having a race. The prize was first pick of the first luxuries they found when they stopped. Maggs was the judge. Ginger thought she'd been offering her a kindness, an excuse to rest, but Maggs needed the distraction as much as anyone.

"We'll never get anywhere if we continue like this," Martin said as he carried a few branches past. Ostensibly, he was talking to Catherine, though his barb was obviously aimed at her.

Maggs turned her face upwards to Marshall. "I'm going to take a look ahead."

"I don't think you're supposed to go far."

"I'll stay within earshot, don't worry," she said.

Maggs picked her way around Ricardo's teams, with their four axes and increasingly blunt machetes. They'd accidentally left a saw behind at their fourth stop, and broken the other at the sixth. She didn't blame anyone, but the earlier bonhomie over the faux contest had been replaced by a weary determination. They'd have to stop soon to find real food and better tools. In the soft soil next to the road, where a rainstorm had created a gulley, were unmistakable deer prints. That was one more thing they needed: a successful hunt. But for that, they needed to stop for longer than a few minutes. It would make them more vulnerable to being followed, but it just couldn't be helped.

A further forty metres down the road, a delivery van had been abandoned on the road. The back was facing her with its doors closed. Someone had taken a paintbrush to its once ubiquitous logo, covering the 'r' and 'v' in U-Drive. Trying to keep an eye on the rear of the van as well as the front, she slowly approached. In front of the van was an old yellow school bus. Another fifty metres down the road was a tan-coloured four-door sporting a moss toupée, facing her way.

It couldn't be an ambush, not a recent one, anyway. She made her way over to the back of the van. While the doors were pushed closed, the lock had been broken. Inside was a sodden mess of fabric and a stench that told her something had nested in there. She drew her tomahawk as she approached the cab. There was too much grime to see inside, so she slowly approached, knocking her axe against the door.

"Maggs?"

She jumped, spinning around, and saw Ginger coming towards her.

"You nearly scared the iron out of my blood," Maggs said.

"And you disappeared," Ginger said, pointing towards the bend, and the now hidden convoy. "What've you found?"

"I've only just begun looking," Maggs said. She reached out and tried the van's passenger door. At first she thought it was locked, but after a third tug on the handle, it screeched open. The odour that seeped out was a mix of jungle and flower shop, partly caused by the semi-dissolved box of laundry powder on the passenger seat.

"Yeesh, that's worse than a locker room," Ginger said. "I guess they ran out of soap. We can get the cars through here."

"Just a minute," Maggs said, her eyes on the school bus. The back window had broken, but that wasn't what had caught her eye. Two holes had been ripped through the chassis. She'd seen that type of damage often enough in recent months to recognise them as being made by bullets, except these shots seemed to have come from inside the bus. The exposed metal was rusted, further evidence that this particular tragedy had begun many months ago. She was tempted to ignore it, but an inner compulsion commanded her feet forward, and to the school bus's open door.

"Bones," she said as she carefully nudged them off the step and climbed inside. "Lots of bones."

Small bones, disarticulated, disordered, and discoloured by the elements. Even if a few weren't still clad in rotting fabric or everlasting plastic shoes, she could tell they were human. The teeth gave it away. She could only spot a few partial sets, all from the lower jaw. There wasn't a single intact skull.

"Bones," she said, backing out of the bus. "Zombies, I think. Shot." She shivered as she looked upwards in search of sunlight to clean her brain, but the trees had joined forces with the gathering clouds to block any hint of mental disinfectant.

"When was it?" Ginger asked.

"Early in the outbreak," Maggs said. "I guess the van contained their extra supplies. It's not worth asking any more questions. Some answers never bring peace."

Her eyes fell on the car. It had been travelling in the opposite direction. It took a moment for her to realise what that meant. She walked over to it. "But there are some questions still worth asking."

"Like?" Ginger asked.

"Well, if this was their scout car, and it went ahead, then turned around, coming back— oh."

She'd wiped her sleeve across the front window. In the driver seat, apparently still belted in, was a desiccated corpse. It was unmoving, but she couldn't tell if it was a zombie or not. She tapped the tomahawk on the glass. The corpse didn't react.

"Dead, I think," she said.

"Let's make sure," Ginger said, raising her crossbow. "You open the door."

Maggs pulled the door wide. Ginger fired. The bolt raised a cloud of dust as it shattered the mummified skull.

"Yeah, clear," Ginger said. "And I think it was dead. Probably a zombie, though. There's a shotgun on the passenger-side."

Maggs's attention had been caught by the thickness of the door. She moved it back and forth. The movement was smooth, and the hinges still took the weight. It was of a far sturdier construction than any of the vehicles she'd briefly driven during the last year. "I think the door's reinforced."

"It's a police car," Ginger said, leaning forward, getting far closer to the corpse than Maggs would have. "I mean, it's got a proper radio, controls for lights, and… oh, hang on, I can't reach. Wait. Ha!"

"What?" Maggs said as Ginger backed out of the car with a wallet in her hand.

"It's a police badge," she said, opening the wallet. "Oh. No. I was wrong. FBI."

Maggs took the wallet, but looked again at the tyres before dismissing the idea of salvaging the car. It would be too heavy, and thus uneconomical. Bulletproof or not, safety lay in getting away from here. In the distance, she heard engines restart. She looked down at the I.D. "Special Agent Naomi Trang."

"And here's her gun," Ginger said, fishing it out of the footwell. "With… four bullets left. She could have shot herself."

"She probably shot the zombies on the bus," Maggs said. "Did she leave a note?"

"I can't see one," Ginger said, pulling the trunk release. "You check the back seat. I'll see if she left any FBI snacks."

Not wanting to reach across the corpse, Maggs walked around to the passenger's side while Ginger went to the back.

"She's not an FBI agent," Ginger called out.

"What do you mean?" Maggs asked as she closed the door and made her way to the back of the car.

"What FBI agent carries fake I.D.s?" Ginger asked. "This one says she's a colonel in the USAF. And this one is for the Department of Energy."

Maggs took them and compared the photos to the FBI I.D. In the military I.D. she was wearing a uniform, but otherwise the pictures could have been taken on the same day. "The names are the same. Colonel Naomi Trang. Director Naomi Trang. If they were fake, why use the same name?"

"A lack of imagination?" Ginger suggested.

The SUV pulled up alongside. "Trouble?" Ricardo asked.

"Midas," Ginger said, which got a puzzled look from Ricardo as well as the passengers in the back. "You told me that's what miners say when they strike gold."

"Oh. Yeah, I did, didn't I?" Ricardo said, a smile creasing his lips.

"Well, it's what we shout now," Maggs said. "I don't know what we've found, but it looks like treasure. Let's get these bags aboard and get moving."

Chapter 40 - A New Hope
Vader

Maggs carried the bags into the SUV, partly to sort and partly to guard. There had been three in the back of Naomi Trang's car, not counting the fully automatic assault rifle, two heavily reinforced cans of gasoline, and a crate of bottled water. One bag contained ammo, smoke grenades, a gas mask, rope, and a bulletproof vest marked with the letters FBI. A second contained US military rations. The third was a go-bag, containing an assortment of survival supplies, a second handgun, a small fortune in worthless dollars, ten gold coins, and padded out with clothes that she hoped would fit her.

There wasn't anything personal in the bags, nor did any of the items look used. The FBI colonel, whoever she was, had died on her way from somewhere with supplies. Maggs took out the wallet again, this time looking beyond the FBI badge. There were two photos tucked inside, both of the same woman with a child. In one, it was a baby. In the other, a boy of around thirteen. She'd aged between the pictures, so it could be the same child, though it might as easily be a sibling. It seemed likely that she'd stopped because of the school bus. Had she known the people aboard, or had she thought she had? A school bus and a van; perhaps her kid had been on a camping trip during the outbreak, though taking kids camping in February seemed like a punishment rather than an education.

Behind the photo was a small, slim envelope, thicker than a credit card and a little larger than a postage stamp. Instead of glue on the flap, there was a rough edge. Where it would affix was a uniform pattern of slightly raised bumps. Inside was a red square of some waxy material and two minuscule strips of paper. Carefully, she extracted the paper. Both strips contained a string of letters and numbers. Belatedly, she thought to raise the red square to her nose and caught a lingering hint of petroleum. It was a fire-lighter. The numbers must be access codes, and Agent Trang had wanted a quick way to destroy them. A frisson of excitement rushed through her, but withered before it had a chance to properly bloom. There was no way of knowing what, or where, the codes were for.

She was about to give it up as one of the apocalypse's eternal mysteries when she turned the wax square over. There was writing in the wax. She held it up to the light, twisting it back and forth, but with the car jolting up and down, she couldn't make the characters out.

"Who has a pen? Something with ink?"

"Do you want to write to Etienne?" Yvette asked, handing her a blue gel glitter pen. "Marshall was telling me about how you won't ever give up looking for him."

"Ah, yes, no, that's not what I need the pen for. Thank you. Do you keep a journal?"

"Sort of," Yvette said. "I'm writing a book."

"Good for you. I tried a few times," Maggs said, as she began to carefully trace the letters. "I could never stop the characters morphing into people I knew. What's your book about?"

"An immortal. She doesn't have any special powers or anything, but she's just been alive forever, and keeps making mistakes. Like the wrong investments, so she's always broke."

"That sounds fun," Maggs said. "Definitely something I'd pick up. It'd be good for a book club, too. People would love to discuss how they would live such a life."

"Like there'll ever be any book clubs again."

"There's nothing stopping you setting up a book club of your own, or publishing the book yourself. The printing presses of the world are all sitting idle, just waiting to be used. Ah, Vader. It definitely says Vader. It must be another passcode. It's a string of numbers, and... I must be misreading this."

"Vader's a place," Marshall said from the front passenger seat where he had been unusually quiet. He waved the map. "It's not far from here."

"Really? How far?"

"Depends on where we are. Five kilometres maybe."

"Then that's our next destination."

The trees pulled back from the road, replaced with new meadows in which the warehouse-style barns were the only clue these had once been fields. Soon, those were replaced by erratic squares of deer-grazed lawn, with an occasional tree rising from an overgrown yard. The clapboard houses had boarded windows, and secured doors, but it was as ghostly a town as any they'd travelled through.

"Stop here," she said when she saw the tattered remains of a Stars and Stripes struggling in the breeze outside a small firehouse. An incomplete barricade ran around the building. Where the barricade was finished, it looked relatively sturdy, but the gaps were wide enough for vehicles to drive right through.

Maggs got out, directing the other vehicles to park while sneaking glances up and down the street.

"Gordon, check inside," Maggs said. "Ric, can you check the houses next door. Anyone not helping, please stand guard. Marshall, up on the roof, please."

He practically flew to the top of the increasingly battered fun-bus. Was he showing off? Probably. There were some instincts that not even the apocalypse could dim. Maggs let her hand rest on the tomahawk as she took in the firehouse's half-finished wall. Steel rebar had been inserted into the concrete of the parking lot, with pallets slid atop them, and cement poured inside.

"About a day's work, do you think?" she asked, though only Chloe was near, and she had her eyes closed.

The nurse blinked. "Sorry, Maggs. What was that?"

"Nothing, dear. You look tired. Sit down."

"I've been sitting too long," she said.

André came out of the firehouse with a grim expression on his face. "Empty. Abandoned," he said. "But Gordon says it's safe. You'll want to see for yourself."

"Everyone stay alert," Maggs said. "No one leaves the lot."

It took a minute for her eyes to adjust to the gloom inside the volunteer firehouse, and another for her brain to adjust to the disorder. Sleeping bags, yoga mats, and folding beds all lay disarrayed in the space where a fire truck should have been. Disarrayed, but not trampled.

"Someone had grand ideas," Gordon said, walking around a partition built between two roof-supporting pillars. "I counted nineteen cots, and another two in the office. The stove in the corner even has a bit of propane left in the tank. There are no bodies or signs of violence. I'd say the mess is because of an animal or two, sheltering here over winter, but come and see this."

Maggs followed him around the pillar to the beginnings of an emergency command centre. On a table, bolts, nuts, and unidentifiable lumps of scrap lay scattered atop a map of the region.

"They had plans," Gordon said, pointing at the map. "That's the road we approached on, and I think that bracket is supposed to be a barricade. Yes, grand plans, that came to nought."

"On that road, but maybe they built barricades in other places," Maggs said. "I don't think it matters. There's enough room to sleep inside, though I suspect we'll have a lot of volunteers for night guard duty. Yes, it's a good place to stay. Depending on what Ricardo finds."

The young miner had a puzzled look on his face when he returned to the firehouse parking lot. "The houses are empty," he said.

"And they've been searched," Ginger said. "Searched, tidied, and the doors have been wedged shut, but each has a big note saying they're unlocked so don't break them down."

"The note's faded," Ricardo said.

"That's… sensible," Maggs said. "So they're empty?"

"Not exactly," Ginger said. "Most of the cupboards are bare, and there's very little shredded packaging. I think the cans and boxes were used up, but the spices and herbs were left behind. So was this." She held up a small tin. "It's coffee."

The crowd, who'd been expecting more bad news, suddenly erupted into cheers that quickly faded into self-aware embarrassment.

"There's some tea, too," Ginger said.

"Yay!" Yvette said. On realising she was the only one who'd cheered this time, she blushed bright red. "What? I don't like coffee," she mumbled.

"We'll have a coffee break as soon as the water's boiled," Maggs said. "Whether we stay here longer will depend on what we find as we look around. The locals clearly abandoned the place almost as soon as they thought of defending it. But maybe not all. Gordon and Yvette, you're on coffee and tea duty. Ric and Ginger, fetch cups from the nearby houses, please. I'd like us to be civilised. And while you're at it, make a note of cushions and blankets, and anything else that'll make the night a bit more comfortable. Georgie, you're in charge of everyone else. I want our vehicles moved to block the gaps in the walls. Use whatever else is to hand to bolster the defences, but don't do anything that'll make it too hard to drive out of here in a hurry. After we've had a break, we'll need to fetch water, so Ginger, we'll want some containers. Off you go."

She went back inside to look again at the map. It really was a small town, but there were a few industrial premises nearby, a wastewater treatment plant, and there was a dam. It wasn't on the main map, but included in an insert in the top right-hand corner. Four large industrial units were situated right next to it, along with a series of notations probably indicating what type of chemical fire might ensue there. Her eyes lingered on the dam. A week ago, she'd have had everyone back into the cars and they'd be there almost faster than she'd be able to contain her excitement. Now, though, they had to get away from here. Far, far away. But first, they needed supplies. Fuel. Vehicles. Food. Agent Trang seemed to have them.

She picked up a pen, tracing the characters on the fire-lighter again. 1770 W-V RD, VADER. If RD stood for road, then it was definitely an address. Vader wasn't a big town. It only took a minute to locate Winlock-Vader Road.

"Midas," she said, circling the road on the map.

Chapter 41 - Beneath the Surface of a Quiet Town
Vader

Ricardo was waiting outside the door to the firehouse. He held out the shotgun they'd taken from Agent Trang's car. "I'm coming with you," he said.

"To where?" she asked, taking the gun.

"You haven't told me yet."

"Well, I'd be glad of the company," she said, and waved to Gordon who was acting as traffic control as their transport was brought behind the incomplete walls. "We're going to scout the town. We'll be about two hours," she called out. Gordon nodded, but was clearly distracted. Everyone else looked much the same, hence why it was taking an age just to move a few trucks a few metres. Yesterday, they'd been exhausted after the battle, and in shock. Though it was impossible to ignore the grief, to each thought had been silently added the caveat 'but I am alive'. Now, as they undertook tasks that would previously have been the responsibility of the recently deceased, the depth of their loss was starkly apparent.

They walked down to Main Street, which looked anything but. The small town's focus seemed to have shifted along with its fortunes, from north-south, to east-west. Like next to the firehouse, the wood-framed houses all had secured windows with notes left on the unlocked doors.

"Left here and then across the railroad," she said. "There's a river to the south of the firehouse. The railroad might be the best way to reach it. I'm not sure. The map wasn't exactly to scale, or up-to-date."

"Are we looking for water?"

"No, for the house the FBI agent carved into a fire-lighter," Maggs said. "Assuming it is a house, though this place looks too small for an FBI office."

"Perhaps it's one of those training facilities where they practiced storming airplanes," Ricardo said.

"Do they really have those, or were they just for the movies? Anywhere that big would be on a map, and would have been noted by the fire crew. No, I don't think it's that. It might not be anything to do with the FBI. Maybe it's a farm, or a friend's home. But she must have been coming from there, and she had guns and food in her car, so I'm hoping we might find what she left behind."

"Whoever left the notes on the houses' front doors would have found it first."

"But what can we do except look?"

They crossed the tracks, passing a cafe and a bar that, in a different universe, would have been a station house.

"Dog," Ricardo said.

To the south was a high fence, concealing an auto-parts warehouse. The dog, a tan-furred setter, had slunk out of a gap in the fence. It moved with deliberate caution, though it didn't appear interested in the interloping humans. The dog froze with its front left paw still raised. It suddenly turned, darted back under the fence, and out of sight.

"Dinner," Ricardo said.

The sound of paws on tarmac came from the left. A pack of dogs, no two of the same variety, bounded out of the trees from beyond the bar. Maggs raised the shotgun, but the dogs weren't aiming for them. They merely sprinted past, and into the fenced warehouse.

"Now I feel sorry for that first dog," Ricardo said.

"Well, better him than us," Maggs said as a clatter came from inside. "C'mon."

She kept the shotgun ready. Possibly, the dogs were playing. Probably, to them, humans were now indistinguishable from inedible zombies. But there was a chance that when their chase was done, they might remember they'd missed out on a potential snack.

The railway line seemed to mark the edge of town. Beyond lay the ubiquitous forests with only an occasional driveway disappearing into the vegetation marking where humanity had briefly marked their presence. There were no barricades or lookout towers. No signs of planting or wood collection. Despite the brush with the dogs, she'd not felt so wonderfully alone in weeks.

"It's nice out here," Ricardo said. "Reminds me of home. I'm going to ask Ginger to marry me."

Maggs recovered quickly from the seven-hundred-degree turn in conversation. "Oh. Good. That's very good."

"Yeah."

She waited to see if he'd go on, uncertain if he was looking for advice or for her blessing. "I think you're a great couple," she said, hedging her bets. Again silence settled, and she could tell it would stay there unless she dragged it aside. "When are you going to ask her?"

"I'm not sure."

"I don't think we've properly adjusted to Roy and Kayleigh's deaths," Maggs said. "I wouldn't rush it, but I wouldn't delay too long. A moment will come, and you'll know when it happens. There'll be no long engagement, though. After you propose, you'll get married the next time we see a church. If you wanted a church wedding."

"Oh. Yeah. I don't know," he said, seemingly regressing into a teenager.

"Perhaps when we get across the river," Maggs said. "We'll find a nice church, or a picturesque spot. We can find some proper clothes and have a ceremony. Assuming she says yes, of course."

"Right. Yes."

"Do you have a ring?"

He put a hand into his pocket and pulled out a small bag. "I've been collecting them. I'm not sure which one's best. I was going to ask Roy for advice."

"I'll look at them in a moment. I think this is the place."

A flash of forest hid the property from the roadside, with over two hundred metres between it and its neighbours. A low gate ran across the driveway, kept ajar by a mound of mulch. A forgotten chain was looped around the left-most railings, while a padlock rusted in the dirt where it had fallen. Ricardo pushed at the gate. The screech of metal rubbing itself raw woke a dozy pair of crows that angrily cawed as they swooped away to a more secluded perch. Maggs tightened her grip on the shotgun, and followed him up the drive. After ten metres of trees, the driveway took a steep left turn, taking them along an ominous avenue carpeted with fallen needles.

"Cameras," Ricardo said, pointing up at a tree.

"It looks like a bat box," Maggs said, squinting upwards.

"Bet it's a camera."

After the drive took another turn, a double garage lay before them, with an attached house just behind. A two-metre-high metal fence, with a rattan privacy screen, was anchored to one wall of the garage and ran around the property. Behind looked like just another two-storey clapboard, painted beige, albeit with smaller windows than most.

"The garage is locked," Ricardo said.

"Probably needs an entry code," Maggs said, pointing to a number pad next to the gate in the fence, and about three metres from the front door. She pushed at the gate. "But this one's open," she said, as it swung inwards with a coffin-creak screech.

Inside the fence was a struggling herb garden. It must have once been lovingly maintained, but between the fence and the house, the shadows were too long for it to thrive without care. The front door was broader than usual, and far more secure. A section of the wooden facade had been removed, revealing another number pad, this one digital, but again, the door was open.

"Hello?" Maggs called.

"Me first," Ricardo said, easing in front of her.

Maggs stepped back as he pushed the door open wide. Just inside was a second set of doors that appeared to be made of glass, but which were impossible to see through. He pushed down on the door handle. It clicked as it locked in place. He removed his hand, but the handle remained depressed. He pushed at the door. It didn't move. The lock clicked again, the handle bounced up, and the door juddered open, releasing a gust of stale air.

"Step back!" Maggs said, hurriedly tugging on his arm.

"What?" Ricardo said, pushing the door open fully even as he stepped back onto the stoop.

"I don't know, but there was a gas mask in the back of Agent Trang's car," she said. "And just remember what happened at the spa."

"We survived," Ricardo said. It was his turn to shout into the house. There was no response. "Want me to try again?"

"Let's go in."

The inner door was far thicker than she'd have expected. Disappointingly, it seemed to be the portal to a very ordinary home. There were photos on the wall, a side table holding a key-bowl and with a military-style backpack, a civilian duffel-bag, and an assault rifle leaning next to it.

"Hello?" Maggs called again, looking up the staircase that bent out of sight, then through the open door on the right, leading into a living room. There was no reply. She pointed to a closed door on the left. "That must lead to the garage. The door next to the staircase probably leads to the back of the house. You check upstairs, I'll look down here."

"Be careful," Ricardo said.

"The same to you," she said.

The living room was tidy and relatively clean. The good armchair had been turned away from the TV so that it now faced the window. The blinds were partially drawn, but even when open, they'd only see the fence and the treetops beyond. By the side of the chair were two neat stacks of books, one larger than the other. The shelves held ornaments, but she couldn't pin any to a specific place or culture. There were no used cups or bowls gathering mould, no attempt at a makeshift fire-pit, or any of the usual debris left behind by gone-tomorrow survivors.

Beyond the living room was an office space converted into storage. A desk was buried behind, and beneath, stacked plastic crates. Inside the nearest were coils of fishing line and lures, all brand new. At the back of the office, a door led into a conservatory filled with bamboo furniture, but it looked less used than the living room. A second door from the living room led into the kitchen, and it was there that she found him, hunched against the fridge, a first aid kit in his lap, the contents strewn about the floor.

"Ricardo!" she called. Instantly, the house shook to the sound of his heavy boots thumping across the floor and down the stairs. "In the kitchen. It's just a body," she added, opening the door connecting it to the entrance hall.

The man had been dead for a long time. His skin was dry and taut, almost mummified.

Maggs pointed to the torn shirt. "I think that's what killed him. A wound across the chest."

Ricardo used his masonry pick to poke the man's shoulder. Slowly, the corpse slid sideways to the floor. "Not a zombie."

"Well, no. How was upstairs?"

"Empty. Tidy. One bedroom looked used." He turned back to the body and gently pulled out the man's dog tags. "He was in the US Air Force. H. Schwartz."

"And the colonel was in the USAF. A few of the photos were pictures of a man in uniform. So… maybe." She stepped back, piecing the evidence together. "A t-shirt, so he died in summer. It looks like a savage swipe across the chest. An animal attack. Probably a bear rather than a dog."

"Could have been a big dog. A *very* big dog."

"But not a zombie. He made it back here, and died while trying to get to his medical kit." Maggs looked again at the corpse. "Naomi, the FBI colonel, had this address inscribed onto a wax fire-lighter, and with two codes."

"One each for the doors," Ricardo said as he opened one of the kitchen cabinets. "There's food, if you like rice."

"Absolutely," Maggs said. She walked over to the nearest cupboard. It contained enough cans for a month, if there was only one person eating them. Next to the sink were a single bowl, a single mug, and two spoons, left to air-dry on a towel. In the cupboard beneath the sink, the S-bend had been removed, and a bucket placed beneath the plug hole. In total, there was about a month's worth of groceries.

"This should last us two or three days," Maggs said. "That's good because hunting around here will be hard with that pack of dogs nearby."

"Or easy," Ricardo said as he opened the fridge. "Empty. Completely empty. And cleaned. Doesn't smell a bit."

"Makes sense, if he was here for a while," Maggs said, looking up at the ceiling. "But if he was here a while, he'd have had some lights on. There's no lanterns, no candles. I wonder if he had a generator. Let's check the garage."

Chapter 42 - Hank Schwarz
Vader

The garage was suspiciously neat. There was no car, but the winter tyres hanging on the wall looked as new as the tools on the rack. Between them, the large plastic barrels contained at least a hundred gallons of water, but that wasn't what immediately caught her eye. Against the rear wall was a workbench. It appeared to be made of oak and very heavy, except it was on a pivot, and had been swung out so it was ninety-degrees to the wall, revealing a sunken hatch in the floor.

"I didn't think the FBI went in for secret bunkers," Ricardo said.

"If they *were* FBI," Maggs said.

On the wall, where it would be hidden when the workbench was in its usual place, was a number pad. It looked digital, and, since the hall was on the other side of the wall, she guessed it was plugged into the same system as the front door.

"Weren't there some code numbers with the address?" Ricardo asked.

"Yes, there were," she said. She reached into her pocket, but then had a thought. With a crack from her knees, she knelt down, leaned forward, and reached for the hatch's handle. There was only the slightest resistance as she swung the hatch upwards. "Unlocked, but heavy," she said as Ricardo stepped forward to shine his light down the hole. She stepped back. "I suppose, without power, Mr Schwartz didn't want to get locked out."

"It looks clear." Ricardo shrugged off his pack.

"Ah, no, don't you even think about it," Maggs said. "I'll go down alone. If one of us has to dig the other out, you're the one with the pick."

The basement was only two metres below the floor. She scrabbled down as quickly as she could, her head pivoting left and right for danger. When she was half a metre from the bottom, she let herself drop.

"It's clear," she said, swinging her light about to double-check her assertion. "It runs under most of the house. It's definitely a bunker, not just a basement. No rooms. Just lots of shelves, a desk, some CCTV monitors… Oh, and a radio. No bed. No bathroom."

The shelves were on casters which could be rolled aside to access the ones behind. It had been left with the fourth set of shelves accessible, on which were weapons cases. They had no lock. The first contained a neat row of shotguns, still smelling faintly of oil. Two were missing. On the shelf above were assault rifles, with handguns below.

"We've got guns down here. At least nine assault rifles. Eight shotguns. And enough ammo to equip an army."

"Agent Trang had a shotgun and rifle," Ricardo called back.

"She did," Maggs said as she rolled the shelves aside. "Food. Military rations. The kind with the self-heating chemicals inside." She left the shelves and walked over to the desk. It was flat pack, wooden, and probably not military issue. Nor was the red-velvet padded chair next to it. Mr Schwarz must have spent enough time in the bunker to think it was worth acquiring a comfortable chair. Probably for when he was sat in front of the radio. Next to the radio were three envelopes. One addressed to Naomi, one to Micheal, and a third to Colonel Spitzer. She pocketed those, and looked around for any other message or logbook, but found nothing. She returned to the ladder.

"Coming up," she said.

When she reached the top, she brushed herself off, though there was even less dust in the basement than in the house.

"There should be a fuel tank," she said. "Probably at the edge of the property. See if you can find it." She held up the letters. "I have some reading to do."

As he went outside, she returned to the living room, wishing she'd had time to boil some water for coffee. She sat in the chair, testing the springs. Definitely well-used. She now understood the furniture and decor. The only time she'd seen the style before had been in the new-development model homes she and Etienne had looked at, briefly, about fifteen years ago. Six months after he'd been promoted to crew manager, and nine months after she'd jumped to the executive ranks, they'd been catching up on their accounts and nearly died when they saw how much money they had left over.

Their lifestyles were far from lavish. She travelled too much for work to want to do it often for fun. He was away too many nights for them to spend their free ones out on the town. Besides, Alma wasn't Monaco, and they weren't teenagers anymore. But to save six figures, after tax, in one year, had left them giddy. A new home had seemed a sensible investment. The model houses, even the most lavish of them, were like this one. Furniture from a catalogue, arranged just like a picture. Decorations that were as inoffensive as plain rice. A paint scheme as muted as a Chaplin movie, and with just as little colour. A house that had yet to gain any character or personality. That's why she and Etienne hadn't moved. Their house was more than where they slept, it was a part of their marriage. As time went by, it creaked, stuck, and leaked, but so did they. It was a home. This place here wasn't.

She laid the letters on the chair's arm before deciding to begin with the one addressed to Naomi.

Dear Naomi,

I'm glad you made it. Hopefully, I'm still alive, and I've left, but maybe you're reading this because I'm dead. If that's how the dice rolled, I'm okay with that. I did my duty, and my duty has been done. No one who knew about the vault can still be alive. Even if they are, they've realised there's nothing they can do with it. I'm going to follow your advice. I'm going to destroy it. Afterwards, I'm going to explore America. I don't know where I'll go. You were right about that, too. I have no roots, no family, and not much of a past to revisit. Not a past I'd want to.

The town's empty. You weren't the last to leave, or the last to say you'd come back. I reckon you got onto that evacuation, both of you, and that's what happened to everyone else who made it to the north. I might try to find you. I might find my feet taking me to some other place. It doesn't matter anymore.

For the first time in my life, I feel old. But not in a yelling-at-the-cashier way. I gave the best part of my life to serving this country and standing up for democracy. Maybe it didn't always come across that way after the news mangled the truth and the politicians stamped on the remains, but I know the world was a better place for my sacrifice. Safer. Until it wasn't. I'm at peace with that, too. I couldn't have stopped this insanity. Again, you were right. One way or another, we'd already doomed ourselves. If it hadn't been zombies, it would have been something else. Either way, my job is done. I'm going to take care of the vault, and then I'm going to find somewhere to enjoy my retirement. I'll fish. I'll hunt. I'll read. Who needs civilisation for that?

I've used as few of the supplies as possible, and restocked from nearby. Everything's here, much as you left it. I hope you find a good use for it.

Hank.

Maggs frowned as she put the letter down. Hank. Hank Schwarz. She assumed it was the same guy who'd died in the kitchen, and she assumed that Naomi was Agent-Colonel Naomi Trang. Beyond that, there was a lot in the message, but most was hidden behind a cypher of personal understanding.

Hank must have written the letter just before he'd died, just as he was planning to leave. Was the vault he wanted to destroy the basement? No, or he wouldn't have left the letters there. And the hatch had been open, so had he come hurriedly back? Hoping the other letters would give more information, she turned to the second.

Dear Micheal,

You made it. Hopefully your mom did, too. But in case she didn't, in case you came here on your own, then I owe you some explanation. Your mom was a true hero. She loved you deeply, and talked about you all the time. I was in her command, and she was the best officer I ever had. We were a top-secret unit. Technically, we weren't even in the Air Force anymore, but contractors for the Department of Energy. I can't tell you why, because people of my pay-grade weren't allowed to ask questions like that.

Our unit was part of Operation Groundhog, one piece of the emergency response to an apocalyptic event. We planned for many scenarios: Yellowstone erupting, solar flares knocking out the grid, asteroids, invasion; if they made a disaster movie out of it, we had a plan. Except for zombies. There was no plan for that. Recently, they had us preparing for a small-scale attack that knocked out the electrical and information grids, followed by raids to steal our most deadly weapons. When the outbreak happened, that's what they implemented.

Our unit, led by your mom, was the last line of defence. In the event of an attack, when defence became impossible, the weapons were to be transferred to a vault we maintained. We were to either destroy the weapons, or ensure they were transferred out of the mainland into friendly hands.

There were other vaults, but the weapons came here. I won't tell you where the vault is, because I've gone out to destroy it. And once it's destroyed, I'm going to start walking, and not stop. The vault's gone. Your mom stayed here because she had to protect those weapons from falling into the wrong hands. She left when she thought that the collapse was so complete, that no one was left to claim them, either friend or foe. I disagreed with her, so I stayed here, at my post.

It turns out, as usual, your mom was right. No one came. There was no invasion. Everything fell apart. I won't romanticise what I did, but I did my duty to the end, and this is the end of America and the world as I knew it. Whatever comes next is up to you. Make it a better world than we did.

The supplies here were for the exfil team that never arrived. Weapons, explosives, food; enough for a small army. Enough to keep you and your friends going while you work out what to do next. God speed. Good luck.

Hank Schwarz

So, Naomi had gone to find her son, but she only managed a few kilometres? That was interesting, in that it showed Hank had never ventured that far north, at least not along that road. The boy must have been in a boarding school if his mother was on permanent deployment here. Or maybe the boy was a man, and had been at university, or in prison. Or a teenager in one of those American military reform schools. No, she'd stopped by a yellow school bus filled with pre-teens.

Regardless, she'd hidden the address and codes in a fire-lighter, and never given it to him. Why hide the address there? Why did she write it down? What exactly was in that vault? She picked up the third envelope.

Colonel Spitzer,

If you were going to return, you'd have done so weeks ago. Australia must be in as bad a shape as everywhere, or maybe it means that the orders are null and void. I think it's the last. There are survivors still here in the state, but there's no government, no America except what part of it we can preserve, and I don't think the contents of the vault need to be saved. I've gone out to destroy it. It's gone.

In case you do come back, or if anyone emerges from a bunker after five years on three rehydrated squares, coming here expecting to find me waiting, consider this my final report. The convoy arrived with the entire stock from the base. No explanation was given why it wasn't shared with the other vaults. The convoy escort and drivers remained at the vault, as per their orders, like me, and like the other guards. Let me tell you, whoever designed it could have spent more time thinking about waste extraction.

After a week, the escort began talking about heading back to their families. For most, that meant the East Coast. When the White House fell, talk became more heated. I tried to persuade them to stay. Not because it was their duty as soldiers, but because as a senior NCO, it was my duty to keep those younger troops alive. They'd lost three people on their way here. There's no way the return journey would be easier. But unlike us, they were young. Unlike us, they had families. Unlike us, they still had that naive sense of immortality that God graces upon every fool who stands up to serve. They left. We stayed. Even Naomi. She stayed until the bombs fell. That's when she went to get her son. That was three months ago.

A week after she left, we received a radio report from General Denning. Or so they said. None of the codewords were used. We didn't reply. Asking where we were broke all protocol, so we assumed the chain of command has been shattered. We shut down the comms.

The submarine never arrived. If you're reading this, you probably arrived aboard it. Well, sorry, but you took too long. This whole project wasn't thought through. The vault wasn't built for habitation longer than two months. The river is a mess. Everyone else is dead. I won't go into details, but you can guess them. All you need to know is that the entire unit did their duty right up until the end.

Lord knows how I'm still alive, but I am. I've seen thousands of walking ghosts march along the highway. I've seen bandits try to rob refugees. I put paid to that, each time I saw it, but too often, I only found evidence of their crimes. I've seen a few people trying to pull something better out of the ashes, but I've not joined them. I felt duty-bound to stay here, to protect the vault. Until now.

There was an earthquake last week, and Mount St Helens released a warning puff of smoke. If ever there was a sign, that was it. The vault's foundations are cracked. Give it another year, and the river will seep in. If the foundations are in that bad a state already, the door might break, or the facility could be exposed to anyone hiking by. I can't bear the idea of some poor kid stumbling across Pandora's box. Humanity might still survive, but they won't survive that. Right now, it seems quiet outside, so I'm going to seal the vault, and end that menace forever.

There are some people who are destined to make things. Some who fix them. Some, benighted souls are made only to destroy. I was made a soldier, and fool that I am, that's what I'll be until I die. So I'm going to make myself useful, and see who else I can help.

Hank Schwarz, United States Air Force, now, finally, retired.

The letters said a lot, and implied an even more intriguing story behind them, but didn't she know it already? The apocalypse had come. The government was unprepared. The military had scrambled to implement the most relevant protocols they could find. It hadn't been enough.

Her eyes fell on the two bags by the small table out in the hallway. They must have been Hank's. She got up and went to inspect them. The backpack contained the military version of camping gear. Clothes, MREs, ammo. No weapons, though. She knelt and opened the duffel bag, then nearly fell over at what she saw. Slowly, she stood, stepping back until her back dug into the wall.

"I found fuel," Ricardo said, before he'd stepped through the door. "Diesel, about five hundred gallons. There's an underground tank beneath a rock garden. What?"

"I found explosives," she said, pointing at the duffel.

Ricardo cautiously opened the bag. "Impressive."

"Don't touch them."

"They're safe. These are a step up from demolition charges. Remote detonators, too. You wouldn't kill zombies with these."

"No. He was on his way to destroy an underground vault and never return."

"There's another vault like this?" Ricardo asked.

"He mentions one in his letters. He doesn't go into details, except that it was a military bunker filled with the best, or worst, weapons the Americans kept in reserve. I don't know what that means, and I certainly don't want to."

"Huh." Ricardo carefully stood up. "Next to the tank were two fuel cans. Both empty. One had its fuel cap open. That's how I found the tank. He was fetching diesel when he was attacked."

"In his letters, he did say he was going to leave."

"What else did he say?" Ricardo asked.

"That he was in the U.S. Air Force. Officially, he was working for the Department of Energy. In reality, he and his team were guarding the vault. Agent Trang was in command of the unit. He lived at the vault. Maybe she lived here." Maggs looked again at the handful of photographs. "Or maybe she didn't. The supplies in the vault downstairs are for an exfiltration team that was supposed to arrive by submarine to collect the weapons in the vault."

"I didn't think we were that near the coast."

"We're not. I suppose they were to come ashore and make their way overland. They were expecting an invasion, not zombies. I guess this was their safe house. After the nukes fell, Naomi went to fetch her son. The rest of his unit either died or fled. Hank wrote the letters three months later. Very soon after, he washed up from breakfast, leaving his dish to dry. He packed his bags, went to fetch fuel, and he died."

"Hank? That's his name?"

"Hank Schwarz," Maggs said. "Are you sure those explosives are safe?"

"They haven't blown up the house yet."

"True, but not reassuring. I'll feel happier when we put them back in the basement. Well, mystery aside, this is good. Very good. Better than good, really. It's everything we need. We'll have to do a stock-take, but we've got food for a week or two, more guns than we need, and enough fuel to get deep into Oregon, maybe even to the border. There's nothing stopping us from leaving tomorrow morning."

"It's diesel."

"Ah, yes. We'll need new vehicles. Georgie won't be happy at leaving the fun-bus behind. Finding new cars shouldn't take more than a day. Can you pack up enough food from the kitchen for a proper meal tonight, and for breakfast. I'm going to take another look in the basement, to see how much food is there. Then we'll go back and share the good news."

Chapter 43 - Night Watch
Vader

"Working hard, or hardly working," Martin muttered as he carried a bundle of firewood past Maggs. She merely smiled, content in the knowledge that she could happily ignore him.

On her return to the firehouse, she'd discovered the pace of work was beginning to slacken as meal-time neared. Clothes had been salvaged, water was being boiled, and the defensive wall had been completed, with the gaps now filled with furniture from nearby. Against bears, and that pack of dogs, they'd be fine. If Dalton were to unleash another horde of zombies, that would be a very different matter, but she thought that was unlikely.

Yvette was in charge of creating a meal from the supplies she and Ricardo had brought back, though Catherine seemed to be helping. Maggs had never got on with Catherine. She'd reminded her too much of the yoga-and-mimosa gatekeepers who'd been the bane of her rise through the corporate ranks. From the lake to the spa, she'd generously offered criticism while studiously avoiding responsibility. But she looked to have thrown herself into the challenge of catering with gusto. The proof would be in the eating, but that was still a few minutes off.

The brief report she'd gathered from Gordon before he'd gone to wash up, was that the town was deserted. Every front door had been secured, and every broken window was already covered. Inside, the pantries were bare. She assumed that had been Hank's work. Though based on when he'd said people had left, and on when he'd died, the missing food couldn't all have been eaten, nor was it in his house. There must be a secondary stash hidden nearby.

Perhaps moving the food to a more secure location had given him purpose during his long months waiting for Naomi, Micheal, or Colonel Spitzer. Had the scent of improperly sealed food on his clothes caused a bear to follow him home? In which case, the food store would be nearby. Not that anywhere would be far away in a town as small as this. Regardless, they were unlikely to find the stash, and she saw no reason to look for it.

"Here you go, Maggs," Yvette said, holding out a bowl. "First course is pasta soup."

"Pasta *and* soup, and it's only the first course? Did you open a restaurant while I was away?"

"We have three courses tonight. Soup, followed by rice and sautéed vegetables, followed by sticky fruit. It was Catherine's idea. Each has a fancy Italian name, but don't tell her I can't remember them."

"It sounds amazing. Smells it, too."

"Thanks. I know the portions aren't huge, but we've got variety."

"This is fantastic. It's a refreshing change from the one-item menus we've become used to. Thank you. And thank her," Maggs added, though she made a mental note to pass on her thanks herself. "She's working out okay? Not being too pushy?"

"No, I'm learning a lot," Yvette said.

"Just remember that you're the boss, not her."

"I am?"

"I told you, you're our quartermaster. You get to boss everyone around except me, Chloe, and Gordon."

"Like I'd try to tell Ricardo what to do. Or Ginger!"

"Maybe start with Marshall," she said, and took her bowl, watching as everyone else lined up to get theirs. The mood was still subdued, though there was a little banter, and even a few smiles. Grief would return, of course, and at unexpected times, but despair had lost its grip.

A sudden breeze from the south rushed through the fire, sending a gust of smoke straight into Chloe's lungs. As she coughed, and Yvette and Catherine rushed to save the saucepans still over the flames, the wind died, and the smoke began rising skywards. They'd need hot-plates from tomorrow, and a generator to power them. And this fire would have to go out just as soon as they finished eating.

Maggs waited until most had finished their first course before she walked to the cooking station and turned to face her people. "Good evening, everyone. There isn't much to say, so I'll keep it brief. Ginger found some beer and soda, so we'll share that out after dinner. Gordon's organised a guard duty roster for tonight, so make sure you've checked with him before going to sleep. It's been a good day. Thank you, everyone, for doing your part. And I'm sure we'd all like to give special thanks to our chefs, Catherine and Yvette, for a fantastic feast."

There were a few cheers. Yvette blushed and hurriedly busied herself with a saucepan, while Catherine smiled.

"Okay, yes, the bar has been set high," Maggs said. "Now for the rest of the update. We have found food, and we've found fuel."

"And weapons," Martin called out.

Reflexively, Maggs's hand dropped to the holstered nine millimetre she'd taken from the safe house. They'd brought back five other handguns for her crew, and six shotguns for those standing watch. The rest had been left behind as she still viewed suicide as a greater threat than an attack by the undead.

"Please let me finish," Maggs said. "It's a government bunker, with government supplies, but they equipped it for ten people, not close to sixty. The food should last us two weeks." She raised a hand to silence the murmur of happy surprise. "I hadn't got to the good bit. There's fuel. A lot of it. Enough to get us across the river and through Oregon. When we leave here, we can just drive as long as there's daylight, and until we're well beyond the range of Dalton. But there's a catch," she added before the chattering grew too loud.

"Isn't there always?" Martin said.

"The fuel is diesel. Finding new cars will be our task tomorrow. After this meal, the fire has to go out and stay out. We'll find a diesel generator and use that for light, heat, and cooking. And yes, because we want to preserve as much diesel as we can for driving, the next few days are going to be uncomfortable."

"But there are guns, too," Martin called out. "Why don't we go back to the spa and get our revenge?"

Maggs blinked away her surprise. Of all the things she'd expected him to say, it wasn't that. "We're not soldiers, Martin. If you want to play Rambo, we won't stop you. Our immediate goal is to get across the Columbia River. Tomorrow, I'll take a team south, by bicycle. We'll scout a bridge, and find a safe spot on the far side. This shouldn't take more than two days, so three days from now, we'll leave. Now, I heard that there's a second course, so let's tuck in."

Maggs took her bowl of spiced rice over to the wall, politely far enough away that people could talk without her having to overhear. Hats took a few steps after her, before deciding there was more food to be scrounged from the crowd than from her. She sighed and looked out at the forest.

Gordon came over, and handed her an energy drink. "This will keep you up."

She put it in her coat pocket for later.

"You didn't mention Longview," he said.

"Martin threw me. I'll say something tomorrow. Not that it matters. Longview is the nearest bridge. We have to try it first. If there are people there… I'm not sure what we'll do."

"What did that letter at the airport say?"

"That's just it, not much. Go to Longview, and there'd be more directions. I don't know if that means there'll be people waiting there, or a note, or how we'd find it, or if they're long gone. They left that message last year. If they returned to Longview, wouldn't they have driven up to the airport to update that note?"

"We can only speculate," Gordon said. "But no, you're right. Since that guy went back to the airport once, he'd have gone back a third time if he could. And if he was able to get to the bridge, he'd be able to go a bit further. Is it the last bridge over the river?"

"Second to last. There's one right on the coast in Astoria. And the Columbia River has a lot of dams and cities upstream. That's a lot of debris that could have washed a bridge away."

"But it's the closest bridge. Even by bicycle, you can be there in a few hours."

"I know. It's just that if it's been washed away, Astoria is probably gone, too. And then we'll have to look eastwards, where we're more likely to run into Dalton. Is it a mad idea?"

"Probably. Which one?" he asked, taking a can of root beer from his voluminous trouser pocket.

"Martin's. To seek revenge by going after Dalton?"

"Yes." He popped open the can, then leaned against an upturned table. "It'd be suicide. First, we'd have to find them, which'd mean we'd lose the element of surprise and the ability to escape, since we'd have burned through our fuel. Second, we don't know how many there are. Third, we got lucky with our escape from the house. Too lucky."

"You think they let us escape?"

"No, not that. I don't think the ones we killed were soldiers. It was easy escaping because they didn't think we could. And if Georgie hadn't been outside, we wouldn't have managed it. But would you put your commandos on guard outside a place filled with hundreds of zombies and a biological weapon? Or would you deploy disposable assets whose only real job is to scream if the zeds break free? You'd keep the real soldiers for when they were needed."

"Like creeping into an occupied building, silently murdering the kitchen staff, and installing a poison gas canister while everyone is asleep?" Maggs said.

"Exactly. That's who we'd be up against. You said the people in the basement were shot with crossbows? There can't have been many soldiers trained to use one of those in a night op, even in the United States. No, our priority is getting as far away as fast as we can, now that we can."

"And we're just leaving Dalton to become someone else's problem," Maggs said. "I hate it, but yes, you're right. What else can we do?"

"Eat our dessert," Gordon said.

"See if Yvette can rustle up a to-go box. I'll save mine for later."

Maggs sat in the dark, reading between the lines of the three letters Hank Schwarz had written. She had returned them next to the radio, adding an unsigned postscript stating she'd found Naomi's body in case Colonel Spitzer ever arrived. Fuelled by warm sugary fruit and the octuple dose of caffeine in the energy drink, she'd had time to reflect on what the letters had implied.

Naomi had a Department of Energy I.D., and Hank was ostensibly employed by that organisation. The earthquake had cracked the floor of the vault, and he was worried about water creeping in. The vault would surely require electricity. There was a dam nearby. Putting all of that together, she could draw a search radius for where this vault might be. But curiosity had killed Schrödinger's cat, doomed Pandora to be reviled as a nosey wench, and for Eve to become a scapegoat for every man who just didn't know when to stop eating. What could the vault contain that would help them? A super-weapon? She barely knew how to clean a shotgun. Food? They had more than they could carry. Fuel? They had more than they could easily take with them. Survivors? Hank said he was the last. A sanctuary? Not one with a functioning toilet, if Hank's letter was anything to go by. Answers? Well, yes, perhaps that. But they were answers to someone else's questions. No, there was no purpose in searching for the vault.

Which didn't stop the three sisters of temptation rolling the questions through her mind, one after the other. At least it was keeping her awake.

She shifted in her chair. The bathroom was beginning to call. She had just decided to risk it, and had begun rummaging in the chair's sides for her flashlight, when she heard a soft whistle of air. It wasn't a loud sound, but it was one she'd been expecting, as the inner door opened, letting air, and an intruder, into the strange little safe house.

Maggs sighed, and abandoned her search for the light in favour of the nine-millimetre pistol in her lap. She was able to track the intruder's footsteps along the hall, to the internal garage door, and across the cold concrete to the hatch. After the first clang of a boot on a ladder rung, there was silence, broken only by the buzz of her tinnitus. The second clang came twenty seconds later, and was far quieter, and far more quickly followed by the third. There were no voices to indicate a second or even third participant. He was alone. She waited. After five long minutes of distant knocking and banging, light suddenly seeped in through the hallway outside.

Muffled by the walls, she heard Gordon shout. "Well, look who the cat threw up!"

She made her way out into the hall, and then into the garage. Gordon and Ginger stood facing Martin, who had just climbed up the ladder. He had a rifle slung over his shoulder, a pistol stuck dangerously down the front of his trousers, and a bag on the floor. The same bag she had helpfully left in the basement next to the racks of supplies, just in case he hadn't thought to bring one of his own. It was empty when she'd put it there. It wasn't empty now.

"I haven't done anything wrong," Martin said.

"Debatable," Maggs said. "Do you have anything else to say for yourself?"

He looked between them and must have finally realised that only Maggs was holding a gun, it was pointing at the ground, and her finger was off the trigger. He went for the pistol tucked into his belt, fumbling the draw, and nearly dropped the gun as he recklessly waved it back and forth.

"Told you," Ginger said.

"He's alone," Ricardo called out from the hall.

Martin's wavering aim settled on Maggs. "Back up, all of you," he said, his words tinged with hysterical panic. "Put your gun on the worktable, Maggs. Then we're going to go outside, just you and me. You'll bring the diesel, and we'll drive away. I'll let you go a mile from here."

"Can we hurry this along?" Gordon said. "I thought I'd enjoy it more, but it's late, and I want to get to my bed."

Martin changed his aim to Gordon, while his expression shifted to confusion. "Back up. Both of you."

"You aren't very well-armed for someone about to wage a one-man war against Dalton," Ginger said.

"What?"

"Oh, that was just talk, was it, just another way of stirring up division?" Ginger said. "You're not going back to the spa. You're just going to drive off with as much as you can carry, eh?"

"I want to live," Martin said. "That's my right."

"Martin, I want you to think very carefully before you do anything," Maggs said. "Think, okay? You hold your life in your own hands. Now, which of our gasoline-powered cars do you plan on pouring that diesel into?"

"I… I'll take the SUV, and take the diesel with me and find another car tomorrow."

"The SUV that's parked inside a wall we made today without a gate," Maggs said. "Moving it would wake everyone up. What you're holding is a gun, not a magic wand."

"Then I'll walk. So what?"

"Martin, put the gun down," Maggs said. "Look around you and think."

The gun wavered. "It's not loaded, is it?"

"Whether it is or not is down to whether you inserted a magazine, but we removed the firing pin from all the guns we left down there," Maggs said. "Clearly, this was a trap. Sadly, it wasn't really a trap for you, but for any followers you might have. I say sadly, because you can see, here and now, just how many you have."

His arm dropped.

"Told you," Gordon said, stepping forward to retrieve the firearm.

"So now you shoot me?" Martin said.

"No," Maggs said. "Now we handcuff you to a folding bed because we all want to get some sleep. Tomorrow, we work. When we leave, you'll remain behind and can do whatever you want. We were never stopping you from leaving, Martin. We'd have given you a gun and supplies. You just had to ask. But you didn't. Instead, you took, and then you threatened us. Think on that, in the days to come."

Ricardo and Ginger escorted their fallen one-time-leader back to the firehouse. Maggs bent to pick up the bag but changed her mind. It could wait.

"I was wrong. He didn't pull the trigger," Gordon said.

"His one saving grace," Maggs said. It was the compromise she, Ginger, Ricardo, and Gordon had reached. If he had pulled the trigger, he wouldn't have survived the confrontation. "Just because he isn't a good person, doesn't mean he's evil like Brass, or like Ezra."

"Or Dalton," Gordon said.

"Yes. They deserve a bullet. Their actions have been their trial, the consequences have sentenced them to death. Martin deserves one last chance to prove that he has some worth in this blighted world."

"And he's blown that chance now."

"No, maybe not. Maybe after some time on his own, with no one to blame but himself, he might change his ways. But maybe not. Either way, we should get some sleep. It really is going to be a long day tomorrow."

Chapter 44 - A Log Cabin with a Scenic View
The Columbia River, March 14th

"What's my dream lunch?" Ginger asked as Maggs passed a bicycle down to her. "Right now, I'd say romaine lettuce with pine nuts and a blue cheese dressing, but no chillies."

"That's impressively healthy," Maggs said. "You wouldn't want something with a few more carbs?"

"When I turned sixteen, my mom took me shopping for a nice handbag and a proper cosmetic set," Ginger said. "It was something her mom had done, and that her grandma had done before her. It was a family tradition, except times had changed. Mom didn't really grasp that until we got to the mall. It was strange. She'd lived in the same world I'd grown up in, but walking around the mall together, it was like we were seeing it for the same way for the first time. I think that was when I first saw her as her own person, you know, not just a mom. And I think she saw me properly for the first time, too, not just as her daughter."

"And the salad?"

"Shopping was a complete blow-out. So I said we should tweak the tradition. Change it from clothes to food. We went for a grown-up meal. I hated salad, but that's what grown-ups ate, so that's what I ordered. It's what I always ordered when I had salad. I miss it."

"Salad greens don't take long to grow," Maggs said, brushing her hands as she walked across the flatbed to the other side where Ricardo was waiting to lift up the next pannier. "Four or five weeks, I think. And there are plenty of pine trees, though I can never remember which ones produce the edible nuts without tasting them."

"What about blue cheese?" Ricardo asked.

"That's going to be the hard one," Maggs said, bending down. "Okay, next. No! Wait!" She straightened as the transporter-trailer blocking the road shifted beneath her feet. Her eyes went to the M1 Abrams. She seriously doubted the civilian flat-bad was rated to carry a tank. The spiderweb straps holding it in place offered little reassurance.

She was glad they were cycling rather than driving. The closer they got to the Columbia River, and the more urbanised the surroundings became, the worse the wreckage got. She'd lost track of how many detours they'd taken through parking lots and across back yards. It was to avoid another frustrating detour that she'd suggested they climb over the flatbed. After all, if an M1 Abrams had managed to remain atop the transporter for a year, a few extra kilos of bike and bags wouldn't shift it. She hoped.

"No, I think we're okay."

"Catch," Ricardo called out, and flung Ginger's bag at her.

"Hey, watch it!"

"Sorry," he said, and actually blushed as he picked up Maggs's bag. "Last one."

Maggs took it and passed it down to Ginger. "Last one," she echoed.

"So, lunch?" Ginger asked. "There's a drive-thru up there. They'd have benches."

They'd brought six self-heating military ration packs with them, along with three cans from Hank's kitchen. Lunch was canned peaches and a pack of crackers from one of the MREs. They'd eaten breakfast in Vader, and had hoped to have dinner there, too, but she'd planned for an overnight excursion just in case. It increasingly looked like the trip would take a lot longer than that.

That morning, explaining Martin's latest betrayal, and then calming the mob, had taken a good hour. Since the prevailing response had been to run him out of town as naked as a mole-rat, she'd had to leave Georgie and Marshall behind to watch the traitor. Even so, she'd still expected to reach Longview by lunch, and be across the bridge soon after. Now, they were lost in the overlapping conurbation radiating from the rare crossing over the Columbia, zigzagging back and forth, with the river still nowhere in sight.

"Sandwiches," Ricardo said, returning to their conversation from earlier. "That'd be my dream meal. Ham, cheese, mustard. Pinch of salt."

"How about a vitamin or two?" Ginger asked.

"I'll have a glass of juice."

"We can grow mustard," Ginger said. "I suppose we might find some pigs."

"I don't mind venison," Ricardo said. "But we're back to the cheese conundrum."

"And the bread," Maggs said, as she looked at her now empty packet of military crackers. "Oh, I do miss carbs."

"We can grow some wheat, can't we?" Ginger said.

"Or maize," Maggs said. "I suppose we'll try growing both."

"Indoors," Ricardo said. "Like that idea you had back at Lac Seul."

"Maybe, yes, if we can find a dam."

"They should have listened to you back then," Ginger said.

"It wouldn't have stopped the plague that swept through Red Lake," she said. "A steady supply of power will be essential to winter farming. Remember the fortress-compound and their power cables along the roadside? I bet that work wasn't done until fall. Probably after harvest, when they realised that they'd be short of food this spring. There's a reason they call these the hungry months."

"I wish we had a chance to make mistakes like that," Ginger said. "I'm getting tired of being on the road all the time."

"We can't stay around here," Ricardo said.

"I know. The Peace Garden, that's where we're heading, right, Maggs?"

"I think so. I don't want to announce a decision until we've ditched Martin. Even then, we've got a lot of land to cross before we reach it. But after we cross the river, I want to take us east. If we ever do cross that damned river."

The sightless corpse lay on its back, both arms extended towards the log wall that had sealed in the road for the last kilometre or so. Roughly trimmed tree trunks were stacked lengthwise, held in place by stout metal brackets, rusting scaffolding poles, and stakes made from the larger branches. Where it was intact, the wall was as high as Ricardo's head. Too often, the supports had given way, spilling tree trunks across the road, as well as down the shallow embankment and towards the industrial warehouses on either side. She was glad they'd come by bicycle; it would be at least a day's work with cable and winch to clear enough logs for a car to reach the checkpoint. Even then, they wouldn't be able to drive across the bridge.

Just beyond the body was a log cabin, placed on the road itself, and a little wider than a lane. It looked like a checkpoint, though the other lane had been left open, without a barrier. From what she could see of the bridge, no barrier was needed. Like the wall, the cabin had been built with unseasoned logs, but these had been saddle-notched at a perfect ninety degrees.

"There must have been a lumber yard nearby," she said, as Ricardo leaned his bicycle against the log cabin's wall.

"They undercoated this sign," Ginger said, having wheeled her bike over to a road sign which now bore a single word in black paint: *Sanctu-*

ary. "A white undercoat, and black painted letters. They look machine-perfect, except they can't be. There are no drips. I think they took the sign down to paint it. I bet that took more than a day."

"So did the cabin," Maggs said. "And the wall would have taken..." She turned around to look back the way they'd come. How long would it have taken if the logs were waiting nearby ready for shipment? How long if the workers were trapped here, terrified by the news of zombies, desperate to do anything if it would quell their sense of helpless despair? Less than a day. A lot less. Maybe just a few hours. And then the despair would have returned, and the workers, the potential defenders, would have had no reason to remain. But someone had.

Like most of the corpse's face, the dead woman's fingers were gone, but she'd died wearing a t-shirt and leggings. Infected during the summer, but the zombie had died much more recently.

"Tables and chairs. Plastic," Ricardo said from the doorway to the checkpoint. "Garden furniture. A couple of electric lamps. There's a broom, too."

Maggs wheeled her bike over to the doorway where a ragged shower curtain had been pinned back. There were a few other items that Ricardo hadn't rated mentioning: a wood-burning stove with a metal chimney that exited just beneath the base of the roof at the rear of the cabin; some pots and pans, all with their lids on; some plastic cups and plates, half of them now on the floor; and a few books and card games on a shelf at the front of the cabin next to the broad slit that looked out on the road.

"No beds," Maggs said. "This was just a look-out post."

"You think they were here?" Ginger asked.

"The people who left that note at the airport? Maybe. At one point." She walked her bicycle onward, scanning the sky. There was no smoke. While that didn't necessarily mean anything, she thought it meant they were too late.

"It's probably better that they're not here," Ginger said as they walked their bikes towards the bridge. "I don't think I'd trust them."

"No. I don't think I'd trust anyone for a while," Maggs said.

"Not until the Peace Garden," Ricardo echoed.

They wheeled their bicycles onwards, their pace slowing as they neared the bridge-block. The wall stretched from one side of the bridge to the other and explained why the road behind them was clear of cars. The abandoned vehicles had been stacked atop one another like bricks, six high in some places. Towering above them was a lonely crane.

Ginger laid her bike down, and began pacing back and forth, staring up at the coils of barbed wire swinging gently in the breeze. "I think I can climb here."

"You're not climbing that," Ricardo said. Ginger merely grinned, and launched herself at the uneven wall of steel.

Maggs turned her back. If the wall had stood through a year of storms, it was unlikely that Ginger's scant weight would bring it down, but that didn't mean she had to watch.

"This is easy. There are support poles!" Ginger called out.

"That's nice, dear," Maggs said, taking in the warehouses on either side of the highway.

"Careful," Ricardo called.

"Says the guy who bashed rocks for a living," Ginger replied.

Maggs smiled. The pair of them were well-suited. She knew from her own marriage, and from witnessing the rise and fall of others', that it was the little differences, the independence and individuality, that helped turn a marriage into a partnership. That thought only reminded her of Kayleigh, Roy, and their baby, and of Etienne. Gloom settled upon her. She turned back to the car wall, where Ginger was already at the top.

"Oh, wow," Ginger said. "It's impressive." She shifted position, leaning forward and raising her left leg as a counterbalance so now only one hand and one foot were supporting her. Ricardo turned around. "Some cars are on their sides, some facing forward. There are supports attached to the bridge towers."

"But how do we get through?" Maggs called up.

"We don't. Hang on." She swung herself around faster than Maggs's heart could leap to her throat, and began dropping from one hand hold to another in a barely controlled fall.

Maggs waited until she was at the bottom before asking, "What did you see?"

"On the other side of the bridge is another wall, just like this one, made of cars and supports. In between, there are two cranes and a whole load of other construction equipment, including three bulldozers. What do dozers drink? Diesel. And construction equipment is designed with the expectation it'll be left outside. We could use the dozers to punch a hole in the wall."

"We'd need to bring the diesel here first," Maggs said. "Then climb over, repair a bulldozer, and create a hole. That's a couple of extra days, if it works, but I suppose it's possible."

"You'd bring the whole thing down on your heads," Ricardo said.

"That's possible, too," Maggs said.

"Well, there's a train over there." Ginger waved to the warehouses east of the bridge. "A train means a railroad, and they use bridges, too."

"What type of train?" Ricardo asked.

Ginger shrugged. "Freight, I guess. Remember that time we found a diesel train in Ontario? There was so much fuel!"

"I don't remember seeing a railway bridge on the map," Maggs said. "But we should look. If there isn't one... I don't know. I think we should have a look at the bridge in Astoria. Since this one is standing, there's no reason to think the other will have been washed away."

"And if that bridge is blocked, too?"

"We'd have to go east, and cross the Cowlitz River first, and then the Columbia. The Cowlitz isn't far from here. I think it runs through the other side of Longview."

"If it's nearby, those bridges would be like this, too," Ginger said. "It'd be crazy if they weren't. Unless they're completely demolished."

"There's no way of knowing without looking," Maggs said.

"Yes, Maggs, but I'm saying, as crazy as it sounds, there is an actual way through this blockade," Ginger said. "Maybe bulldozing our way through the wall isn't sensible. Maybe it's not safe. It might be the only way. We've got two weeks of food, yes? Only two weeks and we've used a day already. We'll use another to get to Astoria. Maybe longer. And then we have to get back. The days add up, all while our food runs down. I'm not wild about the idea, but maybe it's our only option."

"We should look for the rail bridge first," Ricardo said.

"Agreed," Maggs said. "Let's do that, and then... I'm not sure." She picked up her bike and wheeled it back down the road, thinking through what Ginger had said. If it wasn't for Dalton, it wouldn't matter. Vader was a nice enough place. There probably were more supplies to be found, and there was always hunting and fishing. On balance, it was a nice a spot as anywhere. But there *was* Dalton and his minions to consider.

She pushed her bike into the log cabin. "We'll want our hands free if we're exploring an old rail yard," she said, as she leaned it against the wall. "We should see if there's a river-side path. It's a long-shot, but something like that would save us a lot of time."

"To go to Astoria?"

"No, to the Cowlitz River. We're here, and it's not far. Maybe we can cross both rivers. We'll see."

They picked their way over the fallen logs, and to the nearest gap in the wall. Her mind was on the map, not on her footing, and she slipped down the shallow embankment and into the overflowing drainage ditch at the bottom. Cursing quietly, she picked herself up.

"There's always plan C," she said as she tried to find solid ground beneath the swamp.

"Over here," Ricardo said, peeling back a portion of the chain-link fence that had already been cut.

"What's plan C?" Ginger asked.

"I hate to say it, and you'll hate me for suggesting it, but we could always go back."

"You mean Martin's plan?" Ricardo asked.

"Not exactly," Maggs said as she ducked to pass through the fence. "Ginger's right." She straightened, brushing her hands clean, before giving her foot a fruitless shake in a bid to rid it of some water. "What we found in Vader gives us a margin, but we don't want to fritter it away. We could just drive back the way we came. We'd give the spa a wide berth, but otherwise follow the roads we know are clear, sprint for the mountains, and then keep on going. We wouldn't look for Dalton, but if he found us, we're well-armed."

"So drive until we run out of fuel?" Ginger asked.

"Basically, yes. We can't leave until we've found diesel-engined vehicles, so we haven't wasted today, but we can't waste tomorrow. Let's find the railroad, and see if there's a riverside path, and if there's not, then we'll talk it through again."

Behind the fence was a tall and windowless warehouse. They followed it to a corner, then down an alley between it and its neighbour, kicking aside a mulch of hats and gloves, water bottles, books, and even a few bags. Beyond, they stepped into an abandoned refugee camp. Rusting tubes and rotting plastic marked where tents had been set up in the parking lot. The weather hadn't been kind to the detritus of flight, making it hard to tell which rags had been coats, and which had been blankets.

"I guess it was a quarantine camp," Ginger said.

"Could be. But why here?" Maggs said, talking more to herself. She picked her way around a tumble of plastic barrels that had once been a watering station. "Oh. Oh, I think I understand."

She pointed towards a Stars and Stripes flying proudly outside a customs post. "This would have been a railway stop for cross-border traffic. This must have been a transit camp for the evacuation."

"But Oregon's in the U.S.," Ginger said as they detoured around another set of derelict tents. "And that place is definitely pre-outbreak."

"I guess it was easier to deal with goods from California here, or goods *for* California, than further north. I can't see any rails, but we're close to the river. Maybe—"

She stopped speaking as a middle-aged man in a grey camouflage uniform, with a swatch of military ribbons across his chest, pushed a broom around the far corner of the customs house. He kept going for a few more paces, pushing an increasingly large pile of detritus before him. She was about to motion they should turn around when he spotted them, waved, and then continued sweeping.

Maggs took a few steps towards him. "Hello," she said.

He paused. "Welcome." He continued sweeping without looking up.

"Hi. I'm Maggs, this is Ginger and Ricardo. We're from Quebec originally."

"You're in the right place if you want to get your passport stamped," he said, before leaning on his broom to properly take them in. "I'm John."

"Do you live here?" she asked.

"Today, yes. Tomorrow, who can say? But I couldn't abide the mess. What brings you to this corner of our blemished world?"

Maggs smiled. They'd been too hasty. They had found the people who'd left the note at Olympia. "We're trying to find a way across the river," she said.

"Ah, of course. It won't be easy here, but not impossible. Few things are, when faced with determination. Why don't you come inside? There are easier crossings. We will share what we have, and what we know."

Maggs's uncertainty must have shown.

"You're cautious," John said. "That's wise. Very wise. But go on your way, if you wish. The choice is yours. But *I* choose to have a break. I've been at this since dawn. Hasn't made any difference. Never does." Shaking his head, he walked towards the customs house, his broom now trailing after him.

"Either we go in, or we run, and don't use a bridge within a hundred kilometres," Maggs whispered.

"We left the others behind for a reason," Ginger said.

"After you," Ricardo said.

Chapter 45 - Custom and Practice
Longview

There were two soldiers already in the customs house. One pushed a mop with metronomic precision. The other stood at rigid attention by the door. Her eyes barely flickered as the trio of newcomers entered. She bore three military ribbons on her hunter-green jacket, but Maggs had no idea what conflict they'd been awarded for. The mop-wielder wore camouflage trousers and a blue t-shirt with duct-tape covering the logo. She had no ribbons.

"We think it was rabbits," John said, waving his arms to indicate the space.

"I'm sorry?" Maggs asked as she looked around at the scratched reinforced barriers and the empty service counter behind them, before settling on the three heaps of swept debris.

"The mess. It was rabbits," John said. "I've seen it up and down the country. The pocket-protector brigade predicted that mice and rat populations would boom after the downfall. But a short breeding cycle and low life expectancy also means little time to adapt after their food supply vanished. Cats did a little better than expected, dogs a little worse, but it was rabbits that were the real miracle. Many buildings became their burrows. Has this been your experience?"

"No. Not really," Maggs said. "We've seen moose, bears, wild dogs. *Lots* of wild dogs. There was an uptick in mice, but that only lasted for a few weeks."

"Eden is slowly returning," John said. "Captain Pakhaüser, we have some new arrivals for the census."

The mop-wielder put down her tool and picked up a camouflage jacket that had been hanging on the back of a chair. She buttoned it up as she walked over to the counter, revealing she *did* have ribbons, and nearly as many as John.

Before the outbreak, Maggs's encounters with the military had either been during active crises where they'd been covered in so much mud that a camouflage pattern had been redundant, or at official functions where they'd worn blindingly bright whites. Since the outbreak, soldiers had dressed much like everyone else, even at Red Lake where they'd had enough electricity to launder uniforms. This was the first time she'd seen a military unit attempt to look as such.

"Please," the captain said, waving vaguely to the other side of the workstation before opening a leather-bound folder. There were already a dozen loose pages in there, each with writing too dense for Maggs to read upside down. The captain picked up a pen and jotted down the time and date on a fresh sheet.

"Can I start with your names, please?" the captain asked.

"You're conducting a census?" Ginger asked.

"As best we can," the captain said. "Your names?"

"Maggs Espoir, and this is Ginger and Ricardo."

"And before the outbreak, where did you live?"

"Quebec," Maggs said.

The captain looked up. "You really *are* a long way from home. Why did you come here?"

"We didn't mean to. We were trying to cross Canada to reach Vancouver Island. We thought we'd find other survivors there because of the evacuation. Roadblocks, landslides, zombies, you name it, all forced us further south."

"Are you still heading to the island?"

"No. We were hoping to find survivors from the evacuation, but we recently found a few notes saying that it collapsed."

"The nuclear detonations ended the evacuation effort before it had truly begun," the captain said. "Where are you heading?"

"We have no destination in mind right now, we're just looking for farmland."

"Of course. You said you found some notes. Have you met any other groups in person?"

"Only bandits, if you can call that a meeting," Maggs said. "Further east, there were a few times we met people on the road with whom we shared some food. Out here, it's only people who tried to kill us."

The captain nodded sympathetically. "We've found the same. Have you ever served in the U.S. military?"

"We're Canadian," Ricardo said.

"Sorry, of course. Have you ever served in the Canadian military?"

"No," Maggs said firmly.

"What about you?" John said. Maggs turned to see John walking towards them, pointing at Ricardo. "That tattoo on your arm looks martial."

Ricardo rolled his forearm over so he could better see the crossed mining picks above a shadowy black ghoul. "It's the Seeking Dark, a mining thing. I was a miner," he said. "And I was drunk."

"We all have our failings," John said, and waved a hand at the captain. "Get to the important part."

"Yes, sir. When did you first arrive in Washington State?"

"No, no," John cut in. "Ask them the *important* one."

"Of course. Have you seen, or heard of, any bunkers or vaults in Washington State?"

"What?" Ginger said.

"No," Maggs said, but not quickly enough. "We barely know where we are."

"Young lady," John said, stepping forward again, this time pointing at Ginger. "You looked at him. Why? What do you know?"

"Nothing," Ginger said quickly. "I've never been here before."

The front door opened, and the armed guard stepped in. "Sir. He's back."

"*Finally,*" John said, the Canadians seemingly forgotten as he headed for the door.

"Sir," the captain said. "What about these three?"

John gave them a disinterested wave. "Oh, give them some food and water. Once they've been tested, they can go."

"Tested for what?" Maggs asked as John stepped outside.

"It's standard protocol," the captain said. "We've got to make sure no one's potentially infectious. Just place your firearms on the desk. They'll be returned when you leave."

"You want our guns?" Ricardo asked.

"No, but I have my orders," the captain said.

There were footsteps behind them. Maggs turned. As John had left, eight people had entered, wearing a mix of camouflage and civilian clothing. All were armed. Two with shotguns, two with assault rifles, the others with hunting rifles. They weren't pointing their weapons at her trio, nor was the captain armed. But they were definitely outgunned and outnumbered.

Chapter 46 - A Long Way from Olympia
Longview

As the guards led them along a corridor behind the reception desk, Maggs kept her hand away from her tomahawk. The soldiers didn't seem to care that they were carrying blades, and she didn't want them to change their minds. The captain led them through an empty office, half-cleared of furniture, and to a heavily reinforced door, set back in the wall.

"I'm sorry for the delay, but this won't take long now that the scouts are back," the captain said as she opened the door. "Help yourselves to food and water."

The outer door was reinforced and windowless. Beyond was an open cage door leading into a large chamber, forty metres by thirty, with no other external doors. The right-hand third had been split into three separate metal cages, while the rest of the space was relatively empty. It was a holding area for goods rather than people, though there were seventeen other travellers already there, most of whom were now looking at the captain.

"Can we go now?" The speaker was an older man with grey stubble one sunrise shy of being called a beard. His tone was more weary than aggressive, but the expression on the larger man standing just behind him was the opposite.

"Soon, yes," the captain said. "Within the hour. Our scouts have just returned. Once the general has finished speaking with them, we can get the testing area set up. After that, everyone who wants to leave can. Or you can join us. There's plenty of food and plenty of work." She left, taking the guards with her.

The captain's news had dispelled any darker mood that might have spread through their grim prison. A young woman wearing every shade of brown slipped out from behind the curtained-off area she supposed was the excuse for a bathroom. Two other detainees were lingering nearby, though it looked as if they had been keeping watch for an occupied friend rather than waiting to use the meagre facilities. Nine were split between the two nearest cells, while the cage farthest away from the door had just one occupant, studiously reading a book. The other four, all men who'd been waiting to confront the captain had now moved back towards the nearby table, on which were an odd mix of soda, bottled water, and pre-outbreak snacks.

Maggs gave a wide smile and a vague wave to the room at large before turning to Ginger. "Why don't you both see what there is to eat?"

Ginger slipped her arm into Ricardo's and walked him over to the table. His sheer size exerted a gravitational effect on the eyes of the bored and curious, allowing Maggs to give the chamber's other occupants a more thorough inspection. Everyone carried sheathed blades or clubs, and was either holding or staying close to their bags. Noticing that, she realised that neither John nor the captain had asked why they were on foot and without supplies. Not yet anyway.

The five in the middle cage didn't appear to be a group, but the four in the nearest cell definitely were, so Maggs decided to make them her first port of call. Three of them were watching her; an old man with more sun damage than a satellite, a muscular man in his late thirties who was eyeing Ricardo with competitive calculation, and a woman in her mid-twenties whose face bore a story of exhaustion and pain. The fourth, another young woman, was lying on the floor, her eyes closed.

"Hello," Maggs said. "I'm Maggs. That's Ginger and Ricardo. We were trying to get across the river." She smiled sweetly, waiting for ingrained civility to do the rest.

"North or south?" the older man said.

"Sorry, in what context?" Maggs asked. "If it's my preferred reading spot, it's facing east, because that's the direction my good view used to be in."

"Don't mind him," the young woman said, dredging up the hint of a smile. "I'm Dessie. This is Grandpa Jack, Booker, and this is Henley."

"She's sick?"

"An infection," Dessie said. "I'm worried she's developing sepsis. The captain said they were sending a doctor, but that was yesterday. You're not a doctor?"

"Sorry, no. I worked for a utility company. Was it a zombie?"

"A poodle," Dessie said. "I'm not kidding. It was an honest-to-goodness poodle. It looked like a ball of fluff, so obviously Miss Darkness-Lives-In-My-Soul had to pet it. She always wanted a dog, but our lease wouldn't let us." She trailed off, lost in memory. Dessie and Henley were about the same age, though utterly dissimilar in appearance. Henley had a lankier build and had kept up the hipster-grunge style that had been popular among those young enough to describe Nirvana as classical music. Dessie was shorter, wearing the standard farmer's uniform of denim and plaid, though the machete at her belt was long enough to qualify as a sword. Both had matching sets of earrings, though. Three emerald studs in their left ears, and a single topaz in the right. Henley's face was flushed, gripped with fever.

Booker's jeans were splattered with dried mud, but his 'Arrest the Whales' t-shirt looked shop-new and a size too small. His thumbs were tucked into his belt, his hand close to a long hunting knife, while his eyes flicked between her and the people gathered around the food table. Jack was at least seventy, as bald as an egg, and more wrinkled than a walnut, but his eyes were alert as he watched the main door.

Maggs held out her hand. "How'd'you do, Jack?"

"Hmph." He took her hand. His grip was firm, and his hand steady. "Were you trying to go north or south?" he asked, peering into her eyes as he spoke.

"Ah, south. Into Oregon. We read there was a checkpoint here. I didn't think it'd be like this."

"Where'd you come from?"

"Quebec, originally. We never planned to cross the border, but you know how it goes. A week ago, we found a note at Olympia Airport saying we should cross the river here. I'm not sure what I was expecting, but it wasn't the military. Could I have my hand back? Thank you."

"You were at Olympia?" Jack asked. "Did you see any other messages there?"

"From… Oh, what was his name. Ronald Reuel something. I don't remember his surname, but he said that his parents were Tolkien fans."

"We call him Frodo," Dessie said.

"Henley does, because she's the only one who can get away with it," Booker said.

"You know him?" Maggs asked.

"We do," Jack said. "And I should have let him come on this damned trip instead of me."

"You're from the refuge in Oregon?"

"I wouldn't call it a refuge as such," Jack said, and there was a note of wariness in his tone. She could guess why.

"How long have you been here?" she asked.

"Since last night," Jack said. "Everyone else was delivered this morning, picked up on the roads to the northwest."

"And did you—" Maggs began, but stopped as all except Henley looked past her to the open cage door.

"Hey gang, how's it going? I'm Ginger. The big man is Ricardo," Ginger said, as she entered the cage-room with a couple of bottles of water. She handed one to Maggs. "Drink sparingly. The toilets are an adventure."

Hellos and introductions were briefly shared, and Maggs was about to ask again what the four were doing before the arrival of the military unit when a loud clacking from the main entrance interrupted her. The door swung open. John walked in with two soldiers behind him. He stopped just inside the open steel-bar gate. The guards took up position on either side. They weren't aiming their shotguns at the detainees, but they had their fingers close to the triggers.

"Some say that life is a test," John began without preamble, "and that the final judgement is given before God, when our lives are weighed in the balance. That was the case once, yes, but not anymore. The mortal world has fallen. These are the end times, when demons stalk the earth, and the horsemen ride among us. At one time, we would have thought such events were fantastical. Yet we are here to witness it. The seals have been broken, the trumpets sounded, the battle fought. And yet, *we* are alive. We are *still* alive. It isn't a miracle. This is something more. This is divinity. We are the chosen few who will turn the battleground into Eden. If we succeed, eternal salvation is ours. If we fail, it will mean damnation for us, but also for all who went before. This is the ultimate test, and it is a great burden to have it thrust upon our shoulders, but we can't shirk, we can't retreat, when we hear the summons, we can only answer amen."

He paused for a response, though the only thing Maggs wanted to give the man was a straitjacket. The lacklustre amen from three of the detainees seemed enough to satisfy him.

"Before we test you, there is one matter to be resolved," John continued. "That of the vault. Where is she? Yes, you." He pointed at Ginger. "Tell me of this vault."

"I don't know anything," Ginger said.

"It's not the vault," a voice said from the doorway. A voice she recognised. Sheriff Dalton stepped into the chamber. "The spa they were hiding in had a basement whose ladder was hidden behind a false wall."

The only thing that stopped Maggs from leaping for his throat was that Ricardo did it first. He pushed past her, but came to a stop in the face of two shotguns aimed at his head.

Ginger grabbed his arm, and tugged on it. "Don't. Not like this."

Maggs stepped in front of Ricardo. "Constant Dalton, the devil himself. You keep poor company, John."

"Explain," John said, turning to Dalton.

"They're the people from the spa," the sheriff said. "The survivors who escaped. Some of them. What happened to the rest?"

Maggs laughed. "They went north. I thought they were fools, that north was where you'd look. I can't believe that Martin, that walking ulcer, was actually right for the first time in his pestilential life."

"She's the hydroelectric engineer," Dalton said. "We need her and her team. They can power up a dam. It'll be far more efficient than generators."

"Maybe," John said. "After they've been tested. All initiates must be tested."

"But, sir—" Dalton began.

John just raised a hand, and Dalton fell silent. "No one who fails this test could pass the next, and that test is coming. It's coming for us all." He turned and walked out. Dalton took one last look at Maggs, mouthing something that she couldn't discern. He hurried after the general as the two guards slowly backed out, keeping their shotguns trained on Ricardo. As they passed through the open bar-gate, one trained his gun through the bars. The other secured the gate with a bike-lock. Only then did they back out through the main entrance, closing the reinforced door behind them.

"Remember when we said we weren't going to trust anyone?" Ricardo said.

"Yes, and we can beat ourselves up later," Maggs said, looking around their holding cell with very different eyes.

"How do you know him?" Jack asked.

"Dalton claimed to be a sheriff working for the US government, and said he'd help us. Except he used an aerosolised version of the zombie virus to murder our friends. About four hundred of them," Maggs said. "This was only a few days ago. That's what they mean by testing. They're going to gas us."

Perhaps she should have kept her voice down, but what she'd said had carried. Two of the men who'd been lurking by the food table ran to the padlocked gate-door, trying to break it open. Her nostrils flared as the air filled with the scent of cherry blossom. She drew her tomahawk.

"This is the test. Close the cage door, Ric," she said.

"What's going on?" Booker asked, drawing one of his two knives.

"That smell, it's the scent of the weaponised zombie virus," Maggs said. "Anyone who isn't immune is about to turn. That's why they left us our weapons."

She'd been addressing Booker, but she'd spoken loudly enough for everyone to hear her. The door of the cage next to them slammed shut, then was pushed open. A fight began as some tried to get in, and others tried to get out.

"You've got to let us in!" an older man who'd shaved his head but kept his muttonchops yelled at Ricardo.

"There are seven in here," Ginger said, stepping up next to him. "You've better odds in the corridor."

Dessie drew her machete. "Why couldn't they have left me my rifle?"

"Hey! No!" Ginger said, turning to the door where Muttonchops slashed a long knife at the bars where Ricardo's hands had been just moments before. The miner had stepped back in time, keeping one foot on the door, and his hands out of reach. Ginger stabbed her machete through the bars. The attacker stepped back.

"You try to come in here, I'll kill you whether you're a zombie or not!" Ginger yelled.

A scream erupted from the next cage. Something zipped past Maggs's ear. She spun, but it moved too fast for her to follow. Not a bullet, but a knife that had missed its target and sailed through the bars to hit the back wall. Ricardo was holding the door closed, and Ginger was watching the corridor. Maggs backed up until she was standing next to Ginger, where she had a clear view of the four Oregonians and the occupants of the cage next door. There had been five people in there before the chaos began. Right now, she could only see the backs of three. All of them were close to the bars. She dismissed them as not an immediate problem. In their cage, Dessie and Jack were still standing on either side of Henley, while Booker had backed up against the wall, a long knife in each hand, waiting for the worst, much like her.

Another scream shook the air, this time from the corridor. Maggs glanced around. The curtain around the bathroom had collapsed atop a woman, on her knees. Her hands flailed. Had she turned? What a place to die. Metal clattered to the floor just beyond the door of their cage as Muttonchops dropped his knife. He fell to his knees, then slumped forward.

"Ric, Ginger, keep that door closed," Maggs said. Turning her back on the door so she could face the other four. Booker was doing the same. His eyes moved from her to his friends and back again. Dessie was watching the next cage. Jack had sat down. He had a hammer in his lap, but he'd hung his head. Henley was still motionless, which told Maggs absolutely nothing.

Another scream came from the neighbouring cage, as one survivor lunged at another.

"Get back!" Booker called out. Maggs swung back to look, but he'd not been talking to her. He'd thrown himself across the room. Henley reared up, her arms flailing. As Booker pushed Dessie away, Henley sunk her teeth into his ankle.

"No!" Dessie called, backing away. Jack stood up. Booker tried to shake himself free. Maggs raised her tomahawk but Jack still had a grip on his hammer, he swung it up, and then down. The sharpened chisel point easily pierced Henley's skull.

"No," Dessie whispered. "No!" She'd backed up to the bars separating them from the neighbouring cage. Hands had reached out, grasping at Dessie's arms. Booker tried to get to her, but stumbled and fell as he put weight on his injured leg.

Maggs dashed forward, tugging Dessie clear before swinging her axe at the undead arms still reaching through the bars. The blade carved into flesh, exposing bone, but there was no sound from the zombie on the far side, only screams and sobs.

"Dessie! Look out," Jack said. Maggs turned around in time to see Booker getting back to his feet. There were no knives in his hand now, just blank rage on his face. Jack was already swinging his hammer, but Booker threw out his arm as he lumbered around. Much larger, younger, and now operating with unthinking strength, Booker's hand caught Jack in the temple, sending him sprawling. Maggs pushed Dessie clear, swinging her axe up and into the side of Booker's head. The blade lodged, and the zombie slowly toppled to the ground.

"Dessie, help Jack," Maggs said as she grabbed the tomahawk's handle, bracing her foot on Booker's chest. "Ginger, how's it looking?"

"Two still active outside. Two alive next door, and one at the end. Over here!" she called out, banging the cage door. Muttonchops lurched towards the bars. Ginger thrust her machete through them, but the blade merely scored a line through his stubbly forehead.

"On three, I'm going to let go," Ricardo said.

Maggs tugged the axe free. She looked over at Dessie and Jack. He was still gathering himself. She was still in shock. Back at the spa, people had turned quickly, within minutes, not the hours it could sometimes take. Neither Jack nor Dessie had turned, and she was just going to hope that would remain the case here.

Muttonchops lunged, thrusting his undead arms through the bars.

"Three!" Ginger yelled. Both she and Ricardo stepped sideways. The door swung inward, and the zombie came with it. Ricardo grabbed the gate with his left hand, stopping it when it reached thirty degrees. The zombie's face banged into the bars, and Ricardo swung his pick into the back of its skull.

Maggs had already darted around him, out into the corridor, where one more zombie was trying to get into the neighbouring cell. "Over here!"

The zombie turned around. Ginger rushed past, screaming, raising her machete over her head as she ducked low and hacked down at the zombie's legs. As the zombie fell, Ginger spun past, flipping the blade so she could plunge it through the monster's face.

"Back here, quick," Maggs said, looking down the corridor filled with bodies and blood, and no survivors. Slowly, her gaze turned to the other two cells. Three had survived in the neighbouring cage, all dripping with blood. In the third cage, the man still sat on his bench and appeared to still be reading. Maggs walked over, uncertain what she was going to ask, or say, and saw he'd wedged the door closed with two knives.

"Are you okay?" she asked.

"If the pen is mightier than the sword, then the knife is stronger than a lock," he said, without taking his eyes off his book.

She didn't have the time for his ostentatious affectation, so walked back towards the main door. It remained closed. She looked up at the security cameras, wondering if they were recording. Probably not.

Dessie was crying silently, holding a homemade mace in two hands as if it were a totem that might turn back time while she looked down at Henley. Jack was back in his chair, holding his face.

"Are you okay, Jack?"

"I just got the wind knocked from me," he said. "I'll be ready."

"Good. I think it's over, and they're just waiting for the gas to clear, but he said something about this being the first test. I wouldn't be surprised if there was more trouble ahead."

"Who is he? You said you met him."

"Not John. We met Dalton. When did they pick you up?"

"Last night. We ran a small checkpoint here last year. A welcome wagon for people heading south. When winter set in, we had to leave, and only returned a few days ago. They turned up last night."

"What happens now?" Dessie asked. "What do they want?"

"They're following a madman, so don't bother asking," Jack said. "In my day, lunatics like that stood by the intersection holding up a sign. I knew some of them. Served with some of them. Too much war, not enough care. Then along came the internet, and now they're everywhere." He took a handkerchief from his pocket and began to clean his hammer.

Maggs looked at the tomahawk and wiped the worst of the gore on the trouser leg of the dead zombie by the door to the cell. And then they waited. She had more questions for Jack, but knew she'd get questions in return, and was worried she might let slip some clue that her people were still alive. Dessie and Jack could probably be trusted. The other three next door, she didn't know. The guy at the end, definitely not.

After another five minutes, the outer door to the detention room opened. Dalton entered with a single guard. Neither were wearing respirators despite the still strong scent of cherry blossom in the air.

"You got tested too, eh?" Maggs said, stepping forward to take control of the conversation.

"Almost everyone has been, yes," Dalton said.

"You bastard! You murdering bastard!" Dessie rushed forward, ducking under Ricardo's arms.

Maggs grabbed her. "I know," she said, pulling her back. "But they have guns and the door's still locked."

Dalton raised his hands in a conciliatory gesture spoiled by the gun in his companion's hand. "I get it. Really, I do. The general will return soon. When he does, listen to what he says."

"The general? You mean John?" Maggs cut in.

"General Denning, yes," Dalton said. "After he's spoken, those who want to leave can. Anyone who chooses to join us, can. If you're wise, you'll volunteer. First, I need to clear away the people who failed the test." He turned back to Maggs, making eye contact as he spoke. "I need a volunteer to collect the handcart."

"I'll go," Ricardo said.

"No, it's fine," Maggs said. "I'll do it."

"You won't need the axe," the soldier said.

Maggs handed it to Ricardo. She turned back to the soldier. "Better?"

The soldier said nothing, but handed a key to Dalton before raising his rifle again. Dalton unlocked the gate and stepped back. "This way, please."

"Oh, after you," Maggs said.

"No, sorry, but you first," he said as he locked the gate after her. When she reached the end of the office-space, she looked around and saw the soldier had remained by the reinforced door to their battleground cells.

"You don't need back-up?" she asked.

"Through there," he said. "You don't want to keep the general waiting."

There was no one in the reception area. Outside, a black pickup had arrived. A cook was frying meat in thyme and garlic. Four soldiers lingered nearby in a tableau that was both intimidating and insulting, one was smoking, two passed a ball back and forth, and the last was cleaning a rifle.

"This was just a temporary base, then?" Maggs asked. "Somewhere you picked because the detention centre made a great gas chamber?"

"I didn't pick it, the general did," Dalton said. "And keep your voice down."

"Why? The general's insane, and you're no better. You're a sadistic killer."

"I'm just trying to stay alive," he said. "Over there. That warehouse. Listen, the general is… he isn't well."

"I can tell. He's a lunatic."

"No, I mean he's got a brain tumour. He was being treated before the outbreak. Zombies came along. Treatment stopped. He thinks God cured him so he can complete this mission. Maybe he went into remission, but he's been deteriorating rapidly for the last few months."

"Then why are you enabling him?"

"It's not me. I'm not the one who gave him his power. She's somewhere in the south. I've never met her, and I don't want to, not if he's anything to go by. The soldiers, they believe in him. Some *really* believe. They're loyal, so be careful what they hear you say. I can't protect you from them."

"Oh, so you're protecting me, are you?"

"I am. So when he asks you to choose, volunteer to stay. Please."

She looked him up and down. He was dressed much the same as when she'd first met him, but she no longer saw a stoic hero fighting the good fight in a bad world, only a broken coward, lost and alone.

"Where's this handcart?"

Chapter 47 - The Second Test
Longview

She wheeled the handcart back to the customs house. Dalton left them to load the bodies alone. Dessie insisted they leave Henley and Booker until last. The other four survivors didn't know any of the dead, or claimed not to. They were all just travellers, picked up in the last week as they were trying to head south. Rather, that's what the three who'd survived in the middle cage said. The reader offered nothing except aloof disinterest.

"We need another handcart," Maggs said, as she looked at the dead.

"I need my rifle," Dessie said.

"A time and a place," Jack said. "And this is neither."

"They murdered Henley! I'm not letting that go," Dessie said.

"What have I told you about emotions?" Jack said. "Time and place, and it's not here. We've got people depending on us, remember?"

The words weren't intended for Maggs to hear, but they did raise an important question. "Jack, when you got back here after your winter hiatus, did it look like others had been staying here? These people in particular."

"Someone had been in the hide by the bridge," Jack said. "But I didn't think anything of it."

"Do you mean the log cabin built on the north side of the Lewis and Clark Bridge?"

"That's it. We didn't leave much there. Nothing that couldn't be easily replaced, but someone had used it, except there was no one there when we arrived. No one alive anyway."

"So they didn't leave a permanent guard at that checkpoint," Maggs said.

"Ah, I see where you're going," Jack said.

"Where?" Dessie asked.

"They don't have many people," Jack said. The implication seemed to revitalise him. "How many did you see outside?"

"Six, and I think I recognised two from earlier. And since they were waiting on Dalton to return there are maybe twenty people here. Maybe thirty. No more. It tallies with my theory that they are trying to eliminate all groups too large for them to control."

"And they're looking for a vault," Ginger said.

"And are ruled by a brain tumour. Quite literally," Maggs said. "The general, John, was being treated for one before the outbreak. Dalton said his condition is deteriorating. It puts his whole broom act into a different light."

"What broom act?" Dessie asked.

"He was sweeping up outside when we arrived. It's such a futile gesture, unless the world you see is different to the one the rest of us live in."

"He can't have long left," Jack said.

"I don't think we can wait for him to drop dead," Maggs said. She paused. Dalton had said the general's name was Denning. She knew that name from somewhere, but couldn't place where. It would come to her. "How did you get across the bridge, Jack?"

"We didn't," he said with a grin.

"Your base is in Washington State?"

"Nope," he said, enjoying the puzzle he'd set. Before Maggs could press him for a straight answer, the door clanked open. The general had returned, along with four guards, the captain, and Dalton.

"You were tested and found to have much left to give," John said. "Yet the righteous must be willing. The chosen must first choose themselves. Stay, or go." He stepped aside and pointed at the door.

"That's me," the reader said, standing up. He finally opened his cell door, and walked out into the corridor, tucking his book into his pocket.

"If you leave, you may never return," John said.

"No problem, bub. I never look back."

The general waved at the door, seeming to lose all interest. The three from the other cell hurried after him. The general barely gave them a glance.

"Anyone else?"

"Maggs?" Ginger whispered.

"We're staying," Maggs said. Behind the general, she saw Dalton close his eyes in what might have been relief. In many ways, that was as disturbing as the general's disjointed words.

"All of you?" John asked, looking at Jack and Dessie.

"I think there's a lot we've yet to be told," Jack said.

"Of course. But you are the chosen. *We* are the chosen. We are…" A deep frown creased his brow. His mouth moved, but no words came out.

"You need to rest, sir," the captain said, moving with practiced efficiency to his side. "Sheriff, take care of the corpses."

The captain helped the general back through the door. The other soldiers followed, until only Dalton was left.

"Your friends have gone, *Sheriff*," Ginger said.

Ricardo stepped past her.

Dalton raised a hand. "There's only one door to this room, and only one door to the customs house. Immediately outside is a small army waiting to get dinner. Maybe you want to think before you act, and listen before you jump into a hole there's no way to crawl out of."

Ricardo looked to Maggs, allowing Dalton to look behind, checking that they were alone. When he next spoke, he kept his voice low. "Bide your time. You'll get fed. Maybe afterwards you'll be lucky enough to get your revenge. I know I wasn't."

"We'll play your game for a while, Constant," Maggs said. "But we won't play it in ignorance. You'll tell us what's going on here."

"Yes, I will. But right now, the general gave us orders, and he did it in front of the captain, so you can't hope he'll forget. We need to dispose of the bodies. Lesson one for survival here, never cross Captain Pakhaüser. She's a true believer."

"Sydney's dead," Ginger said, but the barb didn't have the result she was expecting.

"I know. Thank you for that," Dalton said.

"Where do we take the bodies?" Maggs asked, hoping to lower the tension before it ripped a hole in the roof.

"There's a mass grave just beyond the warehouses. It's still not full."

"We're not putting Henley and Booker in there," Dessie said.

"Dig a grave for them if you want," Dalton said. "No one will mind."

Ricardo pushed the overloaded cart out of their caged killing room, with Ginger helping to steer. Dessie stayed close to Jack who'd waved away all offers of help. Maggs followed at the back, just in front of Dalton, trying to work out what to say. The office, again, was empty, but immediately outside was a near carnival. There was no music, but there was plenty of talking, laughing, and, yes, praying. She counted eleven people gathered around the fire, and it sounded like there were more hidden out of sight. There was certainly one sitting atop a warehouse to the north, legs dangling over the building's edge.

Dalton pointed them northwest, between two warehouses where a channel had been pushed between the debris. "The graves are behind there."

Jack grunted. Maggs wondered if he was going to say something, or if it was just age and injury. How far could he run? For that matter, could she run? There was a second rooftop sentry, this one on a building to the east. If there were two, there might be more. She would have to assume more.

The abandoned bags had been picked up and stacked along the alley's walls. Those on the very top of the stack bulged. They were probably waterlogged, but she'd bet they were filled with the junk previously spilled from other bags into the alley. Crows cawed a warning as they reached the alley's end, and their chorus was taken up by a flurry of gulls. The mass graves were in a squashed circle of undeveloped land just short of a branched ending of railway tracks. Four bald mounds rose skywards, each covered in a ratty growth of green. Next to them was a pile of dirt, an abandoned excavator, and a partially submerged pit, already containing three bodies.

"Shoo!" Dessie said, waving her arms at the birds now waiting atop the excavator.

Maggs brushed her hand through the air, trying to banish the cloud of midges that hovered nearby.

"There's some shovels over there if you want to dig a grave," Dalton said. "But don't take long. Half an hour, at most."

"You're leaving us?" Maggs asked as Dalton turned around. "You're not worried we'll escape?"

"No." He looked around. They were alone, but he still lowered his voice. "The gate's guarded. There's a sniper on that rooftop. They expect you to run. The general thinks trust is important."

"This is another test?" Ginger asked.

Dalton shrugged. "They never end. *Never*." Head bowed, he walked away.

"He's defeated," Jack said while Dalton was still within earshot. "Seen it before, usually the culprit is a bank. Dessie, why don't you find a shovel."

"Help her, Ric," Maggs said. She took a cautious step forward to look into the pit. Enough water had filled the bottom that some bodies were completely submerged.

"We dug this last year," Jack said, inching a little closer to the edge. "The pit was for the zombies we killed while we waited. We put about twenty in there. Covered them with dirt before we moved out, but thought we'd be back sooner, and that we'd need to add more bodies. I didn't come to look at it yesterday. Should have done. You're right, Maggs. They were here before us, during winter. There must be about forty new bodies in there. Come on, then, if we're not running, we might as well get this done."

They wheeled the cart close to the pit, causing a small avalanche of gravel and grit from the very edge to cascade downwards.

"This isn't safe. Find us a pole or something, Ginger," Maggs said. She took a step back from the edge and looked up at the rooftops, staring at the guard watching them.

"You dug all these pits?" she asked.

"No, just this little one," Jack said. "The larger ones were already here, dug by the crews who barricaded the bridge. We arrived in fall. But it was later than we realised. Winter came early. We had to pull back."

"Why here? If the bridge is blocked, why did you come here?"

"Because the bridge is on the maps. It's where people would come. Last year, we couldn't spare many people to search. This year, there's no need. People have found their farms. Only those for whom farming has failed will take to the road. Those that do, that come south, or go north, need to cross the river. We couldn't monitor every bridge, but this seemed the most likely place to meet people. I wish I'd been wrong."

"We found farms in the north, near Olympia. It was a real community. Thousands of people. They built a central fortress and operated at least a dozen satellite farms. Dalton, or the general, killed them in early December, the same way they killed my people."

"With that gas?" Jack asked.

"Yes," Maggs said. "And with trust. We wanted to believe there was a government who would help us. Dalton arrived in his sheriff's car, talking about a bunker in Cheyenne Mountain and tens of thousands of survivors. We so desperately wanted to believe him, we didn't question it. From what we gathered, the fortress people thought the same."

Steel bit into dirt close to the railway tracks. They'd found a shovel. Dessie was digging. Ricardo stood nearby.

"Dessie and Henley, they were together?" Maggs asked.

"They were. Met in a coffee bar when they both skipped out early from the same Halloween party. She was a good girl, Henley. Had some strange ideas, but isn't that what youth is about? She said that after they've taken everything from you, when you've been reduced to skin and sorrow, you still had your sense of identity, so you had to hold on to it even tighter. Maybe there's some truth in that. She didn't deserve this."

"He's going to pay for it," Maggs said.

"Ah, you're just like Dessie. She's a lawyer. One of the good ones. Worked for peanuts, taking on the corporations who thought money had more rights than people. And what I told her, and what I told Henley, is that out in the real world, the villains don't always get caught, victims don't always get justice, and people often don't learn from the past."

"Last year, there were fifteen thousand of us up at Red Lake in Ontario," Maggs said. "We'd really thought we'd survived the worst, until plague swept through. About five hundred survived. We still don't know what killed everyone. That's why we came west."

"And Dalton killed the rest of you?"

"They came in at night, used crossbows to kill anyone who was awake. I suppose they used night-vision, too. And they plugged an aerosol canister into our air circulation system. But the night before, they sent hundreds of zombies against us so we would use up our bullets. The morning after the battle, Dalton brought an engineer to look around, so he could work out whether the building was airtight enough to kill us off. They are professionals, at least at this."

"But they aren't soldiers," Jack said. By the railway, Dessie stopped digging. Ricardo reached down, offering a hand. She hesitated, but took it, and he took her place in the hole.

"Are you sure they're not soldiers?" Maggs asked.

"Positive. One of them is wearing a Korean War ribbon, and he can't be more than twenty-five."

"Ah. Did you serve?"

"Long ago. Very long ago. I spent the last fifty years farming. Twelve thousand acres, plus some orchards, and a fishing lake. I left it to my son and moved to a retirement place. Quiet spot. Small. Everyone was into crafts and baking, book clubs and day trips to the ocean or down to the redwoods."

"It sounds nice."

"It was, in its way. I hated it. After the outbreak, Dessie and Henley came to pick me up. Our farm had been overrun. My boy was dead. It was just Dessie and Henley left. Them and a pack of survivors who thought mowing a lawn once a week meant they understood the land. Ah, some aren't so bad, I suppose, but they were all heading north, trying to get on the evacuation. It was all long over by then, of course."

"Do you think this will do?" Ginger asked, returning with a length of scaffolding pole in her hands. Ricardo was now shovelling dirt as fast as any machine, while Dessie sat with her head in her hands, her eyes on the growing heap of soil.

"Perfect," Maggs said.

They added the dead travellers to the pit, put Henley's and Booker's bodies back on the cart, and took them over to the grave. It was already deep, though not head height.

"That'll do," Jack said.

"Are you sure?" Dessie asked. "Shouldn't it be deeper?"

"She won't be disturbed," Jack said. "Best get them put to rest before we get called away."

There was no gentle way of lowering the bodies in, so they did it quickly. Booker first, Henley second.

"They look peaceful there," Jack said. "Fill it in, please."

Ginger took the shovel from Ricardo, who was breathing hard, his sweat turning the dirt into streaks of mud.

"Should we say something?" Ginger asked.

Maggs looked over at Dessie, then down at the awkwardly entangled bodies. She couldn't help but think of all those like Fern, Roy, and Kayleigh, who never got a grave. Those like Tatiana and Alexander, whose fate would never be known. Those like Nana and Harmony, and like her dear Etienne, who she could hope were still alive, and yet whom she feared were long gone.

"The best revenge is a long life, lived well," Jack said. "You both taught us how to live well, and so we will. You won't be forgotten. Rest now. Be at peace."

The grave was almost full when a squeak of wheels marked Dalton's return. With him was one of John's crusaders, pushing another handcart, containing the bodies of the four travellers who'd opted to leave rather than join the general's insanity.

Chapter 48 - The Soldier's Lament
Longview

"Shall we fill it in?" Ginger asked, after they'd tumbled the four new bodies into the mass grave.

Maggs turned to the sheriff. "Well, Constant, should we fill it in, or do you expect more unfortunate travellers?"

He shook his head. "Leave it. There'll be more."

"Do we know their names?" Dessie asked. "Shouldn't we mark them down somewhere, or at least read them out."

"I kept names at first," Dalton said. "As I cleared out my town, I wrote down the names of every zombie I killed. I figured, one day, they'd go up on a memorial. I filled a book before I realised that day's never going to come. I don't keep names anymore."

"Then we should say a few words," Dessie said. "We can't just leave them like this."

"She's right," Jack said, turning to the uniformed young man who'd accompanied Dalton. "Go on, soldier, why don't you lead us in prayer?"

The sight of the corpses hadn't shocked the youth, but he blanched at the idea of having to speak in public. "I don't know any prayers."

"And what would your general say to that?" Jack said. "There's always the soldier's prayer. Hats off. Come on."

The guard hurriedly pulled off his baseball cap. Dalton, a little more slowly, a little more cautiously, removed his Stetson, but never removed his hand from the hilt of his holstered sidearm.

While Jack intoned the words, Maggs bent her head, but raised her eyes to the roof of the nearby warehouse. The sniper appeared to be standing at attention. Interesting. So was the absence of ribbons on their young guard's chest and his evident lack of a religious education in this camp of extremists.

"Amen," Jack said. "Unless you're firing off a salute?"

"We're not allowed to waste the bullets," Dalton said. "Leave the cart. I'm going to take you back to the customs house."

Mealtime for the cultists seemed to be over. Only four remained by the smouldering grill, talking quietly. As their group of prisoners came into earshot, one who seemed to be leading the discussion straightened her back, and motioned for silence. She had a single row of ribbons on her chest. The others only had one or two citations. Was that book in her hands a Bible? It looked too thin, and they didn't get close enough to see. Perhaps that was part of their indoctrination. Perhaps not. Maggs was still undecided when they reached the customs house.

"Food is waiting inside," Dalton said. "I have to speak with the captain, but I hope to return, otherwise you shouldn't be disturbed tonight. That's one of—" He stopped as if catching himself from saying something he'd regret. He shook his head. "Calvin will be right outside if you need anything."

Maggs watched Dalton walk off, trying to guess at what he'd almost said until the guard, Calvin, pointed at the door.

"Please," he said. He sounded scared. He looked terrified. But not of her. She went inside and listened to him lock the door behind her.

The other four, who'd entered first, were gathered around the counter where Captain Pakhaüser had written their details in her census.

"It smells like meat," Ginger said, inspecting the saucepan waiting on the inspection counter. "But I'd want to know what kind before I ate it."

They were alone, Maggs realised. There were no guards inside. Jack took the saucepan, sniffed, and nodded to himself. From an inside pocket, he took out a small leather case and removed a folding cutlery set. He speared a lump of meat with the fork, and began to chew.

"It's not people, if that's what's worrying you," he said.

"Grandpa! I told you to stop saying that," Dessie said.

"What? I'm saying it's *not* human flesh," he said.

"You *never* say that," she said. "Especially not when people are eating."

"None of us are eating this," Jack said, putting his bowl aside. "It's black bear, and one that needs a bit more tenderising and a lot more cooking."

"How'd you know what people taste like?" Ginger asked.

"He's joking," Dessie said.

"You hope," Jack said, but it had broken the tension.

"Were you a soldier?" Ricardo asked.

"I was."

"Which war?" Ricardo asked.

"Does it matter?" Jack said. "When you get down to it, they're all the same. Blood, chaos, and confusion. It robs you of your innocence, destroys you, even if you survive. You change so much, if you're lucky enough to get home, you'll never recognise it. There's no redemption in a foxhole, despite what the preachers like you to think. That's what gets me about these people wearing ribbons like they're accessories. It's disrespectful. Medals are for funerals. This lot, they're wearing length-of-service awards as if it meant they raised the flag on Iwo Jima themselves."

"Oh, so that's where you served," Ricardo said.

Jack spluttered. "How old do you... oh. Very funny," he added when he saw Ricardo was smiling.

"Let's go back to you and man-flesh," Ginger said.

"Don't. Once he starts, he doesn't stop," Dessie said with a rueful shake of her head, but her personal loss had been moved from the forefront of her mind, at least for now.

The little light from the setting sun that made it through the small and opaque windows barely added shape to the shadows, but darkness was near. "Ginger, Dessie, why don't you look for a back door, and make sure we're alone in here. Jack, Ric, and I will fetch the bags from the holding cells, and see if there's any edible food left down there."

"We're going to escape?" Ricardo asked.

"Definitely," Maggs said as they headed into the ransacked office. "We just need to work out how. Hopefully, we might find a hidden gun or two in someone else's bag. Though I suppose, if they had one, they'd have used it."

"They searched our bags when they brought us in," Jack said. "They didn't do that for you?"

"We came here empty-handed, leaving ours in the log-cabin checkpoint on the bridge," Maggs said. "You kept your gear with you?"

"Most of it is still down by the river, a little further west. We kept a hidden stash just in case of an emergency, including my spare rifle. Put that in my hands, and I'll show them what a real soldier can do."

"We've got to get out first," Ricardo said, as he opened the door leading down to the holding cells.

The killing room was worse without bodies. Bloodstains and discarded blades gave the impression of a massacre of hundreds. Not that the reality hadn't been bad enough. It was like the spa, like at so many places she'd seen, where there'd been so much death in such a short space of time that the specific details were incomprehensible.

She picked her way over the still-drying pools of blood, towards the cell at the far end, but had to stop halfway. The buckets used in the curtained toilets had spilled. She turned her back, trying to recall what book the man at the end had been reading. He'd been so confident in his survival. The other three, who'd been in the middle cell, had simply wanted to escape. The man at the end had been different. Calculating, careful, and certain that he didn't need whatever protection these cultists offered. Where had he come from? Where was he going?

"I'd rather eat these than stew," Ricardo said, holding up a display box from the food-table.

"Me, too," she said. "What is it?"

"Candy disguised as health food," he said. "Almonds, honey, oats. Chilli, too, for some reason."

"Perfect. Grab anything that's not contaminated," she said, as she went into the middle cell and picked up the bags of the travellers who'd turned into the undead. As she took them up to the entrance, she wondered what had happened to the bags of those who'd been executed. Not claimed as treasure, or these bags would have gone, too. Dumped, then? It made no sense. And therein lay the danger. She was trying to ascribe rational behaviour to people following an irrational leader.

She carried the bags back up to the office. Ricardo had followed her out, a single box in his large hands. He put it down. She raised an eyebrow, while he lowered his voice.

"The vault they're looking for is the same one as in Hank's letter," he said.

"I know," Maggs said. "But we will say nothing about that. Not now. Not ever. Only a few of us know what was in the letters, or even that there were letters. And not a word about Vader, either. Not yet."

She returned to the charnel house where she found Jack sitting in the cage in which Henley and Booker had died, a soft leather satchel open in front of him.

"Is that Henley's?" she asked.

"Booker's," he said. "Don't know where he found it. He was always carrying it. Said it was the perfect bag. Never rubbed. Lightweight. Waterproof. The strap was the perfect length. He'd wax lyrical about it for hours, all while waxing the bag. He said it proved civilisation was due to collapse because we kept on trying to improve on perfection."

Maggs waked over to the wall and ran a finger down the scar left by the thrown knife that had come within a hand's breadth of ending her sorrows. She bent down to pick up the blade. Double-edged, with a blade twice as long as the handle, and that was too short for her to properly grip. Even with practice, it would take an expert to injure a person.

Against a zombie, it was less effective than throwing a brick. It was well-balanced, though.

"He had a point," she said, turning the blade over in her hands. "Who in the world actually needed throwing knives? You can't hunt with them. You can't really defend yourself with them. I mean, if you miss, all you've done is given your attacker a weapon. And yet, there was a market. Just because there's a demand, doesn't mean there needs to be a supply."

Jack laughed. "Sorry. You just reminded me of someone. A few years ago, an English girl came to stay with us. A student. She was doing an exchange program. Dessie was her local guide. I picked her up at the airport because Dessie never remembers to check her oil. The accommodation they were supposed to put her up in had been condemned while Kim, that's her name, was in the air. The college's alternative was a disgrace, so she came to stay with us on the farm. I insisted. Taught her to shoot. Taught her to hunt. Taught her a bit about life somewhere there isn't a castle around every corner." He pointed to the knife. "One Saturday, we went to a fair. A guy there was doing knife tricks, spinning a story about how he'd learned them while in the Marines. He was poor choices wrapped in bad tattoos and worse breath, the kind of person who'd try selling life insurance to Lazarus. When he caught wind of her accent, he started pestering her, trying to make her part of the show. She said, over in England, they used swords, and she knew just where to stick one. Ah, hadn't thought of her in a while. We were going to visit England, me and my wife…" He trailed off, lost in the cumulative grief that comes to those cursed to outlive those they love.

"No one can take our memories from us," Maggs said as she slipped the knife into her pocket. "But this is no place to recall them." She reached down and took his arm. "There are three bags up there. Take a look inside and see what we can use."

She walked him as far as the door before returning to the executioner's chamber. Here and now, grief was dangerous. Ricardo was correct: the general was looking for Hank's vault. Gordon knew that she might not make it back tonight. This time tomorrow, he'd start to worry. The day after, he'd come looking. She'd told him not to, but knew he wouldn't listen. Whether she was alive or dead, if Gordon rolled into the same trap they had, her people would be discovered, and so would Hank's safe house, with the letters that gave a clue as to where the vault was.

She had to stop Gordon from coming here, which meant getting back to Vader, destroying the letters, and the safe house, and then getting everyone away. To do that, they had to escape.

Chapter 49 - Moonlight Concerto
Longview

Jack had emptied the bags onto the floor, except for Booker's and Henley's, which remained untouched to one side. The first priority was clothing. There wasn't much to choose from, but Maggs grabbed what she could and quickly changed. She'd never been one to get attached to clothes, but she would miss that coat; it was the nicest one she'd found in weeks. She emptied the pockets, surprised at how much junk she'd collected in only a few days, slipping the knife, some string, and a precious half-pack of tissues into the pockets of a plaid fleece. It wasn't her colour, though at least this one wouldn't show the blood as easily. There were no shoes that fit, so with her old shirt as a rag, she began cleaning the worst of the blood off her boots.

"Were there any guns?" she asked.

"No. Not that I was expecting one, but you live in hope," Jack said as he opened a paperback, flicking through the pages. "Nothing."

"You do that, too?" Maggs asked. "Looking for diaries and letters?"

"Of course. I've got to get my news fix from somewhere, and this way is a lot more reliable than cable TV." He held up a phone. The screen glowed, showing most of a photo of three children. The youngest couldn't be older than nine, yet all three were holding axes, with a felled tree in the background. "It looks like a recent photo, doesn't it? It could be older, but it's probably taken within the last year." He dropped the phone. "The benighted thing is locked. Why did everything have to be computerised?"

"It was the millennials' revenge on your generation for making housing so expensive," Dessie said as she and Ginger returned.

"Is there a back door?" Maggs asked.

"There is, but it's locked from outside," Ginger said.

"With a chain," Dessie said, her voice now full of resolve. "There are skylights that form part of an emergency ventilation system."

"Can we climb up?" Maggs asked.

"Yes," Ginger said. "But there are three problems. First, the glass has been painted over. Second, as best we can tell, they sealed the top from the outside with foam, like they did at the spa and the other gas chambers they used. Third, the mechanism to open them must have been electronic because we can't find it."

"And fourth, we think there's someone on the roof," Dessie said.

"If we can't tunnel down, climb out, or use a back door, we'll have to use the front," Jack said. "I'll pretend to have a heart attack. We'll get the guards to come in." He bent down to pick up a knife from among the discarded possessions. "And then we leave."

Before they could discuss the pros and many cons of his plan, a shout came from the reception area. "Hello." It was Dalton.

"I didn't even hear the door open," Maggs said as she stood up. She walked through the office and into the lobby.

Dalton was alone, but the door was open, and she thought she could hear voices outside.

"If you've come to offer us more dinner, we'll pass," she said.

"No. I'd like to clear the air. I think we got off on the wrong foot."

"Wrong foot? You murdered Kayleigh and her baby!" Ginger said.

Maggs raised a hand. "We'll hear you out. Say what you have to."

"Not here," Dalton said. "I thought we could go for a walk. Just you and me."

"You've got to be kidding," Ginger said.

"No," Maggs said, looking at Dalton more closely. "He's serious. Okay, yes, I suppose we do have a few things to discuss."

"Maggs—" Ginger began, but Maggs held up a hand. "It's a trap, or it's not, and this is the best way to find out."

"You should bring the axe," Dalton said.

"Oh, so this is another test?" Maggs asked.

"No. Not tonight." He turned and left.

Two guards sat at a picnic table outside, about ten metres to the left of the doorway. She recognised Calvin, the guard who'd brought the four extra bodies to the mass graves. The other man, also about twenty, looked nothing like a soldier and even less like a religious convert. His hair was scraggly as if he'd just begun to grow it out. His hunter's camouflage was too long on the arms. His uneven stubble barely covered his spots. Where the first guard stood as she and Dalton came out, the scruff merely glanced at them, before returning to a card game that involved dice and a notepad.

Dalton gave them a dismissive wave before walking off through the abandoned refugee camp, away from the cars. Maggs followed slowly, taking in everything. Twilight was slipping into night, making the other lights easier to see. The card-playing guards had two lamps, as did one of the warehouse-roof sentries who was walking back and forth. Otherwise, there was no one around. Even the four guards who'd been lingering by the grill had gone. In the distance, she could hear music faintly playing.

"Are you taking me back to the graves?" she asked when it became clear Dalton wasn't going to initiate the conversation.

"It's quiet and not overlooked," he said.

She stopped. "My jailor wants to take me to a mass grave because it's not overlooked? I think I've come far enough."

"I didn't mean it like that," he said, turning to face her. In the gloom, his features were entirely hidden by his hat. When she'd first met him, the hat had made him seem dashing. Now, it seemed nothing but a childish affectation.

"What *did* you mean?" she asked.

"That I'd like a few minutes where I don't have to watch what I say the whole goddamn time."

"The railway tracks, then," she said. "Not the graves." She took the lead, angling towards the alley between the warehouses. "How much of what you told me was a lie?"

"None of it," he said.

"You *are* a sheriff?"

"I am. I was."

"There are hundreds of thousands of survivors?"

"Maybe. I'm not sure. I think there are. I just haven't seen them."

"And you're based out of Cheyenne Mountain?"

"No. Okay, sure, some of it was exaggerated. Some details were changed. But if you take what I said as a whole, it's mostly true."

She said nothing more until they were out in the dead ground. She knew the spot she wanted, just beyond where they'd buried Booker and Henley, and where the tracks stretched eastwards through a loading yard filled with empty freight wagons and little else. She perched herself on the narrow platform the drivers would use to climb aboard their locomotives, and where she had a view of the warehouses.

"Stand in front of me, and take your hat off," she said.

"What? Why?"

"Let me see your eyes. Thank you. It's not the most salubrious of spots, but it matches the air between us. Go on, take your shot at clearing it."

"I know an apology will never be enough. I don't even know where to begin. I am sorry. And I'm angry at ever having been thrown into this nightmare. Zombies, nuclear war, and the complete collapse of everything should have been enough. But no. Of course, bad people would take power, and use violence and fear to entrench their positions because that's what they've always done. Now there's no concern for law or morality to hold them back."

"At the spa, when we were attacked by zombies, that was you?"

"Brewster, but yes. It's how he softens up the targets. If they're overrun, all to the good. If not, he gets a look inside when giving advice on how to improve the defences."

"So he can work out whether you can gas us. I found the canister attached to the air pump. I know that's how you did it."

"Yes."

"Where is he? I haven't seen him?"

"Brewster? On a survey mission for the general. He comes and goes. He knew the general before. When the general dies, Brewster will take over."

Maggs nodded and looked up at the rooftops, counting the lights.

"In Olympia, we found hundreds of zombies stuck in a mall," she said. "Was that you?"

"Them, yes. Me? I suppose so."

"Well, go on, explain it. You wanted to talk, so get on with it."

"They don't want any large groups who might be a threat to their holy mission."

"But why not just kill us? Why turn so many into zombies and leave them trapped in buildings up and down the countryside?"

"You know, at first, I think it was to prove that they could. You'd have to ask the scientists. That's Brewster's team. They… they're worse than the captain. Worse than the general. The undead are their new army."

"He thinks he can give the zombies orders?"

"No, he just unleashes them, like he did on you."

"Why?"

"It depends on who you ask. The general thinks the outbreak is a test from God. Those who are infected, the zombies, will be cured when the final battle comes. Leaving them alive is his way of creating a holy army. Brewster thinks people are inherently untrustworthy. Rather than recruiting an army that will rebel if it isn't paid, he wants to use the undead. They're traps, basically. Sometimes it's easier leading your enemy to the undead than the other way around." Dalton raised his hands. "I know.

It's madness. I don't know how much point there is in rationalising any of this."

"A lot, I'd say, since the general might be sick, but the rest of them aren't. Okay, what's next for the five of us?"

"Usually, we'd move you to separate farms, so if one runs the others could be punished."

"In other words, slave labour on a plantation. But you said usually."

"Yes. I think I can get you transferred south, away from the general, to repair a dam."

"Ah." That got her full attention. She thought back to the spa and the interest he'd shown when she'd told him who she'd worked for. "Where exactly?"

"I was hoping you would tell me. We have plenty of oil, but no other source of electricity. I was hoping you could repair a dam."

"Probably. Why does the general want electricity in the south, and not up here?"

"He's not in charge. Not anymore. He's in self-imposed exile, chasing visions about some government vault that contains the hidden treasures of humanity. The grail, Longinus's lance, you name it, just as long as that name is part of Christian mythology. I know it's not real, but the captain believes in the general's visions. Brewster... I'm not sure what Brewster thinks. I try not to have anything to do with him."

"Who is in charge if it's not the general?" she asked.

"I don't know her name. I've heard people call her Tippy, or the doctor, and I think it's the same person. She's a NASA scientist, and she and the general pulled things together at Cape Canaveral. From what I've heard, they control the U.S.'s entire strategic fuel reserve, the Gulf of Mexico, most of the Mississippi, and have a presence in the Atlantic. There's a lot of rumour, and even more legend, but I don't know how much to believe."

"Have you met her?"

"No. But I have met her people. Sometimes she sends them to monitor the general. Sometimes he kills them. You saw him on a really good day. And when he's having a good day, the captain has a good day. When he's having a bad day, you want to be in a different state."

Maggs scanned the rooftops as she processed what he was saying. There were two lights now.

"How many people are in the south?" she asked.

"Hundreds of thousands. I don't know how many. No one does. Whenever they find people, they move them to a farm, like you saw with the Connollys. Except, by all accounts, it's worse down there. Real slavery, because there's more oversight. More overseers means the slaves have to work harder to keep their masters fed."

"And that's who you want to throw your lot in with? Replacing a dying, and deluded, general with an astronaut who wants to bring back the Confederacy?"

"I… No. It's… look, it's more complicated than that. You've travelled across the continent, yes? How many large groups of survivors did you meet?"

"None, unless you count people who shot at us before we could even say hello."

"Right. And the evacuation failed. There's no one left here in the north, or in the south, or along the East Coast."

"In part, thanks to you."

"Entirely thanks to the general, the captain, their scientists, and this woman down in Louisiana who's supporting them. This is it. This is all that's left of North America."

"What about Mexico, or the Caribbean?"

"There are some farmers around the Gulf, and that's all. North America, the richest continent on the planet, is home to a few small groups and to this one large group. If anywhere in the world was doing better, where are they? Where are the planes? Where are the looters? This truly is what humanity has become."

"Then there's no one at Cheyenne Mountain?"

"I don't know, but I don't think so. There are rumours. Or there were, before the *unbelievers* were weeded out. The general thinks, when he's found the vault, his weapon will help remove Tippy's enemies who are hiding in a bunker, but I don't know if there's any truth to that, or if it's just another one of his visions."

"And this is who you've decided to throw your lot in with? Why not walk away?"

"Because I can't. I couldn't walk away when the outbreak occurred. Nor could you, right? You said, after you heard the news, you went to work."

"I did," she said.

"To keep the lights on? To keep people safe? Same with me. I could disappear off to some cabin in the woods, and you'd better believe I want to. What then? Find other survivors? Fall in love? Have kids? And what do I do when, five years from now, the captain turns up to test them? Is immunity genetic? Would my kids have it? Would yours?"

"That's no longer a question I have to worry about," Maggs said.

"Right. Sorry. I mean that I don't want to leave this to be a problem for the next generation. When the general dies, Brewster will take full control of the scientists. Forget some Holy Grail, his aerosolised virus is the real weapon, the real threat. The captain will control these extremists, and I'm sure she'll want her church to grow. They'll go looking for other converts to test, and so the nightmare continues. I can't stop them if I'm hiding in the woods."

"But you're not trying to stop them now."

"I'm just one person. What do you expect me to do?"

"Kill the general. Kill the captain. We'll do it now. You and me."

He laughed and pointed east. "Go ahead. They went that way. The general and the captain left a few hours ago to meet up with Brewster."

Maggs looked around, then back up at the roofs of the warehouses where she could only see one light now, but there was another, at ground level, to the north, moving between the buildings. She turned back to Dalton. "How would powering up a dam help?"

"Because it's too damned hot around the Gulf in the summer. Farming output is terrible. Slaves or no, they need better farmland. Tippy wants to move everyone north, I know that. She was looking along the East Coast, but she's not found anywhere yet. Wherever we can provide a functioning electricity supply, that will become the new capital."

"And you want to become the bringer of light in their new church?" Maggs asked.

"No, because this new capital will be too vulnerable to attack by the general, or Brewster, *or* the captain with their new weapon. Don't you see? The general will die, Brewster will take over and want to rule in the south. It would be easy for him to persuade the captain to smite all the unbelievers. Tippy won't allow that. She *can't* allow it. She'll have no choice but to kill them all and destroy the lab. Then we've only got to figure out a way of dealing with her." He smiled.

"It's a lot of suppositions," she said.

"I know," he said, putting his hat next to her. He pulled himself up onto the platform. "But it really would take an army to destroy them. I haven't got that."

Maggs looked up. The stars were coming out. Somewhere, maybe, Etienne was looking up at the same sky. Much closer, Gordon would be, too.

"Can we walk? I'm cold."

In silence, they walked around the warehouses, taking a path close to, but not beneath the handful of lights strung up in the refugee camp's ruins. Maggs waited until they were near to the road before she leaned against a wall. "When you first came to the spa, you could have asked for our help."

"Sydney was there to make sure I didn't. But even if I had, what help could you have given? Your group wasn't an army, and that's what you'd need to take out the general. You'd need an even larger one to wipe out the southerners. There is no army. Not here, not anywhere. It's just us, so what do we do? Leave it to be someone else's problem, or deal with it the best way we can?"

"What a world." She thought for a moment, running through what he'd said, weighing up the options. "I kept the lights on. I suppose that means it falls to me to turn them back on again. But it's all five of us."

"I'm sorry?"

"Ricardo and Ginger, and Dessie and Jack, too. Jack's too old to be much use on a farm. But there's plenty of work at a hydroelectric plant he'd be well-suited for. He's still got a steady hand and a keen eye, and that's what a linesman needs. Dessie is fit and, more importantly, small. She can get into the places Ricardo can't."

"Oh, right. Sure," he said. It was his turn to be wrong-footed. "You're not going to fight it?"

"If I were to say no, you'd find a way to tell Tippy about me yourself. You'd get her backing for the plan, and I'd end up being threatened or tortured into doing the work. There's no one so ruthless as a true believer, because to them, whatever they do can't be evil because it's done with the blessing of their god. Ezra didn't understand that, and it's why he was doomed to fail."

"Who?"

"Oh, the preacher we had in our group. He didn't actually believe in anything. Before the outbreak, he had a mega-church where he bought his sermons in bulk so he'd have more time to work out which jet to buy. I'm not kidding."

"No, I've arrested a fair number of those."

"And I bet they didn't believe in anything beyond living as comfortable a life as they could, thinking it was their due. That's what Ezra was like. Martin was the same. A CEO born with a drawer full of silver spoons. To him, every interaction was a transaction, not a moment of contact with a thinking, feeling human being. Brass wanted the respect offered to a general, but didn't know how to be a soldier, let alone how to treat them. And it wasn't even that they wanted a better life for themselves, just that they wanted to make sure no one else had as good a life as them. They were doomed to fail, it was always just a matter of how many others they'd pull down when they fell. But a true believer, that's different."

"I know. They can't be reasoned with, or placated, or managed," Dalton said. "If there was a way, I'd try."

Maggs nodded. In the distance two lights approached each other, two sentries who seemed to be combining their patrol. Or were they calling it a night, now that the general and captain were away?

"You're right," she said. "We have to think of future generations. And I want to be clear that my goal is to do what I can to get the planet back on the right path. It might be impossible, but I want your word you'll do the same."

"You have it," he said, and grinned. "You have no idea how relieved I am."

"We haven't done anything yet," Maggs said. "And there's so much to do."

"We need to pick a dam first. If you can identify one, I'll head out tomorrow to scout it. If it's still secure, I can pick you up in a day or two. All of you," he added.

"I need a map. And I need a drink."

"I have both in my trailer. It's nothing fancy, but it is home."

He led her back across the abandoned camp and towards a dark warehouse close to the road. As he led her around the side, down a litter-strewn and nearly pitch-black alley, she began having reservations. After all, he was a mass murderer, if not a serial killer, and she was just a prisoner being led to the back of a warehouse. Except the warehouse turned out to be a garage. The vehicle doors were closed and secured with a chain and padlock. He opened the door, stepped inside, bent down, and turned on a lantern. The light was dim, but between the stacked crates, there was a tanker, a bowser, a fifth-wheel caravan, and his sheriff's car.

"This is where you live?" she asked, as he walked up to the caravan, sorting through the keys on his chain.

"It's not much, but it's home, and I'm glad that I have one."

Inside, the caravan was as clean as anywhere could be when water was a luxury. The door opened into a lounge area, containing a table, currently folded back, surrounded by a U-shaped bench-seat and a swivel chair that looked like he'd installed it himself. The other wall was dotted with cupboard doors, some of which looked recently installed. Para-cord netting had been attached to the outside, giving extra storage space. A semi-rigid curtain sealed off the remaining half of the trailer, presumably containing his sleeping area. She slipped into the bench seat. He hung hat on a hook on the door.

"A drink, then," he said, and opened one of the cupboards. Inside was a sink and a second set of cupboards, these with doors that slid back on themselves. He took a bottle from one and glasses from another. "Is bourbon okay?"

"After today, I think I'd enjoy motor oil. But yes, that would be nice, thank you." He put a glass in front of her, then took the chair on the other side of the table.

"This is how you live? Going from place to place?" she asked.

"Following the general's visions," he said, speaking low, though she doubted anyone would hear, even if they were standing right outside. "He tested us, of course, and the group I was with. I was the only survivor. He trusts me because I'm a cop. The captain distrusts me for the same reason. I'm an outsider here, just like I've always been. I drive around finding potential converts, while he hunts for his vault. His tomb. We're supposed to go up to the Olympia Peninsula next."

"I'd be careful. We found a note from someone who'd gone there after the outbreak. She left because of disease. Didn't say what kind. Didn't *know* what kind. I don't think you'll find anyone alive."

"Good." He slumped in his chair, swilling the amber liquid back and forth in his glass.

"It must be tough," she said. "You can't trust anyone, so you can't talk to anyone."

"And they give me minders. Sydney was the most recent, and that kid was nothing but prejudice, resentment, and conspiracy theories."

"And while I empathise, that doesn't mean all is forgiven. You've got a long way to go before then. But we both have jobs to do, so let's start there. Let's get the lights back on. Do you have a map?"

He nodded, downed his drink, stood, and walked over to one of the wall-mounted racks, pulling out a stack of driving maps. "Where do you want to start? What about Hoover Dam? It'd be nice to head homeward."

"Sorry, it's too big. Did you say she has a few hundred thousand farmers?"

"So I've heard. I wish I'd seen it, but other than the fuel convoy, the only people who come here stay for good. There was a team here from the south, but the general killed at least one of them. Since then, they keep their distance from him, and since I do the same, I've not run into them."

"You mentioned that. How did he kill them? Was it one of his tests?"

"No. He used a baseball bat, Capone-style. Like I said, you saw him on a good day."

She opened the maps, laying them out in front of her while he fixed himself another drink. She picked up her glass and downed it. "Woah, I'd forgotten how this stuff could burn." She held out her glass. He topped it up, and she placed it back on the table. "We want enough power for half a million people. That will give us room for growth. Transmission to outlying farms will be difficult, and by outlying, I mean within fifty kilometres. Power transmission isn't really about cables, it's all about substations and transformers. We'll have to repair or repurpose existing ones. That'll be labour-intensive, but I suppose that won't be a problem."

"Sadly not."

"And I think our fifty kilometres should be a straight line, rather than the diameter of a circle. A river valley, I think, as we'll find a river near a dam, and we'll find a road nearby. Plus, that solves the water issue. Texas is a possibility, but their entire grid needed an upgrade, and there's the issue of the summer heat."

"And the south does have more zombies."

"It does? Idaho, then. If I've got to pick somewhere right now, I'd go for Brownlee on the Idaho-Oregon border. I suppose it's a day or two's drive from here. There's plenty of good farmland. The facility's output was five hundred and eighty megawatts. That alone should be enough, because we'll be using far less than before. But there are some more, and smaller, dams further east in Idaho. That would give us a zone for settlement and expansion over the coming decade."

"Idaho? Yeah, I'd be happy to see fries back on the menu. I'm sold."

She pushed the map aside. "I'll need to see it for myself."

"You mean you should come with me."

"I know what to look for. If Brownlee is no good, we can continue on to the next dam. In a week, we can drive south and pitch the plan to this scientist. If you have to keep coming back and forth to whatever farm I'm on, it'll take months."

"I don't know if that will be possible. The general wouldn't mind. The captain will think you're trying to escape."

"She'll have my people as hostages, and I'll be able to get them out of captivity sooner. What if we left before they come back? Who could stop you from leaving? You're in charge, aren't you?"

"Me? Ha! Sergeant Jesse Lee is. He was a state trooper from California, so naturally he hates me. He's a nasty piece of work, and the reason I keep my trailer locked up."

"Oh." She picked up her glass and took a small sip to mask her disappointment. There would be no chance of Dalton sneaking all five of them out.

"Our best shot is to ask the general tomorrow, and hope he's in a good mood," Dalton said. "If he's not in a good mood, we probably won't see him. You'll have to go to wherever they send you, and I'll head on to the dam alone. I can pick you up in a few days. Oh, and you should give me your tomahawk. Assuming you want to keep it."

"My axe? Why?"

"In case they send you to a farm. All blades get confiscated. Clothing, too."

"Ah." She remembered Meredith, the woman at the Connolly farm, dressed in clothes from a history book. She drew the axe with its blood-stained finish. "I've only had it for a few months. But it is the best I've found in a while."

He opened a small cupboard and revealed a small armoury containing blades, cudgels, and guns, each on its own mount.

"You've quite the collection," she said, standing up to better see. Closer to him, she could feel the heat radiating from his body. "Shall I put it here?"

"Uh, yeah."

Maggs slotted her axe onto a slot next to a narrow-bladed knife. She reached into her pocket and took out the throwing knife she'd taken from their cell. "You should have this. It's a throwing knife. I'm terrible with it. Been trying for months. I can't get it to stick in the target."

He took it out, examining it, while she took out a small pistol, and then put it back.

"It's properly balanced," he said. "A nice piece. You're probably holding it wrong."

"You'll have to show me how to do it properly. Do you have any music?"

"Music?"

"Why not?" she said. "We've done as much planning as we can for now. Let's just be human for a few minutes." She turned her back to him, picked up a long stiletto with a handle moulded to look like a snake. It would be ridiculously uncomfortable to hold.

"Do you like Bach?"

"You don't strike me as a fan of the classics." She picked up a butterfly knife.

"My brother's a pianist. Was." Dalton said. He opened a cabinet, revealing an old CD player. "He was good. Very good. This is him, playing."

Maggs stood, and walked up behind him, laying her left hand on his back. As the cabin filled with the old melody, she undid the clasp on the knife, one-handed, using her fingers to stop metal from hitting metal as it opened.

"He *is* good," she said.

"He—"

And as Dalton half turned, she punched the blade into his neck. She wrapped her left arm around his, half-trapping him as she dragged him slowly back, keeping him off-balance as she twisted the knife. He struggled, trying to reach the wound. Blood pulsed over her, hot and fast, a fountain spraying the wall and cupboards as she began easing him to the ground. His legs kicked, and his arms thrashed, but increasingly weakly. She stepped back, and looked down at his body, meeting his gaze until he was still.

Chapter 50 - The Eye of the Storm
Longview

Maggs braced herself on the table, not allowing herself to sit. There was no joy in this small measure of revenge, no invigoration, no peace. She took a deep breath and stepped over the body, pulling back the curtain at the caravan's far end. Beyond lay a made bed with red and grey sheets. A green plaid shirt hung on the door. The single shelf held nine paperbacks and a worn but recently polished banjo. It was tidy and clean enough under the circumstances, but it didn't look like a space he'd ever shared. She returned to the living area, bent down, and gripped the corpse beneath the shoulders, slowly dragging the body behind the curtain while the concerto played in the background.

Two brothers. One a professional pianist, the other a Vegas-adjacent cop. Was the banjo an heirloom of their childhood? Had it been a happy home full of laughter and music? Had Dalton been overlooked in favour of his prodigal brother? Why hadn't Constant Dalton ever changed his first name?

Two towels hung across the partition of the box-like shower cubicle. She took them both, mopping up as much of the blood as she could. When they were both sodden, she dumped them in the shower tray. She took a moment to examine herself in the half-size mirror on the cubicle wall. The blood now staining her coat was too obvious. She dumped the coat atop the towels, picked up a sponge, and ran a little water into the sink. The tap worked. She wasn't surprised. Dalton had lived apart from these people he travelled with. Apart, and alone.

After she cleaned the blood from her face and hands, and dried them on the bedding, she opened the closet, looking for a coat. There were only two. The winter parka was too big and bulky. The arms on the brown suede jacket were too long, but it would do. There were two outer pockets, but only one inner pocket. She'd need a bag. A small one that she could hang around her neck. Quickly, she hunted around until she found a drawstring, nylon shoe bag. She hung it around her neck, and pulled on the jacket, tightening the bag's cord until it was out of sight. Good enough.

She stepped out of the bedroom, pulled the curtain closed, and took in the scene. Two glasses on the table. She added the bottle. Yes, maybe if someone glanced inside from the doorway, they might not notice the blood, but see the glasses and closed curtain, and jump to the conclusion she was sure Dalton would have happily leaped at. It might buy her a few minutes, and it was all she could do.

The armoury was a sad sight. Knives with ornate handles, guns with scroll-work barrels, and a hand-cannon whose recoil would dislocate a shoulder. A taser, flash-bangs, and smoke grenades rounded out his collection. She disregarded all of those, and picked up three compact pistols and a plain semi-automatic. Another minute was wasted checking they were all the same calibre.

In a drawer below the cabinet was a box with twelve shotgun shells so there must be other weapons in his car. A shoebox contained loose cartridges. Two other boxes, one half full, contained nine-millimetre bullets. She finally sat down at the table and loaded the magazines while the pianist played on.

As she mechanically inserted the bullets, her gaze fell on the damp bloodstain. If only there'd been another way. When she'd asked for music, he'd picked something played by his brother. They'd only had a handful of brief conversations, but he'd mentioned his ex-wife often enough for her to tell that the divorce had been a pivotal moment. Whoever he'd been before, however good or not, his world had fallen apart before his neighbours had turned into the undead. Constant Dalton had been a broken man desperate for affirmation, and for affection, but at heart, he wasn't evil. He *had* been naive. His scheme was all crust and no filling. If this Tippy woman had wanted to restore a hydroelectric plant, she had the people to do it. No, she suspected Tippy *wanted* the general to search for the vault. Dalton had made a lot of assumptions, but all based on his belief that the vault *didn't* exist. From the letters Hank had left behind, she knew that it did.

When Gordon came to look for her, he would get caught. She'd said her people had gone north. That lie would be exposed. And with a gun to any of their heads, she knew she'd tell them about Vader and Hank. Preempting it by volunteering the information wouldn't save them, either. For one thing, with fifty-seven survivors, they outnumbered the general's troops here. Besides, Tippy wouldn't let the general keep whatever was in the vault. She'd probably kill everyone who knew it existed.

No, Dalton wasn't evil. He'd even taken the first tentative steps towards redemption, but they were too few and too late. To save her people, and to protect future generations, the safe house and the letters couldn't be discovered, so she had to escape. Since she couldn't trust Dalton, he'd had to die.

The music came to an end. She got up and switched the player off. Now came the hard part, but one way or another, in a matter of minutes, it would be over. She slipped one of the compact pistols into her right pocket where she could easily reach it. After a moment's thought, she slipped another into her left. The other two guns, and some ammunition, went into the bag hanging around her neck and tucked under her arm. Her tomahawk went back into its sheath. She buttoned the coat, picked up Dalton's keys, took a half-empty bottle from his drinks cabinet, closed the cupboard doors, and left the caravan.

Outside, she stood on the steps, waiting for her eyes to adjust. The warehouse was empty and unlit, but she could hear music in the distance. People were still up and about. What she needed was a distraction, and there was one right in front of her. Potentially, anyway. A tanker. She'd seen it, but not really thought about it, when she'd entered the caravan, being too focused on what she would have to do next.

The tanker contained diesel, according to the signage on the back, and the dial said it was nearly full. Fuel from the south, she supposed. It was still attached to the rig, and that would certainly have space for the five of them. The idea of driving away was beguiling, but it was too big a risk. On the other hand, a fuel tanker might be the distraction she needed. Wishing it was gasoline rather than diesel, she undid the latches on the emergency release, stepping back as the toxic liquid began gushing onto the floor. How would she ignite it?

Cursing herself for not considering that before she opened the valve, she hurried back into the caravan and took a smoke grenade from the armoury cupboard. She remembered stories about those starting fires. Or would a flash-bang be better? Would either be enough? It would take more than just a spark. She grabbed two of each, putting them into the bag, hoping the answer would come to her in the next few minutes. With that done, and the clock well and truly ticking, she made her way outside, and out of the warehouse, securing its door with the padlock.

She sauntered casually back to the customs house with a contented smile on her face. Not once did she look up, because she didn't want to give the snipers any reason to look down. Outside the customs house, the two guards still played their game. The scruffier one stood, reaching for his gun before she held out the bottle.

"A gift, boys," she said, putting it on the table. "Courtesy of Dalton."

"Thanks," the scruff said, while the other guard, Calvin, looked a little puzzled.

"The sheriff isn't with you?" he asked.

"He has to finish a report for the general. Well, for Tippy, really. Something to do with supplies. Anyway, we've mended our fences. As long as the repairs hold, I'd say things are going to be a lot easier around here." She sighed, and hoped it didn't sound too theatrical. "But I still need to let my friends know about our change in plans. Would you mind?"

She waved towards the door. The scruff slouched over to the door, undoing the padlock and chain.

"Thanks, boys. I'll shout if I need you," she said, and stepped inside, and then to the side where she was out of the glare of their lantern.

"Maggs, what happened?" Ginger asked, running over.

Maggs shook her head, motioning to the door as she listened to the chain being put back in place. She pointed towards the office even as Dessie and Jack came out of it. Maggs ushered them back inside. "Where's Ric?" she asked quietly.

"Working on the hinges to the back door," Ginger said.

"Go fetch him," Maggs said as she fished the guns from her pockets. She shrugged off the coat and unhooked the bag.

"Is that blood?" Jack asked.

"It's not mine," Maggs said. "I hope it wasn't too obvious. No matter. Dessie, grab our gear. One bag each, and not too full. We'll just need food and water for a few days, but speed is a priority."

"Do you want to tell us what's happening?" Jack asked.

"Yes, but I'll tell everyone all together. We're escaping, and in about five minutes. Sooner if— ah, there you are!" she said as Ricardo and Ginger returned. "Can we get out the back door?"

"Yes, but I need another two hours," Ricardo said.

"I just released the valve on their diesel tanker. It's currently flooding the inside of a warehouse. Any sentry walking nearby will smell it, and then we'll have real trouble. Jack, can these grenades ignite diesel vapour?"

"Maybe. Depends. We didn't have flash-bangs when I served. Could have done with them. Basically, we want to start a fire, and these could do that."

"Let's hope they do. There are two snipers on the rooftops, to the left and right. They have lights, so I'm guessing there aren't others with night-vision. Lights at the same elevation would negate night-vision, right, Jack?"

"Yes. Dessie, empty that bag. Stuff it with torn paper. Dry paper. And some cloth. Dry cloth."

"How many sentries are there?" Ricardo asked.

"I saw three lights on patrol. One light was by the main entrance. I don't know how many people are with each light. The general has left, and so has the captain, along with a lot of their people. There are some still about, and most are still awake. I'd say ten at least. The door here is locked. There are two guards outside. This is going to get rough. There's no time to explain, but the general is taking orders from someone further south. Someone worse. Someone sane."

"What's the plan?" Jack asked.

"Get the guards to unlock the door. You head to the road, where we left the bikes at the log-cabin checkpoint. I'll start the fire, and we'll rendezvous there, and if I can't make it, you drive off and I'll hide out in the ruins."

"I'll start the fire," Jack said.

"You can't run as fast as me," Maggs said.

"I can run faster than both of you," Ginger said.

"And *you* don't know where the warehouse is," Maggs said.

"We stick together," Ricardo said. "And we've run out of time, right?"

Maggs stood up. "By the door, Ric. Remember, there are two of them," she said, and crossed to the door herself. Yes, they were out of time. She breathed out, trying to remember the meditation techniques she'd never really learned, and slipped the safety off the pistol she'd kept for herself.

"Help, help!" she said as she hammered on the door. She had to repeat herself. "Quick!"

Ric stood on the far side of the door, a knife in each hand. She heard footsteps.

"What is it?" Calvin called from outside.

"They didn't take kindly to the new plan," Maggs said. "You've got to let me out before I have to kill another of them. The old man's dead." She was improvising now, but hadn't that been the case for this whole last year? "Hurry. That girl's got a gun!"

The door opened. The two young men rushed in, guns held high but far from ready. Ricardo grabbed the scruff, while Maggs thrust her gun into the face of Calvin. Jack, Dessie, and Ginger stepped out of the shadows, guns raised.

"What's going on?" the scruff asked.

"Cover them, I'll do it," Jack said, stepping forward when he saw Ricardo's hesitation at killing someone in cold blood.

"Wait," Maggs said. "Take their guns."

"We don't have time," Ginger said.

Maggs turned to the two guards. "I don't think you're true believers, and I don't think you've been with the general long enough to drown your souls in blood. I'll give you a choice. I can kill you now, or we can leave you alive. Obviously, the captain will execute you for your failure, but you could always run. Take your chances. Find a cabin in the woods. Finish your card game. You don't have to be evil, and you don't have to die. Utter a sound, and you will."

"Dessie, there was a roll of tape behind the counter," Jack said. "Quick now."

"Sorry," Ricardo said as Dessie and Ginger quickly taped the two guards' ankles, hands, and mouths.

"Don't worry. I understand," Maggs said. She turned to the guards. "There's some knives over there, and we'll leave the door unlocked. Cut yourselves free, run, and live good lives, please." She turned to her group. "Everyone ready?"

Jack raised the rifle he'd taken from the scruffier guard. "I am now."

Chapter 51 - Smoke and Flames
Longview

Maggs eased the door open by less than a hand's breadth, looking outside for lights, listening for sound. All was still, but she could only see a fraction of the camp, above which rose the distant strains of a guitar.

"The board's set," Jack whispered, "time to move."

"Follow me," she said. "Lights on. Swagger, don't skulk. Try to look like we're guards heading to bed."

With her back straight, she sauntered across the open ground, angling away from where the vehicles were parked. She avoided looking at the rooftops. If the snipers saw them, they'd probably shout before opening fire. Wouldn't they? It was the same with any ground-level patrols. Wait for them to call out before they started running. Walk, don't run; she repeated that to herself as she took step after step, focusing on listening for danger's approach. Sounds she would ordinarily be able to dismiss as mere background were amplified into a tormenting symphony to which guilt overlaid the memory of the piano concerto.

By the time they reached the cover of the first warehouse, she'd aged a thousand years. Her back was prickling with sweat, and her hands were beginning to shake. Rationally, she knew that was the adrenaline wearing off, but she still wanted to stop, to sob, to scream, to sleep.

"Now we can run," Ginger whispered from behind her.

"Walk, don't run," Maggs said, automatically. "Watch your footing."

Her feet decided to ignore the advice, finding some last reserve of energy to turn her walk into a skipping, slipping, sliding dance between the debris. She knew she was making too much noise, but also knew that time had run out. She could already smell the diesel fumes.

At the end of the warehouse, she came to a staggering halt. There was dead ground in front of her, but she could see the garage containing Dalton's trailer and the fuel tanker.

"Lights off," Jack hissed.

Maggs jammed her thumb against the flashlight's button even as she looked around. The sudden absence of light left multi-coloured circles in her vision. She was about to ask what Jack had seen when she saw it herself. A light to the left, still distant, but bouncing around, reflecting off unseen objects. It was definitely a patrol. Were they approaching? She couldn't tell.

"Where are we going?" Ricardo asked, his voice low.

"There, just ahead," Maggs whispered back, pointing to the garage. "We throw. We run, okay?"

"I've got the bag," Dessie said.

"Give it to me," Maggs said.

"I know where the ring-pulls are. You know where it needs to go. Show me," she said.

"Did she just call them ring-pulls?" Jack muttered.

"Hey, who's down there?" The voice came from above, a hesitant shout but which came with a beam of light, searching for them in the darkness. It was a powerful beam, but was shone down on the alley's midpoint.

Maggs grabbed Dessie's arm, and ran. The sniper must have seen the movement as the light speared across the dead ground, sweeping left and right as it searched for them. A shot rang out. Instinctively, Maggs ducked. It was Dessie's turn to grab her arm and drag her onward.

"You never hear the shot that kills you," she said. "Where's the door?"

As Maggs looked about for the entrance, she realised the sentry's searching light had gone out. Who had fired that shot? It didn't matter because she could hear voices in the distance. The words were indistinct, but the tone was more irritated than aggressive.

"There," Maggs said, running to the door.

Dessie overtook her and reached it first. "It's locked."

"I've got the key," Maggs said, and began searching her pockets. It seemed to take an age before she found it. The yells weren't so far away and were getting more urgent. She got the door open. "Ready?" she asked.

But Dessie was already swinging the bag, casting a trail of smoke as she threw it inside.

"Run!" Dessie said.

This time, they grabbed each other, and sprinted towards the others. How much time did they have? Would it work? The voices were shouting now, and they were getting near. What if it didn't work at—

Night turned to blinding day. A roaring ocean pounded on her eardrums. Her hands hit something cold, wet, and hard. A wave of heat billowed outwards, enveloping her. She seemed to tumble upwards. The ocean receded, replaced with a grinding screech, rising in pitch. A hand tugged at her arm, hard, pulling her along. Ice cold rain pattered on her arms and neck. The grinding screech rose in pitch, too high for her to hear, and with a silent pop, her hearing was back. She could hear shouts, screams, gunshots, and laughter. That last was coming from close by. She looked over and saw Ginger was by her side, holding her up, tugging her along, laughing manically, though with little humour behind her eyes.

Ahead, Jack was in the lead. He was nimble, if not quick, leading them down an alley between two warehouses.

"Where's Dessie?" Maggs wasn't sure if she said it aloud or only thought it. If Ginger responded, Maggs didn't hear her. She half turned and saw a fierce white blaze behind her, and the silhouette of Ricardo, carrying Dessie over his shoulder. Ginger tugged on her arm. She turned around just as something landed on her neck. This time it didn't feel ice cold, but burning hot, a sensation that spread throughout her body.

When they reached an old ambulance with smashed windows, Jack stopped.

"Take five," he said, bracing his newfound rifle on the hood. Maggs leaned against the wreck, the cold rusting bodywork a balm against her neck and hands.

"Dessie. How's Dessie?" she asked.

Ricardo knelt, laying her down. "Alive. Unconscious," he said. "Some burns."

"Let me see," Jack said, handing his rifle to Ginger.

Ricardo offered Maggs a bottle. She took it, wincing at the sharp pain in her hands. "Thank you," she managed, before pouring some in her mouth. She rolled herself across the side of the ambulance until she was standing next to Ginger and had a view of the inferno. The orange-white glow was about two hundred metres distant, with flaming debris still rising and falling around it, almost like a fountain, hammering onto the surrounding warehouses. She couldn't see the fire itself, but it was already spreading.

"That's gunfire," Ginger said.

Maggs hadn't heard it. "There was ammo in Dalton's caravan. A hundred rounds. Maybe more."

"No, that's a lot more," Ginger said. "What else was in that warehouse?"

Maggs shook her head. "I don't know. I don't remember."

"We should move," Jack said. "Can you carry her?"

"From here to Montreal," Ricardo said.

"It won't be that far," Jack said. "But it'll be hours before she can walk."

Ginger handed Jack back his rifle, then took the half-empty bottle of water from Maggs's hands. She hadn't realised she was still holding it. Ginger pulled off her scarf, doused it with water, and then tied it loosely around Maggs's neck. "That'll help with the burns."

"Burns?" Maggs asked, and as she did, her body decided to finally let her know about them. A grating pain began pulsing across her left hand, the left side of her face, the back of her neck, and the back of her head, and she knew the pain would only get worse. "Let's go."

"Where," Ricardo said as he bent to pick Dessie up. "She can't ride if she's unconscious."

"Ride?" Maggs asked, her brain fuzzy.

"We have to forget the bikes," Ginger said. "There were only three of them, anyway. Let's keep going this way, and before something else blows up. Jack, you better lead. I'll stick with Maggs."

"No bikes," Maggs muttered as Ginger helped her up. For some reason, that was important. It was bad. Why? What had she forgotten?

"Careful," Ginger said, taking her arm as Maggs stumbled.

"Sorry," she mumbled as the pain grew worse. A kaleidoscope of horrors filled her mind, backlit by the conflagration behind them. All the pulsating pain jumbled everything from the last few hours with the mental agony of the last year.

"Watch out," Ginger said, tugging her to one side.

Maggs shook her head, regretting it as a wave of pain tore across her face. It seemed to be in her mouth, her teeth, her eyes, everywhere. But through the pain, she saw a shadow above them. "Is that the bridge?"

"I guess so," Ginger said. "It's really burning now. I don't know what was in there, but it was more than just fuel."

"Must be ammo," Maggs said. Ricardo, immediately in front, was carrying Dessie like she was no weight at all. She couldn't see Jack, but trusted that Ric could. She turned, shaking off Ginger's arm. "It's okay. I'm okay. I was just a bit dazed."

The pain was still there, and it was agony, but thinking no longer felt like wading through maple syrup. Behind them, the fire was spreading. She could still hear ammunition cooking off. They must have kept their main armoury in that warehouse. The bridge was now behind them, and seemed to act as a dividing line in the night sky. Above, she could see stars. Behind, there was nothing but a smoky shroud, glowing faintly orange as it reflected the blaze.

"Maggs, come on!"

"Just a moment," she said. Shadows danced everywhere, as the fire grew. How fast would it grow? How far? One of the shadows was moving more purposefully than the others. Her hand moved more slowly than her brain, reaching for her pockets, her belt, looking for a gun, but she had none. The shadow stopped, just close enough that she could make out the silhouette of a person. A shot rang out. The silhouette disappeared, seeming to vanish back into the shadows.

"Don't stop," Jack said, walking past them both, his rifle still raised. "Don't let her stop. Keep going. Keep walking down this path. I'll watch the rear. We're safe, but we're not home yet."

Maggs wasn't sure how far they'd walked, or for how long, before Ricardo stopped, and laid Dessie down inside a partially built log cabin. It was identical in style to the one by the bridge, though this structure had no roof.

"How long do you need?" Maggs asked while Ginger tried to make Dessie comfortable.

"Five minutes," Ricardo said. "But it really depends how far we're walking."

"Not too far," Maggs said. "We need to hide in the ruins. They'll think we've gone further. Rest your arms."

Maggs wanted to rest, too, but she knew if she sat, she'd never get up. She shuffled back outside, looking back the way they'd come.

"How are you holding up?" Jack asked. She'd not heard him approach.

"My brain's full of mist. I ache everywhere. But I'm upright. I don't know how much longer I can walk for. We should find a house. Somewhere to hide for a day, until Dessie can walk, and where we can defend ourselves."

"We can't. Not here. If they find us, they could burn us out. Not that I think they'll be looking. Not for a while. You said the general left?"

"I… Yes. Yes, that's what Dalton told me," she said, reaching back into the depths of her memory.

"Then we've got until morning. It'll take until then for them to reorganise, count the dead, and salvage whatever they can, if they can salvage anything. These aren't real soldiers. They're not even conscripts. They had one job last night, to guard us. They failed, spectacularly. They won't want to stick around."

"But the general will return in the morning. Maybe not early, but Dalton was expecting him back. We should hide in the ruins nearby, because they won't think we'd stop. Besides, Ricardo can't carry Dessie much further, and I won't be able to walk much further than that."

"That'll be far enough," Jack said. "Earlier, you said there was someone worse than the general in charge. Do you know anything about him?"

"Her. Her name's Tippy. She's a scientist, and she's more ruthless than the general. They ran a refuge in Florida together, just after the outbreak, but she sent him here to get rid of him. Exile was the word Dalton used, but the general went willingly, bringing his followers with him. She still sends him fuel and things."

"Where is she, do you know?"

"Somewhere around the Gulf of Mexico. Dalton said there are hundreds of thousands of survivors there. Slaves."

"What did he want with you?"

"Dalton? To set up a resistance movement. Use Tippy to destroy the general, and then to help him kill her. It was a foolish idea that sprang from his own desperation. If she wanted the general dead, she could have killed him. Poisoned him and his followers. I think she wants him alive but out of the way. Or, she wants Brewster and his lab-rats who made the weapon, and she wants Captain Pakhaüser and her army. She might also want them to find this lost vault. I'm not sure. We were all going to be sent to slave labour on a farm. Dalton couldn't stop that. Ultimately, I couldn't trust him to help us escape. He wasn't evil, but he watched evil happen, thinking he had no choice."

"Ah, so he was one of those short-sighted fools who believe the world is split into binary choices, someone who thinks it's best to pick the lesser of two evils, that type?"

"Something like that. I didn't take any pleasure in killing him."

"Of course not. But you don't need to explain yourself. The hardest lesson I had to learn was that sometimes, the real mission is different from our orders."

Maggs mulled that over. "Are there any other lessons?"

"Greed comes with a cost. Have you ever seen one of those heist movies set during a war? They change the cast, and the war, but the plot always stays the same. A unit finds themselves behind enemy lines with a life-changing amount of cash. They can call for an evac, or they can walk out of the jungle, rich men. Once upon a time, at least once, that story wasn't fiction. I was the only survivor." He glanced around. "Everyone else in my unit died, but I came back rich enough to buy a very large plot of prime farmland. That was fifty years, and at least three lifetimes, ago and I still wish we'd just walked away. That's my secret. What's yours? I know you've been holding something back. What is it?"

"Ah." She looked up at the orange glow. It seemed to be spreading across the sky, but that was merely a reflection of the flames off the low-hanging smoke. It would be visible in Vader come morning, she was sure of it. "Fifty-seven of us survived the attack on the spa. The others didn't go north. They're only thirty kilometres away. They'll see the smoke come morning. They know where we went. They'll come looking. I need to get a warning to them."

"I see. Then you can't have Dessie or me slowing you down."

"We're not leaving you," Maggs said. "We'll find a bicycle, and I'll send Ginger alone, and… I don't know. We'll figure it out."

"I already have. The big man's five minutes are up. The good news is he's only got another kilometre to walk."

"To where?"

"To my other secret. We've got a boat."

This time, they walked in a clump. Jack was a few steps ahead, holding the rifle as if he were hoping for someone to shoot. When he raised a warning hand, it was to point at the abandoned cranes standing guard over a desolate chemical plant.

"It's through there," he said. "Just after that bollard."

He led them across the overgrown scrub and to a metal fence that had been cut and then re-secured with binding wire. "Give me a minute."

"You cut a hole?" Maggs asked, talking to keep herself focused. She'd begun to shiver, and she knew that worse was to come.

"We expected trouble," Jack said. "Not quite like this, of course. I thought it might be a few bandits who'd want to take what little we'd brought up. And we only brought up a little so we'd be happy to give it away." He peeled back the wire.

Ginger had to help her through. Maggs had lost all sense of whether she was too hot or too cold. She just had to hold on for one minute, and then for one minute more. Maggs kept her head lowered as Ginger helped her between the abandoned vehicles. There seemed to be a lot, but she didn't have the strength to question why. Jack led them to a steel-framed boathouse.

"This is us," he said. "Ginger, give me a hand."

The doorway was hidden behind a metal sheet. The sound of it dragging along the floor sent an odd spasm through Maggs's ears. One more minute, she told herself. Just one minute more.

Immediately inside was an office. She collapsed into a chair as Ricardo followed Jack through the door.

"You don't look good," Ginger said.

"I'll be okay," Maggs said. "We've got to warn Gordon. Make sure he doesn't come here."

"I know," Ginger said. "Don't worry. Just close your eyes for a minute."

Maggs didn't dare. She knew that if she slept, it would be hours before she woke. If they didn't get away before dawn, they'd be caught.

"You should come with us," Jack said.

Maggs blinked, uncertain if she'd fallen asleep or not. "No," she said. "No, we have to get back to our friends. I have to. Are you going to be okay getting Dessie home?"

"I've got my *good* rifle now. I'm not going to argue with you, but I will ask what your plan is."

"Get back to our people," Maggs said. "Get them safe."

"Yeah, we wanted to cross the bridge, but that's out," Ginger said. "I think we'll drive as fast as we can for the mountains, and hope that we don't bump into the general. We've got guns, though, so I'm not too worried."

"Well, I am," Jack said. "There's too few good people in the world. Fewer still now. You're about thirty kilometres away?"

"I think it's a little less," Ginger said.

"About twenty kilometres west of here, along the river, there's a town called Skamokawa. There's a little island, and lots of jetties. I've been there a few times now. Nice little place. Cycle back to your people and get them to drive there before dawn. In forty-eight hours, I'll come back, and we'll pick you up. If all is well, hang a lamp from the bridge to the island. If it's not well, hang two lights or none. Understand?"

"Sure. Okay. Thank you," Ginger said.

"We'll come back every night for a week. That's your window."

"No, we'll be there," Ginger said. "And thank you, really."

"No, thank you. You saved my granddaughter. I better go or I might lose the tide. I'll see you in a few days."

Maggs forced her head back, but he'd already gone.

"I've got his medical kit," Ginger said. "We need to clean the skin and bandage it, but I think that we should wait a bit. The good news is he's given us some proper painkillers."

"We need bicycles," Maggs said.

"Yes, we'll fetch them," Ginger said.

"We have to find them first."

"Jack told us where to look," Ginger said. "Didn't you hear him? Here. It's the pills. I'm going to hope two will do for now. We don't want to knock you out completely. Maybe three. Yeah. Probably best you take three."

Her throat felt on fire even after she swallowed. The pain slowly receded, but her mind didn't clear. There was something important. Something she'd forgotten.

"On your feet," Ginger said.

Ricardo was waiting outside, next to three bicycles.

"Can you manage this?" he asked.

Maggs tilted her head back, stretching. The air felt warm, and her feet felt light. There was still pain, but she could ignore it.

"We should have sent her with him," Ricardo said as he helped her onto a bicycle.

"Maybe. I don't know," Ginger said. "Let's head west for a while, follow the coast, then go north. A different route might be easier."

She didn't remember getting on the bike until she realised she was lying in grass, the bicycle tangled in her legs.

"I told you," Ricardo said.

"Yeah, three pills was too many," Ginger said. "I'll stay with her. Go back to Gordon. But help me get her… there, that house looks as good as any."

Epilogue - Letters, Old and New
Skamokawa, March 16th

Maggs looked over the top of her book and smiled at Etienne. After a long week of work, there was nothing quite as satisfying as an afternoon at home with her husband. Etienne smiled back. They were warm, they were safe, they were together. What else mattered? She returned to the book, but the words didn't come into focus. When she looked again at Etienne, his warm smile had faded into a concerned frown. His face grew indistinct while the room itself grew brighter.

"Etienne? Etienne!"

"Rest, Maggs," a voice said. A young voice. Firm, but gentle. "Just rest."

The brightness faded, and the room came back into view, but it wasn't her home, and the face looking down at her wasn't her husband.

"Chloe?"

"That's right. You're safe now, Maggs. Try not to move."

As the last echoes of the dream slipped into memory, a great weariness settled across her body. It was an effort even to blink.

"Where… where…" The rest of the words faded before they reached her mouth.

"You're safe, but you shouldn't move. You've got burns over half your body."

When Maggs tried to sit up, a wave of fire engulfed her.

"Please, Maggs. I've got something for you to drink. It's water and opium. We don't have anything to inject you with, so we've ground up some pills. It'll help, but we've got to sit you up so you can drink it, and that's going to hurt."

"Where am I?" she croaked, still trying to find a lighthouse in the mental fog.

"Skamokawa, where your friend, Jack, told you to come," Chloe said. "We're in a house overlooking the Columbia River. Everyone's here. You've been unconscious for twenty-seven hours. The rendezvous with our new friends is tonight."

The words were like flames, burning away the mist. And as they burned, so did her skin. "There was a fire."

"You escaped from the general, blew up their base, and tried to cycle back. I've no idea how you managed to even get on a bike. Ginger and

Ric found a house to put you in. Ginger stayed with you, and Ric came to fetch us. We're all here. We're all safe and waiting for a boat. Now, I'm going to help you sit up so you can drink. It's going to hurt, Maggs. It's going to hurt a lot, but you need to drink this, and then the pain will stop."

It did hurt. A lot.

When she next became aware of the room, the light seemed softer. Her mouth felt like a desert. She let her eyes roam the space, trying to make sense of it. Was the ceiling really lime green? The walls were pink. The giant wooden wardrobe looked as if it belonged in a museum. Hand-carved, she was sure. Wooden chair legs rattled on the other side of the room.

"You're awake! I'll get Chloe." Yvette darted briefly into her field of vision before bolting through the door.

Maggs opened her mouth, wanting to ask if there was anyone else in the room, but couldn't find the words. Slowly, one horror at a time, the past came back to her. Ear Falls. The spa. The customs house. Dalton. The explosion. Jack. Dessie. Henley and Booker. Roy and Kayleigh. Fern. Etienne. The door opened. Chloe entered. Yvette nervously followed behind.

"Hi, Maggs, you're looking better," Chloe said. Yvette's face gave the lie to that.

"Where… talk. What's happening?"

"I'm going to sit you up so you can drink some more," Chloe said. "Then I'll tell you everything, though we don't have much news to share."

It was agony to move, a roaring sea of pain utterly engulfing her. She couldn't even manage to scream. Slowly, oh so slowly, the pain subsided, and she found she was sitting, her skin prickling with sweat except where it burned.

"Drink this first," Chloe said, as she stirred the contents of a small cup. "Just swallow it straight down. Ready? Just blink, don't nod."

Maggs winced and opened her mouth as Chloe poured a little of the liquid into her mouth. It was bitter and gritty on her tongue.

"Swallow, Maggs," Chloe said.

How? She couldn't remember. She juddered her head backwards, and that produced a searing pain that seemed worse in her cheek, but her mouth seemed empty.

"Okay, now we'll try another sip. A larger one this time," Chloe said.

Slowly, she drank the medicine. Afterwards, she felt nothing but exhausted.

"It'll take a few minutes to kick in," Chloe said. "As soon as it does, you're going to drink this." She held up a cup.

"Sorry, it's watermelon," Yvette said.

"You need vitamins and electrolytes, and there's sugar in it, too," Chloe said. "Once we're in Oregon, we'll sort out some better treatment, but for now, we're just going to keep the pain away and keep your wounds clean. I'm going to make sure there's clean water for your wash. Yvette's going to stay with you." Chloe turned to the young woman. "Give it about ten minutes. If there's a problem, shout. Marshall will come and find me."

"Marshall's here?" Maggs asked.

"Outside the door," Chloe said. "I'll be back soon."

"He's been outside since you came back," Yvette said. "He slept out there."

"Where are we?" Maggs asked. It hurt to talk, with pain in her cheek, her jaw, and even her teeth, but there was an odd sinking feeling in her stomach. It wasn't unpleasant, just strange, as if her lower half was slowly falling away, taking the pain with it.

"We're in Skamokawa," Yvette said. "We're waiting for a boat to arrive this evening. Your friend, Jack, said he'd come here."

"Jack. Jack and Dessie."

"Ricardo told us everything. Well, Ginger told us everything. Ricardo sort of growled a lot, you know, like he does. We're all here, including Martin. Ricardo insisted we bring him. He didn't want to leave him behind in case the general found him."

"Good. Good." She could remember the general now. She remembered Dalton. She remembered the heat from his blood pulsing over her hands.

"It's a nice house," Yvette continued. "A *big* house with a little jetty. Seven bedrooms! It must have been a big family. We brought a diesel generator with us, so we've got heat and light. Everyone's having a wash, and trying to clean their clothes so we look presentable when we meet these new people. Gordon wants to create a good impression." She leaned forward a little. "I think he wants to keep everyone busy."

"What happened in Vader, with you?" Maggs asked. The pain was lessening. It was still there, but it felt like a wall was being built between her mind and the torment.

"Not much at all," Yvette said. "We found diesel trucks easily enough. They're all very old. Some people had to ride in the truck bed, but Gordon thought that was better until we had time to look for a bus or something. Georgie wasn't happy about us leaving the fun-bus, and I thought that was going to be our biggest problem until Ricardo arrived yesterday morning."

"By bicycle."

"Exactly. He told us how you were injured, about Jack and how he was coming back with a boat. And about the general, Dalton, and the bridge. We loaded up and were on the road in about twenty minutes. We picked you up and came here. I suppose we arrived an hour after dawn. Maybe a little later. Ginger then explained everything properly, because you know how Ricardo can be."

"Everyone's here? Everyone's safe?" Maggs asked.

"Yes. Though three cars did speed by on the highway earlier. It runs right through the town. You can't see it from the house, but we could hear them. Georgie was on watch, and she *did* see them. They were driving west, doing at least sixty. At least three people in each car. They must have been the general's people. Ginger thinks that he returned around dawn and sent people looking for you. We think that group were going to Astoria to watch the bridge."

"The general," Maggs muttered. Something nagged at the back of her mind. Something important. Something she had to do.

"Yes. We stayed very quiet after that. Except for Ginger, Georgie, and Ricardo, we all stayed indoors. They've been keeping watch on the highway. The cars didn't return, and no one else has come this way. Now, we're just waiting."

Maggs nodded. It hurt to move, but it became easier with practice. "Thank you."

"You should drink your magic potion," Yvette said.

"Magic?"

"It's what my mom said whenever I was ill. She always called medicine a magic potion. That way, you don't mind taking it." She picked up the glass. "Do you want to try a straw? Chloe said it might be easier, but she wasn't sure about… I mean…"

"What?"

"Well, let's try it. If it hurts too much, just say."

Maggs was glad she couldn't see herself, and doubly glad she couldn't feel much of herself either. She didn't even feel the end of the straw when Yvette placed it between her lips.

"Suck."

Maggs did. It took a few tries to remember how, but the drink disappeared, leaving only a lingering fruity taste on her tongue.

"Good," Yvette said, and sounded pleased. "You should rest."

"I've rested a lot."

"Then I'm going to move my chair. No," she added quickly. "Don't move your head. You don't want to put any pressure on the left side of your face."

"It's bad?"

Yvette's face contorted in a battle between honesty and uncertainty.

"Doesn't matter," Maggs said. "It'll heal."

"Yes, exactly," Yvette said with forced bonhomie. She disappeared from view, and reappeared awkwardly carrying a wooden chair with a back almost as high as she was tall.

"Old furniture," Maggs said.

"The house is full of it," Yvette said. She picked up a notebook from the chair and sat.

"You were writing?"

"My book. Yes."

"About a vampire."

"More an eternal," Yvette said, talking quickly as she looked at her book and very definitely not at Maggs's face. "Her friend's in trouble, and she wanted to help her, but that would mean flying to Paris, and she doesn't have a passport because she doesn't have a birth certificate. I don't know about the story now."

"Know what?"

"If people would want to read a story about planes and passports and things. I wanted to write about the mundane problems extraordinary people would face. The sort of problems most stories gloss over. It's just that it's not… well, none of it seems relevant now, not like the letters you write to Etienne."

Letters to Etienne. Her journal. It was in her bag, and that was sitting inside the log cabin on the road leading to the bridge. If the general was searching for them, he'd surely have found it. When had she last written an entry? Was it back at the spa, or had she written anything since? So much had happened, but it had only been a few days since Fern and the others had been murdered. Had she written about Vader? It was hard to remember. After finding the safe house, that night, she'd sat up waiting for Martin's inevitable betrayal, and then she'd gone to sleep. She'd thought about Hank's letters, but she hadn't written about them, had she?

"Did you destroy the safe house?" she asked.

"What? What do you mean?"

"Hank's house," Maggs said. "The house with the fuel and medical supplies, did you destroy it?"

"No. Why, were we supposed to?"

"General Denning. That's where I saw the name."

"What? Where?"

She didn't answer. Hank's letter had mentioned General Denning, and not in a good way. It was after the general had tried reaching him by radio that Hank's unit had gone silent. She'd added a postscript to the letters, and then returned them to next to the radio just in case Colonel Spitzer ever returned. Not that she'd expected it, but it was a way of absolving her guilt for taking the supplies. On reading the letters, she'd been able to guess where the vault might be. Not its exact location, but the clues were all there. To the general, who knew what he was looking for, it would be as good as a map marked with an X.

Would they find Vader? If they found Vader, would they find the safe house? She couldn't know, or for how long and far the general would search for her before returning to his quest for this vault. Did it matter? He'd attempted radio contact with Hank Schwarz after the bombs fell, so had been searching for over a year. If he'd not found the vault by now, perhaps he never would. And did that matter when he had a weapon as terrible as any ever unleashed on the world?

"Maggs?"

"It's all just hitting me, everything that's happened."

"It's a lot, isn't it? Do you want to sleep, maybe?"

"I don't think I can, not yet."

"Then maybe you should write it down in a letter. I mean, I'll write, you dictate. Sometimes it helps to trap the words on paper. My mom said that, too."

Something in Yvette's tone dragged her back to the present. She looked at the young woman and saw the fear and exhaustion in her face, but she also saw the determination. After a year of radiation and starvation, of plague and despair, of betrayal and desertion, and of the sleepless war against the undead, nearly everyone had died. What did she have to show for it? She'd not reached Vancouver Island. She'd not found Etienne. Everyone she'd once known was gone. Almost everyone she'd met during this last year was now dead. But it was the same for Yvette. She'd not given up. Nor would Maggs. Not ever.

She didn't know what she should say in a letter, but she knew where to begin. "Dear Etienne..."

To be continued...

www.ingramcontent.com/pod-product-compliance
Ingram Content Group UK Ltd.
Pitfield, Milton Keynes, MK11 3LW, UK
UKHW020755020625
6184UKWH00053B/1044

9 798285 133056